# Flowers for Elizabeth

### H. H. Vangh

*Flowers for Elizabeth* by HH Vangh

This is a work of fiction. Names, characters, businesses, places, events and incidents are either the products of the author's imagination or used in a fictitious manner. Any resemblance to actual persons, living or dead, or actual events is purely coincidental.

ISBNs0996080635

978-0-9960806-3-7 (print)
978-0-9960806-4-4 (ebook)

Published by Clairvoyant Publishing Inc.

### *To my father*

You passed on at such a young age and never got a chance to see your children grow up. I know that you're on the other side and will always be watching over us. There's not a single day goes by that we don't think of you.


### *To my mother*

You have been left lingering alone in this world for so long. You have raised nine of us as a single mother. I'm so sorry that it took me so long to make you proud of me.

# Prologue

May 25th. It was a boisterous evening as usual, and the city wasn't yet ready to surrender itself to the stillness of the night. The spectacular vast horizon line carved the perfect division between the darkened sky and the beauty of the crowded city in silhouette.

The full moon was luminous as it smiled graciously down onto the earth below. The brilliant colors of the starry sky, along with the thousands of glowing lights, made the city sparkle brightly in the twilight.

The restless streets were actively entertained by the pleasant noises of car stereos and horns. The voices of people yelling at each other as they frantically tried to get where they needed to be were a symbol of harmony to those who lived in the city.

A red convertible was heading down on Broadway, speeding and cutting through the traffic lanes. The driver's vision was blurred. His cluttered mind was spinning wildly out of control as he thought of nothing else but his destination. Suddenly his phone rang.

"Hey, dude!" said the angry voice on the other end. "Where the hell are you?"

"I'm on my way," the driver mumbled.

"Hurry up! They're getting pissed! What the hell is taking you so long?"

"I just took another hit! I'll be there in about fifteen minnn. . ." Suddenly, his voice elevated to a high, screeching scream: "Oh, shit!!!" And then everything went silent.

**Fast Forward . . .**

May 25th. Darkness had given way to dawn. On the horizon, golden rays of red and orange washed across the sky like a flood of paint. The vibrant colors of the crimson sky stretched for miles across the horizon, like a masterpiece painted just for the human eyes. The presence of the sun opened up a glowing curtain of light for the earth below as it began to wake. The warmth of the rays began to heat up the earth, melting away the morning mists.

From a distance, a black limousine gradually maneuvered along a curvy road and came to a stop at the bottom of a large grassy hill.

On top of the hill, a tall oak tree stood proudly with its branches reaching out, shadowing most of the hilltop. Underneath it stood an upright, lonely headstone with a picture of a beautiful young woman embedded into it. The large, old tree was her only companion and protector, shielding her from the ravages of the rain, the wind, and the sharp rays of the sun.

Suddenly the limousine door opened, and the driver got out of it to assist his passenger. An elderly man slowly emerged from the vehicle holding a bouquet of fresh flowers in one hand and a shiny, brownish cane in the other. He had a full head of grayish, silvery hair. His fragile face was darkened with countless age spots, and deep lines and wrinkles from years of sorrow.

He walked a few steps, his pensive eyes never once focused on anything else as he steadily gazed up the hill at the tree. He stopped and stood still for a moment, trying to straighten out his back. Then he hunched over and slowly began to walk again.

With the support of his cane, he struggled up the hill, stopping several times to catch his breath.

"Do you need help, sir?" the driver called out to him.

"No. I've done this every year," the old man replied in a shaky and raspy voice.

It took him a while, but he finally reached the top of the hill. Standing silently by the headstone, he stared at the picture of the woman for a few minutes. Then he released a soft, painful sigh as he laid the bouquet next to her. Gently touching the picture with his fingers, he began to speak to her. "Hello, my dear. How are you? You still look more beautiful with each passing day."

Carefully, he laid his cane on the ground. Then he lowered his right hand, grabbing hold of the green, luscious grass to support his body as he slowly sat down beside her. "I've missed you," he said. "I've missed you every day for all these years."

Overcome with sorrow, he whimpered and then sobbed silently. He leaned against the headstone and closed his eyes, silent and alone like a lost child. But in his heart, he was not alone—he was now with her again. Keeping his eyes closed, he fell asleep beside her.

A beam of light trickled through the protection of the tree, casting a warm, sharp ray that cut across his face. He opened his eyes and realized it was late in the afternoon. Although he'd lost track of time, he didn't seem to care.

"It's four o'clock, sir!" the driver called up to him. "You'll miss your flight if we don't leave now!"

The man didn't want to get up. He didn't want to leave her. He wanted to cry hysterically like a child who didn't want to be parted from his mother. But he knew he had to leave.

Wrapping his arms around the headstone, the old man gently kissed the picture of the woman. A few tears quietly ran down his rough, rugged face as he managed to say his last words to her. "You sleep now, my dear, and I promise I will see you again."

# Chapter One

It was May 25th, a beautiful Saturday morning in Atkins, a large and bustling metropolitan city located on the east coast of the United States.

The sun had just spread a blanket of gold and red flames across the sky. The misty breeze was still sweet, calm, and gentle. But the streets were already congested with vehicles bumper to bumper here and there. Hordes of pedestrians, shoppers, and street vendors filled the pavement and crosswalks as they came and went about their business. The sounds of blaring car stereos, car horns, and the noise from the nearby construction sites created a deafening but lively noise. Vehicle exhaust combined with the sweet smell of food from the mobile food vendors, markets, and restaurants, filling the air with a sweet, pungent odor that only a regular city dweller could enjoy.

In the midst of all this chaos, not too far from the city's center, was Iris Park, an enormous and beautiful tract of land named after the wife of the city's founder, Mr. Joshua Edward Atkins. It was not only known for its thousands of acres of beautiful lush grassland, but also for the tranquility of its trail systems, bridges, streams, and lakes. It had a large zoo and an amusement park as well, creating a sanctuary for the residents from the normal hustle and bustle of city life.

Richard Bennett, a man in his mid-twenties, was navigating hurriedly through a maze of markets and street vendors as if he had done it thousands of times before. He knew exactly which corner to turn and even how many steps to take to get to Progressive Fusion, an eatery/coffee shop owned by his friend Nancy.

Richard was a ruggedly handsome man with light brown, wavy hair. His eyes were shaped like fresh almonds with the color of the deep, blue sea. His cheekbones were high and masculine. His nose was slightly bent from many years of training and sparring in the sport of kickboxing. However, his lips were full and lively, and when he smiled, they curved up uniquely at the corners, showing off a seductive, charming little smirk. He stood exactly six feet tall, and his broad shoulders were wide, showing off his powerful body. His laughter was quite pleasant, and his charming personality could easily make any stranger smile.

He was across the street from Nancy's restaurant and had already noticed a huge line of people waiting to get inside. "Wow, business is doing awesome," he said proudly.

He was actually surprised at how successful the business had become. About three years ago, it was just a small upstart coffee shop. But, after numerous successful advertisements and renovations, it had become one of the most popular hangouts for the young people in the city.

He crossed the street and continued walking to the front entrance where Rebecca was standing. Rebecca Mahon was a shy but easily approachable young woman. With her tall, slender body, she seemed to be wearing clothes that were a one size too big for her. She had been working for Nancy ever since the business started and was now assistant manager.

"Hi, Becca, is Nancy in?"

"Hello, Richard," she smiled pleasantly. "Nancy is inside waiting for you."

As Richard went inside, he noticed that the place was filled to capacity. Every table was full, and there were still people sitting at the counter, getting their morning dose of caffeine and waiting for their turn at an available table. He looked around the room and spotted Nancy at the end of the counter, shouting out orders to her employees.

As he looked at her now, it felt like it was just yesterday when they'd first met as freshmen at Fillmore College. He recalled their friendship over the years, knowing that his memories with her were some of his fondest. She was not only a great friend to him, but also like the sister he had never had.

He smiled teasingly as he approached her. "Hi, Nance, it sure looks like business is doing great."

"It's too busy! I don't know if I should thank you or smack you for your crazy ideas," she replied with a teasing smile.

Nancy Caitlin Madison was a very quick-witted, outgoing, and fun-loving person. She was not afraid to speak her mind and could be straightforward and blunt at times. She was always optimistic, and she loved the people around her. Her spirited personality could uplift anyone who needed her comfort and solace. Five feet tall and voluptuous, she was a one-of-a-kind girl with a beautiful and generous heart.

He laughed loudly and was about to say something, but she interrupted him. "Richard, I'm sorry I didn't have your regular table reserved for you. I was too busy, and when I finally got around to it, someone was already sitting in it."

"Hey, don't worry about it. I'm not in a hurry today. By the way, who is sitting at my table?"

"Well, take a look for yourself," she replied as her eyes directed him.

He peeked through the mass of humanity in the room and noticed an amazingly beautiful woman sitting all by herself at his table. His head instantly tilted back and he had to blink his eyes a few times for a better focus on this stranger who had taken his favorite spot.

From afar, he could see that this woman looked like she was in her early twenties and seemed to be of Asian descent. Even though her face was looking down and her eyes were fixed on a book, he could still steal a glimpse of her from the side. Her dark eyes were round, sparkling brightly, and seemed as if they could warm even the coldest of winter nights. Her porcelain-like skin was flawless. Her soft, luscious lips were erotically plump and alive as if they were the nectar freshly squeezed from the petals of a newly bloomed rose. Her high cheekbones stood out perfectly to match the shape of her straight and slim nose. Her long, black hair fell over her shoulders like radiant sunshine on a bright day.

Sitting there like an angel in the sun beside the window, she seemed to him like a perfect painting. In his eyes, this woman was beyond stunning.

She sat there in silence, sipping a cup of coffee and reading a book. Every so often, she would lift her head up to let her dark exotic eyes wander about the room, surely hypnotizing any man who dared to look at them. He watched in amazement as first one man and then another who approached her were politely cast away like unwanted fish being tossed back into the ocean.

Nancy noticed the delight in Richard's face as he stared at the strikingly attractive woman. "She's gorgeous, isn't she?" she asked.

He stood there motionless, and without even moving his eyes away for a second, he simply nodded in total agreement.

"Well, what are you thinking about?" she asked in almost a whisper.

"I don't know," he whispered in return. "I'm thinking about going over there, but I'm afraid I might get brushed off just like one of those other guys."

As he stood there, gazing at her with approving eyes, she suddenly looked up and their eyes met. He quickly looked away, frantically searching about the room for some kind of refuge from this awkward situation.

A few seconds later, he glanced back helplessly and noticed that she was still looking straight at him. He knew he was caught red-handed and felt a hot sensation rushing through his body. Although his mind was telling him to look away again, he was kind of glad he was caught.

She looked directly at him and gave him a gorgeous smile that revealed a hidden dimple on her left cheek. Her lips were full and plump with a flush of sweet cherry-red, and my, how they quirked up when she smiled.

His heart was pounding so fast that he felt it was going to leap out of his chest. His knees were getting weaker, and he felt as if he needed to grasp on to something to hold himself up. Finally, he found the strength to turn away and started a conversation with one of the costumers at the counter.

After a while, he turned back to her, only to discover an empty table. To his disappointment, she was no longer anywhere to be found inside the restaurant.

Jeanie, one of the waitresses at the restaurant, was going to clear the table to get it ready for him, but he told her to leave everything exactly the way it was. He sat in the exact seat she was seated in earlier and could still smell the aroma of her sweet flowery perfume. Hypnotized by the remnants of her scent and her captivating smile, he found himself continuously looking out the window, desperately hoping to get a glimpse of her again.

Several hours later, he found himself walking east on Washington Avenue, heading toward the Lower Town District. The Lower Town District used to be a thriving industrial neighborhood in the late 1920s and lasted up until the early 1970s. Over the course of time, most of the companies along the avenue were either shut down or moved overseas for cheaper labor. Now, the area that was once known as the "Mecca" of the city was filled with abandoned warehouses, cheap hotels, and run-down apartments. This part of town had now become a slum and a popular hangout for drug dealers, muggers, prostitutes, and anyone who had nothing better to do.

Lost in his thoughts, he had no clue as to why he was walking in this part of town or why he continued on. His mind was restless with the thought of that beautiful woman from the restaurant earlier, and how she made him go weak in the knees with just a simple smile.

As he continued walking with the thought of her still lingering in his mind, he suddenly stopped dead in his tracks. He couldn't believe what he had just spotted. There she was, that same beautiful woman from the restaurant, walking east on Washington Avenue, on the opposite side of the street from him.

From afar, he could tell that she was definitely much taller than any Asian woman he had ever encountered. Her long, slim legs and nicely curved hips were perfectly displayed by her low-rise skinny jeans. She wore a tight pink T-shirt that perfectly hugged her slender body, showing off the fullness of her chest. *This woman's body is just as perfect as her face*, he thought.

The only blemish he could see was a huge, ugly multicolored cloth bag she had strapped onto her shoulder that would clash with any kind of apparel. He wondered how she could carry that huge bag around so effortlessly without stopping to rest.

He curiously watched her as she strolled down Washington Avenue, stopping for a bit to look at street signs and to stare at the surroundings. It was obvious to him that she didn't live in the city. Several times he wanted to approach her and ask if she needed help with directions, but he decided otherwise, fearing her boyfriend suddenly appearing from out of nowhere. Not that he was scared, but he didn't want to set himself up for embarrassment; so he dropped the idea and just continued watching her from afar.

He wasn't trying to follow her. He just happened to be walking this same way, and it was a coincidence that their paths happened to cross again. So, he decided to just keep an eye out for her safety. Heck, this part of town was not a good place for a woman to be walking alone.

As he walked and continued watching her from across the street, he noticed a scrappy-looking guy eyeing her and cautiously following her. Richard's intuition wasn't wrong when he first glanced at the goofy guy. He knew exactly what was going to happen, so he crossed the street and picked up his pace toward them.

As soon as the woman reached the alley, about mid-block between Gardener and Cromwell Streets, the guy finally caught up with her and pushed her into the alley. Richard sprinted as fast as he could now, hoping to get there in a timely manner.

When he finally reached the alley, he could see that she was holding on tightly to her bag and was in a tug-of-war with her assailant over it. Richard had to quickly make a decision about what to do, but then held back as he noticed that the robber had pulled out a small knife and was threatening her with it.

Instantly, Richard ran toward him and tried to kick the knife away from his hand, but he missed. Luckily, he accidentally kicked the guy in the head instead, sending him down to the ground.

Slowly the assailant got back on his feet, but he was still dazed by the blow and was stumbling about. Richard gave him another powerful kick, this time to the side of his chest, and sent him flying back to the ground again.

"Do you want some more?" Richard shouted. Coughing and muttering, the man got up and staggered away.

Still pumped up with adrenaline, Richard was shaking and breathing rapidly. He took several deep breaths to compose himself before he turned to the woman.

"Are you Okay, ma'am?" he asked in a deep, calm voice.

She just sat there on the pavement, silent except for her rapid breathing. He moved a little closer and tried to help her up. She hesitated a little, so he paused and stood still, fearing that if he moved, he would just scare her even more.

"I ... I was so scared. I thought he was going to kill me," she managed to say in a shaky voice.

He carefully knelt down next to her and stared directly into her eyes. *My god! Those eyes of hers are so attractive they are practically sinful,* he thought to himself. He slowly reached a hand over to brush away a lock of hair from her face. "Well, he is gone and you're safe now."

"Thank you," she whispered.

"I'm just glad I was here at the right time and was able to help. My name is Richard, by the way."

The color on her face had finally returned, reviving the flawless glow in her cheeks and the sheer, pinkish flush in her lips. She looked at him with a deep sense of gratitude and returned a genuine smile. "I wish we didn't have to meet this way, but it's a pleasure to meet you, Richard. I'm Elizabeth."

After a few moments of gazing at her with admiration, he noticed that she was getting a little uncomfortable. He quickly shifted his eyes to her bag. "What are you doing in this part of the city?" he asked.

"I was looking for a hotel."

He gently took her hands and helped her back to her feet. "This part of the city is not safe, and the hotels here are not decent. If you don't mind my help, I will get you to a decent hotel."

He took her bag, swung it over his shoulder, and then reached a hand out to her. She agreeably took it, and they both walked away from the alley.

He could tell that she was still unsure if she should be going with him, so he decided to put her mind at ease with some small talk. "First time in this city, I take it?"

She glanced at him with a nervous smile. "Yes, I arrived early this morning."

"So, what brings you here?"

Again she turned to him, this time looking a bit more relaxed. "I was offered a job, but I arrived two days late so someone else got it. Then, a modeling agency offered me a position; however, their criteria were not in my favor, so I declined it."

He let out a light chuckle. "If you don't mind sharing, I'd love to hear why their criteria were not in your favor?"

She giggled with a slight tone of embarrassment. "Well, let's just say that there are so many different talents and various projects in the modeling industry. Some prestigious agencies have clean and clear visions; however, others do not. Nude is just not in my favor."

"Smart move," he said, trying to sound nonchalant.

She glanced at him and sighed out loud. "I'm not so sure if that was such a smart move when I'm left with no job, no money, no place to stay, and no way of getting back home."

"And where is home?"

She looked straight ahead before quietly replying, "Minnesota."

They walked on for about a block when she turned to him with a curious expression. "If you don't mind, may I ask you a question, Richard?"

"Not at all," he replied, smiling.

She looked away as she began. "I stopped by a restaurant this morning to enjoy a few sips of my morning dose of caffeine. While I was there, I saw a handsome man who I just realized now looked similar to you. Was that man you, by any chance?" She glanced back at him with a flirtatious smile.

"Ahhh … so, you did notice me!" He laughed out loud.

"I thought you looked familiar." She giggled softly. "So what are you doing in this part of town, then?"

"I often take long walks around the city. When I got here, I saw you and then I saw that goofy guy following you. Perhaps I was your savior, sent by God?" He looked her straight in the eye and winked teasingly.

"Ahhh … perhaps it was God's plan set forth for us to meet this way. How creative!" She returned that tease with a captivating smile.

They continued walking for a while, and then she turned back to him. With genuine gratitude, she said, "Thank you, Richard. I mean it sincerely. I don't know how I could ever repay you for your kindness."

Richard smiled and continued walking for a moment. He thought about asking her to have dinner with him, but he wasn't sure how to word it. He didn't want seem too direct or too blunt, so without even looking at her, he jokingly said, "How about you have dinner with me and we'll call it even?"

He wasn't sure how she would reply to that, so he continued calmly walking. To his surprise, she excitedly replied, "Yes, of course! Where would you like to go, and what are your preferences on food?"

He let out a slight laugh, pleasantly amused at the way she responded. "Just follow me and we'll be there in about thirty minutes."

As they walked on, she began to relax and got a bit chattier. "So, what exactly do you do for a living? Are you a kickboxer?"

"No, I'm in the advertising business," he replied, chuckling.

"Your kick back there was amazing," she said. "You fought like you were a professional fighter."

He chuckled again, this time with an embarrassed expression on his face. "Actually, I was aiming for his knife, but I accidentally kicked him in the head instead."

She laughed out loud. "Well, you fooled me. But anyways, thanks to your bad aim, you saved both of our lives."

Richard was known as a friendly, outgoing, and kindhearted person who could easily enjoy any conversation with anyone, but nothing had come close to this lively conversation he had with Elizabeth. He discovered something about himself that he hadn't known before: even the most boring things suddenly became exciting and interesting to him when Elizabeth talked about them.

As they walked and continued chatting, he found himself deeply enthralled by her character. She was so open-minded and easygoing, and could make anything and everything sound intriguing. And he was sure that even if she just stood there and breathed quietly, she would still be the most beautiful sight in the world. He was, in fact, bewitched by her in every way: her physical attributes, her generous nature, her quick-wittedness, and the liveliness of their conversations. He didn't want this wonderful experience to end and was desperately thinking of how he could prolong it.

They walked for a couple of minutes without saying anything to each other. She noticed through his facial expression that he was deeply engrossed in his thoughts.

"What are you thinking about?" she asked.

"What?" he replied, as if she had suddenly startled him.

"You were awfully quiet, and it seemed like your mind was elsewhere."

"Oh, I was just thinking about how heavy your bag feels and I can't believe that you carried it all day," he replied teasingly.

She giggled softly. "I had no other choice. But now I have you to carry it for me." She returned his smile with a playful wink.

"So, what do you have inside this bag?"

"Everything a woman needs. That ugly bag has been with my family for years, and I take it with me everywhere I go. It sort of reminds me of my family."

"And where are they?"

"Huh?"

"Your family," he said. "Where is your family?"

"Oh, they're back home," she quietly replied and suddenly became a little reserved. He noticed her abrupt change in emotion, so he decided to drop the subject.

They arrived at the outskirts of Iris Park, and he decided to prolong his time with her by going into the park to walk the trails.

"Where are we going?" she asked, even though she already had an inkling of what he was planning to do.

He looked at her with an earnest and hopeful expression. "I'm not hungry yet. Is it all right with you if we walked in the park for a little while?"

"Yes, of course." She smiled sweetly. "To tell you the truth, I was just about to ask you the same thing. I really wanted to walk in this park with someone so they could show me some of their favorite spots. I thank you for doing this."

He smiled graciously. "It will be my honor to be your guide today."

# Chapter Two

They entered the park and had been walking for a few minutes when Elizabeth stopped to admire the scenery around her. Wildflowers were in full bloom with an endless variety of bright and lively colors. The sight of bees and butterflies tending to each of the flowers like nature's little gardeners fascinated and intrigued her.

She smiled sweetly as she gazed at a tree where a mother bird nestled comfortably with her young ones in her nest. She chuckled softly as she looked down at the lush green grass and saw fearless rabbits and squirrels scurrying about, busy gathering nuts and stealing scraps from the nearby picnic tables. She gasped excitedly as she looked to her right and saw a mother duck leading her ducklings to a small stream nearby, and closed her eyes as she listened in on the steady and soothing hum of insects.

The tranquility of her surroundings, the trees, and the flowing streams left her breathless. How she appreciated just indulging in the gentle scents, sights, and sounds.

Richard patiently stood by her side, admiring how this woman had wholly immersed herself in the beauty around her. Although he had walked these grounds hundreds of times before, he had never once stopped to truly enjoy the park's tranquility until now. What an honor it was to have this chance to experience the serenity of this place through her eyes.

They walked side by side along a small paved trail and had just passed the picnic area when he became aware of the admiring, and perhaps envious, eyes gazing at them. He knew that someone very near to his side was to be blamed for that. *Such an attention thief,* he thought to himself, and smiled proudly. He knew these feelings well, for many times he had encountered couples and felt envious of the guy who had the luck to walk beside a beautiful woman. And he knew that Elizabeth was much more dazzling than any beautiful woman in the park that day. Emerging from his reverie, his eyes brightened just a bit as he continued strolling slowly alongside her.

"This city was built around the park," he said.

"Oh really?" she said, glancing curiously at him.

"Yes," he replied. "The city's founder, Mr. Joshua Edward Atkins, saw the beauty of this place and constructed the city around it. The park served as a sanctuary for the residents of this great city," he explained.

"Mr. Atkins had great vision."

"Indeed he did. He named this park after his wife, Iris, who died after giving birth to their third child. This place represented her beauty and serenity."

Eventually they came upon a small, curvy trail at the bottom of a large hill. Although it took them a while to reach the top, she seemed profoundly thrilled to have had the opportunity.

At the top stood a large bench made of bronze. Next to the bench was a sign that read, "Atkins Peak." Looking down from this place, visitors could appreciate the beauty of Mother Nature in all directions.

Slowly she gazed along the horizon and was thrilled with the beautiful sight—soft, puffy clouds lounged comfortably in a pool of greenish-blue sky, shadowed by a veil of mist painted lightly across the horizon. With the refreshing afternoon breeze brushing against her bare skin, she closed her eyes and felt as if she was halfway to heaven.

"This is my favorite spot," Richard said, sensing how pleased she was with this place. "I often come here to be alone. If you look down from here, you have a full view of everything inside the park."

"And much more beyond the park," she added breathlessly.

She looked down and saw a large lake near the southern entrance of the park. The trail they were on previously seemed to extend to the lake and loop around it. On each side of the lake were two smaller lakes, which were connected to the larger one by a series of small running streams.

She sighed softly, feeling a pain in her heart as she was reminded of home. Her throat and chest tightened, so she quickly cleared her throat. "What are the names of those lakes?"

"The large lake is called Lake Iris," he replied, pointing. "To the left is Lake Josephine, and Lake Harriet is to the right. Mr. Atkins named the lakes after his wife and two daughters. Josephine passed away at age eight and Harriet at age twelve. People say that in his later years, Mr. Atkins spent most of his time sitting up here looking down at the lakes. I guess the lakes reminded him of his family."

"What an unfortunate story," she said as she continued gazing at the lakes. Then her eyes shifted back to him. "Did he have any more children?"

"A daughter named Caroline. She married Samuel Maxwell and they had a daughter named Jane. Jane married Edward Lucas. Jane and Edward had only one child, Judith, who married a man named Thomas Norwood. Judith and

Thomas also had only one child, Annie. Annie married Robert Cromwell and they had two children, William and Beatrice. William was killed in the war. Beatrice later married a man named Charles. They had three children but only one of them, Victor, survived to adulthood. Victor is married to a woman named Doris."

"So, Victor and Doris are still living?"

"Yes. They live in a huge mansion by the ocean about twenty miles south of the city."

She looked at him, intrigued. "How is it that you know so much about the family? Are you the city's historian?" She smiled teasingly.

He laughed. "Well, let's just say that I know my history," he replied proudly.

They went to the bench and sat for a while. She almost fell asleep while basking in the pleasant warmth of the sun.

"Are you tired?" he asked softly.

She glanced at him and smiled, a little embarrassed. "Yes, it's been a long day."

He pointed to his shoulder. "Well, why don't you lean on me and take a short nap?"

She looked at him and smiled sweetly. Then, she gently placed her head on his shoulder and slowly drifted off to sleep.

"Wow," he whispered to himself.

He sat there quietly, trying as much as possible not to move, to avoid waking her. He slowly lifted his other hand and gently brushed a lock of her hair away from her face and tucked it behind her ear. He could barely believe what was happening to him. If he only had one moment to remember for the rest of his life, this was it. Yes, this moment would overshadow every accomplishment he had achieved in his life thus far.

Then suddenly he felt lonely—despairingly lonely at the thought of her leaving after this evening. He dreaded the emptiness he would feel.

Desperately, he tried to come up with an idea. What could he do or say to make her stay with him longer? Maybe he could let her sleep a long time, then take her to dinner and chat with her into the wee hours of the morning. Perhaps then it would be too late to go looking for a hotel for her? Maybe then it would be appropriate for him to ask her to stay at his apartment for the night? *Yes, that would be the plan*, he thought to himself with a satisfied smile.

It was about a quarter to six, and he was getting very hungry. He hadn't had anything to eat all day and now a loud growl rumbled from his stomach. He was a bit embarrassed by it and hoped that the growling wouldn't wake her.

She had been napping for a long while when she suddenly stirred as if she was uncomfortable. Her eyes slowly opened. "How long was I out?" she asked without moving her head off his shoulder.

"About two hours," he replied softly.

"You should have woken me up instead of letting your tummy do it for you." She chuckled.

"Pardon my rude stomach," he apologized, blushing. "It has no manners."

"Do you want to go eat now?"

"With you, I'd do anything!" He winked at her.

Progressive Fusion was not far away. As they approached, she looked at him with a funny expression. "Let me guess, this must be your favorite restaurant?"

"Well, it's the closest one to us." He chuckled. "Besides, their dinner menu is fantastic."

"When did you discover this place?"

"I've been eating here ever since it first opened about three years ago. The owner is a good friend of mine from college, and I helped her get the place going."

They went inside, and Richard spotted Rebecca at the counter. "Hey Becca, is Nancy still here?" he asked.

"She's right over there," Becca replied, pointing to a table at the end of the room.

Nancy looked surprised to see him, and she was even more surprised to see him accompanied by the gorgeous woman from earlier in the day.

"Hey Nance, you got a table?" he asked, his eyes hinting to her for some privacy.

"Absolutely, follow me," Nancy replied nonchalantly. She strategically placed them at a corner table far away from the windows and far enough from the other costumers to avoid interruptions.

"Here are your menus. I'll be back to take your orders." Nancy gave him a quick wink before she turned and walked away.

Elizabeth was amazed at the food. Nancy's signature sirloin steak was seasoned with dry, freshly crushed black pepper, salt, butter, and basil. It was juicy and tender, and grilled just perfectly in her opinion.

"What is your last name, Richard?" she inquired, savoring a bite of the steak.

"Bennett," he replied, "What about yours?"

She let out a sudden laugh. "You know Richard, if we were to be married, my name would be Elizabeth Bennett."

He looked at her with a puzzled expression. Grinning, she said, "*Pride and Prejudice* was one of my absolute favorites."

"Oh, gosh, you're right! *Pride and Prejudice* was one of my favorite books, too. You're right, 'Mrs. Bennett,'" he said jokingly. But, in his heart, he was wishing that someday he might actually have the opportunity to call her by that name.

As their conversation continued, he was astonished by her intellectual insights and the way she spoke so eloquently. Not only did she value communicating with him, but she also valued his perspectives even when she begged to differ. She seemed to be well-rounded in every way—no matter how the table was turned on her. How he loved that she chose to carry on such a deep and meaningful conversation with him—Richard Bennett. What's more, she was so humble and down-to-earth.

"What is your nationality, Elizabeth?" he asked, looking at her with a deep sense of curiosity.

"I'm Hmong," she replied, smiling.

Perplexed, he tilted his head a little to the side and squinted his eyes, hoping to get more information. "Pardon my ignorance," he said sheepishly, "but could you please explain what 'Hmong' is?"

She grinned politely and began to explain. "Most people don't know who the Hmong people are. To most Westerners, we're just Chinese. But the Hmong people are not Chinese. They are nomadic and peaceful people who lived in China for thousands of years. They are loyal, self-sufficient, and fiercely independent. They are very family oriented and live together in huge communities. According to some scholars," she continued, "the Hmong people originated from the southern region of China. But according to others, the Hmong people originated from Mongolia. Over time, they gradually migrated south, all the way to Southeast Asia. But, there was no written history anywhere, so anyone could speculate."

"So, do all Hmong people look like you?" Although he was sincere about his question, she found it humorous.

She let out a chuckle. "Actually, my grandmother was French, and she met my grandfather at a refugee camp in Thailand, where they both worked as doctors."

"This is very interesting. Please tell me more about your grandparents."

"My grandfather was a well-respected man and a great doctor in Laos. During the war, he worked in a secret military base built by the Americans. After the base fell to enemy hands, he fled to Thailand along with thousands of other Hmong people. He stayed at a refugee camp and worked as a doctor at the hospital. My grandmother was a very beautiful and intelligent woman who grew up in a small city in France called Cheroy. She went to college and became a doctor in her thirties. She joined the Red Cross and came to the refugee camp, where my grandfather worked. They met, fell in love, got married, and my father was born two years later."

He asked her about her parents, but could see that she was a little hesitant to share that information. He also sensed that she suddenly felt reserved and uncomfortable, so he dropped the subject.

They were still deep in conversation when she glanced at her watch. "Oh, my gosh! I can't believe it's nine o'clock already! I suppose we should get going, or I'll be spending the night in the park somewhere."

He paused for a moment, trying not to give away his plan. With a comfortable smile, he joked, "The park is quite spacious. Do you suppose it has room for two?"

As she laughed, he leaned over and said, "Elizabeth, I'm more than grateful that I had the opportunity to spend the whole afternoon with you today."

"The pleasure was all mine, Richard," she replied with a genuine smile. "Thank you for your time and effort to show me around. I enjoyed it wholeheartedly."

He looked at her and said, "I have never had such profound conversations with anyone in my whole life. I feel like I've already known you for years. If you don't mind, please accept my offer to take one of the rooms in my apartment for the night."

She pondered the idea for a few seconds. "You're too kind, Richard, but would you really take in a stranger to spend the night at your apartment?"

"Are we strangers?" he asked, grinning.

"You're right," she said sweetly. "I feel like I've also known you for years, but this is …"

"As you said earlier," he interrupted her, "perhaps it was God's plan set forth for us to meet this way. I've never felt so close to someone so quickly before, but there's nothing to hide. I'm so glad we met, and I appreciate your precious time today. If you're not comfortable with me being in the same apartment with you, I could go to a friend's place for the night. I just want you to have a good night's rest after all that walking earlier."

"Are you sure you don't mind?" she asked, as if she was seeking reassurance.

"I'm sure."

She smiled sweetly, then turned away and glanced around the room for a few seconds. When she looked back at him, she saw that he was still gazing intently at her. She smiled again, and then gave a quiet, simple nod.

"Is that a yes?"

"Yes," she replied, nodding again.

After what had happened to her earlier that day in the alley, she should have been more careful, but she didn't feel spooked by him at all. Instead, she felt like he was a good friend and that he really just wanted to help her. Somehow, she had a good feeling about him, and through their conversations today, she felt she had already developed a sense of trust in him.

As they walked out of the restaurant, she turned around to look behind her several times.

"What are you doing?" he asked as he noticed the concerned expression on her face.

"I'm looking for that waitress to come after us for skipping out on the bill," she replied.

He laughed.

"What's so funny? We could go to jail, you know," she said in a serious tone.

"I'm sorry," he said. "I forgot to tell you that dinner was on the house. Nancy never charges me for eating there."

She reached out and playfully punched him in the shoulder.

"You like to hit people, huh?" He chuckled.

"I only hit the ones that I really like," she said, smiling.

They talked, laughed, and enjoyed each other's company as they walked down Park Avenue to his apartment.

"What is the name of your neighborhood?"

"It's called 'Highland Village,' and the residents here called themselves 'Highlanders,'" he replied.

"Is it a safe neighborhood?"

"It's a very safe neighborhood. The majority of the residents are wealthy or pretty well off."

"Are you wealthy?" she asked.

"No, I'm just a little well off." He looked at her with a charming smirk.

On the sidewalk was a street vendor selling flowers. "Would you like to buy a rose for the lady, sir?" the vendor asked.

Richard stopped. "Hmmm ..." he said, before taking out his wallet and handing the man a bill. "This batch here, please." Richard pointed to some lively red roses inside a bucket.

Elizabeth's eyes widened as she watched Richard hand the money to the man. Because of the darkness, she couldn't see what kind of bill it was, but she could see how the man frantically grabbed all the flowers from the bucket and wrapped them into a huge bouquet.

Richard took the flowers and politely presented them to her. "To the most intriguing and beautiful woman I've ever had the pleasure of meeting."

"You're not joking?"

"Do I look like I'm joking?" He smiled sweetly. "To you, from yours truly."

Still surprised, she joyfully accepted the bouquet and whispered, "You are too much. Thank you, Yours Truly."

# Chapter Three

Even before they reached the enormous, beautiful white building, which was located on Park Avenue between Sampson and Gorman Streets, Elizabeth's intuition had already told her that it was Richard's home. The building occupied almost the entire city block, and it resembled a huge, elegant hotel.

"Let me guess," she said as her eyes widened and her brows rose. Pointing a finger at the building, she said, "That's the home of Richard Bennett?" She smiled teasingly as her gaze shifted from the building to him.

"We'll see." He smiled in return and continued walking.

As they approached, he could see she was mesmerized by the spectacular Victorian-style appearance, so he explained to her, "This building has twenty floors. The second through nineteenth floors are each occupied by twenty apartment units. Ten huge penthouses make up the twentieth floor. When we walk inside, you will see that most of the main floor is occupied by an enormous lobby, several small gift shops, and a restaurant."

The red carpet walkway to the main entrance was covered by an elongated white canopy, stretching all the way from the entrance to the sidewalk. At the two giant double-glass doors of the main entrance stood two men dressed in grayish military-style clothing, complete with campaign hats.

Martin Schrieffer was a retired police officer who had been on the force for forty-five years. He could have retired twenty-five years into his career; however, he continued to work to avoid sharing his pension with his ex-wife. After forty-five years, he was forced to retire, and his pension was shared equally with her. Because of this, he had to work as a doorman for the building to supplement his income. Due to his lively personality, he was a great fit for this position. One of his greatest attributes was that he enjoyed talking to people, and he could talk for hours about everything and anything.

Gary, on the other hand, was a young man who had been working for the building ever since he was in high school. He was a very quiet person and spoke only when spoken to.

"Good evening, gentlemen," Richard said as he and Elizabeth approached.

"How are you doing tonight, Mr. Bennett?" Martin cheerfully replied. "Say, who is this lovely young lady?" His eyes fixed delightedly on Elizabeth.

"Martin, Gary, this is Miss Elizabeth," Richard said politely.

"It's a pleasure to meet you, Miss Elizabeth. Such a beauty you are!" Martin said excitedly.

"Thank you, Martin." Elizabeth smiled pleasantly. "It's a delightful pleasure to meet you as well."

Richard knew that Martin loved to chat with everyone, and if they stayed there a minute or two longer, Martin probably would talk all evening. So, he politely inserted himself into the conversation before Martin began again. "Well, you guys have a good night," he said as he quickly led Elizabeth away toward the doors.

As they approached the main lobby, Elizabeth stopped to take in the exquisite sight. The impressive landscaping inside the lobby consisted of some live plants, a variety of exotic flowers, and even a few indoor trees. In the center of the lobby was a small pond with a fountain in the middle, shooting a constant gush of water about fifteen feet into the air.

They walked about twenty yards north of the pond and stood next to a giant glass wall. Her eyes traveled inquisitively up it, and she noticed that it stretched all the way to the top floor. It also had a constant gush of water running down from it, simulating a gorgeous and calm waterfall.

At the bottom of the wall sat a cozy fireplace surrounded by eight elegant white antique French-style sofas. The low, dull light inside the lobby combined with the flickering flames from the fireplace created a romantic atmosphere.

He noticed how captivated she was. "Beautiful, isn't it?" he said softly.

"I've never seen anything this majestic before, Richard." She continued to stare in amazement.

"My thoughts exactly, but this morning, I saw something far more beautiful than anything in this room," he said as he stared at the giant wall.

Flattered, she quickly glanced at him and gave him a gentle, teasing nudge.

They continued to the front desk, where the assistant manager greeted them. "Good evening, Mr. Bennett."

"Hello, Tony. Please meet Miss Elizabeth. She will be staying here for a while and will need a keycard to the elevator."

"It's a pleasure to meet you, Miss Elizabeth," Tony said politely. Then he turned to Richard. "Of course, Mr. Bennett," he said, quickly reaching for a keycard and handing it to Richard.

"Why do I need a keycard for the elevator?" she asked curiously.

"Well, there's an elevator that goes directly to the top floor only, and it requires a keycard to use it," he explained as they continued to the elevators.

Richard's apartment was located on the top floor at the southeast section of the building. The elevator opened into an eight-by-eleven-foot foyer paved in smooth, glossy, white marble tiles.

As they entered Richard's apartment, Elizabeth noticed a sitting room to the right that contained two elegant, Italian-designed black armchairs surrounding a dark mahogany console table. On top of the table sat a lonely accented arrangement of wild silk flowers, accompanied by a dark finished framed wall mirror a couple of inches above the flowers.

The sitting room opened into a huge, contemporary-style great room. The large, ceiling-high windows and vaulted ceilings promised its occupants the feeling of a safe haven. The luxurious furniture was a perfect choice, creating a warm dynamic in which one could feel instantly at home. The entire interior design allowed its resident a sense of warmth and comfort.

The modern-style kitchen was another marvel. The elegantly carved cabinetry had a dark cherry glazed finish. In the center of the kitchen stood a large, rectangular-shaped island accented with glossy black marble countertops. A few feet behind the unique island was a set of matching stainless steel refrigerator and stove standing against a rectangular stained glass backsplash, complementing the dark cherry glazed cabinetry and black marble countertops.

In the center of the dining room sat a single table in a dark cherry finish accompanied by six uniquely hand-carved chairs on each side, plus one on each end. It was much too large for one person to dine at, she thought.

She stood there for a moment, intrigued by the large rooms. "Wow, it's enormous," she gasped.

"Well, it's just a place to sleep. I live in my office the majority of the time," he said modestly.

"Do you mind if I look around?"

"Not at all," he replied kindly.

She went straight to the kitchen and stood there for a few moments, admiring the exquisitely smooth surface of the marble countertops. Opening the refrigerator, she noticed that there was nothing inside except a couple of water bottles and a carton of orange juice.

"Do you cook?" She looked at him with a curious expression.

"No. Not once since I moved in here three years ago. To tell you the truth, I'm not even sure if the stove is still working." He smiled.

She laughed at his silly reply and went over to the living room and sat on one of the couches. "Mmmm. This is so soft and comfortable," she said as she slowly sank into it.

He went to the couches and sat across from her in silence, smiling pleasantly as he looked at her.

She frowned slightly. "Is there something in my teeth?"

"No," he replied, chuckling. "I was just thinking about this morning when we made eye contact for the first time. You were very calm, but I was so intimidated that I seemed to freeze for a moment. I couldn't return your smile then; therefore, I'm returning your smile now."

"It's too late. The first impression is always the best." She looked straight at him and laughed as she added, "You already captivated me with your awkwardness this morning."

He broke out in laughter. How this woman managed to keep him mesmerized all this time amazed him.

They chatted for a while, and then he showed her to her room so she could take a shower. He wasn't sure if she was going to come back out, so he went back to the couches and sat there, desperately hoping that she would bid him good night before she turned in for the evening.

After an agonizing twenty minutes, which seemed like an eternity to him, she returned wearing a towel over her head. She had on a tight white T-shirt that perfectly hugged her body, showing off her firm breasts and revealing the lower half of her slender waist. A pair of tight pink shorts exposed her gorgeously smooth long legs and stunning curvy hips.

He stood up slowly. As much as he wanted to, he couldn't keep his eyes from staring intently at her.

Blushing, she said, "I'm sorry. I didn't have anything else to change into. This is what I wear when I sleep. I hope you don't mind."

"Hmmm… Let's just say that you make that sleepwear look quite glamorous," he said teasingly, but in his heart, he knew she was more stunning than any woman he had ever seen.

She smiled and went to sit across from him. He sat back down and passed her a cup of cappuccino he had just made. Taking a sip, she quickly complimented him. "Mmmm, this is delicious."

"Thank you. I'm glad you approve. People have told me that making cappuccinos is one of my best talents."

She laughed and took another sip.

The silence that followed made her feel a bit uncomfortable. She glanced away, letting her eyes wander around the room as she tried to come up with something to keep the conversation going.

"I guess the advertisement business is doing very well for you to be able to afford to live like this?" She glanced back at him flirtatiously.

"Well, I have many clients," he said.

"So, what is the name of your firm?"

"It's called the Bennett Group."

"Bennett Group?" She pondered. "So, does that mean you're the owner?"

"Yes, I started the business five years ago."

"Wow, I'm really impressed."

Silence filled the room once again. She glanced at him and then quickly looked away, pretending to be admiring one of the pictures on the wall. After what seemed to her like a long time, she turned back to face him and saw he was still gazing at her. Shyly, she tried to divert his attention. "It's awfully quiet in here, Richard. Are you tired?"

"Not at all," he replied.

*Why won't he contribute to the conversation?* she wondered, feeling a little frustrated. And the way he was looking at her now was making her a bit uneasy. Her eyes wandered around the room for a few seconds before returning to him. "This is such a cozy and comfortable place, Richard. It's very neat and clean. Are you a neat freak?"

He chuckled lightly. "No, I'm actually a messy person, but I do have a maid that comes in here every Friday morning."

"So you live alone, you go for long walks, you don't cook, and you spend most of your time inside your office. You just don't really have much of a life, do you?" she joked, trying to keep the conversation going.

"That sounds about right," he said with a charming laugh.

She squinted her eyes, intrigued. "Well, you're a handsome, sweet, and generous guy. You must have a special someone?" She broke off eye contact and looked away, a little embarrassed after asking that.

"I did, until a little over a year ago," he replied. He looked at her, curious. "What about you? Do you have someone?" he asked, hoping she would say no.

She sighed softly. "I guess we're in the same boat. I've spent most of my time being alone, going for long walks and traveling. I don't have much of an opportunity to meet and fall in love with anyone."

"This world is filled with many lonely people like us. We just need to meet up and make it two less lonely people in the world, right?" He winked at her.

"I agree!" She chuckled, amused at his silly pickup line.

As their conversation continued, he found himself more and more fascinated by her. There was a strong urge within him to know why she was alone and traveling so much. "So, what do you do for a living?" he quickly inserted into the conversation.

He noticed her look away nervously, as if she wanted to drop the subject. Then her voice took on a rather alienated and mysterious tone. "I'm a traveler, I guess. I have been on this long journey for a while, and I still don't know when I will reach the end. It's such a lonely way to live, but I don't know what else to do."

The room was silent again as he tried to comprehend what she had just told him. He could sense the distress, emptiness, and loneliness in her voice. Even though they had only met and been together for a day, he thought he knew almost everything about her already. Perhaps he was wrong? Now he felt as if he had not even begun to scratch the surface. Who is this beautiful, smart, near-perfect woman?

There were so many more questions he wanted to ask her and so many more things he wanted to know about her. He made a promise to himself that he would be patient with her. He'd be a happy man, he thought, if only he could spend the rest of his life discovering everything about her.

"So, how long have you been traveling?" he asked.

"Five years." She sighed and again she looked away for a moment before looking back at him. "Have you ever been on a long journey?"

"No, I can't say that I have. Sounds like it'd be fun."

Her smile was tinged with anguish. "Well, it was fun in the beginning. But later on, the road became longer, bumpier, and lonelier. After a while, I kept wishing that it would end, but it didn't. I guess I will have to just continue on down the road and see where it'll lead me."

He pondered silently for a few seconds. "How long are you planning to stay in the city?"

She let out another sigh as she looked down at her cup. "One, maybe two days," she replied faintly. Then, she quickly looked up at him. "I'm not sure at this point."

With that being said, he felt a slight sense of hope. "Perhaps I could convince you that your journey ends here in Atkins." He gave her a charming grin. As corny as it sounded, he had to put it out there and see how she would react.

She turned her head to look around the room again. A few moments of silence followed. Finally, she looked back at him with an irresistible smile. "Perhaps."

The conversation continued into the late evening, and he noticed that she was getting very tired. "Well, I guess I'll turn in for the night now," he said, rising from the couch and stretching. "You've had a long day, and you need to get some rest. Sleep well, Elizabeth."

"Thank you for everything, Richard."


Richard lay in his bed in disbelief. Was she really in his apartment, sleeping in the next room? His heart pounded excitedly as he recalled the hours he'd spent with her. Even though he had just met her, he found her to be exceedingly charming and beautiful. And her delightful sense of humor had only served to draw him closer to her.

As he reveled in his thoughts, a feeling of dread came over him. He had promised her that he'd help her find a hotel. After that happened, would she still want to see him? He needed a way into her heart first, he decided.

He rolled over to look at the clock on his nightstand: 2 a.m. The world outside was peaceful and dark. Through the window he could see a half moon peeking out, surrounded by a few visible stars. He could hear the rustling sound of leaves on the trees, even though his apartment was on the twentieth floor.

He tossed and turned in bed, his mind shifting back and forth like a TV remote control switching from one channel to another.

"Wake up, Richard," she whispered in his ear.

"Good morning," he said softly as he looked into her despairing eyes. "What time is it?"

"It's noon. Thanks for everything. I must go now." She frowned. "I must go now, Richard." She began to weep.

He was confused, not knowing why she was crying, but her cries grew louder and louder, so loud that he bolted upright in bed.

"Was that a dream?" he whispered. Then he heard it again—the sound of crying coming from her room. Running down the hall to her door, he reached out his hand and was just about to knock, but then stopped. He stood there momentarily to see if the crying would stop, but he heard it again. Now she was screaming as if she was afraid.

Immediately he opened the door, ran to the bedside, and turned on the lamp. She was still asleep, curled up into a ball. He hesitated, unsure of what he should do. Finally he decided to just gently wrap his arms around her. "It's Okay," he whispered to her. "It was just a bad dream. You're safe now."

He didn't know whether or not she was awake yet, but slowly her crying subsided. He felt her tense body shaking in his arms and noticed that she was also sweating profusely. As he continued to hold her, she wrapped her arms around him and buried her head in his chest. Silently, she stayed there, resting in her safe haven.

"Would you like for me to stay here until you fall asleep?" he asked, stroking her hair.

She slowly nodded. Was she embarrassed, scared, or just tired? he wondered. It didn't matter to him. What mattered was that she felt safe and comfortable in his presence.

Gently he laid her back on the bed and reached for the blanket to cover her. Next, he pulled up a chair and set it next to the bed. He watched over her in silence, admiring her angelic face as she drifted back to sleep. If only she knew how much he adored her. If only she knew how much he wanted to protect her and to be her safe haven forever.

# Chapter Four

Richard slowly opened his eyes to the bright light of the sun shining in through the windows. He suddenly remembered going into Elizabeth's room and supposedly watching over her while she slept, but now, somehow, he was in her bed and covered by her blanket. He quickly sat up and frantically looked around the room for her, but she was nowhere to be found. Fearing that she might have left, he got out of the bed and started toward the door.

As he opened the door, he was overwhelmed by the sweet fragrance of fresh coffee brewing, along with the delicious aroma of bacon.

"Elizabeth?" he called out as he entered the kitchen.

"Good morning," she replied sweetly from the dining room. "Breakfast is ready. Why don't you go wash up, and we'll eat together."

After what she went through last night, how could she be in such a good mood? he wondered. And where did all that food come from? He quickly went into his bathroom and did his usual morning wash-up routine, except this time he did it in half the time it normally took him.

He settled himself at the dining room table, across from her. His eyes widened with surprise as he examined the food on the table. The breakfast entrees included bacon, sausages, sweet breakfast rolls, and a ham, egg, cheese, and vegetable omelet. Off to the side of all of those amazing dishes was a salad of assorted fruit.

"I'm impressed!" he said, delighted. "What time did you wake up to go shopping and cook all this?"

"A couple of hours or so before you," she replied with a smile. She noticed that he was still staring inquisitively at the dishes, and she wasn't sure why he hadn't started eating. "Aren't you going to eat?"

"May I?" he quickly replied, as if waiting for her permission.

"Of course you may." She chuckled softly and smiled.

He stuffed a forkful of the omelet into his mouth and was astounded by the taste of it. "Again, I'm impressed!" he said. "This omelet is so delicious! I've never tasted anything like this before. What did you put in it?"

"I added a few different Asian spices to it," she replied. "I was hungry this morning, so I walked to a nearby market to buy some food to make breakfast for us. On my walk, I also spotted an Asian market, so I stopped in to get some seasonings."

"You should've woken me up. We could've gone to a nearby restaurant and grabbed breakfast," he said, trying to be apologetic. But in his heart, he was elated to have this opportunity for a home-cooked meal—the first meal ever cooked inside his apartment, and it was by none other than Elizabeth.

"I didn't want to wake you," she kindly replied, "and besides, I've missed my cooking." She continued with a soft giggle, "You were right about your stove. I was having a heck of a time trying to get it to work."

He chuckled as he took a sip from his cup. "Mmmm…the coffee is perfect, by the way."

"Thank you. I've been told that making coffee is one of my best talents," she joked.

As he sat there, watching her watching him enjoying his meal, a feeling of completeness filled his heart and he couldn't help but ponder how his life would be after she left. A rush of sadness came over him as he thought about his life before he met her. Ever since he moved into his apartment, he had never once thought about cooking for himself or even sitting at this table to enjoy a meal. Each day would start with breakfast at a restaurant and end with dinner at a restaurant. How he would love to wake up to this every day for the rest of his life. His lonely apartment would be so much lonelier now without her.

After breakfast, he offered to wash the dishes while she cleared the table. He still wondered how he had ended up in her bed, so he decided to ask her about it.

"Leverage and technique. You're not the only person with martial arts training," she teased, trying to prolong his curiosity.

"Really?" he said, even more curious now. "Just how did you do it?"

She giggled softly. "It was simple. I woke up and you were already in bed with me."

Confused, he stiffened his back and frowned a little. "I'm sorry, I didn't mean to…"

"Oh no, it's quite all right," she interrupted. "Thanks to your snoring, I woke up in time to make breakfast for us." She gave him an adorable wink.

"I snored?"

"Well, just a little," she replied. With earnest gratitude, she quickly added, "To tell you the truth, it gave me some comfort."

They went into the living room and sat down. He noticed that she wasn't as lively as she had been earlier. He was planning to ask her about the nightmare, but now he hesitated. If she wanted to share, perhaps she'd bring it up. Instead, he sat there quietly, hoping that she would talk to him about it.

They sat in silence as she looked around the room. She glanced at him as if she wanted to say something, but then held back. He didn't know what to say to her either. He suspected that she probably wanted to talk about leaving, but his heart couldn't bear the thought of that.

Discreetly, he looked up at the clock and noticed that it was almost eleven. He had promised her yesterday that he would help her look for a hotel in the morning. What should he do now? How could he prolong his time with her yet again? Suddenly he blurted out, "Would you like to go on a tour of the city?" He had no idea where that came from. Perhaps it was tucked away in his subconscious somewhere? Desperately, he waited for her response.

She looked at him and saw that his eyes were fixed intently on her, filled with anticipation. "Go with you?" she simply asked.

"Yes, I'm your tour guide for today," he replied weakly. Then he quickly added, "I grew up in the city, and I know just the places that you'd love to see."

As silence filled the room again, he felt a rush of panic. *What if she took offense to that?* he thought. What then? As he waited for her response, he felt a surge of anxiety from deep inside him.

After an agonizing couple of minutes, she finally turned to him and smiled. "That's a great idea. I would love to go with you."

The day couldn't have been more splendid. The warm sun and cool breeze were just perfect for a walk.

"Where should we go first?" she asked excitedly when they were outside the building.

"Well, you already saw the east side of the city yesterday," he replied. He gently took her hand. "Today let's roam the west side."

They strolled several blocks along Park Avenue until they came to Summit Drive. As they approached the intersection, she stopped abruptly, her nose catching a whiff of the strong, pleasant aroma of fresh coffee and the sweet, buttery perfume of a nearby bakery. The fragrance was so powerful that she could almost taste the pastry rolls and the rich coffee.

After they turned the corner, her eyes sparkled as she noticed an endless array of shops, restaurants, food venders, and fruit markets alongside the street.

As they slowly navigated through the maze, stopping every time he noticed her eyes growing wide, he became increasingly captivated. Until now, he'd never known someone so appreciative of even the smallest things in life, and she had opened his own eyes to life's multiple wonders.

A few hours passed, and they came upon an elderly man playing a small electric piano. He was sitting out in the sun, far enough away from the markets and vendors to not disturb or harm their businesses. His old, white T-shirt was stained with orange spots in the front. His scarred and rugged cheeks were flushed and seemed burnt from being out in the sun. His sad eyes looked as if they had endless stories to tell, yet his face lit up as Richard and Elizabeth approached.

What intrigued her most was that this talented man, who played the piano so elegantly, was missing a few fingers on each hand. Still, he effortlessly serenaded her with a wonderful, angelic sound.

Silently she stood near him, amazed as he played one of the most enchanting pieces of music she had ever heard. Tears came to her eyes as once again she was reminded of home, her loved ones, her family … She wiped away a tear trickling down her cheek. Reaching into her purse, she took out a hundred-dollar bill and gently placed it into his raggedy hat, where only a few dollars and coins were visible. Then, she leaned over to him and whispered a word of thanks for the heartfelt music.

Richard was left speechless as he observed all of this. Many people had come and gone without even noticing this man, yet here she was, pouring out her gratitude to him. Richard was in awe, again, at how appreciative she was of small things.

Later they came upon "Maya's Designs," an elegant boutique. He noticed that Elizabeth was staring admiringly through the glass window at a mannequin covered in an elegant black knee-length dress.

"Would you like to go inside?" he asked.

She glanced at him and smiled politely. "Richard, I'm just window shopping."

He chuckled. "As a man, I often wonder why women window shop. Where's the enjoyment in that?"

She laughed softly. "Well, we have great imaginations."

"Do you know what I would really enjoy?"

"What?" she asked.

"I would really enjoy seeing you in that dress. Will you do me the honor?" He took her hand and led her inside.

A female clerk approached them. "May I help you?"

"She would like to try on that dress," Richard said, pointing to the mannequin in the window.

"Of course, sir," the woman politely replied. "That's the only one of those dresses we have left inside the store. It'll take me a couple of minutes to get it for you."

Delighted, Richard watched Elizabeth's expression as she waited patiently. Her dark, exotic eyes glowed with anticipation as she smiled like a child who was waiting for her turn to ride the carousel at the amusement park. How he wished he could see her like this every day, for the rest of his life. Then an idea came to him, and he knew what his next move was going to be.

The clerk came back with the dress and handed it to Elizabeth, who glanced at the price tag, her eyes widening. "Richard, this dress is three thousand dollars!" she gasped.

"Go try it on," he said with a charming smile.

She happily made her way to the dressing room, dress in hand. To complement it, she asked the clerk to bring her a pair of black Gucci stilettos, along with a necklace and earrings.

While she was inside the dressing room, Richard grabbed a black suit from the racks in the men's section and went into another dressing room. He quickly tried it on and came back out moments later. Handing the clerk his credit card, he then went to the dressing room to wait for Elizabeth.

He waited anxiously, his heart pounding. He was so nervous that he could no longer recall whatever idea he had come up with earlier.

Moments later, she walked out of the dressing room wearing the elegant garment. The way it showed off her womanly curves was enough to excite any man who looked at her.

She slowly took a few steps toward him, her black, silky hair swaying from side to side as if it was dancing in midair. Her exotic face was more beautiful than ever, and the color of her skin was sun-kissed and flawless.

"What are you doing?" She giggled as she noticed the black suit.

"I wanted to dress up to match you, but seeing how stunningly beautiful you are, you've just knocked me down by a few notches," he exclaimed proudly.

She gave a soft laugh but sincerely said, "You look stunning, Richard. Most handsome, indeed, and I'm not joking."

"Glad you approve."

"So, how do I look? And please be honest." She smiled inquisitively.

Hypnotized, his eyes frantically wandered about every inch of her magnificent body. He was right for being so nervous, because she was simply stunning. As much as he tried, he couldn't think of anything or anyone who could compare to this precious and unique creature standing just a few feet in front of him.

"Well?" she said as she slowly inched closer to him.

His heart was pumping faster as she moved closer, smiling that same gorgeous smile that had captivated him since the moment he first saw her. He wanted to reach out, grab her, and pull her into him for a passionate kiss. But he hesitated. If he kissed her soft, plump lips, he wondered, would he be able to withstand their sweetness?

He looked at her earnestly as he began to speak. "As I look at you right now, there is not a single star in heaven that could compare to what I see before me. That dress has finally found its rightful owner." He paused for a moment and then slowly reached out a hand to tenderly caress her cheek. "And my heart has finally found its rightful owner as well."

His words made her blush, and she stood there in silence, smiling and not knowing what to say. Luckily, the clerk approached them and handed Richard his credit card.

"Would you like me to wrap these up for you, sir?"

"No," he said, glancing at the clerk. "We are going to wear these for the rest of the day. But, we will need a shopping bag to carry our other clothes in."

"Of course," the clerk replied. "I'll be right back."

Elizabeth stood there, stunned. "Richard, this dress is so expensive. You don't have to buy it."

He reached out a hand and stroked her black, silky hair, gently combing through it with his fingers. "This dress could only be worn by you. It would be a great disservice if someone else were to wear it." Then, with a playful yet daring smile—the kind of smile he sensed she couldn't resist—he added, "Besides, we'll need these clothes where we're going."

She frowned slightly. "Where are we going?"

"We're going to an elegant restaurant," he replied.

"Really?" she said as her face lit up. "You're just full of surprises. I really love that in a man. Thank you."

Then she surprised him by embracing him tightly and giving him a soft, passionate kiss. The touch of her tender lips covering his sent a flutter of sparks through him, enticing every sense as his body began to quiver. She pulled back to gaze at him, her smile warm and affectionate.

He was right! Now that he had kissed her lips, he truly was unable to withstand their sweetness. How she could leave him craving for more seemed so unfair. But the thought of him being able to kiss those lips again and again for the rest of his life was profoundly enticing—he knew that from now on, he was not going to lose her, and he was willing to do anything to make her stay.

They left the store and continued on Summit Drive back toward Lake Avenue. As they turned the corner, Elizabeth paused to gaze up at a huge white building that resembled a French-style château, about mid-block on Lake Avenue. Above the entrance was a huge sign that read, *La Fleur de Paris* (The Flower of Paris).

He noticed that she was still intrigued by the building, so he reached for her hand and gently squeezed it. "Let's go inside," he said softly.

At the entrance, they were cheerfully greeted by the doorman. "*Bonsoir, monsieur et madame* (Good evening, Mr. and Mrs.)," said the doorman as he opened the door for them.

"Do they speak French to everyone here?" she asked, curious.

"Yes, this is a very prestigious restaurant, and they want their costumers to have the full experience."

"*Ah, bonsoir, Monsieur Bennett* (Good evening, Mr. Bennett)," said Jack, the maître d'.

"*Bonsoir*, Jack," Richard replied, trying to impress Elizabeth with his

French. Even though he didn't know much, he did know enough simple French words to understand short and simple conversations.

Jack looked at Elizabeth with approving eyes. He smiled kindly and turned to Richard. "*Ooh là là, vous êtes un homme chanceux d'avoir une belle dame avec vous ce soir* (You're a lucky man to have a beautiful lady with you tonight)."

"*Oui*, Jack," Richard replied.

"*Et où avez-vous trouvé cette charmante créature* (And where did you find this lovely creature)?"

Richard gave Jack a confused expression, thinking perhaps that Jack was asking him where they would like to be seated. So, in his broken French and thick American accent, he struggled to reply that he wanted a corner table.

Elizabeth smiled graciously at Jack. It seemed to her that Richard had no idea what Jack was saying. She didn't want to embarrass him, but she just couldn't keep silent any longer, so she kindly budged in and came to his rescue.

"*Vous devez pardonner mon copain, il a essayé de m'impressionner et il n'a aucune idée de ce que vous venez de dire* (You must forgive my boyfriend, he tried to impress me and he has no idea what you just said)." She winked at Jack and they both chuckled.

"*Ah, vous pouvez parler français* (Oh, you can speak French)?" Jack asked, surprised.

"*Oui, ma grand-mère était française et elle m'a appris* (Yes, my grandmother was French and she taught me)," she replied.

"*Ah, excellent*," Jack said.

Richard watched in amazement as Elizabeth continued the lively conversation in French with Jack. He felt intimidated by her ability to speak the language so fluently; however, he was mesmerized by how her words just slipped through her lips so effortlessly, like water flowing down a river. His heart pounded rapidly in his chest as he listened to the conversation. He suddenly felt lightheaded, as if he was floating in midair. What an attractive woman she was! And although he didn't understand much of the French, there was one word that he was sure of: "copain" definitely meant "boyfriend." He smiled approvingly at the thought.

Soon they were seated at a secluded corner table. He sat quietly, gazing across the table at her, a slight tinge of embarrassment painting his face in a dark pink. Although she noticed it, she kept her eyes focused about the huge room, trying to avoid eye contact with him.

After a while, the silence felt awkward, so she finally looked at him and said, "I apologize for not telling you that I could speak French."

He let out a soft chuckle. "I was trying to impress you, but I ended up being impressed by you. I should have known when you told me that your grandmother was French."

She laughed. "I love it that you tried. I found it very attractive."

He leaned closer to her. "The more time I spend with you, the more I'm fascinated by you. You truly astound me."

As the food was being brought to their table, he sat quietly and listened as she gave him a detailed history about every dish, what region in France it came from, and whether the taste met with her approval.

"How do you know so much about this? Are you a chef?"

"No," she replied modestly, smiling. "I was just interested in food, so I studied a lot about it."

"You never cease to amaze me, Elizabeth."

As the wonderful evening drew to a close, Richard became very quiet as he contemplated his next words. He thought long and hard about what he was going to say to her without making it sound like he was asking too much. Finally, he slowly leaned over to her. "I have to apologize for breaking my promise about finding you a hotel today. I was having so much fun, I completely forgot about it. Would you consider staying another night? Or am I asking too much?"

She gave him an inquiring look. "You just can't get enough of me, right?" she joked.

He chuckled for a second and then looked her straight in the eye. "No, I could never get enough of you. You have inspired and bewitched me in more ways than any woman ever could."

She smiled graciously. "Thank you for such a wonderful day, Richard." Then, she reached out her hands to gently cover his and added, "Yes, I would love to stay another night."

After thanking Jack for the wonderful dinner, they took a cab back to Richard's apartment, where they continued their conversation, staying up into the late hours of the night, chatting about nothing and everything.

It was getting very late, and he could tell that she was getting very tired. "We had a long day. We should try to get some rest tonight," he politely suggested.

She hesitated a little, as if wanting to argue her way out of going to sleep, even though it was obvious that she was exhausted. Perhaps the dream she had had last night scared her so that she didn't want to sleep?

After a slight pause, he looked at her with a comforting and understanding expression. "If you like, I could sit by your side and watch over you while you sleep?"

She was a little reluctant, but her fatigue finally won her over and she quietly agreed.

She went into the bathroom to change into her T-shirt and shorts. While she was doing that, Richard went into his room and changed out of his clothes and into his pajamas. When he entered her room he saw that she was already in bed. He moved a small love seat next to her bed and sat there quietly. "Good night, Elizabeth. Sleep well."

"Thank you, Richard. Thank you for being so thoughtful," she replied as she slowly drifted off to sleep.

***

She had been sleeping less than an hour when she abruptly woke up. "Richard?" she called out in a panicked voice.

"I'm right here," he replied softly. He reached over and turned on the lamp. "Try to go back to sleep. I promise that I will not leave you." He reached out a hand and gently touched her cheek to reassure her.

Letting out a deep sigh, she said, "Richard, would I be too rude if I asked you to climb into bed with me? It's just that I had another dream—"

"Of course not," he interrupted.

He lifted the covers and slowly climbed into bed with her, gently moving his body next to hers. She took his arm and placed it underneath her head. Curling her body up next to his, she held him tightly as she slowly drifted back to sleep.

He felt as if he was dreaming, but he knew he wasn't asleep yet. Just holding her in his arms sent sweet sensations through every vein in his body. He couldn't explain the overwhelming joy in his heart and desperately wished that he make this beautiful moment last forever.

Questions popped into his head. *Who is this angel? Where did she come from? And why did it take so long for her to come into my life?* He contemplated these deeply as his fingers gently brushed a lock of her hair away from her face.

If only he could control his fate in this lifetime, he would make every moment be as perfect as this one. But then, he decided, regardless of what his fate brought about, he was going to make it happen. Yes, he had made up his mind and heart—no man, no creature, not even God was powerful enough to break this promise.

# Chapter Five

It was early Monday morning. The sun had peeked over the horizon, casting a warm beam of light through the window. Richard awoke and basked in its brightness. Elizabeth's breathing was soft and steady, and the sight of her peacefully asleep filled him with profound comfort.

Even as he savored the moment, he was again saddened at the thought of her leaving. If only he didn't have to meet a new client this morning, he would stay and treasure this peaceful moment forever.

He slowly got out of bed, trying his best not to disturb her, and then quietly went to his room. When he was about to leave, he peeked into her room and marveled at the sight of her, still sleeping so peacefully. *This must be her first peaceful sleep in a long while*, he thought. He carefully closed the door and then left his apartment.

Richard's firm occupied the entire thirtieth floor of the Maxwell Building, which was located on the corner of York Avenue and Midway Parkway. It employed thirty people, including three managers. One of the managers was his childhood friend and ex-girlfriend, Angela Denning.

Angela was a beautiful blond woman with a slim, attractive figure. Her eyes were deep-set and lovely like the blue sky on a cloudless day. Her lips were like a fully blossomed rose. If only her heart were similar to what was displayed on her face, she would have been a complete and most desirable woman. But she was a woman with many flaws.

Angela came from a very wealthy family. Her parents were the owners of the Eastern Shore Shipping Company. Being the youngest child and only girl in the Denning family, she was spoiled to the core. Her boorish, self-centered, inconsiderate behavior had made her a repugnant person—one that no one wanted to be around.

For twenty-five years of her life, she had friends who came and went, but she never cared. Still, there was one friend whom she had always cherished and was desperately trying to keep.

Ever since they were children—from playing hide-and-seek in their backyard, to going to the fair, to going to their first dance in junior high school, and attending prom together—Richard had always been her dearest friend, as well as her heart's desire.

To her, he was her world. However, his heart knew what it wanted, and it saw her in a different way. Richard's desire burned only dimly when he was with Angela.

With her education and family connections, she could work for any corporation in the city. She chose, however, to work with him. Her selfish heart wanted him to be with no other woman, and by being with him every day, she could attempt to manage his life. To Angela, he was already hers and she was his, regardless of how he might feel.

But Richard was focused on other things this morning—an intense feeling of joy about the past two days with Elizabeth, and the urge in his heart to be with her. He quickly walked down the hallway to his office and didn't even notice his secretary, Samantha, standing in front of the coffee machine.

"Good morning, Mr. Bennett!"

Jumping slightly at the sound of her voice, he wheeled around. "Oh, good morning, Sam!" he said, startled. "Is everything ready for the meeting?" he quickly added.

"Yup!" she replied in a friendly tone. "Everything is ready. The client will be here at ten o'clock. All of the reports and papers are on your desk."

"Excellent! Do I have any calls or messages this morning?"

"No, but Angela is inside your office." She rolled her eyes. "She seems pissed as always."

"As always," he chuckled and continued to his office. Quietly he opened the door.

Angela was sitting at his desk, going through his emails on his computer. "I would appreciate it if you would let me read my emails first," he said calmly, trying his best to not sound annoyed.

Startled by his sudden appearance, she immediately stood up and got out of his chair. "Where the hell have you been all weekend?" she snapped at him. "I called you and your phone was off! I came to your apartment and that old fool, Martin, refused to let me inside the building! He kept mumbling on and on about me not being on the guest list!"

"Angela, this is not the time."

"Tell me!" she snorted. "Why did you take me off the guest list?"

"Look, we have a very important meeting in about an hour!" he replied sharply. "I'm not in the mood to argue with you right now! We'll talk about this later. Now, would you please leave?"

She gaped at him as if he had just grown fangs and was about to bite her. Still furious, she stormed out of his office, almost knocking Sam down as she came in through the door.

"What a bitch," Sam whispered softly, setting a cup of coffee on his desk.

"You got that right," he replied.

"Why don't you fire her?"

Richard sighed. "Because she is very good at what she does, and our families have known each other since before we were born."

"Man, I feel sorry for her secretary and the people that work for her," Sam said as she walked out of his office. He laughed at the comment and began reading the reports on the client.


Richard sat impatiently inside the conference room with his two other associates, James and Thomas, as they waited for the client to arrive.

James Selby was a childhood friend of Richard and had been with the firm since it started five years earlier. He was shorter than Richard, but very heavily muscled. He considered himself quite a sharp dresser, even though he wore shirts that were one size too small to proudly show off his chest and biceps. He claimed to be a very charming individual and quite the lady's man. He'd never had a serious relationship and seemed to have a different girlfriend almost every month.

Thomas Ellison, on the other hand, was a loyal and talented man. He had been with Richard's firm for less than three years, yet he had already made management. He was happily married to his high school sweetheart and they had three children together.

Richard got up a couple of times to pace around the room, then sat down again. He reached for a pencil and started to tap it on the table, then put it down and began to twiddle his thumbs. He repeated this a couple more times.

James and Thomas looked at each other and smiled amusingly, for this was the first time they had seen Richard act like that before a meeting.

"Are you that nervous, Richard?" James said.

"Something seems amiss here. Perhaps you're in a hurry to go somewhere?" Thomas joked.

Richard smiled, somewhat embarrassed, and relaxed a little. He didn't know he was being that obvious.

"Is Angela going to be here?" James asked.

"I don't know, but we can start without her," Richard replied.

Just then, Angela stormed into the room. She stomped her feet loudly as she crossed behind James and Thomas to seat herself right next to Richard. She turned and fixed her eyes furiously on him as if she were about to choke him to death.

Finally Mr. Marx and his associates arrived. Everyone briefly greeted each other and then sat down to do business. Marx Dentistry was a new chain of dental clinics and had opened seven new clinics throughout the city. Because of the success rate of Richard's firm and his family connections, the Bennett Group was commissioned to advertise their business.

Richard sat there, pretending to be listening to Marx's explanation about his business and his expectations. But in truth he was completely preoccupied with Elizabeth. How his heart yearned to stop everything right now and run home to be with her.

As Marx continued his speech, Richard thought about another joyous and memorable evening with Elizabeth. Then an idea came to him. He knew how much she loved surprises, so he thought that after dining at Nancy's, he would take her to the outdoor movie that was shown at the park every Monday night, near the City Museum. *That's it!* he thought. *That will make her so happy!* He almost said it aloud, but stopped himself after Angela turned to look at him. He smiled at the thought, and even after an hour of sitting in the room, the gleeful expression on his face hadn't changed a bit.

As soon as the meeting ended, Richard rushed into his office without saying anything to his associates, sat down, and called his home phone. But there was no answer. He called several more times and still didn't get an answer. *Did she leave?* he thought anxiously.

"Richard, let's go get lunch and talk about what happened earlier," Angela said as she entered his office.

"Not right now, Angela," he replied. "I have some important matters to attend to and I will be gone for the rest of the day." He rose from his chair and rushed to the door.

"What 'important matters' are you talking about?"

"It's nothing that concerns you," he replied as he raced down the hallway.

"Richard! Richard! *This* matter is certainly not over!"

Within thirty minutes, he was back inside his apartment and noticed that Elizabeth was neither in the living room nor the kitchen. Almost out of breath, he called out to her, but heard no reply. He went to her bedroom and knocked on the door. "Elizabeth?" he called, but there was no answer.

Stepping into the bedroom, he could still smell the sweet scent of her perfume lingering in the air. The bed was neatly made. He checked the bathroom and noticed that everything was neatly stacked and put away. He came back out to the bedroom and noticed that her ugly cloth bag, which she had placed next to the dresser, was gone.

All of the sudden, a strange realization hit him like a punch in the gut. His mind began to spiral, and a rush of pain gripped his chest. He quietly sat on the bed for a while, trying to make sense of what had just happened.

Perhaps she had left to find a hotel nearby? He walked briskly out of her bedroom and went over to his computer to do a search on all the hotels in the area. He called every nearby hotel but was told that nobody named Elizabeth had checked in.

He left his apartment and ran through the lobby so fast that he almost knocked Martin down at the front entrance.

"Martin, did you see Elizabeth down here earlier? Tall, black hair, beautiful eyes?"

"You mean the beautiful woman with you the other night? How could I forget such a gorgeous face?"

"Yes!" Richard replied impatiently. "Did you happen to see her down here earlier?"

"Sure did."

"Did you see where she went?"

"Well, she bid me good-bye, wished me a great afternoon, and then she left, heading toward the park, I think ..." Martin scratched his head, trying to recall. "Umm, Mr. Bennett—"

"Thanks, Martin!" Richard yelled back as he hurried toward the park.

He wanted to be calm and positive, but his heart reacted otherwise. His heart felt tight and heavy, so heavy that he needed to exhale through his mouth. He regretted leaving for work that morning. If only he had remained in the apartment, perhaps he could have convinced her to stay a couple more days. Perhaps he could have given her a reason to stay forever.

While walking quickly toward the park, he was filled with a mixture of hope and despair. He longed to find her just taking a walk and enjoying a breath of fresh air. However, he felt dejected after searching for a few hours, only to discover that she was nowhere to be found.

Slowly he began to accept the fact that she might have left him. Heartsick, he started toward Nancy's. He needed to be with someone. He needed a friend. He needed Nancy.

As he walked through the door, Nancy noticed that he looked different. She saw his sagging face and the misery in his eyes.

"Hello there, stranger," she said pleasantly. "Where is my good friend, Richard?" she added, trying to be comforting.

He looked at her and attempted to smile, but he could barely manage to get one corner of his mouth to curve upward. With a woeful expression, he simply replied, "Hey, Nance."

"Go have a seat, and I'll be there in a couple of minutes."

He shuffled to his regular table and sat there silently. His heart ached as he stared out the window, hoping to see Elizabeth walking by. He was so preoccupied that he didn't notice Nancy had come over to him with a cup of hot chai.

"Well, how bad is it?" she asked, seating herself across from him.

He looked at her and let out a deep sigh. "It's awful, considering that we clicked perfectly right from the beginning. She is charming, funny, smart, generous—everything a man could ever want. These past two days have been the best days of my life thus far. I was on cloud nine. It's more than I could ever imagine."

"It sounds beautiful, Richard. So, what happened?"

"I left for work this morning thinking that I'd just be gone for a few short hours and that when I returned, she'd still be there, waiting for me. But when I returned, she wasn't there."

"You didn't say anything wrong, did you? Or perhaps she was upset over something?"

"Well, I did promise her that I'd help her find a hotel. She couldn't possibly be upset about that, since we both agreed that we'd look for one today."

He also told Nancy about Elizabeth's strange nightmares. Even though he wanted to be more optimistic, Richard and Nancy both came to the conclusion that maybe there was more to Elizabeth's life than what she had shared. Maybe she was running away or hiding away from someone, and didn't want to endanger his life at the same time.

"I wish she could have stayed." He let out a long, despairing sigh.

"Oh, Richard. You're the most wonderful guy I've ever known. I have a feeling that she'll be back."

He smiled faintly. "Thanks, Nance. Thanks for cheering me up."

"Are you hungry? Do you want something to eat?"

"No. But thank you for asking," he replied. Sighing again, he added, "I guess I'll have to go back to that big, lonely apartment."

Nancy reached over and took hold of his hand. "Hey, try to think positive. Like they say, losing is nothing, but giving up is everything. I definitely hope my good friend doesn't give up that easily."

"Thanks again, Nance. I'll let you know what happens." He got out of his seat and slowly walked toward the door.

It was another beautiful, calm evening. The night sky was clear and the temperature was perfect for a walk in the park. The streets were filled with cars and people—some busy finishing up their last activities of the evening, others just out for a breath of fresh air. The neighborhood was abuzz with its usual pleasant sounds, but Richard heard nothing as he continued on his long, lonely march back to his apartment.

His cluttered mind refused to focus on anything except Elizabeth. He found himself missing her so much that he was almost in tears. What had happened to her? Why did she have those nightmares? Was she was afraid of someone? Was she hiding from someone? Who? Was she running from the law? Was she running from a jealous, crazy boyfriend?

Perhaps he should have pressed the issue a little bit more when they were together, but she was very reluctant to share her personal life with him. It didn't matter to him now. None of that mattered to him anymore. He didn't care if she was running from the law; he'd accept her flaws. It didn't matter if she was running away from a crazy boyfriend; he'd protect her. If she had hidden secrets, he'd love her unconditionally.

He was so absorbed in his thoughts that he walked right past Martin at the doors, not hearing anything Martin said to him.

As he got out of the elevator, he was struck by a strong, delicious aroma in the hallway. He sniffed a couple of times, detecting a mixture of fresh cilantro, onions, and tomatoes. Perhaps a splash of coconut? He quickly tilted his head to see where the smell was coming from, but couldn't pinpoint it. In his mind, he was thinking that someone must be eating well tonight.

As he approached his front door, he realized that the smell was coming from his apartment. Frantically he opened the door and noticed that the room was dark, except for a few candles burning dimly on the dining table.

"Elizabeth?" he called out, hoping to see her inside, and not a crazy boyfriend setting up an ambush.

"You're late," came a sweet voice from the dining room.

He quickly turned on the lights and saw her sitting there at the dining table, flashing her gorgeous smile. She was wearing the same elegant black dress that he'd bought her the day before. Her hair was in a seductive updo with a few curls waving down her cheeks, making her look even more stunning and sophisticated.

"Do you normally come home this late?" she asked, frowning slightly.

He just stood there, frozen like a statue. His facial expression was a combination of shock and relief. "No," he managed to say, and continued to stand there, dumbfounded.

She was expecting him to be a little surprised, but didn't expect him to be this shocked. "Okay, why don't you go wash up and I'll set the table for dinner," she said sweetly.

He walked into his room still feeling confused. Had she in fact been here this whole time he was out searching for her? No, Martin had seen her leaving. What had happened? Regardless, he was profoundly relieved. He couldn't believe that his heart had gone from feeling so much sadness and despair to being overwhelmed with happiness, all in a matter of minutes.

Not surprisingly, dinner was fantastic. It was not his ordinary dinner of mashed potatoes, steak, salad, or soup. These were some of the most delicious foreign dishes he had ever tasted, making his tongue dance delightedly in his mouth. How he loved the bite-size, tender sirloin steaks she had sautéed with garlic, ginger, tomatoes, onion, lemongrass, and cilantro in exotic sauces and spices. Not only was this woman beautiful, both inside and out, but her cooking skills were phenomenal.

After dinner, they went to the living room. He sat across from her so that he could again have a full view of her. Gazing at her admiringly, a grin spread across his face as he thought of what had happened earlier this afternoon. He thought about how he was planning to surprise her with dinner and then a movie at the park, but instead she had surprised him with a wonderful meal.

She glanced at him and he looked away. Then his eyes moved quickly back to meet hers. "Is something the matter?" she asked, smiling angelically.

"Oh, was I staring?" He chuckled. His eyes were again fixed on her and he made no effort to look elsewhere. So what if he was staring? This woman set his heart aflame!

"You seemed exhausted earlier. Did you have a rough day at work?" she asked.

"Sure did. I thought that I had lost something very dear to me, but it turned out that it was here all along."

She giggled softly. "It must have been something very special for you to be running around searching for it all day."

"How did you know?" He grinned, blushing.

She laughed. "When I came back from the market, Martin told me that you were running around frantically looking for me. Did you think that I'd left?"

"Yes," he replied. "So, I searched for you all day. Why didn't you answer the phone this morning?"

"I wasn't sure if I was supposed to answer the phone, so I let it go to voicemail. Then I went to the market to get something to cook for dinner."

"When I came back, you weren't here. I checked your room and your bag was gone, so I thought that you left."

"I took the bag with me so that I could carry groceries in it," she said, smiling amusingly. "I put all my clothes in the drawers and in the closet, but I guess you didn't check?"

He laughed loudly. "You know, it didn't dawn on me to check the closet."

After a few second, he leaned forward and said, "Will you please answer the phone from now on?"

"Sure, I'll do that for your sake."

This is why he couldn't imagine himself without her. These two days with her had brought an overwhelming happiness to his life. He needed to tell her about these feelings for her. He needed to ask her to stay, but how? What if she thought this was too soon to have such feelings? He must think of a way—a genuine way to tell her how much he adored her and wanted her to stay with him.

They stayed up into the late hours of the night again, until he noticed that she was very tired. But she seemed hesitant. Was she afraid to go to sleep? He paused for a moment and then looked at her, staring straight into her tired eyes. "If you're comfortable sharing, I'd like to hear about your nightmares."

She looked at him with a horrified expression. "Why do you want to know?" she asked, almost in a whisper.

"If you're not ready or comfortable, I will understand and will respect that. I just thought that if I knew, I might be able to help you."

She was very reluctant, but somehow she knew that she would have to tell him. She clasped her hands together tightly as if for comfort and sighed deeply. Then she quietly began. "For five years now, I've been having the same nightmare. There is always a bright light from the window, and then two bright, ghostly beings come out from it. They grab me and try to pull me to the light. At first they were very strong and they almost got me to the light several times. But for the past few years or so, they have gotten weaker, and I was able to fight them off each time. In the past two nights, they came again for me, but I was fortunate to have you there to be with me."

"Do you know the reason why you are having this dream?" he asked, trying to understand.

"I don't know, but these recurring dreams happen the same way every time. That is why it's so hard for me to sleep at night," she replied despairingly. "In the beginning, the nightmare occurred only once in a while, but it has become more frequent throughout the years. Honestly, I haven't been able to sleep peacefully for such a long time now," she said, small specks of tears forming in her eyes.

He saw through her tears that she was fearful, desperate, and at a loss. He slowly got up from his seat and walked over to her. As he sat next to her, he reached out his arms and gently pulled her into him for a soft, comforting embrace.

"You're safe here with me, that much I can promise you." With these words, he vowed silently in his heart that if there was ever anyone he needed to protect with his life, it would be her.

# Chapter Six

Richard sat inside the conference room with James and Thomas as they worked on a slogan for Marx. With all three brains clashing all morning, nothing was getting accomplished. Everyone was getting hungry and frustrated.

Richard was agitated. He didn't like the ideas presented by the other two. "You guys had all day yesterday, and this is the best you could come up with? We have to try harder! This is not going to cut it!" He spat fiercely, then caught himself and apologized. "I'm sorry. I didn't mean to take it out on you guys. Let's go have lunch and come back to this later."

On his way down the hall to his office, Richard was still stressed. He wanted nothing more than to call Elizabeth. He had missed her all morning and wanted to talk to her. He knew that simply hearing her voice would be enough to reduce some of his frustration.

"Mr. Bennett! Wait!" Sam called out.

"What is it, Sam?" he replied, irritated and tired.

"There's someone in your office waiting to see you."

"Do I have an appointment scheduled?"

"No, sir. She said she was here to see you, and then she went inside to wait."

He grumbled loudly. "Sam, I'm not in the mood to talk to anyone right now."

"I'm sorry. Would you like for me to go tell her to leave?"

"No." He sighed deeply. "I'll go see what she wants."

He entered his office, and there to see him was none other than Elizabeth. She was sitting in one of the chairs at his desk with that contagious, captivating smile he loved so much. Just the sight of her lit up the glooming morning, and he felt his stress and frustrations subside.

"Hello," she said cheerfully. "I hope I didn't intrude on your busy schedule."

"No, not at all," he replied politely as he walked over to her. "I'm thrilled to see you here."

She continued smiling as he approached her. "Are you hungry?" she asked. "Starving."

She directed his eyes over to the coffee table, where she had placed a huge brown paper bag. "I suspected you might be, so I brought some leftovers. I thought we might eat lunch together."

Grateful, he reached out a hand to gently caress her cheek, thanking her for coming. "Thank you for being so considerate, Elizabeth. I really needed this."

She smiled sweetly at his passionate gesture. Then, she got out of the chair and walked over to the table.

While she was unpacking the food, he asked her how she had found his workplace. "It was actually very easy. Your face is plastered on billboards all over the city. All I had to do was point to a billboard and the cab driver took me here." She winked at him, and he laughed as he seated himself next to her.

Just as they were about to start eating, James charged into the office. "Richard, are you ready?" Catching sight of Elizabeth, he froze. His jaw dropped, and his eyes widened. He stood there awkwardly and couldn't say another word.

"James, this is Elizabeth."

James smiled. "No wonder Richard was in such a hurry to leave yesterday. I would have done the same myself."

Elizabeth chuckled at his comment. "It's nice to meet you, James."

Richard glared at James as if hinting for him to leave, but Elizabeth's generous nature wouldn't allow it. "Would you like to join us?" she asked. She noticed that he was still a little hesitant because of Richard. "Come join us, please. There's plenty of food," she insisted as she held out a plate for him.

"Sure, don't mind if I do," James said as he walked over and sat right across from her.

As James began to fill his plate, there was another knock on the door. "Richard, are you ready?" Thomas peeked inside.

Richard let out a frustrating sigh. "Thomas, this is Elizabeth."

"Hello, Thomas. Please join us," she said kindly.

Thomas smiled at them, walked over, and sat next to James. As he accepted the plate from Elizabeth, his eyes gazed straight at her. "It's a pleasure to meet you, Elizabeth. I didn't know that Richard was planning to have you bring lunch for us. What a nice surprise."

She laughed sweetly. "Actually, Richard didn't know it either. He was just as surprised as you are," she said, glancing at Richard. Richard smiled lovingly at her and continued eating his food in silence.

"This is delicious. Where did you get it?" James asked.

"Actually, this was leftover dinner I made for Richard last night," she replied, delighted by the compliment.

James looked at Richard with a fascinating gaze. He had no idea what

Richard had done to earn the affection of this beautiful woman, and he was very curious to find out. "Well, Richard is a very lucky man," he said with a touch of envy.

"Agreed." She winked at James.

Thomas dabbed his mouth with his napkin and added to the compliments. "Wow. I must applaud you for your cooking skills! It's indeed better than anything I've ever tasted."

"Thank you for the kind words. I'm glad that you like it," she replied graciously.

Richard ate quietly, trying to enjoy his lunch and paying less attention to his two colleagues, but he couldn't help feeling a bit uncomfortable sharing Elizabeth with them. He wished that they would just eat quickly and leave, but they were both fixated on her and seemed to be interested in whatever she said.

James caught a glimpse of Richard gazing at her lovingly, so he quickly asked, "So, Elizabeth, how did you and Richard meet?"

She turned to Richard and grinned. Then she looked back at James and replied, "I was at a restaurant one morning, and I suddenly looked up to see Richard staring at me. At least I thought he was looking at me, but he must've been looking elsewhere, because when I smiled at him, he simply looked away. Feeling a bit rejected and embarrassed, I left the restaurant. A few hours later we met again, and we've been with each other ever since." She leaned against Richard and gave him a gentle nudge.

"Well, I didn't know that Richard was such a charmer, considering that he has no social life whatsoever. He hasn't been out on a date in over a year," James said playfully.

She quickly glanced at Richard and giggled. "Maybe you might learn a thing or two from Richard. He is the most charming, sweet, and considerate man that I've ever known. These the qualities have completely captivated me."

Upon hearing her words, Richard's heart melted. This was the first time that she had expressed out loud how she felt about him. Perhaps there was hope. He looked at her admiringly, his smile growing even wider.

As Richard continued quietly eating, he was suddenly anxious, as if he were going to be implicated in a crime. He couldn't help but worry that Angela might walk in on them at any time. He became fearful, not knowing how Elizabeth would react to Angela's temper and boorish behavior. Suddenly he wished that Elizabeth hadn't stopped by.

Just as he feared, Angela suddenly walked into his office and stood near the door. He took several long deep breaths as he braced himself for a firestorm. James and Thomas suddenly became very quiet.

Seeing Elizabeth sitting by Richard's side, Angela's posture stiffened as she scowled at the two of them. James and Thomas straightened their backs and looked sideways at each other, preparing for the inevitable.

James cleared his throat loudly as the thumping of Angela's heels clacked on the floor like a jackhammer, getting louder with every step as she got closer to them.

She stopped right in front of them, her eyes fixed on Elizabeth as she spoke harshly to Richard. "Well, well, well! Just as I thought! Caught red-handed!"

Richard looked at her and tried to sound calm. "Angela, please meet Elizabeth."

"How do you do, Angela?" Elizabeth said, offering her hand.

Angela ignored Elizabeth as she turned to look straight at Richard. She glared at him with fiery eyes. "So! Is she the reason why you didn't answer my phone calls, and why you took me off the guest list?"

Still attempting to be calm and cool, Richard said, "I don't feel I owe you any explanation, Angela. I'm sure you know very well the answers to your own questions. And if you don't, try to think of some reasons why you might believe I would do such things."

"Tell me! Is this the tramp that you're cheating with?" Angela spat out.

It took all of Richard's strength to stay composed and not lose it in front of Elizabeth. He calmly looked back up at Angela and stared intently into her eyes. She could tell by his infuriated expression that she had gone too far. She thought that he was going to yell at her, and as she braced for an argument, he calmly said, "First of all, she's not a tramp—she is way too classy. I haven't cheated on you, because you and I are not dating. I took you off the guest list over a month ago because I was appalled by your rude behavior toward the employees in my building. The reason I didn't answer your phone calls was because I don't enjoy any conversation I have with you. Every time I speak with you, I get irritated and annoyed by your behavior."

Angela tilted her head to one side and gave him a dirty look. She was breathing heavily, and her once flawless makeup was now blotches of brownish lines as the sweat trickled down her face. "I gotta get some air! This matter is not over, Richard!" she spat as she stormed out of the room, slamming the door behind her.

Both James and Thomas remained quiet but were not surprised by the whole ordeal. They knew Angela too well.

Elizabeth, on the other hand, sat bewildered, trying to make sense of what had just happened.

Though he had tried to be calm, Richard's face was awash with embarrassment, anger, and fear. He wondered what was going on in Elizabeth's mind. Angela had made him out to be a dirty, lying loser who had been caught cheating on his girlfriend. Had he lost Elizabeth's trust? He feared she might storm out of the office and never want to see him again.

As confused as she was, Elizabeth remained composed. She even managed to muster a cheerful smile. "Let me guess, overly possessive girlfriend?" she quipped, trying to make light of the situation.

"'Overly possessive' is an understatement," Richard replied, gently adding, "and she is not my girlfriend."

She looked at him sincerely. "You're a good man, Richard. I applaud you on how you handled it."

He let out a sigh of relief. "I appreciate your understanding."

"I don't blame her for being so angry," she continued. She paused and touched him on the arm. "I would have felt the same way if I saw you in here, eating lunch with another woman. But then, I would have taken a more civil approach to the situation."

This is why he was so head-over-heels for her. Even though he had only known her for a few days, he loved her ability to understand and make light of a tense situation. She was the total opposite of Angela.

"It's about time Angela woke up," James pitched in, trying to support his colleague. "She has been after Richard ever since they were little. The only reason she works here is because of him."

"Different day, same crap," Thomas said, rolling his eyes.

Elizabeth laughed. "So then, how do you guys get any work done around here with so much commotion?"

"We try to ignore her, or at least I do," James replied.

Elizabeth smiled and then glanced at her watch. "Oh wow, it's getting late. I must get going," she said as she got out of her seat.

"I'm so sorry," Richard said helplessly.

"There's nothing to apologize for, Richard. I understand," she said with a comforting smile.

"Are you going back to the apartment?" Richard quickly asked, hoping that she wouldn't be looking for a hotel.

"No," she replied. "I think I'll walk around the city a bit more and do some window shopping." Then she whispered to him, "And yes, I will be home waiting for you."

As she turned around and started toward the door, Richard stood up and and grabbed her hand. "Hold on for a second, Elizabeth." Then, he called out to Sam to bring in the company phone.

A minute later, Sam walked in with a cell phone. He took it from her and handed it to Elizabeth.

"Oh. Why?" she asked, puzzled.

"In case you get lost. You could use it to call me. My number is on speed dial," he said.

She took the phone from him and then leaned over to give him a gentle kiss on the cheek. "Thank you. Good luck on your project."

As she headed again toward the door, she heard a voice behind her. "Wait!" She quickly stopped and turned around to see James approaching them with his phone. "I want a picture of the two of you together."

"Sure," she agreed and stood next to Richard for the picture. Just before the snap, she suddenly reached around Richard's waist and pulled him in for a tight hug. "Richard's a dead man if Angela happens to walk in right this minute," she joked, and they all burst out laughing.

James's eyes were still wide, and his jaw dropped down a few inches as he watched her walked away.

"James, close your mouth," Richard said teasingly.

"Wow! What a woman," James said in amazement. "How did you manage to find a gem like that?"

"I saved her life."

"Is that right?" James looked at him, curious. "What the heck did you do?"

"She was getting mugged, and I beat up the mugger," Richard explained. Then, he let out a deep sigh and added, "I think she feels indebted to me. Maybe that's why she's stayed with me for these past couple of days."

"Wow, lucky for her. And very lucky for you," James said. He looked at Richard and added, "You know, Richard, you might have saved her life, but I think she saved yours as well."

"What do you mean by that?"

"Just look at yourself, buddy. You've spent most of your time in this office. You haven't been out on a real date in over a year. Now, you can't wait to get out of the office. You're in love, my friend. I believe she was sent here to save you."

Richard sighed again. "You're right. I am in love. I love her very much." He cleared his throat. "Enough of that. Let's get back to work."

They stayed in his office for over an hour, picking each other's brains and trying to come up with a slogan, but nothing spectacular came of it. No matter how hard Richard tried to stay focused, he was always thinking about Elizabeth. Just the thought of her could make his heart dance restlessly. He took a deep breath.

"You okay, Richard?" Thomas asked.

"I'm fine," Richard faintly replied. "James, do you mind if I take a look at that snapshot?"

"Is someone on your mind?" James said teasingly as he took out his phone.

Richard stared at the picture and laughed at how surprised his face had been when she gave him that unexpected hug. The camera caught them just at the right moment. *How precious*, he thought.

He couldn't stop admiring her beautiful and captivating smile. There was only one person he'd ever met whose smile could make his heart pound nonstop, and that one person was none other than Elizabeth. "That's it, that's how you smile," he gasped in excitement.

"I've got it, guys!" Richard exclaimed. "I've got the perfect slogan!"

"What's that?" Thomas asked.

"If you two agree," Richard continued, "I'd like to use Elizabeth's smile for this slogan. Let's get a picture of her smile and use it with the phrase 'That's how you smile.' That will be our pitch to Marx. What do you think?"

"Not a bad idea at all," James said, nodding.

"In fact, it's a great idea," Thomas agreed.

"Perfect! You two work on it. I have to get out of here," Richard said as he rushed to the door.

"Hey! Where are you going?" James yelled after him.

"I'm going to go be with my girl for the rest of the day! And keep everything confidential! It will reveal itself in due course!"

"Boy, I can't wait to see the look on Angela's face when she sees this," James said to Thomas, and they both laughed.

# Chapter Seven

Elizabeth roamed from one street corner to another, admiring the many varieties of clothing boutiques on Smith Avenue. Her eyes widened with excitement as she wandered from shop to shop, peering through the smooth glass windows.

As she indulged herself in the latest fashion displays, there was one item inside a store called "Summer Boutique" that caught her eye. While she stood outside the window looking at the gorgeous red sundress on a tall and slender mannequin, she suddenly heard a voice behind her say, "Would you like to go inside and try it on?"

Startled, she turned around to discover Richard standing behind her. She gave him a gentle slap on his chest.

"How did you find me?" she asked, laughing.

"Well, your phone has a GPS locator built in, and I could use the service to find you anywhere in the city."

"Don't you have to work?" She squinted her eyes in curiosity.

"We came up with the perfect slogan. James and Thomas are busy working on the project. Now that I have the rest of the afternoon off, I wondered if I could be of use to you in any way." He gave her one of the sweetest grins she had ever seen from him.

"In any way?" she asked, chuckling.

"Any way you'd like," he said. "So, where would you like to go?"

She smiled sweetly at him as she looked into his deep blue eyes. "I'm happy to go anywhere you'd like, Richard."

"No. Today is your day. You tell me where you want to go, and I'll take you there," he said as his fingers gently combed through her long, silky black hair.

"So, *every* day is my day, right?" she said, elbowing him slightly.

"A foolish man is happy because he is offered the world, but a real man is happy because of what he is able to offer to the world. If every day makes you happy, I'm more than willing to give you every day of my life." He winked at her as he carefully said the words with the most passionate tone that his heart could muster.

Elizabeth swooned, and gently wrapped her arms around him. "I'd like to see Chinatown," she said softly.

While they were walking up Smith Avenue and heading toward Lee Boulevard, she spotted a music store that piqued her curiosity.

"Would you like to go inside?" he asked politely.

"Wow, you're good! Are you a mind reader or a psychic of some sort?" she joked.

"When a man is in love, he knows his woman's world inside and out." He looked at her to see if she understood what he had said.

"And when a woman is in love," she replied, "she just wants to be by her man's side." She turned her face halfway to meet his and smiled teasingly.

"That sounds fair enough." Richard grinned as he opened the door for her.

Elizabeth headed straight for the piano section as if she was a regular customer and already knew where everything was. Without hesitation, she went straight to a beautiful grand piano.

He could see in her eyes how she admired its fine design and its smooth, shiny black surface. Even though she was silent, her expression said it all. He could sense her deep desire to feel the glossy, weighted ivory keys.

Elizabeth closed her eyes as she slowly stroked a few keys with her fingers.

"Do you play?" he asked.

"Just a little, but not very well," she replied modestly.

She remained quiet for the next few seconds, just brushing her fingers on the keys. A sense of peacefulness rushed through her veins as she was reminded of home once again. She felt a deep longing—a longing that she couldn't understand or describe. She was sure about one thing, though. She knew how much she missed her family. She missed sitting at the piano with her brother and grandmother on an early Saturday morning, playing tunes while her mother prepared breakfast.

"Will you please play something for me?" he asked, noticing the sadness in her eyes.

She sighed as she slowly sat down on the bench and placed her right hand over middle C. She lightly tapped out an octave.

"Is that all?" he asked with a chuckle.

She glanced up at him and giggled softly. "I'm just warming up."

He stood next to her with his eyes fixed on her fingers, anticipating the wonderful sounds they were about to make. She closed her eyes again for a brief moment and then started to gently stroke the keys with her fingers.

He was hypnotized as he watched her fingers dance effortlessly along the keys, applying just the right amount of pressure and creating the most angelic sounds he had ever heard.

In the middle of the song, her fingers sped up and flew through the keys so fast that his eyes couldn't keep up. Toward the end, she slowed down and softened the pressure as the sound quietly faded.

*What flawless execution*, he thought. Yet again, another one of her hidden talents had left him speechless. He felt that she had poured out her heart and soul into the song for him. He stood in silence for a moment, trying to compose himself before he said another word.

"Wow! That was simply beautiful. It sounds like music from heaven," he complimented. "What is the name of the song?"

"It's a song that my mother wrote for my father," she quietly replied.

"How long have you been playing the piano?"

"Ever since I was about four years old," she said, blushing slightly. "My mother was a classical pianist, and she taught me."

"And you told me you only play a little." He chuckled lightly. "You never cease to amaze me, Elizabeth."


The entrance to Chinatown was on Lee Boulevard, a block to the east of Smith Avenue.

As they approached, her eyes lit up. Hordes of Asian people were scattered everywhere, filling up the street and sidewalks as they went about their business. She gasped excitedly upon seeing two giant golden statues of Chinese dragons standing on either side of the street, holding a huge sign that read, "WELCOME TO CHINATOWN." The sign must have been thirty feet high and stretched all the way across the street.

Elizabeth's jubilation did not go unnoticed. Richard grinned broadly as her eyes took in the vast array of Asian restaurants, grocery stores, herb stores, bakeries, and bubble tea shops, as well as other stores selling everything from rare merchandise to pots and pans.

The mixture of food, burning incense, garlic, chili peppers, and exotic spices created a potent aroma through the whole area.

She closed her eyes as she deeply inhaled the smells. "This feels like home," she whispered contentedly.

"There's a Chinatown in your hometown?"

She glanced at him and quietly replied, "No, but there is a vast variety of Oriental shops and restaurants, and this is what it smells like on the streets during the summer."

He patiently walked beside her as they wandered along the street looking at all the merchandise on display. About an hour later, they found themselves at an intersection where an elderly Asian woman holding a black plastic bag approached them. He stood next to Elizabeth and listened in as the two women carried on a lively conversation.

He watched as Elizabeth reached into her purse, took out a hundred-dollar bill and gave it to the elderly woman for a pair of black high-heeled shoes. When Elizabeth was offered the change, she refused to take it, and the elderly woman bowed repeatedly to thank her before walking away.

"You didn't even try them on," he said, puzzled.

"It's okay," she replied. She sighed deeply as she watched the old woman slowly stagger away. "I sure hope I'm not her only customer. I don't know her story, but I'm assuming that the poor woman has been walking around all day, trying to make some money for her family." She looked at the pair of shoes in her hand. "I'll just give these away to someone else."

He was filled with great respect and appreciation as he watched her explain why she did what she did. *What a compassionate woman*, he thought. Her generosity inspired him.

"Elizabeth. Come with me," he said, taking her hand and quickly leading her toward the elderly woman. "Tell her that I would like to buy the last three pairs from her."

Elizabeth translated his message as Richard removed three hundred-dollar bills from his wallet and handed them to the woman. The woman's face was filled with gratitude as she repeatedly bowed to him. With a tear running down her cheek, she said something to him. His eyes turned to Elizabeth to translate.

*"The wonderful things you do for others will not be forgotten. They will accompany you and guide you throughout your journey."* Then Elizabeth hesitated.

"What else did she say?"

She smiled embarrassingly and continued, "She will always pray for the growth and prosperity of our love and marriage."

Richard's heart swelled with warmth. For a split second, he even felt like it suddenly grew wings and was flapping off into the sky. He kindly thanked the woman for her gracious and generous words before they walked away.

As they continued down the block, he hoped that someday this woman's words would come true. He always knew that he possessed a kind heart, but until now he didn't realize just how powerful the art of giving was. Perhaps he didn't fully comprehend what he'd meant when he said that a real man is happiest not because he is offered the world, but because of what he is able to offer to the world. Now, he understood the true meaning of those words. Again, he was a step behind her. He knew for certain now that he didn't want to lose her, not even if he was offered the world.

"So, what language were you speaking when you were chatting with the nice, elderly lady?"

"Cantonese," she said nonchalantly.

"Is that Chinese?" he asked, somewhat embarrassed.

She chuckled and smiled. "Well, the Chinese language has many dialects. I only know two: Mandarin and Cantonese."

They continued to walk the strip for a while, and he decided to give her some historical facts about Chinatown. "When the city was first built, the first Asian people to live here were the Lees. They started a laundry business in this area."

"So the street was named after them?"

"Yes. Over the years the Asian population increased, and then this area began to bloom with many other shops and restaurants. Mr. Atkins dedicated this area to the Asian community and called it 'Chinatown.'"

They came across a small clothing boutique, and he noticed that the sign above the shop was written in some sort of Chinese characters. She read the sign and said, "Oh, the writing is in Mandarin. Could we go in there?"

"Like I said, today's your day, my darling," he joked, hoping she wouldn't take offense to his nickname for her.

"Thank you, sweetheart," she replied teasingly. He smiled, pleased with her flirtatious reply.

As soon as they entered the shop, he stayed back to allow her time to browse around. While he was standing near the register, a female clerk asked him if he would like to try on a suit. He respectfully declined and browsed a little while, waiting for Elizabeth. The clerk, however, seemed somewhat annoyed. Then, she turned to another woman, who was also standing by the register, and they began a conversation.

He noticed that as they chatted, they would occasionally turn toward him and smile. However, he hadn't the slightest clue as to what they were saying, so he just looked at them and gave them a pleasant smile in return.

Elizabeth had noticed this and was deeply surprised that the Chinese women seemed to be making fun of him. She quickly approached them and said to them in Chinese, "I don't understand the rude and imprudent mocking of a genuine customer when perhaps the owner should show gratitude and respect to anyone who made the slightest effort to stop in. Perhaps one should learn from those whose businesses are a success."

The bewildered expressions on their hot, burning faces were so intense that he could easily figure out what had just happened. With a huff, Elizabeth turned and quickly walked toward him, grabbed his arm, and led him toward the door. She turned back to the women and said something again to them as she and Richard walked out of the shop.

"Thank you," he said.

"I apologize on their behalf, Richard. Not all Chinese people are like that, but some can be so rude when you browse inside their store without buying anything."

Again, he was in awe of this woman. "Well, at least you let them have it.

They'll think twice before they do that again," he said triumphantly. He gently placed his arm around her waist and they continued down the block.

It was later in the afternoon when they finally walked to a small restaurant named Pho Anh. Inside, they were greeted by a middle-aged Asian woman who led them to a table near the windows. She was a jolly sort who was more pleasant than the last two women he had encountered.

He scanned the menu and noticed that it was written in some sort of language that didn't resemble any Chinese characters he had seen on the many store signs outside. So he sat quietly, trusting that he was in good hands with Elizabeth.

Elizabeth, on the other hand, was carrying on a cheerful conversation with the woman who had seated them. She turned to look at him and smiled warmly. "I hope you don't mind that I ordered for the both of us. I'm here for a particular dish that I miss very much."

"Great! I'd love to try that dish as well."

After the woman left, he asked Elizabeth what language she was speaking to the woman.

"It's Vietnamese."

"You speak Vietnamese too?" he asked, surprised.

She chuckled at his facial expression and replied very modestly, "Yes, but just a little bit."

Intrigued, he asked, "How many languages do you speak?"

"You're going to have to find out yourself," she teased.

He laughed softly. "Well, so far I've found out that you can speak Chinese, Vietnamese, English, and French. Oh, and could you please say something in Hmong?"

"Sure. *Kuv hlub koj* (I love you)," she said.

Raising his eyebrows, he leaned toward her and asked, "What does that mean?"

"It means that you are cute," she chuckled softly, knowing she was not being fully honest with her translation.

"How is it that you've come to know so many languages?"

"My family migrated from China to Vietnam, and then to Laos, then to Thailand, and finally, to America. My grandfather could speak Hmong, Vietnamese, Chinese, Laotian, Thai, French, and English. My grandmother could speak French, Spanish, English, and Hmong. Growing up, my grandfather always stressed the importance of being multilingual. His philosophy was that a person's value is not how smart they are, but how many languages they could understand. If a person is multilingual, people will depend on him or her for translations; therefore, he or she will always be in demand. I'm fortunate to have this advantage when looking for a job," she explained with an adorable smile.

"Wow, I applaud you. And I can't help but feel a little intimidated by you," he said as he reached across to hold her hands.

The woman arrived and set down two huge bowls of rice noodle soup. She also placed a large tray in the middle of the table that was filled with bean sprouts, lime slices, green onions, cilantro, lettuce, and several sliced-up jalapeño peppers.

He paused to slowly inhale the delicious aroma of the mixture of the broth, herbs, spices, and meat from the soup. "What do you call this?" he asked.

"Pho," she replied.

"Please share with me what all is in this dish."

She looked at him with a delightful smile and explained. "Pho is a Vietnamese soup with a mixture of white rice noodles and a variety of side dishes, including meats, vegetables, herbs, and spices. The broth is made from a slow simmering of beef bones and a variety of authentic spices. What makes a delicious, hearty bowl of pho is what is added into the broth. The spices added into the pot usually contains clove, star anise, coriander seed, fennel, cinnamon, black cardamom, ginger, and onion. The meat choices include thin slices of round-eye steaks, fatty flank, brisket, slow-cooked beef tendon, tripe, and beef meatballs. Pho is served with a mixture of condiments that include fresh limes, green onions, cilantro, bean sprouts, lettuce, crushed and fried garlic, fish sauce, spicy chili sauce, and hoisin sauce."

"Wow. All of that in *here*?" he exclaimed with a surprised look as he pointed to his bowl.

"Yes." She smiled. "Although pho is originally from Vietnam, it is one of the Hmong people's authentic foods. When families and friends gather for a party or for whatever reason, one of the most popular main dishes that is cooked is a big pot of pho broth with the many varieties of side choices."

She picked up a pair of chopsticks and a soupspoon with a short, thick handle and set them next to him. "Some people like to eat this soup just as it is, plain. But for me, I like to add spices, herbs, and different sauces into the broth," she explained as she poured a mixture of the fish sauce, hoisin sauce, and chili sauce into the soup. She sipped the broth, made a funny face, and continued to mix in more sauces along with some bean sprouts, cilantro, and a splash of lime juice.

He looked at her and chuckled.

"What's so funny?" she asked, smiling.

"By the time you're done mixing everything, I should be already done eating my soup."

She giggled loudly. "It usually takes me about five minutes, if not more, to get it to exactly the way I like it."

"After you're done adding those things, could you please give me a helping hand? I'm not sure I could do it myself, and I'd love to have it taste the same as yours." He gave her a flirtatious wink that set her heart aflame.

She burst out laughing, tasted her soup once again, and then slid it over to him. "There! It should be perfect now. You can have mine."

He tipped his head down as he lifted a spoonful of broth to his mouth. He slowly sipped just a little bit of it, but felt that he needed to slurp a whole spoonful in order to understand the true taste of this soup that had made her so homesick. There were no words that could describe this refreshing spoonful of spicy liquid. The seasoning was perfect.

He slowly lifted up some noodles with his chopsticks and slurped them down. *Whoa!* He was delighted with how soft and slippery they were and found himself craving more.

"So, how is it?" she asked curiously.

"It is soothing to the soul as well as the body, mind, and spirit," he said earnestly.

As he sat there eating his soup and watching her, a deep emotional rush again overwhelmed him. He was so madly in love with this woman in front of him and couldn't imagine himself without her. The thought of her leaving him was so unbearable that he couldn't bring himself to accept the possibility that it might happen. He needed to tell her right now how he felt about her. He looked at her for a moment and then set down his spoon. "Elizabeth?"

She lifted her head up to look at him. "Is something missing?" she asked, squinting her eyes in curiosity.

He leaned toward her, looking straight into her hypnotic eyes, which stared intently back at him. He sighed deeply and then he began. "Elizabeth, would you consider staying with me for a little while longer? I know that it's an awkward and perhaps inappropriate question to ask, but I really enjoy being with you and can't see myself being without you."

She glanced away for a moment and then back at him. She could already sense that he had feelings for her. "Why do you ask such a question? What are you implying, Richard?"

With a warm, affectionate expression, he chose his words carefully. "What I'm implying is what every man in my position would want, and that is to gain the love, trust, and respect of the woman who has bewitched him in so many ways."

"Is that how you feel? It has only been a few days, Richard. You hardly know me."

"That is true. But every day I discover something new and interesting about you. You fill my every moment with remarkable adventures, and you not only inspire me, but you make me feel whole. In the last few days, I've felt more joy than I ever have in my life. When I'm with you, I feel like I have finally found myself."

She looked deep into his blue eyes and gave him one of her teasing smiles. "So then, how many days do you believe you'll be able to handle me?"

"However long forever is," he quickly replied. "People say that when they're in love, they can give the stars, the moon, and the world. I'm just a man, a human being. I'm not going to make such tall promises. However, I will try to give you whatever it is that will make you happy."

She didn't expect that his feelings for her were this strong. But then, her feelings for him were equally as profound. She sighed softly and said, "I will stay with you for as long as you want. I don't expect much from a person and won't ask for much." She paused for a second, and then added, "However, my heart does fear one thing, and it is the most important thing to me." She paused again, this time looking straight into his eyes. "The one thing I fear the most is to be hurt by the one person who claims to love me the most."

He gave her the most earnest of expressions—one only a man who is deeply in love could give to the woman who meant everything to him. Every emotion, every passion, every sincerity, and every admiration he had for her deep down in his heart was in his expression. He carefully professed to her, "If you promise to let me know what it is that will bruise your heart, I promise that I will lock those things up so that I never come close to hurting you with them."

# Chapter Eight

Angela was at her office earlier than her usual starting time, hoping to see Richard. She had already gone to his office twice this morning, and he wasn't there. She knew that he had changed. He had been late for work for the past couple of days, and one day he didn't show up at all. He hadn't answered her phone calls, and wouldn't even allow her to set foot inside his apartment building. She knew that it had something to do with Elizabeth, and the more she thought about them, the more furious she got. So, she decided to go back to his office to settle things with him.

"Where's Richard?" she snapped at Sam.

"He hasn't come in yet," Sam replied calmly.

"It's eleven o'clock in the freaking morning! Doesn't he have a business to run?"

Sam held her breath for a second and then slowly let it out. "I'm sorry, ma'am. He said that he'd be in sometime in the afternoon."

Angela was frustrated and didn't know what else to do. She quickly turned around and stormed back to her office, yelling at anyone who didn't get out of her way quickly enough.

"Is she in her special time of the month?" a passing co-worker asked Sam.

"She seems to be in her special time of the month every day. It's a good thing her office is way on the other side of the building," Sam replied, and they both chuckled.

It was almost noon when Richard finally arrived at work. He was in a most cheerful mood. It was certainly obvious to everyone that he had been quite a happy guy lately: the way his face brightened when he smiled, the way he greeted others, and even the way he walked. He whistled joyfully and did a little dance in the hallway on his way to his office.

"Good afternoon, Mr. Bennett," Sam chuckled, amused at his silliness.

"Good afternoon, my lovely assistant! What a splendid day!" he replied cheerfully.

"Sure is, Mr. Bennett!"

He paused for a moment before saying to her in a delightful manner, "Sammy, you've been with me for three years now. You don't have to call me sir or Mr. Bennett anymore. You're like a big sister to me, so from now on, I want you to just call me Richard."

"I'd like that, Richard," she replied. She was somewhat confused, but at the same time felt delighted to hear such inviting words. "Richard, I'm giving you a heads up. Angela is on a rampage today."

"So, what else is new?" he laughed. "Will you please tell James and Thomas to meet me at the coffee shop on the corner of Rome and Central? I'd rather we have our meeting over there for safety reasons. Today is too beautiful a day to be ruined," he said, trying to stay as positive as he could.

He walked away, but then stopped and turned back around. "Oh, and by the way, Sam, don't tell Angela about this." He winked at her and then headed to the elevators.

Just a few minutes after he left, Angela came storming back to Sam's desk. "Is he in yet?"

"You just missed him. He left about five minutes ago."

"I've got to find out what the hell is going on here!" Angela spat out furiously as she stormed into his office.

She went straight to his computer and quickly went through his emails. Finding nothing that would satisfy her, she pulled open the drawers to his desk. She had no idea what she was looking for, but she felt so frustrated and helpless that she didn't know what else to do.

Just when she was about to leave, she spied a small yellow sticky note hanging on the wall behind his desk. The note had a phone number on it with the name "Elizabeth" written above it. *Ah-ha*, she thought. She quickly picked up the desk phone and dialed the number.

As the phone rang on the other end, she felt numb and sick to her stomach, just thinking about Richard being with this woman. She had an urge to yell at her and tell her off, but that would defeat the purpose of this phone call. She would have to play it cool and get this woman to meet up with her. *I've never lost a face-to-face battle with anyone yet*, she assured herself, *and I certainly will not lose to this woman.*

"Hello?" answered a female voice.

"Hello? Is this Elizabeth?" Angela quickly asked, trying hard to be polite.

"Yes. This is she."

"Hi Elizabeth, this is Angela. I'm sorry about the other day. I am just not myself lately. I hope you'll understand and forgive me for being so rude."

"Oh, hello, Angela," Elizabeth said pleasantly. "It's nice to hear from you. There's nothing to be sorry for. I can understand why you acted the way you did."

"Thank you for understanding. By the way, I was just wondering if you could spare some time. I'd like to go for a cup of coffee with you and have a little chat."

"Sure. Just let me know when and where to meet you."

"There is a coffee shop called Gourmet-Gourmet Coffee about two blocks north of Park Avenue on Gorman Street. Could you meet me there in about an hour?"

"I would love to. I'll see you then."


Elizabeth hung up the phone and paused for a few moments to think. She already knew why Angela had called. She could sense deep anguish in Angela's voice and knew that this meeting might not be pleasant. After a few minutes pondering about what might happen, she left the apartment and was soon walking up Park Avenue, on her way to Gorman Street.

She entered the coffee shop and saw Angela sitting alone at a table by the windows, staring silently out the window like an abandoned, lonely girl.

Elizabeth walked straight up to Angela and greeted her politely. Angela stood up to welcome her and gave a smile in return. "Thank you for coming," she said pleasantly. "Would you like anything? Coffee?"

"No, thank you," Elizabeth replied.

They both sat there quietly for a moment, just looking at each other. They each knew why they were there, but neither of them knew what to say to the other or how to begin. Elizabeth had already seen the angry and temperamental side of Angela, so she tried to remain positive and composed.

Angela sized Elizabeth up, looking her up and down, wondering exactly what it was about this woman that had captured Richard's heart.

Finally, Angela let out a big sigh. "Elizabeth ..." She stopped and sighed again softly as if she couldn't think of another word to say.

"Please go on. I'm all ears." Elizabeth assured her with a smile.

"You must know why I asked you to come here, right?"

Elizabeth nodded and maintained her polite tone. "I do have an idea what this meeting is about, and I'm pretty sure it is as difficult for you to begin this as it is for me. However, I must also assure you that whatever it is that you have on your mind, I will try to understand. Therefore, please remember that we both must keep this discussion as civil as possible."

Angela raised her eyebrows and gave Elizabeth a condescending look, then quickly shifted gears. "I've loved Richard all my life. He was my first love and the only man I want to marry."

Elizabeth kept smiling pleasantly. "Someone once said that loving someone who doesn't feel the same is like reaching for the stars," she said softly. "You'll never reach them, but you just keep trying for the sake of trying. Do you know if he feels the same way as you do?"

Angela glanced away, pondering the question. She looked back and replied, "I understand unrequited love, and I will never fully know his heart or the secrets he keeps hidden in it, but I do know that he does love me. He may think that he's not in love with me, but I do believe that he does love me. He needs me just as much as I need him."

Elizabeth empathized with Angela, but felt that she was being forceful and controlling in her handling of the matter. She chose her words carefully so as to not offend Angela in any way. "Love can be a poison if its potion is too strong. It is like squeezing water in the palm of your hand: the tighter you squeeze, the more it'll leak out of your palm. If you truly love Richard, perhaps you should think about letting loose just a little to prevent him from walking farther away."

"What do you mean by *that*?" Angela interjected sharply. "You want me to let him go so you can have him all to yourself, right?"

Elizabeth smiled pleasantly and was surprised at how quickly Angela became offended. "I'm sorry if you took it the wrong way. I'm just—"

"Let me tell you something, Elizabeth," Angela interrupted. "Richard and I are *perfect* together. We are both from respected and wealthy families. We practically grew up together, and our families are very close. I can help him with his business and make it even more successful. When we get married, our fortunes will double, making us the wealthiest people in the city. I know that he is enchanted by you, but do you feel you have the very best to offer him?"

Elizabeth sighed deeply, and then slowly replied, "I don't have many possessions or much money to offer him. In fact, I don't even have a place to stay. If there were something I could offer him, it would just be my heart and my undying love. With just these two simple conditions, I can grant him the trust, respect, and love that he is so desperately searching for."

Angela knew that her semi-civil approach was not going to discourage this woman. *Game on*, she thought—*time to change tactics*. "Look!" she said harshly. "I'm telling you to back off! I don't want you to get in the way of our path! Richard and I are destined to be together!"

Elizabeth just sat there, calm and composed. "I don't know much about destiny, so I don't know who is destined to be with whom, but I do know that there must be a reason why our paths have crossed, too. There must be a good reason why you, Richard, and I are living and breathing under the same sky. So, if you believe in destiny, then perhaps you will understand and accept fate as it was written for you if your destination is a little off."

With those words said, Angela instantly became irate. Her expression was now furious. "I'm warning you! If you interfere with my dreams, I will make sure you meet an awful fate!"

Unfazed by the threat, Elizabeth calmly replied, "With that being said, I would like for you to keep in mind that I do not control what goes on in

Richard's mind and I do not have the key to unlock his heart. Therefore, if he has had me locked up in his heart already, maybe it is best that I just surrender and be that prisoner. Maybe he and I were in fact meant to be."

"I've had about enough of this! Just what are your plans, anyway?" Angela's voice was so loud now that a few people turned to gaze at them.

Elizabeth remained composed, showing Angela that she wasn't affected by her boorish behavior. "My plans are simple. I just want to meet a wonderful man, fall in love, and get married. I want to spend every moment with him and cherish those moments for the rest of my life."

"I'm sorry to spoil your plans, but Richard is mine. Look! I've been by his side for all these years. I will not give up that easily. If you want to fight with me for him, then we're on!"

Elizabeth smiled again at Angela's threat. "Love should come naturally. If one has to fight, then it's not love. Life is too short, and one must never spend even one day fighting. I'm sure someone out there has been waiting all his life for you. I hope someday soon he will cross your path and grant you the love and happiness you deserve."

No matter what approach Angela used, it seemed like she couldn't defeat Elizabeth. Elizabeth seemed to know what she was talking about, and as much as Angela wanted to deny it, the things Elizabeth said did make a lot of sense.

Elizabeth decided to go for the knockout blow. She glanced at her watch and then looked back at Angela. "If you would excuse me, I have a very important task this evening. They say that one of the many ways to keep a man happy is through his stomach. Dinner is our very special moment. I must go home and prepare for that special moment."

"You're living with him?" Angela asked, infuriated.

"Yes, for now. Like I said before, you will have your chance with someone else who will cherish his every moment with you," Elizabeth said politely as she slowly stood up and left the shop.


Richard came back to his office in the same pleasant mood as earlier. Sitting down at his desk, he picked up his phone. As he pressed the numbers, Angela blasted open the door and stood there in full fury.

"Whoa! Good afternoon, Angela. Are we a little temperamental today?" he joked.

She walked straight to his desk and stopped in front of him. "So she's living with you now? *Why?*" she asked furiously.

"Her name is Elizabeth," he calmly replied.

"Why is she living with you, Richard?" she demanded.

"I asked her to stay with me. I practically begged her to stay."

"Do you make a habit of asking every bimbo you find on the street to stay with you?"

"Elizabeth is not a bimbo. She is, by far the most beautiful, affectionate, generous, intelligent, and understanding woman I've ever known."

Angela scoffed and slowly leaned over his desk to give him a provocative smirk. "For your information, I had a little chat with your Elizabeth today."

Richard's cheerful mood suddenly shifted. He could hear his heart pounding, and his eyes widened in full circles. "I just hope to God that your chat with Elizabeth ended on good terms," he said in a half-threatening voice.

"My story hasn't changed all these years, Richard. What I told her was what I have said to every woman who jeopardized our relationship in the past."

"What did you say to her?" he demanded harshly.

"Don't you think that a woman as intelligent as she is would have some sort of a scam going?"

"I don't know what you mean."

"C'mon, Richard. A man as smart as you are?" Angela barked. "You met barely a week ago, and she already believes it's her duty to cook for you. She is already dreaming of marrying you and spending the rest of her life with you. That's just a little too easy, if you ask me!"

Angela's plans to discourage him had backfired on her. Thanks to her revelation, he now knew Elizabeth's true feelings and intentions. If Elizabeth had any reservations about their relationship, she would have revealed them to Angela.

His heart began to soften, his aggression faded, and he began to relax. There was a deep, liberating feeling in his heart as he leaned onto the backrest of his chair.

Angela stood there bewildered. "I don't know what's on your mind, but I do hope that my words knocked some sense into you. You and I both know that you are a smart man."

He breathed a deep sigh of relief, and then calmly said, "You just might be right, Angela. Thank you for pointing out my shortsightedness. I will make the necessary adjustments. Now I have some work to do, so if you don't mind excusing yourself."

Angela's face was filled with satisfaction as she turned around and started toward the door.

"Oh, and one more thing, Angela," he said as she turned around to look at him. "Please don't interfere anymore. This is a delicate matter, and I want to handle it carefully."

Angela smiled optimistically as she walked out of his office. And this time, she didn't slam the door behind her on her way out.

Richard was about to call Elizabeth when his phone rang. He glanced at it and was thrilled to see that she was calling him. He cleared his throat and then answered cheerfully, "Hello, honey."

She chuckled loudly. "Hello, pumpkin."

He laughed. "So, how was your day?"

"I had a very fruitful and animated afternoon," she replied with a slight giggle.

"That's great news," he said. "It seems we're both under the same sunny sky."

She laughed softly. "So, what time will you be coming home?"

"In a little while," he replied. "Is something the matter? Do you need something?"

"Oh, just wondering when I should start dinner. You didn't eat already, did you?"

"No, I've been saving myself for your cooking. I'm just finishing up on some of the details for this project. I'll come home in a little while."

"There's no need to rush. Dinner will be ready when you get here."

After he hung up the phone, he felt the now-familiar rush of completeness in his heart. He felt like his dreams had been fulfilled and that there was nothing more he needed in this lifetime.

As he sat there wondering what he had done to deserve such profound happiness, he suddenly felt a strong urge to be with her. The project didn't matter. He needed to go home.

So he left the office and started on his way back to the apartment. While he was walking down Gorman Street, he saw the same street vendor who was selling flowers a few nights earlier. He went over to him and bought a beautiful bouquet of fresh flowers.

On his way up to his apartment, Richard could barely contain his excitement. *So, this is how it feels to be in love? The long and lonely days at work, the urgent desire to return to his waiting love, the thrill of coming home to his beautiful woman—is this what it feels like to be in love?*

He took a deep breath as he entered his apartment. Elizabeth was in the kitchen and had just finished cooking dinner. He walked quickly up to her and handed her the bouquet.

She was delighted with his considerate thoughts, and she gave him a hug to thank him. "How sweet and considerate of you, Richard!" she exclaimed. "I was home and bored most of the day. Surely, I don't deserve this."

"I love coming home to you. This simple gesture is not even enough to express my gratitude," he replied passionately.

He went to the bathroom to wash up and then quickly returned to help her set the table. After dinner, they went over to the couch and sat for a while. He sat next to her and had his eyes fixed on her the whole time.

"So, how was your afternoon?" he asked.

She smiled sweetly back at him. "I received a phone call from Angela. She asked me to meet up with her at a coffee shop."

"Oh, yeah? Did you go?"

"Yes, I did."

"And how was it?"

Elizabeth cocked her head slightly. "Well, it started out pleasantly. Then it just sort of went south from there." She chuckled.

"I hope you stood your ground."

"I tried my best to avoid any arguments, but as you know, she is so easily provoked. Everything I said to her, no matter how harmless, was met with an enraged response."

"Welcome to my world."

She laughed softly. "So, how close are you two?"

He looked at her earnestly before carefully explaining. "We grew up together. I was her first date to the junior high school dance, and we went to prom. We dated for a while, but it didn't work out. We're still friends, but I think that she wanted much more than that. Our families, especially my mother, wanted us to get married, but I just couldn't see myself being with her for the rest of my life."

"Why don't you tell her that so that she'll stop torturing herself?"

"You probably noticed when you chatted with her earlier. Angela is not a rational person. She is insensitive and greets everything with fire. Every time she and I discussed our relationship, my story, as well as my heart and mind, never changed. I have always been firm about the words I use, and those were that she and I could never be more than just friends. Some things are just not meant to be, but she took my words as a challenge."

He paused, but before Elizabeth had the chance to say something, he said, "Well, that's enough about Angela. I wanted to ask you something."

"Yes?"

He looked at her enthusiastically. "You know that I've been working on that new project, right?"

"Yes, you told me. How is it going so far?"

"It's going great. And I've found the perfect person for it." He looked at her playfully.

"That's great! I hope everything works out."

"Well, there is just one little glitch."

"Hmmm... I'm guessing this perfect person is Angela?"

He laughed. "Trust me, it's not her. It's someone special. I haven't asked the person yet. And I'm not sure if that person will be willing to help me out."

"Richard, you're good at what you do. I'm sure you'll find a way," she assured him. "By the way, what is it that you want that person to do?"

"I want her to smile."

"Really? All you want is for that person to smile?"

"Yes, and that's the entire project."

"That's it? Well, that should be simple enough. I can't think of any reason why people wouldn't love to smile. It is such a healing thing to do. How did you come up with that idea?"

"Well, I see a certain gorgeous smile every day, and I want all the people in this city to be as mesmerized by it as I am." He winked at her.

She laughed loudly. "So, you want me to model for you?"

"Yes, very much," he replied. "I want to capture your glamorous smile and put it on billboards throughout the city."

She hesitated a little—and then smiled at him. "I would be honored, Richard."

# Chapter Nine

It was early Monday morning. Richard, James, Thomas, and Angela were inside the conference room, waiting for the arrival of Marx and his associates. Richard was looking forward to this moment, when he would finally have the opportunity to reveal his project to Marx. He was a little nervous, not because he thought it was going to fail, but because he knew what was going to happen as soon as the meeting ended and Marx left the building.

Angela was as anxious as Richard was, if not more so. She couldn't wait to see the project, because for the first time ever, she had had no involvement in it at all. Richard had insisted on working on it by himself, saying he'd reveal it on the day of the clients' arrival.

Although they were both sitting there quietly, James and Thomas were grinning from ear to ear, anticipating the look on Angela's face after Richard revealed his idea. However, both were also concerned because who knew what kind of commotion she would cause after the clients left the building.

Finally, Marx and his associates arrived and were led to the conference room by Sam. Elizabeth was standing outside the door, waiting for her cue to enter the room, when Sam came back outside to stand next to her.

"Are you nervous?" Sam asked.

"Not really," Elizabeth replied. "I don't have a script to read from, but all I have to do is smile. And I will be sure to give them my very best smile."

"Man, I would pay big money to see the look on Angela's face once you enter the room," Sam said with a slight chuckle.

Elizabeth looked at her. "I'd love it if you'd go in with me to keep me company."

Sam hesitated. "I'm not sure if I am supposed to go in."

"I'm giving you the okay—that is, if you're comfortable going in with me."

Richard opened the door. Elizabeth suddenly grabbed hold of Sam's hand and they both entered the room together.

Angela's eyes widened in surprise as soon as she saw Elizabeth. Her jaw dropped, and her face turned so red that she looked like she might explode. She opened her mouth as if to say something, then closed it with an enraged frown.

James and Thomas reveled in the perplexed expression on Angela's face. For years they had been arguing with her, and this was payback. If only they had a video camera to capture this moment.

Richard stood in complete admiration as he watched Elizabeth chatting away with Marx and his associates, bedazzling them with her gorgeous smile and lively laughter. The clients were ecstatic about the project and were in total agreement that it would be a success.

Despite her rage, Angela took a few deep breaths as she patiently waited for the meeting to end. Her heart pounded heavily and her throat began to ache from not being able to express her anger, but she kept herself composed for the sake of Richard's business. Everyone but Marx knew exactly what was going to happen as soon as he and his team left the building.

Just as Marx and his associates were about to leave, an older gentleman entered the room.

"Oh, hello, father," Richard said to the man. "Mr. Marx, I'd like to introduce my father, Victor Bennett."

Victor Bennett was the son of Beatrice and Charles Bennett, the descendant of Atkins that Richard had told Elizabeth about the day they met. Victor had had two siblings, a brother and a sister. His brother passed away at birth and his sister died at age seven, leaving Victor as the only surviving child in his family.

Even though he was born to a family with great wealth, Victor was humble and down-to-earth. It was said that he had Atkins's heart, a kind and warm heart that held a great love and respect for others, especially those who were less fortunate.

He was in his earlier sixties, but was very energetic and actively involved in many charitable foundations in the community. Due to his generosity, commitment, and devotion, he was very well loved and respected by the people of the city.

As Victor and Marx chatted, everyone inside the room breathed a sigh of relief. They knew that as long as Victor was in the room, Angela wouldn't go on a rampage.

"Your son is a genius," said Marx to Victor. "And he has great eyes. That lovely young lady there," he added as he pointed to Elizabeth, "will bring a lot of clients to our business."

"She most certainly will," Victor said after he looked at Elizabeth, too.

"Richard," said Marx, "I want you to launch this project as soon as possible."

"I'm working on it, sir," Richard replied.

After Marx and his associates left the room, Richard quickly gestured for

Elizabeth to come over for an introduction. "Elizabeth, please meet my father, Victor Bennett."

"My goodness, you are very beautiful," Victor said as he took her hand and gently squeezed it.

"You are too kind, Mr. Bennett." She smiled shyly. "It's an honor to meet you."

"Elizabeth is my…" Richard stopped short, not knowing what to say next. He wanted to tell his father that he had found the woman of his dreams, but he was unsure how she would react to that. He didn't want to make her uncomfortable.

Elizabeth noticed Richard's hesitation. "I'm his newfound friend," she quickly interrupted. "We have been seeing each other for about a week now." She flashed a confident smile that made Richard beam. The expression on Richard's face was that of a man who was madly in love. He reached an arm around her waist and pulled her closer to his side.

"I'm delighted to hear that Richard has finally found himself a wonderful girl," Victor said proudly. "You take good care of him now, for he's the only son I've got."

She giggled softly, glanced quickly at Richard, and replied, "I will do my best."

The truth is, Victor also loved Angela like a daughter. For all the years that he had known her, he had learned to accept her for who she was. Never once had he complained about her attitude. He had never compared her to anyone else, nor had he ever asked that she change. However, there was one thing he knew of her, and that was the fact that she was a lot like his wife, Doris—cold, cruel, and snobbish.

Even though Victor didn't express it aloud, he really wanted his son to find someone that would instill a good set of moral values in him—someone who would encourage him to have a sense of commitment to the community, as Richard was the last descendant of Atkins. He didn't know Elizabeth yet, but he hoped that maybe she could be that great woman by his son's side.

Meanwhile, Angela was in total disarray, unable to believe what had just happened that morning. Only a few days earlier, she thought that she had set Richard straight about Elizabeth's true intentions, and was optimistic after that conversation. Now she felt betrayed, and powerless to do anything about it. Elizabeth must be manipulating Richard and playing with his emotions, she thought. "That bitch," she mumbled quietly.

She was so lost in her thoughts that she didn't notice Victor had come over to greet her. Quickly, she snapped out of her trance and greeted him.

"Hello, Mr. Bennett. It's nice to see you, as always," she said quietly, trying to conceal her anger.

"You look a little pale, are you not feeling well?"

"Oh, I'm just a little surprised to see you. That's all," she replied faintly, forcing a smile.

"Well, it's always a pleasure to see you. Richard had invited me over for lunch, so I came here to eat lunch with them."

"By 'them,' do you mean Richard and that woman?" Her voice rose sharply as she gazed at Elizabeth and Richard talking and laughing with each other.

Victor turned his head in the same direction and suddenly realized that it would be risky if he invited her to join them. From past experience, he knew that if she came along, there would probably be a huge commotion at the restaurant. However, being the kind and considerate person that he was, he decided to extend the invite and hoped that she would just decline it. "Yes, with them," he said. "Would you like to join us?"

Angela's heart sank. Having lunch with Richard and his father would mean the world to her. How she missed those times when she was Richard's first priority, his favorite person in this world. But she knew that things had changed. He was not the same Richard anymore, and if she joined them for lunch, she wouldn't be able to control her emotions and would just make a fool out of herself in front of Victor.

"Thank you, sir, but I have a lot of work to do. You go and enjoy yourself," she said with a trembling voice, trying very hard to hold back her tears. Then she slowly got up from her seat and left the room.

Victor sensed her pains, and he felt a little heavyheartedness himself. He loved Angela, but deep down he had wished many times for Richard to keep his options open. He wanted Richard to meet someone who would see eye-to-eye with him and someone who would share the same philosophy about life.

After seeing Angela's enraged expression toward Richard and Elizabeth earlier, Victor realized why Richard had asked him to come over. Richard already knew that a huge commotion would start as soon as the client left the building. But with Victor being here, Angela was going to be humble, and that would give them the opportunity to leave building without any disruptions.

"Clever boy," Victor said silently. He smiled amusingly as walked over to Richard and Elizabeth. He placed a hand on his son's shoulder to assure him that he understood and approved of the plan.

Richard looked at his father and smiled. Father and son seemed to know one another well enough to have a whole conversation without having to say a word.

The plan did work well. Angela did show humility in front of Victor, which gave them plenty of time to leave the crime scene without getting caught.

Angela was trying her best to not be annoyed, but she was dying inside. Her heart felt like it had just been stabbed by the world's longest and sharpest knife.

She couldn't sit still, she couldn't stand still, and her heart was beating out of control. She had to do something, or she felt she would suffocate.

She stormed into James's office and saw that he and Thomas were laughing hysterically at something as they ate lunch together. Upon seeing her, they immediately became silent, and the expressions on their faces seemed to indicate that they knew a gunfight was about to start.

"Did you guys have anything to do with this?" she snorted with a trembling voice that almost made them leap out of their seats and run. "Even though we have our differences, I just trust that you two didn't have anything to do with this!"

They took a moment to gather their wits before James finally answered, "I'm just as stupefied as you are, Angela. We were kept in the dark until this morning, too, and I didn't know that Richard was going to incorporate his girlfriend's alluring smile into this project. But then, you have to admit that it sure looks like it'll be a great success. That's what any business is about—success, right?"

"Look, Angela," Thomas quickly added, "no one knows Richard more than you do. His stubbornness is absurd! Even if we disapproved of his involving Elizabeth in the project, you know that we wouldn't be able to stop him."

Angela was still not satisfied. "Again, I just trust that your laughing wasn't at my expense!"

"Look, we have no idea what you're talking about! We didn't do this to you! Your anger should not be directed at us!" James said in a stern voice.

Angela stormed out of the room. She was furious, and her heart felt like it was bleeding when she thought about Richard and Elizabeth. Their laughing and giggling made her sick to her stomach. Was this a losing cause? she wondered. No wait, she told herself. She was not just anyone—she was Angela! She wasn't going to just sit idly by and cry like a baby. She might be down, but she was not out.

Doris, Richard's mother, was now her only hope. Doris adored her immensely, and she would be willing to go to battle for her. Angela knew that if she got Doris involved, she would be able to even the odds.

Doris Algren Bennett was a beautiful woman with very strong features. Even in her mid-fifties, she was still a very elegant woman who profoundly adored the finer things in life. She was the daughter of Maude and Jackson Algren, who were in the retail and hotel business. The Algren family owned several hotels in the city, including the luxurious five-star Palm Hotel, which was located on a hill on Starlight Boulevard, overlooking Iris Park. The Algren family also owned several high-end boutiques on Summit Drive and many other shops throughout the city.

Doris was the younger of two sisters. Because of this, she was pampered and spoiled by her parents. Even though Maude and Jackson were kindhearted people, Doris did not inherit their generous nature. She was cold, selfish, self-centered, and cruel. Because of her unquenchable thirst for wealth and power, she married Victor, who was the only surviving child of the wealthiest family in the city, and the sole heir to the Atkins fortune.

Doris cared about very few people in her life. However, there was one person in her life whom she cared deeply about, and that was her son, Richard.

Angela decided to call Doris. After all these years of trying to win Richard's heart, she decided she had nothing else to lose now. "Ma'am, I'm so crushed," she sobbed with a trembling voice. "My heart is shattered, and my dream with the only man I've loved all my life had just been ruined. If only you could imagine the pain I'm going through right now. I'm desperate."

Angela described the whole ordeal to Doris, while adding her own embellishments about Elizabeth's intentions and how she had brainwashed Richard. She infused a despicable picture of Elizabeth into Doris's mind, painting her as a homeless bimbo who used her body to sleep her way to Richard's fortune.

"Don't despair, my dear. I will take care of this myself," Doris assured her. "You are the only woman my son will ever need in his life. I will see to it that it stays that way."

"Thank you, ma'am. I'm sorry to trouble you, but you're my only hope. He is too blind to realize that she is just after his fortune."

"Hang in there, sweetheart. From now on, I want you to be strong and polite to Richard. I want you to pretend that this issue isn't bothering you. You try to win him over with your kindness, and I will take care of that woman."

"Yes, ma'am," Angela replied sobbingly. "It's not going to be easy, but I will try." Angela hung up, feeling ecstatic and confident. She had great trust in Doris, and she believed that if Doris got involved everything would work out in the end.

Inside Nancy's restaurant, in a secluded corner in the back, three very cheerful people were seated. Richard, Elizabeth, and Victor chatted happily as they shared some of their fondest moments and most inspirational stories.

Victor watched with approving eyes as the two lovebirds exchanged admiring expressions in front of him. "I hope that in seventy years," he said sincerely, "you will be as loving, affectionate, and devoted to each other as you are today. You both have my blessing for a flourishing and golden future."

Richard was profoundly touched by his father's heartfelt words. "Thank you, Father."

Victor looked at Elizabeth. "So, if you don't mind my asking, where did you meet my son?"

Elizabeth smiled pleasantly. "Well, it was in this very restaurant. I was eating breakfast one morning, sitting at that table over there," she said as she pointed toward a table by the windows, "when I noticed two stunningly handsome eyes staring at me. So, I stared back. I looked him straight in the eyes just to see what he was going to do next. Little did I know that my heart was going to be hypnotized by him that instant." She looked straight at Richard. "I must've scared him a little, because when I smiled at him, he suddenly looked away. I felt a little dejected by that, so I left the restaurant. However, luck must have really been on my side, because I saw him again a few hours later. Wow, twice in one day!" She winked at Richard. "Later that day, I found myself in an alley with a stranger who tried to mug me, and Richard came to my rescue. He then offered to show me around the city, bought me dinner, and even offered me a room at his apartment to stay for the night. Mr. Bennett, your son is not only my hero, but he is also the most generous man I've ever known."

Victor nodded. "That is truly a remarkable story. I've never seen Richard this happy before, and it gives my old heart such comfort. My dreams are for him to meet a good woman, get married, and give me some grandchildren before I pass on."

Elizabeth smiled at Victor and glanced at Richard. Richard's face blushed slightly at what his father had just said. He became awfully quiet now, not because he couldn't find any words to say, but because he was silently praying for his father's dreams to come true. He wanted to marry this woman, to have a family with her, and to grow old and gray with her until death—although not even death would part them, he thought.

"May I ask you a personal question, dear?" Victor asked. "If you're not comfortable, know that you're not obligated to answer."

"Please ask, Mr. Bennett. I'll do my best to answer."

Victor paused for a second, and then he carefully said, "What do your parents do for a living?"

Elizabeth looked at Victor with a cheerful and earnest expression. "My father was a well-known and much-respected doctor. He was also very active in the community and started a clinic in my hometown to provide free medical services to poor families. He also started a charitable foundation to help the poor and to help many Hmong refugees assimilate into their new lives in the United States. Years ago, he traveled to Thailand and started a clinic inside the refugee camp near the city of Nong Khai, to provide medical services for Hmong refugees. He was also very outspoken about the human rights violations by the communist Laotian government toward the Hmong people that were still living in Laos. My mother was a classical pianist and a lawyer. She often volunteered for my father's foundation and provided free legal assistance to many poor people. She also traveled with my father everywhere around the world to give presentations about their clinics and the foundation, and to inform people about human rights violations."

Victor sat mesmerized by what he'd just heard. He looked at her and humbly said, "Your parents are remarkable people. I'm fascinated by their conviction, their commitment, and the compassion they've shown toward others. They've done more than I'll ever do in my entire life. I'm truly humbled and amazed at the work they do."

Richard was also amazed—for this was the first time Elizabeth had talked at length about her parents to him. "It must have been hard for you with your parents constantly leaving home?" he asked.

She turned to him and smiled sweetly. "Yes, it was very hard for me and my brother because we missed them dearly. But we understood what they were doing and were very proud of them. My dream was to carry on their work someday."

Richard sighed deeply. "I've been living in the comfort of my world and never really thought about the suffering of others. I'm truly blessed to have met a woman with so much conviction. It grants me the opportunity to open my eyes and to reach out to those who are in need."

Victor was extremely pleased at the moral conviction his son was learning from Elizabeth. That was the underlying principle on which the city was built. "Whenever you're ready to carry on that work, dear, you'll have my full support," he said earnestly.

"Thank you, sir. You truly are a great man with many great words. Your support means a great deal to me."

After lunch was over, Victor gave Elizabeth a hug. "Thank you for a wonderful time, my dear. You should come down to the house. Doris and I would love to have you over for dinner sometime soon."

"Thank you for the invite, sir. Perhaps we'll do that one of these evenings."

After Victor left and Richard and Elizabeth sat back down, he noticed a puzzling expression on her face. "What's the matter? You seem confused."

She smiled at him. "I was just thinking."

"About ... ?"

"You told me a story a while back about one of Mr. Atkins's great-great-granddaughters, Beatrice, who had a son named Victor, and he was married to a woman named Doris."

"Wow, you have a good memory," he said, chuckling.

She laughed softly and continued, "So, I concluded that you're a descendant of Atkins."

"Yes, and I apologize for not telling you the whole story at the beginning. I just didn't think it was important. Besides, I didn't want you to have the wrong impression of me."

She took his hand and gently held it. Then, with an earnest and loving expression, she said, "People say that the first impression is always the best. My first impression of you was that you were the most wonderful, caring, and generous man I have ever met, not to mention the fact that you were my hero."

Just then Nancy she walked up to their table. "How's everything?" she asked.

"The food was awesome, thanks to a great chef!" Elizabeth said enthusiastically.

"I'm glad to hear that," Nancy replied, smiling. Then, she hesitated a little bit before she said to Elizabeth, "I was just wondering ... Richard told me about one of your dishes—'beef laab.' He said it was the most delicious thing he had ever tasted. Would you consider teaching me how to cook it?"

"It would be a pleasure," Elizabeth kindly replied.

"I just have no manners at all." Nancy chuckled. "I hope I'm not asking too much, but I really want to try it."

"Of course," Elizabeth said. "Just let me know when you're available. We will have a fun and enjoyable cookout together."

"Great! Would it be too much trouble if you come over tomorrow?"

"No trouble at all. I'll be there sometime in the afternoon. Is that okay?"

"Thank you, Elizabeth," Nancy replied excitedly.


After lunch with Elizabeth and Richard, Victor went straight home. When he arrived, he was greeted by the housekeeper, Marie.

"Hello, Marie. What a beautiful day!"

"It sure is!" she agreed. "Hope you enjoyed the magnificent sunshine."

"I sure did, thank you. Where is Mrs. Bennett?"

"She's in the solarium, sir. I'll get your tea ready and bring it out to you."

"Thank you, Marie."

Victor loved all of his servants and treated them with dignity, kindness, and respect. He always remembered to thank them regardless of how big or small their task was, and he could always engage in lively conversations with them about anything.

Doris, on the other hand, was very different. She was not easily approachable, and was often cold and cruel toward her workers. She always carried a bell with her and expected their full attention when she rang.

Victor walked into the solarium and noticed Doris sitting at the table, reading a book and drinking her tea. He casually walked over and sat across from her.

"So, I heard that Richard has found himself a new love interest," she said nonchalantly while her eyes were still fixed on her book.

"Seems like it. She is quite a lovely and intriguing young woman from a very modest and fascinating family," he said approvingly.

She suddenly put down her book and gave him a challenging glare. "Do you mean to say she's from a middle-class family?"

He took note of her facial expression because every time she had that look, it meant that she already had a sinister plan in the works. He leaned forward and looked her straight in the eye. "Yes, and I have never seen that boy this happy, so you better not do anything to disrupt their relationship or I will not forgive you," he warned her sternly.

She continued to glare at him. "Come on, Victor. You and I both know that the only person qualified to marry our son is Angela."

"Well, thank God he doesn't see it that way."

"What do you mean by that?"

"What I mean is that I would rather see my son happy and have a loving and lasting marriage."

"With Angela's wealth, status, and family connections, they will succeed far beyond any of our expectations," she proudly exclaimed.

"Are those the only things that matter to you in life? Money and power don't always equal wealth. The way I see it … a healthy marriage means a wealthy life. I don't want my son to go through thirty years of what I've been through."

She frowned at him, then picked up her book and continued to read in silence.

# Chapter Ten

Richard's day began in the early morning. Even before the first light of dawn, he was already in his office, eager to finish the project. He was in a spirited mood and wanted to finish up so that he could spend the rest of the day with Elizabeth and Nancy.

He wrapped up quickly and was just about to call Elizabeth when he heard a knock at his door. "Richard? Are you in?" Angela peeked into his office.

"Yes, I'm here," he answered.

That's odd, he thought. She had never bothered to knock on his door before. The majority of the time, she just barged right in. *What is she up to?* He pondered this for a few seconds as he braced himself.

To his surprise, Angela seemed to be in a frisky mood. "Good morning, Richard," she said pleasantly as she walked in.

"Hello, Angela. How are you?" He frowned curiously.

"I'm doing well. I was wondering if you wanted to have breakfast with me this morning." She held out a big plastic bag in front of him.

"Angela, what are you doing?" he asked, continuing to give her a skeptical look.

"I just wanted to have breakfast with you. That's all," she replied as she walked to the coffee table. She turned around and noticed that he was still sitting at his desk. "Come on, Richard," she said, giggling amusingly. "I'm not going to poison you."

Hesitantly, Richard rose from his seat and joined her. "Look, if you are going to fight with me about yesterday, I'm really not—"

"Oh, no, no," she quickly interrupted. "It's all water under the bridge. It's probably too late now, but I wanted to apologize for the way I acted. I was childish and selfish. I should have taken your feelings into consideration. Please understand that I'm just here to make amends." She noticed that he was still skeptical and trying to figure her out, so she quickly added, "Look, Richard, I'm not going to lie to you. I was shocked and angry that you involved Elizabeth in this project."

He opened his mouth to explain, but she interrupted him again. "Please hear me out. I had all day yesterday to think about the project, and it really is a great idea. We are in a business that requires creative and successful ideas, and we should not let our personal differences affect the outcome. The bottom line is that it looks like it will be a success, and I'm happy for you."

Upon hearing her words, he felt a slight sense of relief, not to mention surprise at her sudden change in behavior—he didn't think she had it in her. It seemed a little strange, but maybe she had finally learned to accept the fact that the two of them were not to be.

"Thank you, Angela. And I'm sorry for my attitude. I know that I've hurt you on many occasions, but I never meant to. You've always been a very dear friend, and I do love you."

She tried to conceal her reaction, but his words had struck her too deeply. As she opened her mouth to say something to him, she suddenly felt a warm stream of tears stinging her cheeks. "Oh, Richard," she said in a soft, trembling voice, quickly wiping her cheek with the back of her hand. "Why do you have to say those things to me? Why do you have to be so sweet, and yet so discouraging?"

"I'm sorry, Angela. Please don't cry." He gently touched her face and slowly wiped away a tear. "You should know that you will always have a special place in my heart."

"What is wrong with me, Richard? What is it that I lack? Why can't you see how much I love you?"

"I know you love me, and I love you too," he said. "But you and I were only meant to be the best of friends."

"But my eyes see only you and my heart knows only you." She was sobbing softly now. "How can I just walk away and pretend our paths never crossed?"

He gently lifted her face to meet his. "I'm truly sorry, Angela. I never wanted you to pretend that our paths never crossed. I will never forget the precious times we spent together, and you shouldn't either."

"Oh Richard, you're too much," she said as she continued to sob. "I'm not going to give up. I'll wait for you. I have a whole lifetime to wait."

"Please don't say that," he softly said. "I'm not that bad of a person to make you wait your whole lifetime. I'd rather see you with someone else who can give you the happiness you deserve."

"How do I find happiness in this pain? I'm deeply hurt, Richard. My heart will never be the same without you."

He gently brushed her long blond hair away from her face. "Please, don't do this to yourself. You are a beautiful woman, and anyone who is fortunate enough to have you in his life is very lucky."

"Why can't you be the lucky one in my life? The thought of losing you is too much. I won't ever give up on you." She rushed out of his office, sobbing.


Angela's plan worked to perfection. Unbeknownst to Richard, she was only there to occupy his time, distracting him from calling Elizabeth while Doris chatted with her at Richard's apartment.

Elizabeth had been about to leave the apartment when she heard the doorbell ring. She opened the door to find an elegant older woman standing outside. "You must be Elizabeth?" the woman said snobbishly as she barged in.

"Yes, ma'am, I'm she," Elizabeth replied in a startled voice as she closed the door behind her.

Doris stared at Elizabeth intently, her eyes scanning the young woman up and down, side to side, as if she were searching deeply for something, perhaps a blemish of some sort. "I heard you were here, that's why I'm stopping by. In case you're confused, I'm Richard's mother."

"Oh, hello, ma'am, it's a pleasure to meet you," Elizabeth said politely and extended her hand.

Doris waved off the gesture with a huff and walked straight to the couches. "I would like to have a little chat with you, if you don't mind."

"No, ma'am, I don't mind at all. It would be a pleasure to speak with you." Elizabeth walked to the couches and sat across from Doris.

Elizabeth watched as Doris's expression became increasingly hostile and resentful. An uneasy tension unfolded in the room, and Elizabeth glanced away for a moment to think of something to say. She turned back to Doris, only to discover that she was still glowering at her.

"May I get you something?" Elizabeth politely asked.

"There's nothing that you have that I would want!" Doris replied sharply.

Elizabeth was taken aback by Doris's rudeness, but she remained quiet, uncertain of what was going to happen next. The silence that followed was suffocating.

Doris looked around the room for a moment. "I'm curious about something," she said, leaning toward Elizabeth and looking her straight in the eye. "It must be *new* to you to be living in such comfort? Well, you shouldn't get too used to it."

Appalled, Elizabeth was unsure how she should respond. She smiled politely at Doris. "I'm not sure if I understand what you mean by that, ma'am?"

Doris frowned angrily and quickly snapped in a harsh, insensitive manner, "Don't insult my intelligence, young lady! I can see right through you! I know what you're planning to do!"

Elizabeth was dismayed by the outburst, but she remained polite. "I'm truly delighted to have the pleasure of meeting you this morning, ma'am. Perhaps if you would be a little bit more specific about the nature of your visit, I would be more equipped to answer your questions."

Doris looked straight at Elizabeth with a furious frown on her face. "I know what you're up to! You know who my son is, and you purposely attached yourself to him like a leech. Do you think that you can sleep your way to our family fortune?"

Elizabeth was stupefied by such hostility coming from such an elegant woman. But she also felt sorry for Doris. *How miserable she must be to have such bitterness in her heart*, Elizabeth thought. She could have matched wits with Doris word for word, but she decided otherwise.

Elizabeth just sat there quietly as Doris continued her verbal onslaught. *What did I ever do to deserve to be treated in this way?* Elizabeth wondered. This woman's words made her feel worthless. Never in her life had she been referred to as a gold digger, a bimbo, a whore. The despicable image that Doris had painted of her was untrue and unfair. She desperately wanted to explain herself, but she knew that Doris would neither listen nor believe anything she had to say.

She wanted to cry to make Doris stop. But she knew that if she started crying in front of her now, the onslaught would only get worse. *Perhaps the only way to stop this woman is to give some of it back to her*, she thought. She patiently waited for her chance to speak.

Eventually Doris stopped. Elizabeth had remained so calm, Doris was unsure if her verbal insults had even gotten to her. "Well?" she bellowed. "What do you have to say for yourself, you bimbo?"

Elizabeth looked steadily at Doris and calmly replied, "I'm sorry if you feel that way, ma'am. It wasn't my intention to sleep my way to the family fortune, as you so elegantly put it. It wasn't until yesterday that I learned that Richard was your son, and a descendent of Atkins. Money may speak loudly in your perspective, but believe it or not, in my book, money is not that important." She paused for a few seconds to consider her next words. She knew that saying them would cause another outburst from Doris, but she had to tell the truth. Smiling, she said, "No offense, ma'am, but I find it hard to believe that you are Richard's mother. Because it was his generous, considerate, and loving character that captivated me, not his money."

Doris was enraged. "Don't you dare try to criticize me!" she snapped. "Do you know who I am? I will not be spoken to in this way!"

"In what way do you want me to speak to you? I've tried to be civil, but obviously the nature of this visit was not about civility."

Still simmering, Doris paused and took a deep breath before calmly saying, "You should do yourself a favor and leave while you still can. I will not allow my son to marry a person like you. He was dating someone else who is far better than you. I will not allow him to marry a person whose conditions are so far beneath his own."

"Richard is a grown man," Elizabeth calmly replied. "He is an intelligent and competent man. It would be a shame for him not to be able to make his own decisions." Then, looking straight into Doris's eyes, she added, "I'm very confident that his decisions will be a great benefit to his and my happiness."

Doris took several more deep breaths to calm herself down and collect her thoughts. For a full twenty minutes earlier, Elizabeth had just sat quietly as Doris ranted on and on, calling her every insulting name she could think of, and yet the young woman seemed unfazed. And now, using only a few words, Elizabeth had gotten under Doris's skin deeper than anyone else ever had.

Doris knew that Elizabeth was going to be much more of a challenge than she had initially thought. But Doris's entire life had been about rising to the challenge and destroying anyone and everyone who got in her way. She now realized that attacking Elizabeth personally was not the answer. She would have to change her strategy. She would have to attack her in the most insensitive way she could think of.

After pondering a while, Doris looked back at Elizabeth and uttered, "You will regret this. Even if you succeed in luring him into your web of lies and somehow convince him to marry you, I will never accept your children. What makes you think that the children of whatever your kind is will be the descendants of Atkins? We are proud of our white heritage. Your children would not be purely white—they would be low, half-bred mutts, hated by every one of my friends and family members. A mixed-race mutt will not be a descendant of Atkins, or the heir to the family fortune. I will not allow you to taint the bloodline of my family with your kind! I will not allow it! Do you hear me?"

Elizabeth bit her tongue and remained silent, woeful at this blatant display of bigotry. It took all her strength to stay calm and composed. She remained silent for a moment, and then she took a deep breath and sighed deeply before she calmly said, "I feel sorry for you, ma'am. I believe you have made your point. I would like to be alone, if you don't mind." She stood up and made her way to the dining room.

Doris got up and walked to the door. "This matter is not over until you leave my family alone. Have some respect for yourself, and get out of this apartment. It's what a respectable woman would do." She slammed the door loudly behind her.

Elizabeth was dejected and heartbroken. Never in her life had she felt this low and worthless. Every word that came out of Doris's mouth cut like a thousand knives, piercing and chopping up her heart into a million pieces.

She sat silently inside the dining room, trying to make sense of the whole ordeal. She thought Victor was one of the most humble and down-to-earth people she had ever met. But Doris was the total opposite, and she was caught completely off guard. She was appalled by the manner in which Doris chose to attack not only her, but her unborn children as well. She thought Doris was one extremely closed-minded woman and was crushed by her insensitive and indignant behavior.

Feeling a need for some fresh air, she decided to walk to Nancy's. On her way there, her mind remained completely focused on the incident and how Doris's words had tormented her. Her heart was broken, not because she felt she was low and worthless, but because she was disappointed that there were such cold and heartless people in the world.

She entered the restaurant and took a seat at the counter. Nancy noticed the lifeless expression on Elizabeth's face as she sat there staring down at the counter. Elizabeth was so engrossed in her thoughts that she didn't notice Nancy had approached her.

"Elizabeth? Elizabeth?"

Elizabeth suddenly snapped out of her trance and slowly raised her head to see Nancy's smiling face.

"Are you okay? Is there something wrong?"

Elizabeth tried to sound cheerful. "Hello, Nancy. I'm all right. Why do you ask?"

"Well, you seem like you're both here—and not here."

Elizabeth forced a smile. "Let's just say that I'm all right now. I just need a little bit of time to sort out some things. That's all."

Nancy handed her a cup of mocha and sat in the seat next to her. "Let me guess, you received a visit from the Wicked Witch of the South, right?"

"You mean Doris? How did you know?" Elizabeth asked, surprised.

"Believe me. I know exactly what you're going through. I received that same visit a few years ago when she thought I was dating Richard."

"Is that right? Were you guys involved at that time?"

Nancy chuckled. "No. I love Richard, but it's not what you think. He has always been like a brother to me. We met when we were in college. He helped me start this business, and we spent a lot of time together working on it. Then a little blond bird tweeted some misinformation into his mother's ears, and that was when she paid me a visit. I was not a kind and considerate person like you—I let her have it! After that, she never bothered me again," Nancy said triumphantly.

Elizabeth giggled and then sighed softly. "I wish I could be more like you."

"Sometimes a coldhearted and bitter person like that needs to be put in her place. She thinks that she has power over people, that she can control every aspect of their lives. She's just a cold, cruel snob. Her nickname is the 'Wicked Witch of the South' because she lives in the Atkins Mansion, south of the city. If it wasn't for her wonderful husband, people would have stoned her to death a long time ago."

Elizabeth laughed at Nancy's animated description of Doris. It seemed that Nancy was even angrier at Doris than she was. "Thank you for making me feel better," she said. "I really appreciate that." Then she let out a deep sigh. "I'm sorry, Nancy, I'm just not really in the mood today for cooking."

"No problem, sweetie. You take care of yourself, and we'll do it some other time," Nancy said, giving her a hug.

"Thank you for understanding. I'm going to go walk around the park for a while and get some fresh air. I'll see you later." Elizabeth got out of her seat and started toward the door.

"Elizabeth!" Nancy called. Elizabeth turned around. "I'm sure you know this already, but Richard is a wonderful person. He's not anything like his mother. He deserves a chance," Nancy said earnestly.

"I know."


Richard finished the project as quickly and as well as he could and left the arrangements to Thomas. It was obvious that he was excited about joining Elizabeth and Nancy for lunch. His facial expression couldn't hide that fact.

"Sam, I'll be gone for the rest of the day!" he shouted to her while running to the elevator.

He arrived at Nancy's restaurant and looked around eagerly for Elizabeth. Waving at Nancy, he called out, "Hey, Nance! Is Elizabeth in the kitchen?"

"Richard," she replied as she approached him in a concerned manner. "I have something to tell you."

He paused for a second before he asked, "What is it? Is everything Okay?"

"Elizabeth was here briefly, but she left a while ago."

"Oh? What happened?"

"Well, your mother paid her a visit this morning, and the rest is a story you're familiar with."

Richard's happy expression suddenly changed to one of concern. He knew what his mother was capable of, so he took a deep breath, held it for a moment and then slowly let it out. "Did she share with you what my mother said to her?"

"No, she didn't, but I just sensed a difference in her mood, and I guessed that it was your mother's doing. She just smiled and confirmed it. You and I both know that whatever your mother said to her was most likely insensitive and malicious."

"Dammit, Mother! Why do you always have to do this to me?" he yelled, getting the attention of several customers.

Embarrassed by the commotion he'd caused, he turned to Nancy and quietly asked, "Do you know where Elizabeth went?"

"She just said that she was going to the park to get some air. I'm sure she could use some company right about now. "

"Thanks, Nance."

Richard's mind was buzzing with questions as he entered the park and ran down the trail. He stopped several times to call her phone, but there was no answer. His heart pounded rapidly, and he feared that he might not find her. What a miserable life he would have if she decided to part ways with him now! How would he go on? He had to find her and convince her that he would do anything to make up for the pain his mother had inflicted on to her.

Suddenly he remembered that Elizabeth's phone had a GPS locator. Taking out his phone, he began to hone in on the signal. It led him to the trail up to Atkins Peak, so he quickly ascended it. And there she was—sitting on the same bronze bench and staring far out toward the lakes. She was too lost in her thoughts to even notice his approach.

He quietly walked toward her and gently sat down next to her. She didn't seem to be surprised or frightened at all. It seemed as if she was expecting him. She turned her head to look at his face and smiled weakly. Then, she slowly leaned into him.

"I'm so sorry," he said gently. "How could I—"

"Richard, you don't need to say another word," she interrupted. "It wasn't you who hurt me." Then she affectionately tried to reassure him. "If you're wondering where my love stands with regard to you, it is still standing as strong as that big tree over there." She pointed to the biggest and tallest tree in sight, about halfway down the hill.

# Chapter Eleven

Richard sat silently in his office. He was so upset that he felt numb. How could his mother, the woman who claimed to love him more than anything in this world, continue to hurt him over and over again? How *could* she? When would she realize that instead of giving her only son love and understanding, she was killing him with her cruelty? The more he thought about his mother, the more stressed out and depressed he became. Luckily, his salvation was just around the corner, because he was going to join Elizabeth and Nancy for lunch. He knew that just seeing them would ease some of the stress.

Just as he was about to leave, his office door suddenly flew open and there was Doris, standing in the doorway. "I'm here to see my son," she said as she stormed into the room.

"Not in the mood, Mother," Richard simply said, without even making eye contact with her.

She quickly walked over to his desk and leaned over it, looked straight at him, and said, "Are you implying that she is more important than your very own mother—the woman who gave birth to you?"

He looked up at her and let out a deep sigh. "I'm not implying anything. I love you very much, but I also love Elizabeth very much—she is the woman my heart desires. She will someday be your daughter-in-law and the mother of my children."

"Yes, *Elizabeth*," she said with a profound sense of bitterness in her voice. "I'm here for that sole purpose. Let's talk about your *Elizabeth*."

"Like I said, I'm not in the mood right now. Besides, I'm on my way to meet her."

"You are not going anywhere until you have answered all my questions!" she demanded sharply.

He glanced away and said, "Will answering your questions change your mind about her?"

"No, but as your mother, I would like to knock some sense into your head."

"You're forgetting that I'm a grown man, Mother."

"Yes, a man who is blinded by lies and deceit! Can't you see why she is attaching herself to you and wants you to be so madly in love with her? It is so obvious! Look, she'd hardly even met you and she had already packed her bags and moved right in with you! A little odd and desperate, don't you agree?"

"You've got it all wrong, Mother. Why can't you just trust me for once? Why can't you just show some real love and respect for me? Why can't you grant me just a little peace and happiness?"

"You're not happy that you were born to a mother like me? Is that what you're saying?"

"That's not what I'm saying. What I'm saying is that I'm blessed to have you as my mother and I love you to death, but Mother, the happiness I share with you is different from the happiness I share with Elizabeth. All I'm asking is for your understanding and acceptance. Can't you see that my days have never been this pleasant? I look forward to going home every evening to be with her. I want to spend the rest of my life with her because that's how much I cherish her."

Doris was a little discouraged by his enthusiastic response. "You are too blinded by her lies. Open your eyes, Richard! Know the difference between the truth and deception," she said as she slowly reached into her purse.

"What do you mean by that?" he asked, his eyes were fixed on the purse.

"Don't you want to find out about her personal agenda?" she said in a mysterious tone.

"What are you talking about?"

Doris took out several photographs from her purse and laid them out on his desk. "What's this?" he asked, trying to avoid looking at the photos. He suspected that it wasn't going to be pleasant and was fearful of what he might see.

"Here is the truth about your precious Elizabeth," she said with a sinister grin. "Look at them, Richard." She pointed at the photos.

He slowly reached down to gather the photos together and carefully examined them one at a time. The photos showed Elizabeth with another man— some showed her involved in a tight embrace and a passionate kiss with him.

Observing his perplexed facial expression, she grinned satisfactorily. She knew she had finally won the battle. Perhaps if Elizabeth was caught being dishonest, this so-called love story would come to an end.

"I hired a private investigator to follow her this morning. This was what your precious Elizabeth was doing while you were at work," she said triumphantly.

"It can't be. This can't be true," he said softly. He was at a loss as he stared intently at the photos. He tried desperately to be optimistic, but the photos didn't lie. It was all there in front of his eyes. He kept staring at the pictures, unable to believe it. "So, who is this man?" he asked despairingly.

"His name is Patrick Sherwood. He is a rich and handsome man, just like you."

He threw the photos back on the desk. "I don't believe it!" he snapped at her. "Do you have to go *this* far, Mother?"

"I will do anything to protect my only son."

Richard shook his head. "Until I see it with my own eyes, you can rest assured that my heart and mind will remain strong," he said defiantly.

Sensing that she was beginning to lose this battle, Doris leaned over and softly pleaded, "Richard, I beg you to open your eyes and see this woman for who she really is. I want you to end this before you regret it."

"That's for me to decide. As your son, I also know what you're capable of."

"This is not a ploy, Richard. The photos don't lie."

"I understand, but until I see it with my own eyes or hear her confessions with my own ears, I'm not going to give up that easily." Although he stood his ground firmly, inside he was dying.

Doris became silent for a moment. Being the cynical person that she was, she already had another sinister plan in the works. She knew that if she couldn't persuade him, then she'd persuade Elizabeth. She let out a deep sigh and said, "If you don't believe me, then will you do one more thing for me?"

"What do you want, Mother?" he said sharply. By now, he was really annoyed with her.

"I want you to agree to let me do a background check on that woman. If everything she told you about herself is true, then I'll back down. Please, Richard, it will give my old heart some comfort."

Knowing his mother and her tricks, he was hesitant. When he was young and naïve, he used to think that his mother had a magical way of dealing with issues and solving problems. But as he got older, his heart and mind begged to differ. And it wasn't until he met Elizabeth that he truly understood what it felt like to have a moral conscience. Through her eyes and heart, he had realized that being aware of one's positive qualities as well as one's faults played an essential role in leading a moral life.

"Well, what is your answer?" she demanded.

Richard was silent. He was concentrating so hard that he couldn't even feel his own breathing anymore. He kept his head down for a long while before finally lifting it and letting out a long sigh. Looking at his mother sincerely, he finally managed to say, "You have my permission, Mother, but hear me out … If anything goes wrong that proves you're the cause of my relationship going sour, then your only son will vow to never forgive you as long as he is alive."

"Good! But understand, if you and that woman don't work out, it would be your own fault, not mine. Oh, and if that were to happen and you felt grateful, don't thank me. The good Lord would deserve those words of thanks even more," she said in an energetic and satisfied manner.

"My investigator is out in the lobby," she continued. "I'll have him come in and talk with you. He's one hell of a bloodhound. He'll find out anything you want to know about her." She quickly walked over and opened the door.

A rugged-looking middle-aged man entered the room. "Good afternoon, Mr. Bennett. My name is Joseph Greene, from Greene Investigations."

"Hello, Mr. Greene. Please have a seat," Richard said.

Mr. Greene went over to the desk and sat next to Doris. He took out a notepad and looked at Richard. "Please elaborate on what you would like for me to find out about the subject," he said.

Richard quickly got out of his chair. "Talk to my mother. She'll tell you everything. I've got to go get some air." Before he got to the door, he abruptly stopped and turned around to say, "Oh, and one last thing, Mr. Greene. Please contact me, and only me, about your findings."

"Yes, of course, Mr. Bennett."

As Richard walked to Nancy's restaurant, his mind was paralyzed with uncertainty. Had he begun to doubt Elizabeth now? Could it be true that she had found someone else, or had she always had someone else, and the two of them were trying to con him somehow? Only an hour ago, he had been so confident about his trust in her. Had he gone mad now?

He tried to be positive, struggling to come up with a good reason for her to show affection toward another man. Whatever the reasons were, his mind was unsettled. He desperately wanted to know the truth.

Elizabeth was in the kitchen of Nancy's restaurant. She and Nancy were cooking and enjoying each other's company. Although they had only known each other for a short time, they had begun to build a strong bond. To Nancy, Elizabeth was becoming like the little sister she never had.

"I'm impressed!" she exclaimed to Elizabeth. "These are some awesome dishes. With your permission, I would like to use these on a special limited-time-only menu for the restaurant. I will even name them 'Elizabeth's Signature Entrees.'"

"I'll be delighted if you do," Elizabeth politely replied.

She glanced at her watch and was surprised to see it was almost one o'clock. She silently pondered why Richard hadn't arrived yet, but didn't want to say anything.

"Hmmm ... Where is Richard?" Nancy asked.

"I'm not sure," Elizabeth replied. "He told me this morning that he'd be here around noon or a little later. Maybe something came up."

"It's not like him not to call. Why don't you give him a call?"

"I don't want to bother him if he's in an important meeting. He'll be here when he's here," Elizabeth replied.


Richard arrived shortly after one, and Jeanie immediately directed him to Nancy's office in the back of the restaurant. Elizabeth and Nancy were inside the office, having set out all the dishes they had cooked. He was pleasantly surprised to see that they were sitting at the table waiting for him.

"Hey, there you are. A little late, aren't we? " Elizabeth said, giving him a charming little frown.

Richard grinned. "Wow! And I was sad thinking that maybe the party had begun without me."

"If it were just me, the party would have ended already," Nancy joked laughingly.

Richard let out a faint laugh. "I'm sorry. I was tied up in a meeting. But I appreciate the wait." He went over and sat next to Elizabeth. He smiled warmly at her, trying to look composed as she filled his plate with food.

Nancy was delighted with Elizabeth's loving gesture. "Does she always fill your plate for you, Richard?"

He looked at Nancy and smiled faintly, trying not to get too emotional. "Every time I'm with her, I feel like she's not only my hands and feet, but also my heart and soul. She even speaks my mind. She's so special to me."

Elizabeth smiled and leaned into him appreciatively.

His eyes welled with tears. It was too overwhelming for him to believe that Elizabeth could love anyone else the way she loved him. He was at a loss. He wanted to trust his heart and believe that there was no one else in her life. But his mind was fixated on the photographs. He needed to know the truth. *Even if that guy in the picture is a boyfriend of hers or something, I will understand*, he told himself, gathering his confidence. He was prepared to handle anything at this point. Turning to Elizabeth, he gently asked, "So, how was your morning? Did you go anywhere today?"

When she looked at him, his heart nearly stopped. Her eyes showed a mix of confusion and fear. For a moment, he thought that he had caught her and that the gig was up. He composed himself, however, disguising his feelings. "Is there something wrong?" he asked, trying to look concerned.

She slowly glanced at him. "Not really," she whispered. "Well..."

"What is it?" he asked.

"It's just that something weird happened to me this morning, and no matter how much I tried to reason it out, I just can't make sense of it," she continued, sounding puzzled.

"What do you mean?"

Nancy's eyes were wide. She had stopped eating and was now staring at Elizabeth, impatient to hear what she had to say. She wondered if Doris might be involved in this. Nancy knew how cruel and manipulative Richard's mother could be, and was ready to protect Elizabeth even if Richard couldn't.

Elizabeth was looking straight into Richard's inquisitive eyes. Then she timidly explained. "This morning, just about an hour after you left, I received a call on the home phone from a man who said that you wanted to see me at Maury's restaurant. He informed me exactly when and where I was to meet you.

I thought it was strange that you wouldn't call me yourself, but I shrugged that off and went anyway. When I arrived, I was greeted outside the restaurant by a man who called himself Patrick. He reached out his hand to forcefully grab mine and held it tightly, pulled me into his arms for a tight hug, and then—he kissed me! I had to use all my strength to break free from him. As I stood there in shock, he apologized. Then, he just casually walked away as if nothing had happened."

"Did you know this guy?" Richard asked in a concerned voice.

"No, I've never seen him before!" she replied, her eyes wide.

Upon hearing this, Richard became so enraged that he could feel his blood pressure rising. "Goddammit, Mother! How could you?" he screamed, squirming restlessly in his seat. He felt as if he were burning from the inside out. He wanted to punch a hole in a wall somewhere, but instead took several deep breaths to keep himself from doing something that he might regret. Then, gently taking Elizabeth's hands in his, he calmly said, "From now on, I don't want you to listen to anyone else except for Nancy and me. Okay?"

"Of course," Elizabeth replied. She looked at Nancy and then back at Richard with a puzzled expression. "Am I missing something here? What is going on?" she asked.

"Nothing, sweetie. I'm just concerned about your well-being."

With a profound sense of relief, Richard gently placed his arm around her shoulder and pulled her closer to him. He knew that he had to be more protective of her from now on, and he was determined to do everything in his power to never allow her to be hurt by anyone.

Nancy sat and ate in silence. She knew that this was Doris's work and was waiting for an opportunity to voice her concern to Richard. When Elizabeth excused herself to go to the restroom, Nancy gave him a frustrated and disgusted look.

"I know, Nance," he said. "I'm going to put an end to this charade."

"So, did something else happen this morning?"

He sighed heavily. "My mother came to my office and showed me some photos of Elizabeth embracing and kissing another man."

Still with a disgusted expression on her face, Nancy looked straight at him. "Richard, are you going to just sit idly by and watch Elizabeth get hurt? I hope you know that she is the most wonderful thing you have ever been blessed with."

"I do know, Nance," he quickly replied. He paused and took a deep breath before he continued. "I had to admit that I was a bit traumatized by the photos and started to doubt her. I'm already feeling a great sense of guilt over this."

"How low of your mother to go this far, especially to hurt someone as sweet as Elizabeth! I understand she wants to protect you, but why does she have such hatred in her heart?"

"It's not just Elizabeth that she hates. She hates anyone who she believes is a threat to my relationship with Angela. But don't worry. I will protect Elizabeth with my life."

"What are you two talking about?" Elizabeth said as she walked back into the room.

"Oh, just sharing a few secrets about you with Nancy, sweetie," Richard said, smiling.

"Yes, and gushing about all this delicious food," Nancy quickly added.

Elizabeth nodded and went to sit next to Richard. His heart was overjoyed with the profound relief that it was all a lie, cooked up by his mother in her attempt to discourage him. He was disgusted at how he had handled his own selfish emotions earlier, but he didn't want to let her know about his mother's reprehensible actions.

On their way back to the apartment, Richard and Elizabeth stopped by the flower vendor and he bought another bouquet of flowers for her. "Richard, you've bought me so many flowers already! We don't even have enough room in the apartment for them anymore," she said jokingly.

"Then we'll have to just rent another apartment for your flowers," he laughed, placing his arm around her shoulders and pulling her against him. She responded by wrapping her arm around his waist as they continued to walk home.

As soon as they entered the apartment, she went straight to the couch to relax. "Ahhh, what a day," she said, sitting down and leaning back into the couch.

Richard lay down on the couch and gently placed his head on her lap, hoping she wouldn't object to it. To his surprise, she was very receptive as she tilted her head to look at him and smiled warmly.

She slowly moved her fingers through his hair and softly touched his face. He sighed as he looked up at her. This was such a beautiful moment in his life. "You know, sweetie, I could stay like this forever," he said. She smiled and continued combing through his hair with her fingers.

Without a word, he lifted up his head and moved slowly up toward her face. Her beautiful dark, exotic eyes were so warm and trusting. He could feel her soft, warm breath against his face now as he inched closer to her. Her luscious, moist lips looked so inviting, but he didn't want to explore them just yet.

He softly kissed one side of her cheeks and slowly made his way to the other side. She closed her eyes and basked in the tantalizing sensation, and then she slightly parted her wet and hungry lips, waiting to receive his.

A moment of extreme ecstasy rushed throughout his body as he laid his lips against hers, tasting their sweetness. He gently reached his arms around to embrace her, placing one hand on the middle of her back and the other behind her head to support her neck as their tongues vigorously intertwined. Electricity raced through them as they continued, and then . . .

"Richard, Richard, please stop," she said softly in between breaths.

He pulled back to look at her. "What is it, sweetie?" he asked with a soft, heavy sigh.

"Richard, let's stop. I'm afraid it might go too far, and I'm not ready yet. Please understand."

His hand cupped her cheek. "It's all right, Elizabeth. I understand." He pulled her into his arms for an affectionate embrace.

Overjoyed by the pleasant sensations running through him, he silently thanked God for granting him the sweetest gift he had ever asked for. He continued to hold Elizabeth tightly in his arms, trying to make this special moment last forever.

# Chapter Twelve

Richard and Elizabeth had been with each other every day for about a month. Every day that they spent with each other made their lives even brighter. Every touch, every breath, and every move was meaningful and beautiful in its own way. Her simple beauty mesmerized him. She was so exquisitely stunning, and his admiration of her was somewhat like that of a devoted bee appreciating a fully bloomed flower. Never had he been so madly in love.

Richard had not heard anything from his mother for a while and had begun to feel more at ease. He was optimistic that maybe the tongue-lashing he had given her the day after that deplorable ploy had somehow deterred her from attempting any more of her dastardly deeds.

Elizabeth sat with him as they joyfully ate breakfast together. He was his usual jolly self, and there was nothing more enchanting to him than to talk, laugh, and enjoy every moment with her. He wanted to stay home with her that day, but he needed to go to his office for a weekly meeting with his managers. He stood up to put on a light jacket, then turned around to look at her again. How he admired and loved this woman! "I will be home around two," he said adoringly. He gave her a soft kiss and then left for work.

Elizabeth cleaned up the table, did the dishes, and then showered. While she was in the shower, she heard the home phone ringing. Thinking that maybe it was Richard calling her, she quickly got out of the shower and ran to the phone, but the call had already gone to the voicemail.

She quickly pressed the message button to hear what sweet message he had left her, but to her surprise, the message said:

"*Hello, Mr. Bennett. This is Joseph Greene, from Greene Investigations. I spoke with you briefly a month ago, and we agreed that I would contact you directly when I finished my investigation of Miss Elizabeth. Well, I'm done and found out some very interesting things about her. Please give me a call, and we'll sit down together to go over the report. Thank you."*

Elizabeth froze. Her mouth dropped and her face went as white as a ghost. Paralyzed, she sank to the floor and stayed there for several minutes. Eventually, she found the strength to pull herself up and stood in front of the phone again.

She replayed the message, thinking that she must have heard it wrong. She listened in disbelief as the words stung her ears again. *Why would he hire an investigator to check on me?* she asked herself, trying desperately to understand. *Why was he so mistrusting of me? Was he worried that I was after his money, as his mother had claimed?*

She had come to believe that everything was going great, and she applauded him for his strong will and committed heart. But now this! This was so unexpected, especially when it was from none other than her Richard—the man she believed loved her so much and had promised her he'd do anything to protect her from harm.

A vision of Doris suddenly appeared before her eyes, and she felt as though she was reliving the same nightmarish encounter with her all over again. She could clearly hear Doris's laughter, and her harsh, cruel words were replaying over and over in her head, like a broken record. But, this time, not only did she feel that Doris was there, but Richard was also there, and was shouting along with his mother those same words that had tormented her so much.

They were shouting louder and louder, and no matter how hard she tried, she just couldn't make them stop. She was completely devastated and was feeling more vulnerable than she had ever felt in her life. Her heart sank, and all she could do now was to break down and cry. She was going to cry as long as she could. She was going to cry until they stopped.

After crying for what seemed like an hour, she got dressed, her heart filled with a strong urge to run away from the pain. After today, she told herself, I will not hear those tormented words again. After today, I will put their minds at ease. I am going to give them what they want.

Richard arrived at his workplace in his typical playful mood. He was with the woman that he so adored. His meals were nothing less than superb. He couldn't wait to go home to her every night. And what was most precious to his heart was the simple fact that he had her in his life.

He was energetic, spirited, and carefree as he sang and casually strolled down the hallway to his office. "Sam, take the rest of the day off," he called out.

"What are you talking about, Richard?" she asked with a confused but entertained expression. "Are you all right?"

He laughed loudly. "My day couldn't be any better. Go out and enjoy the rest of the day. I'll answer the phone myself."

"You don't have to tell me twice." She quickly grabbed her purse, got up from her desk and made a dash for the elevators.

He laughed as he watched her leave, then went into his office, sat down, and turned on the radio, which was already set to his favorite music station. Leaning back in his seat, he placed his feet on the desk and impatiently watched the huge clock inside his office ticking away one slow second at a time.

"Richard? Are you in?" Angela said as she slowly peeked into his office.

"What can I do for you, pretty lady?" he replied in a cheerful tone.

Angela giggled softly. "Hmmm . . . anything you want, but for the time being, I just wanted your approval on this project. It's for the Larson Company."

"You don't need my approval. I trust you, Angela. You're good at what you do." He smiled pleasantly.

Angela began to feel a little remorseful. She couldn't believe that after what she had done to him, he had shown no ill will toward her. She sighed deeply, and then said, "Look, Richard, I'm sorry about what your mother did. If I had known, I wouldn't have spoken to her."

He smiled sweetly. "It's all right, Angela. It's all water under the bridge."

"Does that mean you forgive me?"

"Already done."

A love song was playing on the radio. He looked up at her with a silly expression. "You feel like dancing?"

"What? What's *wrong* with you today?" she said, half-confused and half-excited.

"I'm just in a dancing mood. Can't a man feel like dancing?" He stood up from his desk, walked over, and grabbed her hands to twirl her about the room.


Elizabeth walked along a small trail inside the park. She was so heartbroken that she didn't know where she was going, nor did she care. She just kept walking until she came to a bridge over a small stream. She slowly walked to the middle of the bridge and stood there for a long while, staring at the peaceful flow of the water below. Her lost, confused, and lonely heart was crying, but her eyes shed no tears.

She continued down the trail until she came to Lake Harriet, where she watched a mother duck playing with her ducklings as if teaching them how to swim properly. She looked to her right and spotted a man down the trail excitedly teaching a young boy how to fish. Behind her she heard some loud chattering and laughter on the trail. She turned her head to look and saw a happy family on their bikes. Everyone seemed to have someone today—that is, everyone except her. She thought of her family and felt despairingly alone. Although she didn't want to be on that road again—that long, lonely, and painful road with no end—she knew that it was inevitable.

She continued down the trail until she saw a beautiful rose garden ahead.

From a distance, she could smell the sweet fragrance of the flowers lingering in the air. She walked straight up to them, enthralled at the sight of such beauty. Each flower was unique in its own way. Each color—red, pink, yellow, and white—added another splash of beauty to the canvas of nature. Some petals stood exquisitely firm and proud as they basked in the warm sunlight, while a few others crouched down sadly, their beauty beginning to wither away as they slipped off their stems, landing softly to cover the lush green carpet below.

"Such is a life," she whispered as the painful emptiness slowly consumed her once again.

She closed her eyes for a moment to deeply inhale the sweet, fresh flowery scent in the air. She took a long moment to indulge herself in all of this beauty around her before she left the garden. Such beauty would only be a sweet memory in her heart after today.


Richard entered his apartment and shouted excitedly, "Sweetie, I'm home!" To his surprise, she didn't reply to him as she usually did. He walked through the apartment and noticed that she was nowhere to be found.

He called her cell phone, and was shocked to hear its ringing coming from the living room. He walked over and saw that she had left it on the coffee table. *That's odd*, he thought. *Why would she leave her cell phone?* He sat down on the couch and tried to think positive thoughts, but instead his mind raced.

After an hour of waiting impatiently for her, he knew he had to do something. He left the apartment and went down to the lobby, hoping that he would run into her there. But to his dismay, she wasn't there either.

Without another thought, he headed for Nancy's. Perhaps his intuition just led him there. When he got to Nancy's and was told that Elizabeth hadn't come by at all, he began to worry about what might have happened to her. It wasn't like her to just go somewhere without telling him.

Next, he went to the park and frantically ran around the trails in search for her. But to his despair, he couldn't find her. He hiked the trail to Atkins Peak, hoping that she would be up there, but she wasn't there either.

He stayed there for an hour, surveying the entire park, thinking perhaps he might catch a glimpse of her walking somewhere. But he still didn't see her. He called the home phone but got no answer.

Finally he sat on a bench, his shoulders dropping, wondering about her whereabouts. Had something happened to her? Did his mother hire someone to hurt her or drag her away? All kinds of crazy thoughts rushed into his mind, as he became fearful about her safety. At the same time, he was furious with his mother. She had to have something to do with this. But then he was also angry at himself. If something had happened to her, it would be his own fault. He had failed to protect her as promised, and he would never forgive himself. He closed his eyes tightly and pressed his fists against the bench so hard it almost broke the skin on his knuckles.

After a while he stood up. Glancing down from the peak, he noticed a woman with long black hair swaying freely in the breeze making her way up the curvy trail. It had to be Elizabeth, he thought. Even though she was too far down for him to recognize her face, he knew that figure anywhere.

"Hey, you," he said, relieved to see that it was, in fact, Elizabeth. "Did you forget to wait for me? Why are you out walking by yourself?"

Her small smile was tinged with anguish. "Am I that predictable, or how did you find me here?"

"I'll have to admit that it did take me a while," he said, frowning and sitting down on the bench. "I thought something happened to you when you left the apartment without your phone."

Without a sound, she went straight to him and sat next to him. He noticed that she wasn't the same cheerful Elizabeth that he had come to know. She seemed withdrawn, distressed, vulnerable—even heartbroken. He put his arm around her shoulders and tried to be as comforting and as supportive as he could. "I'm sensing some gloominess in the air. Is everything all right?"

Without looking at him, she replied sadly, "Everything's all right. I'm just feeling a little homesick."

Sensing her despair and her longing for her family, he tried to cheer her up by saying, "Would you like to go visit your family? Maybe we could go together?" He hoped that this might comfort her.

Instead, she looked at him with quivering lips and teary eyes. "Oh, Richard, I don't have a family anymore," she replied in a trembling voice. She melted into his arms and began to cry.

He squeezed her shoulder tightly. Then, in a warm and soothing tone, he softly said, "If you don't mind, please tell me about it. If you're not comfortable and ready to share, however, I'll understand."

She remained quiet for a moment and then slowly raised her face to meet his. With tears leaking out of her desolate eyes, she began to speak. "Both my parents and my little brother were murdered. They were killed when someone bombed our family's clinic in Thailand. My grandfather died when I was ten. My grandmother died five years ago. I'm the only one left in this world. I miss my family so much. I miss having them with me in my times of sorrow. I wish they were here to guide me through." She broke down into tears and began crying again.

Bewildered at what he just heard, his heart sank and he suddenly felt a sharp pain in his chest. Elizabeth had been a strong, pleasant, and cheerful person while they were together. To see her like this, to see her breaking down in front of him, baffled him and melted his heart.

He now knew that she was more complex than he could ever imagine. She had confined this painful sorrow deep in her heart, masking it with a cheerful smile. He now knew that deep down inside the heart of this strong, loving, and seemingly happy woman was an indescribable pain. How he wished that he could bear all of that pain, so that she could be truly happy and honestly display that cheerfulness she showed the world.

He was at a loss for words and didn't know what to say to make her feel better. He hadn't known that she was left all alone in this world. He didn't know … He realized he didn't know much about her at all. His chest began to tighten, his eyes swelled, and his lips began to quiver. He couldn't utter another sound, so he just continued to hold her tightly as she wept quietly in his arms.

A few minutes later, he gently lifted her head up and softly wiped away her tears. "Don't cry anymore, sweetie. You have me now."

As he slowly wiped away her tears, she said softly, "Richard, I have a confession to make. I'm sorry I lied to you when we first met. I wasn't here for a job. I was running away. I was running from the pains and sorrows in my life. I just didn't know how to cope with it, so I ran away from it. I'm so sorry."

Again he pondered what she said. Was this the "long journey" she had been talking about earlier that she had been traveling on for so long and that had become "longer, bumpier, and lonelier"? His heart struggled to comprehend the pain that she'd had to endure all by herself. He knew that she desperately wanted this journey to end. And he was going to make it happen. He wanted her pain and torment to end forever. He wanted to spend every day making her happy, for the rest of her life.

He held her tightly in his arms, trying to be as comforting as he could. Then he stared deeply into her eyes and softly said, "I understand, sweetie. I'm sorry, too, that I didn't know what you were going through. I didn't know how much pain you had in your heart, but I'm here for you now. You don't have to cope with it alone, and you don't have to run away anymore. I promise you that no one will hurt you anymore—not me, not anyone."

*But you did*, she told herself.

He continued to hold her as they sat at the peak together until the sun had finally vanished below the horizon. In her heart, this was her last sunset with him. This was going to be her last memory with him.

Elizabeth was quiet the whole time during the walk back to the apartment. He led her to the couch and gently sat her down. Then he went into the kitchen to make a nice warm cup of cappuccino and brought it out to her.

"Thank you," she said quietly.

As she drank from the cup, an even deeper rush of sorrow overwhelmed her, confusing her. How could this man be so sweet and so wonderful but yet so cynical and so mistrusting? she wondered. She was going to ask him about the phone message, but she was too hurt from it and her mind was already set on leaving.

Richard sat down beside her. "Are you feeling any better, sweetie?" he whispered, hoping she was calming down.

"Yes, thank you," she softly replied. "Richard, I'm truly sorry for what I've put you through. I hope someday you'll find it in your heart to forgive me."

"There's nothing to forgive. That's what love is—to be understanding," he said as he gently ran his fingers through her hair. "Maybe it would help to watch a movie together?"

She looked down at the coffee table and let out a sigh. "I'm sorry. I'm kind of tired right now."

He caressed her face and smiled warmly. "I understand," he said soothingly. "Why don't you try to get some sleep? It has been a long day for you."

She smiled despairingly at his loving gesture and softly replied, "Thank you. You have a good night." She rose from the couch and went into her room.


Elizabeth lay in her bed thinking about the phone message. She thought about Doris's words and how they had hurt her. She thought about Richard, the man that she loved more than anything. How could he *do* this? Was he thinking of her in the same way his mother was? How could she prove to him that she was *not* a despicable woman? Maybe her leaving would prove to him that she was not just interested in his money. She remembered how Doris had called her bimbo, a whore. Did Richard think of her that way as well? She loved him so much; it would destroy her to think that he thought of her in that way. She decided she wanted to be with him one last time before she left. She wanted to prove to him that she loved him for who he was, not for his money.


Richard tossed and turned in his bed, thinking about Elizabeth and how it must have been so sad and painful for her to be left alone in the world. He couldn't begin to comprehend the pains she had endured. He was not in her shoes, so how could he be more understanding of her situation? He vowed to love her more now than ever before, being there for her so that she didn't have to suffer alone.

As he lay there entrenched in his thoughts, he heard a soft knock on his door. "Richard? Are you asleep?" She slowly peeked into his room.

He quickly sat up and went to the edge of the bed. "No, sweetie, I'm still awake," he replied quietly.

Entering his room wearing a short, white, silky nightgown, she walked straight up to him and stood before him. He sat there in silence, staring up at her beautiful face. She smiled warmly at him and whispered, "How much do you love me?"

He took a deep gulp of whatever was clogging his throat. Then, with the most sincere and passionate feeling his heart could muster, he replied, "I love you more than anything in this world. I love you more than life itself."

He noticed her satisfied expression. "What about you?" he asked. "How much do you love me?"

She closed her eyes for a second and then slowly opened them to look straight into his eyes. She sighed deeply before she softly murmured, "I love you enough to give you the one thing that means everything to me." He squinted his eyes as he looked at her with a puzzled expression.

A seductive smile spread across her face as she slowly slipped off her nightgown to reveal her magnificent, bare body to him. He longed to look her over in all her beauty, but his eyes remained fixated on her face.

All those times he had stared at her, wondering if he might ever see that entire beautiful body. Now that she was here, in front of him like this, he was afraid to even take a quick glance at it. He just sat there in a deep trance.

"Richard," she whispered.

He suddenly snapped out of his trance and glanced at the beautiful goddess before him. Indeed, God's creation had surpassed any of his greatest imaginings. He looked up at her face and hesitated a little, then he softly asked, "Sweetie, are you sure you want to do this?" She looked down at him and slowly nodded.

With her approval, he reached out both hands to place them on her hips. He moved his hands gently up and down, caressing her soft, silky skin, feeling every inch of her womanly figure. Then he slowly moved his hands up to her chest and gently caressed her firm breasts. He could feel his heartbeat racing faster as he tenderly moved his fingers in circular motions around her nipples, feeling them harden beneath his thumbs. He felt a rush of heat through his body as he leaned forward and replaced first one thumb and then the other with his wet and hungry tongue. He couldn't stop now, even if he wanted to. His tongue stroked her eager breast, as he switched from one to the other in perfect succession, inducing them to full arousal.

Her eyes were closed, and her lips began to quiver. He stopped for a moment to observe that she was fully enjoying what he was doing. Softly he kissed her silky skin and then moved up to her neck, each stroke of his lips sending sweet sensations through her veins. She squirmed ever so lightly in his arms as he continued the motion.

His lips finally found hers and he parted them gently with his tongue, slowly intertwining her tongue with his. They devoured each other passionately, barely able to stop and gasp for air.

He gently placed his hands on her back and slowly laid her down on the bed, proceeding to plant soft, quick kisses up and down her body and sensing her body jerk each time he touched her with his lips. He kissed her belly and moved toward her breasts again, taking them inside his mouth, one at a time. He patiently suckled them, teasing them as her body tensed in ecstasy.

He slowly let his right hand slide down below her belly to discover new treasures. She couldn't help but moan deeply as soon as his fingers found her beautiful, sweet wetness. This was the secret spot he had been waiting to explore for so long—his paradise, his love, his life—his Elizabeth.

As his fingers worked magically on and around her most precious treasure, she moaned softly. How could she have thought that she was in Heaven earlier, when it was nowhere near how she felt right now? This was the point of no return. She was so hot, wet, and ready for him.

He slowly parted her legs as he gently moved on top of her. His heart throbbed with anticipation. He took her lips in his and began to kiss her deeply and passionately. He pressed his body tightly against hers and slowly entered her.

Her body tensed up and she winced. Groaning softly, she tightened up her legs and gently pushed her hands against him to allow her more time to accept him deeper into her.

Seeing the expression on her face and feeling her extreme tightness, he abruptly stopped. She slowly nodded as she looked up at him with teary eyes to confirm his suspicion. He quickly and passionately embraced her. "Oh, Elizabeth," he said, almost in a sob. "I love you so much."

Now that he knew, he wanted to make her first time a truly unforgettable experience. Being extra gentle, he entered her ever so slowly, steadily making his way deeper into her. He gently continued the motion until he was all the way inside and she began to relax.

She was moaning softly now, tremendous pleasure surging through her body with his every thrust. He could feel the electric sensations intensify with every movement. As the point of climax was reached, he let out a euphoric cry.


After lying next to each other for a while in bed, he pulled her into his arms and kissed her lips again, tenderly touching her face and brushing away a few locks of her hair. "I love you so much, Elizabeth. I don't know what I would do without you."

Her eyes were filled with tears as she thought about her plan to run away. She remained quiet for a moment before turning to look up at his face. He could see the tears forming in her beautiful eyes as her mouth opened. "I'm sorry, Richard. I run away every time I get hurt. Will you please forgive me?" She let out a soft sob.

He gently pulled her closer and placed her head on his shoulder, slowly wiping away her tears. "There's nothing to forgive," he passionately replied. "You have given me everything I ever wanted. There's nothing more I could ask of you. I thank God every day for sending you my way."

# Chapter Thirteen

The night couldn't have been more beautiful. The moon was bright, full, and simply gorgeous in the night sky. It was just sitting there, staring straight at them through the large glass windows.

Richard tried not to fall asleep. It would mean that in the blink of an eye, this special night would be over. He wanted to stay up to enjoy every minute of it.

He was still looking at the moon when all of the sudden, he found himself standing in the middle of a beautiful, lush green meadow, all by himself. He turned around in a full circle to glance at the surroundings. The sun was high in the sky, and other than a few birds soaring far off along the horizon, he was alone.

He couldn't remember how he got there or why he was there. It was a beautiful place—too beautiful to not have someone to share it with, he thought. He thought about Elizabeth and how painful it was going to be for him to be in this place without her. How was he ever going to endure the pain and sorrow of being in this place all alone? He felt a deep sense of despair as his heart sank down to his weakened knees.

"Elizabeth?" he called out to her, but heard no replies. He called out to her several more times, and more frantically: "Elizabeth! Elizabeth! Elizabeth!"

He abruptly woke up to the sound of his own voice, and quickly turned to see that she was still sleeping beside him. The sun was now peeking through the window, casting its glow on the two of them. The soothing warmth of her body immediately comforted him, and his despairs melted away. She was like an angel—a real-life angel that had just rescued him from this nightmare.

As she lay there sleeping soundlessly, he was mesmerized by how beautiful and peaceful she looked. How he wished that he could bear all of her pain and sorrows so that her heart could be as peaceful as his was at this moment. Then, he thought about his own dream and tried to comprehend how it had felt to be in that place, all alone. *Is this how she feels?* he pondered. *Is this how she feels when she has to endure all of her suffering alone?*

After that strange dream, he wanted to keep her closer to him—now more than ever. He had missed her so much already, even though she was right there beside him. "I love you so much. Please don't ever leave me," he softly whispered to her.

Then he began to tenderly touch her bare body, moving his hand up and down in complete admiration of how beautiful she was. He slowly reached his arms around her and gently held her for a while, silently thanking her for being there. He wanted to make love to her again and again—from dawn to dusk, and then start all over again when night fell. He began to slowly kiss her, waking her up and arousing her again.

After their early morning delight, he didn't want to go to work. He wanted to stay in bed with her, hold her, kiss her, and then make love to her again, but Angela was giving a presentation to a new client and he had to be there for it.

Hesitantly, he got up, showered, and got dressed. Leaning over the bed, he caressed her cheek once more before he left. "I will be back shortly," he said with a loving smile.

"I'm so sorry, Richard. Please forgive me," she said quietly.

He tenderly touched her face, slowly stroking her cheek. "There is nothing to forgive," he said sweetly. "You are my world, my happiness, and my life."

She looked at him, small tears forming at the corners of her eyes. She stared deeply and intently at him, as if trying to implant an everlasting picture of him inside her heart. She passionately kissed him, and then whispered softly in his ears, "I will miss you, Richard. I will miss you always and forever."

"Is that a promise?" he asked, assuming she was going to miss him while he was at work.

"Yes," she replied faintly.

He passionately kissed her again, and then left.

Richard arrived at his workplace, eagerly wanting to see Angela's project. He headed straight to her office and went over the details with her.

"This is going to be great!" he said ecstatically.

"Thank you," she replied, sounding surprised. "My, aren't we cheerful today?"

"Is it that obvious that I'm the happiest man in the world?" he said, grinning broadly.

"I'm happy for you, Richard. Whatever you took this morning, I want some too," she said chuckling. He laughed and gave her a big hug.

***

Elizabeth packed everything she owned into her cloth bag and left behind everything that Richard had bought for her. Exhausted and heartbroken, she just wanted to leave the memories of him behind her.

She went to the dining table and sat there for a while. A deep sense of sorrow overwhelmed her, and her eyes began to glisten with tears as she started on her goodbye letter. She loved this man so dearly and wished that she could just trust her fate. *But what is fate?* she asked herself. Maybe *this* was her fate—to always have to be on this journey and see where the road led her. It was a cruel fate, but she had no other choice but to endure it alone. She cried over and over as she carefully worded the letter.

After the meeting, Richard went straight to his office and called La Fleur de Paris to reserve a table for the evening. He wanted to take Elizabeth there for a special night together. He knew that it was probably too soon, but he couldn't wait any longer: he wanted to propose to her and make her his wife as soon as possible. Cass Jewelers was not too far away from his apartment, and on his way home, he could stop by to pick out a ring for her. He was thrilled with his plan and could hardly wait for the afternoon to be over.

Sam knocked on his door and then peeked into his office. "Excuse me, Richard. There's a Joseph Greene here to see you."

"Ah, send him in, Sam," he said. It had occurred to him that the investigator might show up one of these days, and although he was curious what Mr. Greene had found out about Elizabeth, he knew that after last night nothing in the report could deter him from his plans.

Sam stepped aside as the investigator entered. "Hello, Mr. Bennett."

"Hello, Mr. Greene. Please, come on in."

Mr. Greene went inside and closed the door behind him. Holding an orange envelope in his hand, he approached Richard and said, "I got the information on Miss Elizabeth."

"I see. Please read it to me."

Mr. Greene took out a single paper from the envelope and stood in front of Richard to read it.

*"Elizabeth Jia Lia Vang was born in St. Paul, Minnesota. Her father was a prominent doctor and a political activist. Her mother was a lawyer and a pianist. She had a younger brother named Charles.*

*At the age of five, she won her first state piano concerto competition and was considered a top prospect. She graduated from high school at the age of fourteen and was accepted to college right away. She graduated college with honors at the age of sixteen. After she received her bachelor of arts, she attended grad school and received a master's degree when she was eighteen.*

*Besides holding a full-time job, taking care of her family, and being in school, she also was very much involved in many charitable organizations.*

*Her parents and brother were killed in a suicide bomb attack in Thailand eight years ago. Other than her grandmother, she was the only surviving member in her family. She lived with the grandmother until the grandmother passed away five years ago.*

*After the death of her grandmother, she received the sum of three million dollars from her parents' trust fund. She sold the house in St. Paul, gave the proceeds to charity, and then simply disappeared."*

Richard raised his eyebrows and let out a huge sigh of relief. Knowing the kind and generous heart this woman possessed, he wasn't surprised at all. He was so profoundly elated that everything she had told him was consistent with the report. At a loss for words, he simply asked, "Is that all?"

Mr. Greene folded the piece of paper and set it on Richard's desk. "I'm sorry, but that would be all at this time. I was unable to find anything else on her—not even a work record or a permanent place of residence. It was like she just wanted to be forgotten. If you ask me, I'd say that she is a very mysterious and remarkable woman. I would like to meet her someday."

Richard was pleased to hear such words. "Maybe you will be able to meet her soon. Thank you, Mr. Greene."

"Not a problem. I'll let you know if I find out anything else. Good afternoon, Mr. Bennett."


Richard couldn't have been more pleased to hear this news about Elizabeth. He had known from day one what kind of a woman she was, and his feelings for her only grew stronger with each passing day. He couldn't wait to prove his mother wrong and rub the report in her face.

He was still engrossed in his thoughts when he heard another knock at the door. "Oh by the way, Mr. Bennett," Mr. Greene said as he peeked back into the office. "I'm sorry to bother you again, but I had left you a message yesterday and didn't hear from you. I just wanted to make sure I had the right phone number. Was the phone number that I called yesterday a good number to reach you at in case I find out anything else?"

"You left me a message?" Richard asked, puzzled. "Which number did you call?"

"The number your mother gave me. She told me that it'd be all right to leave a message if you're not there. She also told me that it would be a good number to reach you if something urgent needed to be discussed. Is there something wrong?"

"Which number would that be?" Richard asked with a tense and frightened look in his eyes.

Mr. Greene walked over to Richard and showed him the number on his phone.

"That's my home phone. You left a message on my *home* phone?" Richard said with a rush of panic in his voice.

"Yes. Is that not a good number to call?" Mr. Greene was dumbfounded.

"Oh my god," Richard gasped in disbelief as everything started to make sense to him now. "No wonder she was so upset yesterday. No wonder she kept apologizing to me. She was planning to leave! This was my mother's plan all along!"

He quickly picked up his phone to call Elizabeth. When he heard no answer, he panicked even more. In the back of his mind, he was hoping that she may have just stepped into the bathroom or out of the apartment, like she did yesterday. However, his heart couldn't relax, and he rushed out of his office, leaving Mr. Greene standing there.

Richard reached his apartment building and flew through the lobby like he was running for his life. The elevator ride up to his apartment was the longest ride he'd ever experienced, and he began pacing frantically back and forth like a knight about to enter the battlefield.

He quickly walked out of the elevator and dashed down the hall to his apartment. He opened the door and called to her, but heard no answers. His heart knotted so tightly that it began to ache. He called out to her again as he rushed into her room.

When she was nowhere to be found inside her room, he remembered to check the closet. A rush of relief filled his heart when he saw that her belongings were still there. Her clothes were still hung up neatly, and her shoes were still stacked nicely in place on the rack. His heart began to relax a little and his breathing was more calm and regular now. *She's not gone*, he thought. *She just went out*, he assured himself.

He called her phone again and noticed that it was ringing from somewhere else in the apartment. For a second he thought that she might still be sleeping in his room, so he ran there. No sign of Elizabeth.

He was suddenly reminded of the day before when he thought she had left and he frantically ran around looking for her all afternoon. Maybe she was just out again, he reasoned. She loved and cared about him too much to do this to him. She wouldn't allow herself to turn his life upside down. She wouldn't shatter his dreams this easily. He thought up every excuse to reassure himself.

He walked over to the home phone to play the message that was left by Mr. Greene. He knew such words would devastate her. He knew his mother well; he knew she could stoop this low, especially when it concerned him. So how could he allow this to happen to Elizabeth?

His heart began to beat faster and his breathing became fast and irregular again as he thought about the hurt he had caused her. Even if she hadn't left, she would be hiding somewhere, trying to cope with her pain alone. He had to find her. He had to comfort her.

He quickly headed to the park and went straight to Atkins Peak, hoping that he would again find her there. But at the top of the trail, all he saw was an empty bench. He carefully scanned the park below, hoping to get a glimpse of her, but to his dismay, she wasn't anywhere in sight. He waited at the peak until the late afternoon hours, still clinging to hope.

Finally the sun set. As the sky transformed from a reddish-orange to a splash of brown and black, his heart sank deeper and deeper. He was suddenly reminded of his dream from the night before, when he was standing all alone in the middle of a beautiful meadow. How his heart ached for her. How he feared losing her.

The long walk back to the apartment was depressing, but he prayed that she was at home waiting to surprise him with another delicious dinner like usual. This small shred of hope comforted him somewhat as he made his way through the dark.

"Hello, Mr. Bennett. How was your evening?" Martin asked, cheerfully greeting Richard as he entered.

"Martin, I had one hell of a day. Did you happen to see Miss Elizabeth?"

"As a matter of fact, I did, sir."

Richard was suddenly filled with excitement. "Really?" he quickly asked. "Did she come back?"

"Well, I saw her this morning. She was carrying that god-awful bag with her. She kissed me on my cheek here," Martin said, pointing to his left cheek, "and it almost made me fall to the ground. She said good-bye to me like she was leaving town or something. And then she asked me to give you this letter." Martin reached into his coat pocket, took out a pink envelope, and handed it to Richard.

With a confused and woeful expression on his face, Richard took the envelope from Martin. Even though he didn't want to give up hope, deep down he knew something was not right. He was dying to read the letter right away, but knew that he might need to be alone for this.

He slowly made his way to the elevators. On the way up, he contemplated if he should read the letter right there in the elevator. *No*, he thought. *I should probably sit down first.*

In the hallway to his apartment, he sniffed the air, trying to detect one of those to-die-for dinners that Elizabeth had waiting for him every night. But to his dismay, he smelled nothing.

He opened the door and slowly walked into his lonely apartment. Tonight was the first night in a whole month he had come home to an empty apartment. Tonight marked his very first night without her.

He went over to the couch and sat in the same spot where she sat every evening, and tried to inhale her sweet scent. He closed his eyes, imagining her smile and how she held him when he came home. Finally, he built up enough strength to open the envelope. Inside was a piece of folded-up pink paper. He slowly unfolded it and read it.

*My Dearest Richard,*

*From the first time I saw you, I didn't know I would fall this deeply in love with you, but I guess my heart knew it best. It was this heart of mine that found a warm place in you. When you held me in your arms, it was my heart that you confined within yours. When you kissed my lips, it was my soul that your lips touched.*

*Even though I have only been with you for a short while, you were not only my best friend and the person that I adored most, but you were also my safest haven.*

*When you first walked into my life, it didn't matter to me whether you were poor or wealthy. I didn't care about wealth, status, or power. Even if you gave them to me, I wouldn't know what to do with them. What I wanted most in my life with you was simple. I simply wanted to be everything to you so that you didn't have to go through life thinking about what could have been.*

*My journey has not been smooth. I have to admit that the roads I've traveled have been quite bumpy, and my days were terribly lonely until the day I met you. From that day on, my heart took quite a turn. I had wanted more than anything to build a home and have a family with you.*

*I would love to hold the key of patience in my hand, but it is time for me to run away once again. If someday fate grants my heart another chance to join yours, perhaps I will meet you again. Perhaps then, my dream of having a family with you will be fulfilled.*

*Please don't look for me. You must be strong, because you are an Atkins and you were destined to be a great man. I'm truly sorry to have hurt you. There's a quote that says, "No man is worth your tears; he who is will never make you cry." The same applies to a woman. If she makes you cry, then she is not worthy of your love. Therefore, please don't shed another tear for me, because I have already done all the crying for the both of us.*

*You must take care of yourself now, Richard, and remember that I will always love you.*

*I will miss you always and forever,*

*Elizabeth*

Two tears glistened at the corner of Richard's eyes and slowly trickled down his cheeks, making their way down to his lips. Several more tears appeared and followed the same paths.

"You're wrong, Elizabeth. I will do all the crying for the both of us," he sobbed.

# Chapter Fourteen

It was just before dawn, and a storm raged outside. The wind howled angrily like a lonely wolf. Lightning flashed furiously across the horizon like daggers trying to split the sky in two, and the rain lashed violently against Richard's window. But he heard none of it. He had been sitting there silently, in the same spot he had been while reading Elizabeth's letter. He hadn't moved much at all, except to slide off the couch to sit on the floor, and his head rested motionlessly against one of the cushions.

His eyes were fixed on the plain, colorless wall, but his mind seemed to be somewhere far beyond it. He felt so heartbroken, so betrayed and so abandoned by his mother that he felt sick to his stomach. How could she, after he had specifically threatened her that if his relationship with Elizabeth were to go sour in any way, he wouldn't speak to her or forgive her ever again?

He hadn't eaten since the previous morning, but he didn't feel hungry at all. He hadn't slept a wink last night, but he was too heartsick to sleep. He had to go to his mother to break the news to her, so he set out even before the first light of dawn.


He appeared in front of his parents' mansion and rang the doorbell repeatedly. Marie came to the door and was pleasantly surprised to see him. "Good morning, Richard."

"Is my mother in?" he asked angrily.

Marie frowned. "She's in the living room with your father."

He barged in and walked a couple of steps past her, then suddenly stopped and turned around. "I'm sorry, Marie, for my rude manner."

"It's all right, honey," she replied pleasantly.

Richard stormed into the living room and found Doris and Victor sitting down on the sofas, facing each other and drinking their morning tea. "Richard! What a delightful surprise to see you," Victor said cheerfully.

"Hello, Father," Richard replied quickly as he rushed over to Doris and threw the orange envelope onto her lap.

"Read it!" he yelled.

Doris picked up the envelope and then turned her head up to look at Richard. "What is this?" she asked, puzzled.

"It's what you so desperately wanted to know!" he fumed. "Everything you wanted to know about Elizabeth is right in there!"

He stood there with his hands on his hips, watching as his mother pulled the paper from the envelope and read it. "She's such a 'bimbo,' Mother! She's such a 'gold-digger'! No, she's just what you *wanted* her to be!"

"Whatever she is, she still isn't good enough for my son!" Doris roared defiantly.

"I'll tell you what she is, Mother! She is the most perfect human being I have ever met! She loves me not for my wealth, or my power, or my position, but for the person that I am, Mother! You pushed it too far this time!" Richard was so overcome with disgust and disbelief that he began to cry in front of them both.

"Doris, what have you done?" Victor asked with a furious expression of his own.

"I'll *tell* you what Mother did," Richard said as he looked at his father. "She harassed Elizabeth. She threatened Elizabeth. She hurt Elizabeth. And she drove Elizabeth away." Then he turned to Doris and said, "You can go celebrate now, Mother, because you did not just drive Elizabeth away. You have also driven your son away. Far away this time."

"Doris, is it true?" Victor demanded as she sat there in silence.

Richard knelt down in front of her and looked into her eyes. She could see the agonizing pain in his teary blue eyes and could sense the despair that she had caused. She was paralyzed, knowing she was not going to be able to console him this time. She was afraid to accept what she had done to her only son. She had to apologize to him, so she lowered her head to look at him with a sincere expression on her face. "I'm sorry, Richard," she said quietly.

Richard abruptly stood back up and laughed hysterically at her words. His eyes were so red she was afraid that if she were to say another word, his eyes might just leak out tears of blood.

"Good going, Mother! Congratulations! You just said you're sorry!" He laughed hysterically again. "Say you're sorry again. That might just bring her back!"

Victor was stunned. He just sat there silently, waiting to see what Doris was going to do next.

Richard wiped the sweat off his forehead with the back of his hand. He was quiet for about a minute, just staring at the wall. No one said anything. The room was so quiet that Doris felt she would even hear the sound of a pin if one were to drop on the soft, plush carpet at her feet.

Richard turned back to her and slowly knelt down in front of her again. This time both of his knees were on the floor, as if he were going to beg her to save his life. He slowly reached out both of his hands to gently hold hers. He looked deep into her eyes as if he could peer right into her soul. With a deep anguish and tearful expression on his face, he softly said in a most painful tone, "Look deep into my eyes, Mother. Examine my face carefully. This is going to be the last time you're ever going to see this face again."

After a long moment of staring into her eyes, he added, "Oh, and by the way, in case you're interested, I will never stop looking for her, even if it takes my whole lifetime. Until I find her and she allows herself to forgive you, you can rest assured that this will be the last time you'll ever see me or hear my voice again. And if I cannot find her in this lifetime, then the Bennett name and the Atkins legacy will end with me. This is a promise." He slowly stood up and then quickly walked out of the room.

Doris felt like someone had just put a knife through her heart. She could still hear Richard's words ringing in her ears. Her son was gone, and her heart was torn. Her life was over. She had made the biggest mistake of her life, and how was she ever going to fix it? Could it ever be fixed? She feared she may have lost her son forever.

"Doris, I warned you!" Victor scolded her. "I told you that this was going to happen, but you just couldn't leave it alone! Now do you see what you've done?" He quickly got out of his seat to go after Richard.

"Richard, wait!" Victor called out as he followed after him.

Richard turned around, and his father gave him a tearful embrace. "I'm so sorry, son. Had I known about it, I would've never allowed it to happen."

"I know, Father," Richard replied, understanding. He pulled away and wiped his eyes.

"She was an angel," Victor continued. "I know one when I spot one. I had just begun to see that you would live a contented life with this angel. I'm just as heartbroken as you are. We will look for her together, you and I. I just hope that someday you will learn to forgive your mother." He put his hand on Richard's shoulder to reassure him.

Victor came back to the living room and sat next to Doris. He gave her the coldest and most bitter stare that she had never seen. It was a stare that jabbed her deep in her heart, and it continued to pierce her with every breath she took. She took one look at his eyes and knew she had better hide her face forever or beg for forgiveness.

She sat in silence as she stared dazed at the floor, trying to think of something to say, but nothing came to her. Richard's words continued to echo in her head, and she began to shake as she realized how far she had gone this time. Her only son was so wounded now that even her pleas for forgiveness wouldn't begin to mend his heart. If he wouldn't forgive her in this lifetime, she would understand.

"I'm sorry, Victor. I just wanted to protect our son," she managed to say shakily with her eyes still glued to the floor.

"*Protect*?" he answered her sarcastically. "You call this *protecting*? Has it ever occurred to you that maybe he was doing better without your help?"

"I just thought that he deserved something much more . . ." she tried to explain, but he cut her off.

"Deserved something much more? Like Angela? Do you actually think that he would be happy if he were to marry a girl who has your personality? I'm sure he has the eyes to see and the heart to know the misery his father has been through all these years."

Doris gaped at him. After all these years of marriage, he had never spoken to her in such a way.

"You . . . you were never happy?" she asked in anguish.

"It's about time you re-examine yourself, Doris. You never seem to realize just how inconsiderate, cold, heartless, and insensitive you are. You have never once shown a bit of compassion toward anyone. In fact, you seem to find enjoyment in stepping on those who are less fortunate than you, and you talk to them with no remorse whatsoever. One who has a heart would understand that money and power don't always mean happiness. Answer just this one question; since you have all the money in the world and with that money, you also have great power. Be honest—are you truly *happy*?"

"Well, I've never—"

"Did you ever actually sit down," he interrupted her again, "and talk to Elizabeth in a civilized manner? If you had, you'd see that she is a very intriguing, loving, warm, and generous person. That is the kind of woman that I would want my son to be with. I want a strong woman who will be by his side, guide him, support him, and love him unconditionally. Do you know why? Because I don't want my son to have to live every day of his life with someone and wishing he could do better! He is a better man than that, and Elizabeth was the angel sent from Heaven to rescue him. Sometimes I wonder what I did wrong to not have an angel sent down to rescue me!"

"Victor, I've never been spoken to in this manner!" she snapped at him.

"Get used to it, because if you don't fix this, you will be spoken to in this manner much more often!" he snapped back at her.

"What am I supposed to do now?" she whimpered.

"You're on your own this time. I'm done talking with you for the rest of the day." He got up from his seat and walked away, but then suddenly stopped halfway and turned around to her and said, "I'll be sleeping by myself tonight." He turned his back on her again and left the room.

***

Richard went to his office and, for the first time in his life, he felt strange and lost in it. He felt as if he didn't belong here and the urge to leave and just run away was overwhelming.

He requested a quick meeting with James and Thomas. They could sense that he was quiet and seemed withdrawn. He wasn't the same Richard they had known before Elizabeth came along, and he certainly wasn't the Richard they had come to know after he met and fell in love with her either. He was a stranger.

"You okay, Richard? Is something the matter?" Thomas asked.

"There is an important task that I'm going to ask you to do for me." Richard spoke quietly, trying to control his voice. However, his eyes betrayed him as they glistened with tears. He breathed a deep sigh. "I will be going on a long journey, and I'm going to ask that you two look after the business while I'm gone. You have always done a fine job, and I'm trusting that you will continue to do so in my absence."

"If you don't mind my asking, how long will you be gone for?" James asked.

"I don't know," Richard answered slowly. "I don't even know where I'm going. It could be for one day, or it could be for the rest of my life. However, I do know one thing, and that is that this journey will be an agonizing one."


He left his office and went to Nancy's. He sat at his regular table, staring out the window, praying and wishing that God would just drop Elizabeth down from out of nowhere. He prayed to see her one more time, even if it was just for a day. No, he'd be happy to just have her with him for a minute or two. He wanted a chance to tell her that he was truly sorry for the pain he had caused. He wanted to tell her that she was the only person in this lifetime to have captured his heart, and that by leaving him, she had taking his heart with her.

Nancy noticed the woeful look on his face and immediately knew that something was wrong. She brought his usual cup of chai and set it next to him. "I smell a whole can of trouble in the air. Tell me the whole story," she said warmly, trying to comfort him.

He slowly looked up at her. "Nance, I really screwed up this time, and Elizabeth has left me for good," he said as his lips began to quiver.

"It isn't like you to hurt her, so let me guess: was it your mother again?"

Richard carefully explained the whole ordeal to Nancy, making sure that he didn't miss even the tiniest of details.

"Oh my god," Nancy simply responded, although she wasn't shocked. She knew how cruel Doris could be. She knew what Doris was capable of doing, and had expected this sooner or later. That was why she kept warning Richard to be more watchful. She gently took his hands in hers and tried to comfort him as best as she could. "Oh, Richard. Maybe she just needed to sort out her thoughts. I don't think that she'll leave you forever. She loves you. As a person viewing things from the outside in, I could see that she loves you very much. Every time she was with me, she talked about you in the warmest and most loving manner. She wants to please you in every way she can. If she were to run away from you now, I trust that she will return to you soon."

His eyes welled with tears. He really did believe that Elizabeth loved him with all her heart, and after hearing Nancy's words of assurance, he felt a little bit relieved. He hoped that Nancy was right about Elizabeth needing time off to sort out her thoughts and that she would return shortly.

"Elizabeth needs me, Nance. I'm the only person she has left in this world, and I promised to protect her, to shelter her, and to give her the love and comfort she needed. I promised to give her the world, and she trusted me wholeheartedly. Now it seems like her world came tumbling down, and I was the cause of it. I'm all torn up inside, and I feel like hell because I failed to keep my promise. I just hope that someday she will find it in her heart to forgive me."

"Richard, you will find her, and then you can explain everything to her. It was just a simple misunderstanding. Elizabeth is a smart and compassionate person, and she will understand. You are not just an average guy. You're not just an ordinary man. You have a loving heart that is bigger than the ocean, and your love for her is greater than anything I could ever imagine. If she can't see that, then that is a flaw of hers. If she cannot forgive you for a heartache that you didn't cause, then you two were simply not meant to be."

"I wish I could just see her and explain everything to her, but I don't even know where to begin to look for her."

"Let's start with some of her favorite places—places she really enjoyed spending time."

He thought for a moment and then he smiled faintly. His eyes lit up. "I know, Nance. You're a genius! I've got to go." He quickly got out of his seat, gave her a hug, and then left the restaurant.

"Where are you going?" Nancy shouted after him.

"I'm going to Chinatown!" he shouted back.


Richard felt as if he was on a mission. He remembered Elizabeth telling him once that Chinatown reminded her of home, so he was optimistic that he would find her there. He was on Smith Avenue again and heading toward Lee Boulevard, only this time he was without her. He kept his fingers crossed, and at times he even felt the need to calm down his excited heart. His mind told him to slow down, but his feet begged to differ. They were making wider and wider strides as he got closer to the music store that he and Elizabeth had stopped at.

Inside the store, his eyes roamed around, making sure that he didn't miss any corner of the room. To his disappointment, she was nowhere inside. He went and sat in the very same spot where she once sat down to play the piano. He closed his eyes and tried to remember the way she had poured her heart out when she had played for him. He could still hear the song vividly in his mind and was still enjoying it when a store employee interrupted him. "May I help you?"

"No, thank you." He slowly stood up and walked out of the store.

As he walked alongside the streets of Chinatown, he could see hordes of Asian people everywhere, going about their business. *How am I ever going to find her in this crowded place?* he wondered. If only he could speak their language, he would ask around to see if anyone had at least seen someone who would fit her description. He even tried a couple of times, but he was instead directed to the restrooms. Perhaps asking where the restrooms were was one of the most popular questions around here, he thought. However, he didn't lose hope. Like he had told his mother, he had a whole lifetime to look for her.

He spent most of the afternoon just wandering around, hoping that he would cross paths with her. But she was nowhere to be found. Once in a while he would spot a woman who resembled Elizabeth, and he'd feel his heart race like exploding fireworks, only to discover the woman was not Elizabeth. Although he didn't want to give up yet, he realized that he needed to take a break.

As he slowly made his way out of Chinatown, another place occurred to him—the restaurant where he and Elizabeth went to have their first bowls of pho together. He turned around to head there.

As he walked in, he was greeted by the same Asian woman from their last visit. She welcomed him with a simple hello and gave him the same warm smile. Then she directed him to a table, but he instead pointed to the same table where he had sat with Elizabeth.

"Where you girlfriend?" she asked in broken English. He was surprised that she even remembered them.

"She's not here. I'm looking for her. Have you seen her today?"

"No. I not see her. Too bad she not here, I have good time talking to her."

He sat there quietly and just nodded.

"You come here to eat pho?"

"Yes."

"Okay, I come back with very special bowl for you."

"Thank you."

Just a moment later, the woman returned with an enormous bowl along with the condiments. He inhaled the aroma and began to mix in the condiments and sauces. He tried to remember the steps Elizabeth went through. He took a big sip of the broth and began to cough and gag.

The woman giggled and walked toward him. She took another spoon and tasted his soup, stuck out her tongue, and squinted her eyes. "Very bad. I get you another bowl, okay?" she said as she took the bowl away.

A few minutes later, she brought out another bowl for him. "Okay, I mix for you," she said smiling.

"Thank you," he replied, embarrassed.

He watched in amazement at how she knew exactly the right amount of sauces and condiments to put into the soup without having to measure anything. She just grabbed a pinch of this, a spoonful of that, a shake, and a twist, then stirred everything together. It reminded him so much of how Elizabeth did it. He suddenly felt a twinge of pain in his heart and tried desperately to compose himself and hold back his tears.

She finally looked up at him with a satisfying smile. "Okay, very good now. You try it," she said as she slid the bowl in front of him.

He took a slow sip and was pleasantly surprised that it was actually very good; however, it was not nearly as good as how Elizabeth did it. He thanked her and ate silently.

After he left the restaurant, he took a cab to Iris Park. He went straight to Atkins Peak, sat down for a bit, then stood up on the bench to glance around the trails to see if he could spot Elizabeth anywhere. Without her, he would not feel the same ever again. How could she come into his life, and then suddenly disappear without a trace? How was he ever going to find the strength to go on from here? His heart had been crushed, torn into pieces. He felt absolutely hopeless, and now he feared he would never be at peace again.

He finally found the strength to get up from the bench and make his way home in the stillness of the night. His steps were unsteady, and he stumbled along the trail like a drunkard. But he didn't care.

The sky began to rumble, and flashes of light streaked along the horizon. A once quiet and still world now suddenly roared with heavy, rolling sounds of thunder. Rain began to slash the world below, blending with the teardrops on his cheeks like a rapidly flowing river. However, he didn't notice any of this. He didn't realize that he was soaked to the bone. He was too lost in his thoughts, and he seemed to be light years away from coming out of it—if ever.

# Chapter Fifteen

It seemed like it was just yesterday when Richard met and fell in love with Elizabeth. He could still remember every line and mark on her beautiful face. He could still smell her sweet scent in the air. At times, he could still hear her charming laughter and loving whispers echoing inside his apartment. What he could not believe was that a month had already gone by. Had he really lived for a whole month without her? Or had he died on the day she left?

His heart had been broken for a month, but to him it seemed like he had been floating in this timeless world of pain forever. How was he going to live the rest of his life without her? He couldn't accept the fact that she was gone. His heart desperately yearned for her love, her touch, and her comfort. His whole being had been damaged by this cruel and harsh thing called love. He once believed that love was the sweetest thing that could ever happen to the human heart, but now love was the thing he feared the most.

He couldn't eat or sleep or think straight. He'd completely let himself go, not feeling the need to shave his beard or to wash or cut his long and greasy hair. His body was deteriorating from the lack of nutrition, but he didn't seem to care. He felt like a lost soul.

He didn't want to go home, and didn't care where he'd end up from one day to the next. He wanted to be alone and invisible to everyone, even those who loved him dearly and those he once loved with all his heart.

The place he once called home was now just a place where he went to lie down from time to time. Many nights he lay on the bench at Atkins Peak, with no thought of going home. At least there his heart could find comfort beneath the stars and his mind could feel somewhat at ease.

His mother, too, was heartbroken. She could only watch her son from afar, and it hurt her deeply to see the pain she had inflicted on him. She felt sick and disgusted by her own actions and feared that she might lose her son forever as he continued to spiral down his self-destructive path. She tried to reach out to him but felt more miserable every time she was rejected by him. She missed him dearly and wanted to try being a loving mother to him now. She wanted to be understanding. She wanted to comfort him and to assure him that she would support him. Most of all, she just wanted to love him, if only he would give her that privilege again.

She had never felt so alone in her life, because she had lost not only her son, but her husband as well. In her sorrow, she had reached out to her husband for some comfort, but he only cast her aside.

Victor's heart was breaking as well, and like his son, he felt hurt and betrayed by Doris. If only he could turn back the hands of time, he'd make sure to protect Richard and Elizabeth from her. How could he allow his only son to be so crushed and miserable? How could he allow Doris to hurt his son in such an atrocious way? His poor Richard was so young, yet now he had lost his will to live a happy and successful life. How could Victor ever forgive himself for allowing his son to walk such a torturous road?

Victor went to Richard's apartment to check on him and try to console him. Upon arriving, he found Richard lying lifelessly on the couch. His eyes were open, but he didn't seem to hear Victor enter the apartment at all. Not once did he move or turn his eyes to see who was coming in. He just lay there staring up at the ceiling. His facial expression revealed that he no longer had anything to live for. He seemed weak and frail lying there motionless, as if he was just waiting for the inevitable end.

Victor's old heart cried out for his son. He couldn't bear to see Richard like this anymore. He lifted Richard up and held on to him. "My sweet and generous son, how could you become like this? Why do you do this to yourself? My old heart can't bear it anymore. If you die, then I'm going to die with you," he whimpered softly.


Richard woke up to a quiet beeping sound. He sat up and noticed that he was inside a room filled with small TV monitors. He felt a slight pain on his left arm when he moved it. Looking down, he noticed a clear IV tube sticking out of it.

"Where am I?" he said aloud. "Did I die?"

He glanced around the room and realized that he was in a hospital. He slowly moved toward the edge of the bed and tried to get up. Just then, his father came into the room.

"Hello, Richard," he said, approaching his son. He carefully placed his hand on Richard's head, brushing away a lock of long and greasy hair. "Are you feeling any better?" he said softly, with a gentleness that only a father could express to a beloved son.

Feeling frustrated and hopeless, Richard faintly replied, "Why didn't you just let me die, Father?"

"Because you're my son, and I love you very much. I want you to live." Victor continued to stroke his son's hair. "You must not be discouraged by life's many trials. You must always remember that problems are only temporary. You will overcome painful moments and will soon treasure all the loving memories of those you've loved and lost. Everyone must struggle first in order to be strong enough to start anew." He looked directly into Richard's eyes. "And you, my son, you are a strong man. You must face these cruel obstacles and defeat them so that you can be strong again and find your destiny."

"I don't know how, Father. I'm weak and tired. How can I just pull myself up and walk this road alone? I'd rather die alone than to have to live alone."

"Don't say that. What happens if she comes back and you're not here to welcome her? You must continue to live every day of your life believing that she will return someday. Live as a happy man. Bake a cake every day to await her arrival if you must, so that when she finally comes back, you'll be there to celebrate her return."

"It has been a month, Father. She's not coming back," Richard said tearfully.

"Whatever happened to your hopes of finding her even if it takes a whole lifetime? Life is like a journey: sometimes you're on a mountain, many times you're walking in the valleys, but you must always remember that when you are down at your lowest point, the only way to go is up. Think of these circumstances as life's rewards. Once you reach the top of the mountain and you are a strong man again, let's hope that she has returned to celebrate it with you."

Richard let out a soft sigh. "I wish that I could just fall asleep and wake up to that celebration."

"Nothing in life is easy, son. If someone tells you differently, then they're trying to sell you something. From now on, you must move on and start living your life the way Elizabeth would have wanted you to. And when she comes back, you'll be ready for her."

"I will try, Father. Thank you."

Victor gently squeezed Richard's shoulder and let out a deep sigh. "Richard, I know that your mother did you wrong, and I was also very upset with her. I also said some things to her that I've shouldn't have said. As crazy as it sounds, you must understand that she was only doing it for you. She wanted you to have everything: wealth, status, power, and happiness. Unfortunately, she was confused about the priorities. Please forgive your mother and try to talk to her. She is truly sorry for her actions and is living in pain every day."

Richard looked wary as he slowly replied, "That would be hard for me to do at this time, Father. Maybe someday, but Mother must remember that she has dug a deep hole in my heart. Until Elizabeth comes back to fill that hole, and if she can find it in her heart to forgive Mother, then maybe I will think about giving her another chance. At this time, all I'm asking is for her to allow me time to heal my pain."

Victor smiled warmly and earnestly said, "You're just as stubborn as your mother." He gently kissed Richard on the forehead and then walked to the door. As he opened it, he turned around to Richard and said, "There's someone here to see you."

"Thank you, Mr. Bennett," Nancy said to Victor, then quickly popped in through the door.

"Hello stranger! Have you seen my sweet friend Richard?" Nancy smiled as she walked up to Richard and gave him a hug.

"Hi, Nance," he said weakly.

"You look like hell, Richard," she joked.

"Hell is nothing compared to how I feel," he answered. "Have you heard anything from Elizabeth?" he asked curiously.

Nancy sighed. "Unfortunately, I haven't, but I'm sure that wherever she is, she's hurting too."

He looked at her with a tormented expression. "There's a deep well in my heart filled with only pain and sorrow. I'm drowning in it, and haven't been able to climb out. I know that there's also a well in Elizabeth's heart. At least I have friends and family to pull me out of it. It pains me so much to think that she is all by herself, drowning inside that well, with no one to pull her out of it."

Nancy gently placed her hand on his face. "Please don't despair, Richard. Elizabeth is a very strong woman. She has lived with pain and sorrow most of her life. I'm sure she'll pull herself out of it. It is you that I worry most about, because you are at rock bottom."

"I miss her," he simply said, then became silent.

"Baby steps, honey. Take baby steps every day."

She gave her friend a compassionate smile. "Look, Richard," she added, "I've never had the chance to experience true love, but I've seen the tremendous passion, the strong bond and absolute devotion that you and Elizabeth had for each other. To me, that is a love beyond all measure. I'm confident she'll return someday."

"Thanks, Nance. Thanks for coming here and making me feel better. I'm just so sorry that it was under such unfortunate circumstances. "

"It's okay, sweetie. I'm just happy to see you and hope that you'll have a fast recovery. By the way, are you hungry? You need to eat something."

"No, I'm not —"

"You need to eat. You're skin and bones," she interrupted him and then she went to the door and opened it. Becca came inside carrying two huge brown paper bags.

"Hi, Richard," Becca said as she walked up to them.

"Hey, Becca," he said, trying to be cheerful.

Nancy brought the bags over, took out several dishes and placed them onto the table next to him.

"What is it?" He frowned as he quickly looked at the dishes.

"I know that my version of it won't be quite as good as Elizabeth's, but at least it'll give you some comfort. Eat up, Richard. You need to put on some weight. I'm not going to leave you alone until you finish a plate or two."

For the first time in about a month, Richard chuckled faintly and then reached for the fork to start in on the beef laab. Nancy was right, it was quite good but could never compare to Elizabeth's. However, she was also right about how it gave him comfort. Even though the food reminded him of Elizabeth and his heart shattered with pain because fond memories began to rush in, the beef laab did make him feel better. He suddenly felt Elizabeth's spirit beside him, looking at him and flashing her usual beautiful smile, except that this time she wasn't there to fill his plate for him.

Nancy noticed the change in his expression. Even though she didn't know what it was he was thinking, she knew for a fact that it was probably something positive, because his face had a sudden rush of a lively color. She smiled happily as she sat there watching him enjoy the food. "Elizabeth's special dishes are a big hit at the restaurant. We've gotten so many requests for them that I had to hire another cook."

He quietly nodded and was just about to say something to Nancy when Becca's cell phone rang. After a short conversation, Becca said, "Nancy, we have to go back. Jeanie called and said that the cooks are fighting again!"

Nancy got up. "Sorry, Buddy, I've got to go back. You take your time enjoying the food. Promise me you'll eat it all, okay? I'll see you later." She and Becca quickly walked out of the room.

Richard was all alone again. As he continued to eat, he reminisced about the times that Elizabeth spent watching him eat. She always seemed to find enjoyment and complete satisfaction in watching him enjoy her cooking. If only she were sitting beside him now like she always did.

Then an epiphany overwhelmed his shattered heart. He felt a sudden warm tear roll down his cheek and stop on his lips. He accepted it and welcomed it into his mouth as he continued to chew his food. Perhaps his father and Nancy were right: Elizabeth would have wanted for him to be strong.

Another tear streamed down his cheek as he thought about her, how she had come into his life and left him—gone without a trace. She had come and made an unforgettable mark on his life. He would forever keep the sweet memories of her in his heart, but life needed to go on for him.

Even though he still felt numb, he knew he needed to continue onward. He needed to strengthen his heart and find the courage to just keep going. It was not going to be easy for him to walk this dark and lonely road without her, but the possibility of fate bringing them together once again someday was enough for him to take that first step. Yes, she was and always would be the light on his dark and lonely journey.

# Chapter Sixteen

One moment at a time, one day at a time, every day for two weeks, Richard felt himself getting better and feeling stronger. He began to eat better and was able to sleep through the night on most nights. He began to appreciate his life and felt almost as if he had been reborn. He began to realize how much he had missed just being present in the world. He was thankful to have made the decision of a lifetime—to survive, to be strong, and to live for Elizabeth.

He decided to return to work. Perhaps it was the best thing for him to do. Keeping himself busy and his mind occupied would help get him through the day.

As he slowly walked down the hall of his building he noticed that all the employees had stopped whatever they were doing to gaze at him. They seemed shocked to see him.

"What's with the stare?" he asked, smiling. "Do I look like a ghost?"

"Good morning, Mr. Bennett! Welcome back!" they said cheerfully.

He continued to his office and saw that Sam was busy playing a game of solitaire on her computer. He didn't want to interrupt her, but then she quickly turned around and saw him.

"Richard!" She immediately got out of her seat to give him a huge hug.

The hug almost sent him tumbling backward. "Hey, easy now!" he said, chuckling.

"You've been gone for so long and I was starting to lose hope. I've missed you so much!" she said as she wiped a tear from her eye.

"I'm not dead, silly. But thank you. It's nice to be back." He handed her a tissue. She took it and blew her nose loudly.

He laughed. "So, what's new around here?"

"Without you around to keep the peace, Angela was constantly fighting with Thomas and James," she said, rolling her eyes.

Unable to come up with a response, he just laughed softly, and continued to his office. When he opened the door, the first thing he saw was a large pot of flowers on his desk.

"Sam, who brought the flowers?" he called out.

"I did," a voice replied from behind him.

He quickly turned around and saw Angela standing at the doorway. He smiled politely.

"Hello, stranger," she said as she quickly walked over to give him a tight, passionate embrace. She knew this was her chance, and nothing was going to stop her now. She pulled back to examine him carefully and said, "You look so thin, Richard." She tenderly rubbed her hands up and down his back.

"I've lost about twenty-five pounds," he replied.

"Are you hungry? Let me order breakfast for us."

"No, I'm not hungry. But thank you for asking."

She walked over to the flowerpot and proudly exclaimed, "I've missed you so much, Richard. I put this pot on your desk and put a flower in it for every day that you were gone."

"Thank you for being so considerate," he said kindly. "So what has been happening around here since I was gone?"

"There's nothing new. James and Thomas are constantly at odds with me."

He laughed. "It's always nice to have a healthy debate. It gives you a different perspective."

"There's nothing healthy about it. I'm losing my mind talking to those two idiots."

"Likewise, I'm sure," James said as he walked into the office. "How are you doing, buddy?" He shook Richard's hand.

"I'll be all right from now on," Richard replied.

"Where are your manners, James?" Angela quickly cut in, annoyed. "Can't you see that I'm talking to Richard?"

"You already had your turn. It's my turn now," James retorted.

"It would certainly help me if you two could come back later," Richard interjected. "I would like some time to myself to catch up on a few things. We'll chat in a little while."

"Sorry for the rude manner, Richard. Welcome back, by the way. All right, we'll chat later," James said as he walked out of the office.

Angela slowly walked up to Richard, looked him straight in the eyes, and politely asked, "Would you like to go out for lunch today?"

"Sure," he simply replied as he turned around and walked slowly to his desk.

She wanted to stay in the room with him, but she knew that he wanted to be alone for now, and she didn't want to be too brazen—at least not yet. She had already won by chasing Elizabeth away. All she needed now was to give him time. She now had a chance to start anew with him, and she was never going to let that chance slip away from her. "There's no way I'm going to let you get away again this time," she whispered quietly.

"Pardon me?" Sam asked as she entered the office and put a file on Richard's desk.

"Oh, nothing," Angela quickly replied. "I was just mumbling to myself." She looked away and left the office.

Richard and Angela went to Maury's restaurant for lunch. As they walked in and were politely greeted by the hostess, Angela did what she had always done in the past. She ignored the greeting, gave the hostess an annoyed look, and then demanded to sit elsewhere when they were led to a table not to her liking. "Can't we get something a little bit classier, like that table over there?" Angela spat out as she pointed to a table that was already occupied by four people.

"I'm sorry, ma'am, but that table is still occupied."

"I want to speak to the manager!" Angela snorted loudly.

"It's all right," Richard broke in to rescue the helpless hostess. "We'll take whatever table you have available."

They were seated at a small table by the window. Richard casually gazed outside as he tried to ignore Angela's complaints to the waitress about the slow service. "Wow, I guess we'll just going to have to spend the whole day here! What fun!" she yelled out.

Finally his annoyance reached its peak. "You do realize," he scolded her, "that there are about twenty tables in here and there are only a few waitresses?"

Angela went silent for a while. Even though she was annoyed and angry at the slow service, she knew she needed to control her vicious side. She glanced at Richard and noticed that he was still annoyed with her, so she apologized. "I'm sorry, Richard. I admit I was a little out of line, but only because the service was slow. I guess I should just be a little bit more patient."

"There's no need to ask for forgiveness, Angela. Please try to keep your temper in check," he answered, still gazing out the window.

She was a little offended by his statement, but she tried to remain composed. She sat quietly for a while before asking, "So, did you and Elizabeth come to this restaurant often?"

Still staring out the window, he nonchalantly replied, "No, we've never been here together. We spent most of our time at Nancy's."

"*Seriously*?" she said. "It's hard to imagine that Elizabeth and Nancy would get along. Nancy is such a *bitch*."

He immediately turned his face from the window to glare at her. "It doesn't surprise me that you'd say something of that sort." He leaned closer to her and added, "Just a friendly note: Elizabeth and Nancy got along quite well. In fact, they were actually very good friends."

Angela was dumbfounded and dejected. He always found a way to contradict everything she said to him. Feeling hurt and desperate, she felt she needed to ask him to explain how she was so different from Elizabeth.

"Angela, there are some things in this world that are best left unsaid."

"I want to know, Richard," she demanded. "What does she have that I don't? Why do you hate me so much?"

"I don't hate you, Angela."

"If you don't hate me, then there's no reason you can't love me. People grow fond of each other if they spend more time together, but it seems like you and I just grow farther apart. Honestly, I'd like to know what Elizabeth has that I don't."

Richard sighed deeply, his eyes drifting back to the window. "The truth is that Elizabeth opened my eyes to see the beauty the world has to offer. She opened my heart to learn how to accept, hope, forgive, and respect. She taught my soul how to see life's possibilities and to take great pride in its rewards. She gave me the strength to see this world in a whole new light. For all these reasons, I was able to create happiness for myself."

Angela's jaw dropped, her mouth gaped, and she rolled her eyes annoyingly as if she were seated across from a lunatic. "Good Lord! What has happened to you? What happened to the Richard that I used to know? "

"People and things change over time, Angela. Some beautiful things wither away. Other things get old and rusty. But some things get better with age. People are the same way. Some become cold, cruel, and bitter as they get older. Others become wiser and begin to see the things around them in a whole new light. Those who take the effort to view things through the eyes of others and to change themselves are better able to shape their destiny. The Richard you once knew doesn't exist anymore. You, too, should look at yourself and make some effort to change some things."

She was appalled by his statement, but she knew she needed to show him that she was willing to change for him. She let out a deep sigh before replying, "I *do* want to change, Richard. I just don't know how."

After lunch, Richard paid the bill but noticed that Angela had left nothing for a tip. *After how she treated that poor waitress, she should have at least left something for her*, he thought. He went over to their distraught waitress and discreetly handed her a hundred-dollar bill. "This is for putting up with her." He smiled, winked at her, and then left the restaurant.

"Hey, do you want to share a cab back to the office?" Angela asked while they were outside.

"No. I'm going to walk home. I'm done for the day."

"Richard, are you crazy? It's a long walk back."

He looked at her with an inspired and determined expression. "Angela, have you ever taken a long walk around the city and enjoyed its beauty?"

"Never. Why should I?"

"Well, there's always a first time. Care to join me?" he said with a charming smile—one that she couldn't refuse.

After about three blocks, she was already complaining. "Richard, please, let's get a cab. My feet are killing me."

"Here, take my arm, then. I will pull you along." She gratefully took his arm and leaned into him as they continued to walk down the street. She hated every minute of the walk, but at least she was making some progress with him.

As they continued along, Richard couldn't stop thinking about Elizabeth and how her eyes glowed radiantly and her face beamed whenever she had walked with him. She could be so appreciative of the simplest things! If only Angela would put in just the tiniest effort—but no, Angela took everything for granted, and for her to give in even a little would be too much to ask.

As they approached Summit Drive, Angela frowned displeasingly as she sniffed the strong odor in the air. "God, what the hell is that smell?"

He deeply inhaled the air and slowly enjoyed its tantalizing aroma for a moment before he replied, "That, Angela, is the smell of life. Can't you see the beauty in this place?"

"What beauty? What's so beautiful about this place? It's just a bunch of people yelling at each other," she sharply retorted.

"Come on. Let's experience this side of life together."

"We're going through *that*?" she asked reluctantly.

"Why not?"

"But that reeking smell will get on my hair and clothes."

"Come on," he said pulling her along. "That's why God made water. You can take a shower later at my apartment if you want."

Angela of course liked that idea. As they made their way through the markets, she became irritated, barking at anyone who got a little too close to her.

Before long they came upon the same elderly man he and Elizabeth had seen, skillfully playing piano despite missing a few fingers on each hand. Richard was standing there silently, enjoying the inspirational music, when Angela scoffed, "Arrrgh! How disgusting! I wonder if anyone has ever told him that he needed a bath. Perhaps soaking himself in a bathtub for a day or two would help?"

Without even turning his head to look at her, Richard slowly walked over to the man and placed a nice, crisp hundred-dollar bill inside the man's raggedy hat. He thanked the man for the uplifting music, turned, and proudly walked back to Angela. With a jubilant and satisfying expression, he asked, "Have we learned anything yet?"

Her face turned a little pale, as she seemed quite disturbed by what he just did. "Don't you know that if you give him money, you're only motivating him to come back here every day to do that same crap?" she said sharply.

Richard felt sorry for her, for she was not a compassionate person and she never would be. *She will always care only about herself,* he thought sadly.

"If only you could see beyond his begging," he said to Angela, "you would be able to see the talent he possesses. You would also be able to see that despite his disability, he still has the will to live and the motivation to share his great talent. Instead of seeing a beggar, Elizabeth would have seen this as an exceptional performance. And instead of walking away, she would have put money in his hat for such a worthy performance."

Angela's jaw dropped again, showing her disgust. She became quiet for a moment, but her silence didn't last long. The long walk was killing her feet, so she nagged at him again, "Richard, we've walked too long. I'm really tired. Could we go to your apartment now?"

He felt hopeless. He wished that she would see eye to eye with him, but there was no winning when dealing with this woman. The more he tried, the more he found himself missing Elizabeth. He became very quiet now. It wasn't until after a long pause that he managed to answer, "We're on our way over there now. Just hang on and keep walking."

About an hour later, they reached his apartment and were greeted at the door by Martin. "Good afternoon, Mr. Bennett." Martin slowly turned to Angela and reluctantly said, "Hello there, Ms. Denning."

Angela rolled her eyes and huffed.

Richard immediately stepped in. "My apologies, Martin. A grown woman with an attitude is a woman who hasn't yet grown up. Please forgive her."

Angela couldn't believe her ears. She opened her mouth, but then immediately closed it again. It took all her strength to restrain herself from saying something rude.

As soon as they entered his apartment, she hurried to the couch, sat down, and propped her feet up on the coffee table. Unbeknownst to her, she was sitting in Elizabeth's spot, so he rushed up to her and quickly moved her to the end of the couch. She was too tired to ask him why he did what he did.

Her eyes wandered about the room. "How I miss this place, Richard, but then I would have felt more relaxed, comfortable, and at home if the scent of a woman wasn't still lingering in here," she blurted out.

"Relax and feel at home anyway, or forever be distressed, because the scent of that woman will remain somewhere close to my heart for a very long time," he retorted.

She bit her tongue again. After some silence, she slowly got up and decided to take a nice, warm shower.

"Go ahead, use my bathroom," he said.

"What's wrong with the other room?" she asked, referring to the room Elizabeth had stayed in.

"It's locked."

Angela's eyes narrowed. "Oh? Why?" she asked.

"I have my reasons."

"Is it because Elizabeth used it?" she said, staring at him.

"If you put it that way, then yes."

"She's *gone*, Richard. The room is finally available for other people to use, thank God."

"I wanted to keep everything the way it was," he replied in a plain and simple tone.

She looked at him with a cold glare. If only her eyes could shoot out flames, he would have been burned to ashes already. Without another word, she stormed into his room to take a shower.

A half hour later, she came out of his room, went straight to where he was sitting, and sat right next to him. He was stunned to see that she was wearing an oversized T-shirt—his T-shirt.

Her smile was seductively warm and charming. The way her body slowly squirmed next to his, the fast and unsteady warmth of her breathing very close to his ear, the burning sensation of her bare skin brushing against his—how temptation could deceive the heart! He hadn't seen her like this in a long time. Her sensuality almost pierced the wall that he had built around himself.

"What are you *doing*?" he managed to ask.

"Just want to sit next to my favorite person in the world," she replied sweetly.

"I meant to ask, what are you doing wearing my shirt?"

"Well, I have no clean clothes to change into, unless you want me to not wear anything at all," she teased.

"The last time you wore my clothes, you ended up spending the night here."

"I did? I don't remember it because it was so long ago. Maybe you should refresh my memory?" She lightly touched his arm.

"I don't want to confuse the situation," he said, pulling away. "You and I both know that we are better off just being friends."

"I'm a changed person, Richard. Please give me another chance."

"Your heart shouldn't make demands, Angela—you'll just hurt yourself. It's only a lie when someone believes he or she has changed for someone else. If you truly want to be a changed person, change from within, change for yourself; don't change for me or anyone else."

"I understand," she replied. "I'm much more mature now. You'll see."

"Let me know when you learn what compassion is, when you understand that no one is perfect in this world, and when you are able to accept that everyone has flaws. To speak so freely with only empty words and to force yourself to believe that those words are true—you're only lying to yourself. You will only hurt yourself in the process."

Angela sighed. "When I realized that maybe I'd lost you forever, I learned that I'd made mistakes, and I have lived with my guilt. I'm guilty of making you run away from me. And if I haven't totally changed to your liking, couldn't you at least consider the fact that I have tried to change?"

"Wake up, Angela," Richard replied. "Accept yourself for who you are first. When you're able to accept that you can't change for anyone else, maybe then you will be able to understand the world around you. Maybe you'll be able to understand that not everyone is like you and me or as fortunate as we are. Maybe then you'll be able to experience compassion and be more selfless. Until then, please do not force me to believe you. For tonight, please go change back into your own clothes and leave. I have nothing more to say." With that, Richard got up and walked out the door.

Angela was shocked at Richard's behavior. His words stung her deeply, and she felt a little dizzy trying to comprehend all of what he just said to her. A tear ran down her cheek as she slowly got up to go change back into her own dirty clothes. She left the apartment very disappointed, but knew she would forgive him very soon, because that was how much she loved him.

# Chapter Seventeen

May 25th marked the day Richard and Elizabeth had met each other for the first time. Five lengthy years had gone by, and still Richard's heart longed for her. He still felt a strong desire for her. He never stopped missing her.

It was a Saturday morning; the sun was shining beautifully on the earth below, the wind was crisp, and the fresh smell of Mother Earth was lingering in the air. This reminded him that spring had finally made its way around once again, but he couldn't understand how he had kept himself moving forward without her for all these years.

On his way to Nancy's, a trip he had regularly taken every Saturday morning for the past five years, his mind was occupied as usual with thoughts of Elizabeth. Briefly, it made a surprising shift from Elizabeth to Angela, and it saddened him to realize that he was never truly happy with his relationship with her. Angela had always been Angela regardless. Though he had hoped that change could be possible, he never fully trusted that a person would ever truly change unless there was a great desire from within. He had now begun to accept the fact that Angela was born with her attitude and character, and she would never change. He needed to accept her for who she was, or forever try to break away from her.

He went into Nancy's and sat at his usual table. Nancy brought him a cup of chai and sat with him. As he sipped his drink and gazed out the window, she could sense the continuing sadness in him. She wanted to say something, but she decided to let him talk.

Without shifting his eyes from the window, he asked her in a soft and desolated tone, "Do you know what today is?"

"Yes, I remembered," she quietly answered.

With small specks of tears forming in his eyes, he let out a trembling sigh. "Five years ago today, I met her inside this restaurant. Today is the day that I'll finally lock away the memories of her deep inside my heart forever. Even though not a day has gone by without me thinking of her, I know that she is not coming back. I must move on and stop these memories from lingering within me. After today, I'll never bring these memories back out again."

"I agree. You have waited for her for five long years, and it's time you put it all behind you now. Life goes on, Richard. I'm sure she has moved on, too," she said, trying to be as supportive as she could.

Silence hung in the air in this familiar, yet strange place. He simply replied, "I know."

Nancy sighed deeply. She wished there was an easier remedy for his pain. She wished that Elizabeth would return, even if it was just for a day, to put the pieces of this puzzle together, but five long years had gone by and Nancy, too, had given up. She cared so much for Richard. It broke her heart to see him in such despair every day.

"I'm so proud of you, Richard," Nancy said sincerely. "You're such a strong man to have lived every day of your life without her for all these years. If it was me, I'm not sure I could handle it the way you have."

"I died every day, Nance. I died a little bit every day since she left. If only my heart could stop beating, too," he said, shifting his eyes from the window to his hands now as his thumbs slowly rubbed the cup in his hands.

"But now your heart is stronger than anyone else's," she said, smiling. She decided to change the subject. "How are you and Angela coming along?"

He let out a deep, agonizing sigh. "She is still the same Angela. She still drives me crazy with her shenanigans. But at least she's always there."

"Am I going to hear wedding bells?" Nancy asked curiously.

"I don't know. She'll probably drive me to suicide if I marry her."

"Have you told her that?"

"I tried many times, but she's incapable of accepting it."

"So what are you going to do?"

"I don't know," he replied sadly. He shifted his eyes back to the window and added, "Maybe I should just run away like Elizabeth did."

"Hey, don't do that. I would miss you too much." She gently reached over and placed her hands over his.

He sat there in silence as his eyes never left the window. He felt like he was suffocating. After what seemed like a good five minutes of just sitting there quietly, he finally turned back to his friend. "I'm going to go for one last walk around the park, then I will lay the memories of Elizabeth to rest forever."

"You do that. Then come back here later and have lunch with me, Okay? I won't eat until you get back."

"I will, Nance. I'll see you later."

He left the restaurant and headed toward the park. As he walked along, staring at the beautiful scenery, he was again overcome with sorrow. This place was a familiar place, yet it seemed so strange to him now. It was once a place so full of life and promise. It was a place where he had set aside his previous memories so that he could make new memories with Elizabeth. He had considered it his safe haven, but now it was a place so strange to him that he almost feared to walk into it.

He felt as if Elizabeth had died and he was here to bury her. His heart began to pound heavily inside his chest and his breathing became unsteady. His eyes glistened as he remembered why he was here. "I'm here to forget her," he said despairingly.

He felt two streams of warm tears leak down his cheeks. Wiping them away with his fingers, he started in on his final speech to her. "Elizabeth . . . I wish I could just be frozen in time as I wait for you here, but that would mean that I'd be left here alone without you for eternity. If only I knew where you were, I'd run to you. If only I knew whether you'd return, I'd wait for you, even if I had to wait my whole lifetime. But I can't bear this pain any longer. My heart has bled for you for too long, and it has dried up. Even though we only shared a brief amount of time together, you gave me enough memories to last me a lifetime. I was blessed with great fortune to have met you, and you have no idea how many times I have thanked the Lord above for giving me that chance. Today I will cry my last tear for you, and then I will finally lay your memories to rest."

He walked along the same trails that he used to walk hand-in-hand with her. He even took a turn around each of the lakes. He wanted to take in every memory he could and reminisce about the wonderful times he shared with her before locking them away forever.

Finally he arrived at the curvy path that lead up to Atkins Peak. He continued on the path and soon was at the top. A little boy was sitting on the bench, but Richard didn't pay much attention, as his mind was too clouded and his heart was too heavy to attend to anything else.

He slowly spun around to observe the beautiful scenery below. Nothing had changed. Everything was still exactly the same as the day Elizabeth left. The brilliant green fields, the freshly blooming flowers, the gentle breeze, the earthy odor of damp dirt from the spring showers—everything was still there. The only thing missing was Elizabeth. And today, he had made the decision to let all memories go and start anew.

Suddenly the boy let out a cheerful giggle. Richard turned to look at the boy and noticed that he was proudly twisting a Rubik's cube in his hands. He seemed to be around the age of four. *Too young to understand the puzzle*, Richard thought. But as he watched, he was amazed at the little boy's skill. Before long, the boy had solved the puzzle. Richard stood astonished at what he had just observed.

He wanted to see the boy do it again, so he slowly approached him. The boy stopped to look up at him. Richard noticed that this boy had beautiful blue eyes. His hair was dark and wavy, and his high cheekbones were a perfect complement to his slim nose. The boy smiled at him, and Richard noted an adorable dimple on each cheek.

*Goodness, what a beautiful little creature he is,* Richard thought, as he suddenly forgot all the sadness he had built up. He wondered what the parents of this little boy looked like. *Whoever they are,* he thought, *they are truly two lucky people.*

"I'm amazed!" Richard exclaimed. "If you don't mind, will you please do that again for me? If I mixed all the colors, could you solve the puzzle again?"

"I'll try my best, sir," the little boy replied with a bright smile.

Richard gently took the cube from him and mixed the colors before handing it back. He was ecstatic as he watched the little boy's tiny fingers work the cube: turning it, twisting it, and turning it again until only solid colors appeared on each face of the cube.

"Wow! You're amazing! What is your name?" Richard asked.

"My name is Edward Bennett, sir," he replied with another adorable smile.

Edward Bennett? Richard thought hard, but his mind was blank. *Wait, could this be … ?* No, that was wishful thinking. If only he were that lucky. "Well, nice to meet you, Edward. So, who are you here with?" he asked curiously as if waiting for a prayer to be answered.

Richard froze as he heard a familiar voice behind him calling out for the boy. "Edward, honey, it's time to go."

Stunned, Richard couldn't move. He was so startled he couldn't turn around. The voice was so sweet and angelic. Finally he found the strength to turn around. And there she was: Elizabeth, his one and only Elizabeth, standing just a few feet in front of him. Her hair was a little shorter, wavier, fuller, and bit lighter in color, but her face was just as breathtakingly gorgeous as he remembered.

"Elizabeth?" he said weakly, as his mouth could only manage to say one word.

"Richard?" she uttered, as if gasping for air.

She was so surprised to see him that she was unable to move or say anything. She stood there staring as her heart excitedly danced. She didn't know what to do or say to him. Should she run and hide? Or gather up some courage to say something to him? Her face turned a little pale as she paused. Finally, she slowly gave him that gorgeous smile that he had missed so much. "Hello, Richard," she simply said.

In dead silence, he took a step closer to her, yet stayed just a step away, fearing that if he got any closer, she might disappear—again. He felt as if his heart had stopped. If she were to run away again this time, he would surely die. "Hello, Elizabeth," he managed to say in a low voice.

Silence filled the air once again as both of them just stood there, staring at each other. *Be still, my heart,* she told herself, fearing that he would hear it pounding in her chest. She opened her mouth to say something, but instead just let out a long sigh.

She closed her eyes for just a moment, and then tried again. "Richard, I don't even know how to begin this," she said weakly. "Each and every time I think of you, I find myself in tears, because the memories I have of you are truly my fondest. What we had was nothing less than a miracle. It was a blessing, a strength that enabled me to go on along many bumpy roads." She slowly lowered her glistening eyes and let out a trembling sigh.

"Say no more, Elizabeth," Richard said. "Believe me, I understand your pain."

She slowly raised one hand up to wipe a tear from her cheek. "I want you to know that even though we were in different parts of the world, you always had that special spot in my heart. You have always been the only one in my heart."

Even though his own eyes were filling with tears, he tried to stop her from crying. "Elizabeth, please don't cry. Every time you shed a tear, my heart aches. Every time you're in pain, my heart carries half of the burden, if not all of it."

"Richard." She sighed again, staring at her feet.

"Yes?" he said as he took a step closer to her. He was now standing right in front of her. He raised a finger to brush a lock of silky, black hair off of her forehead and then let it slowly trail down to touch her lips. How he hungered to take those lips in his, but he just stared at her in silence.

"There's something you need to know," she said faintly. "I have wronged you in many ways. I have kept a very big secret from you, and I don't even know how to begin to tell you this."

"You don't have to explain anything. I'm just so overjoyed to see you."

"You are a father, Richard. Edward is . . ."

He gently placed his hand on her cheek. "You don't have to say anything. It's a miracle, a dream come true for me. Never once in my life did I think that I deserved something as beautiful and breathtaking as this moment. Your returning here is already a dream come true for me, let alone bringing me this beautiful creature that we created together." He reached his hands around her waist to pull her close and said to her with a soft sob, "Do you know how happy you make me feel?" He didn't even notice the tears rolling down his cheeks.

He held on to her so tightly that he feared he might hurt her. His mind knew he should be a little gentler, yet his heart refused to let her go. He feared if he let loose, she might slip away once again, like grains of sand slipping through his fingers. His lips slowly covered hers and he kissed them passionately, as if he was never, ever going to let them go again.

Then he stopped and looked at her with tearful eyes. Just as before, this woman could leave him speechless simply by gazing at him. He smiled sweetly. "So, he's about four, I'm assuming?"

Suddenly he heard a little voice behind him say, "Mommy, who is this man? Why does he have the same name as my father?"

Richard turned around and looked down at Edward's curious little face. A mixture of joy and sorrow overwhelmed his heart as he looked down at his son.

Elizabeth smiled warmly at Edward and then she softly said, "Edward, this is your father."

Edward looked up at Richard with a confused but intrigued expression on his little face "Are . . . are you my father?" he asked slowly.

"Yes. Yes, I'm your father." Richard dropped to both knees and warmly embraced his son.

Elizabeth's heart was joyful and liberated as she watched Richard hug his son. Overcome with emotion, she began to weep quietly.

# Chapter Eighteen

It felt like a dream to Richard. He was still in disbelief that his Elizabeth had returned. His life without her, the struggle to go on alone, the endless pain in his heart, the dried-up tears, the lonely nights, the longing in his heart for her every passing day, and the multiple prayers he'd sent to God—and then, here she was. Was this just his mind playing tricks on him? Or had God finally answered his prayers by sending her back to him? Whatever the reason, he thanked God for granting him another chance with her.

He sat silently on the bench, staring at her in complete admiration. Without shifting his eyes, he slowly lifted his hands to her face and tenderly caressed her cheek. He had forgotten how soft and delicate her skin felt. How he had missed touching her and holding her in his arms!

He slowly moved his hand up and gently combed her soft and silky hair, and then brushed a strand over her ear. "If this is only a dream, then I'll pray to God to never let me wake from it," he said passionately.

She gently touched his face with her fingers and ran them down to his quivering lips. "This is not a dream. I'm really here. And your son is here too," she said in a warm and comforting tone. Overcome with joy and gratitude, he pulled her into him and held her in his arms.

After a long embrace, he relaxed back against the bench and reached over for her left hand. As he folded his hand into hers, he jumped a little. Looking down, he noticed a diamond on her ring finger. His heart suddenly sank. He wanted to ask her about it, but he was too afraid of what he might find out. He agonized silently but decided to be patient. He knew that she would eventually tell him the story behind it.

He tried to conceal his worry with a faint smile. "I'm so thrilled to see that you decided to come back. There are no words that can describe the happiness that I'm feeling right now," he said, trying to sound cheerful. "I know that you have just returned, but if you don't mind sharing, where did you go after you left me?" Perhaps this question would lead her to talk about the ring without him having to ask her directly about it.

With her eyes fixed on the ground, she let out a soft sigh. After what seemed like forever, she replied, "I went to England and stayed in a little town called Hamilton. My grandmother took me there once when I was a little girl. It's a beautiful and peaceful little town. Edward was born there."

"And you stayed there all this time?"

"No." She glanced away for a second and then she looked at him. "After Edward was born, we moved around a bit."

She paused, as if she was trying to think up something else to add. "I promised Edward that when he was old enough, I would bring him to America to see the city of Atkins. I drew a line on the wall of every place we lived in and told him that when his height reached the line, we would come to Atkins. He measured himself every day, and about three months ago, he ran up to me and excitedly told me that he had finally reached the line on the wall. I had to keep my promise."

He chuckled. "Thanks to you, he is one precious child. You are raising him well, and I can't put into words how proud I am of you."

"Well, he was always a very good boy, and it hasn't been that difficult raising him. I guess he does take after his father." She smiled her teasing smile.

This made him laugh loudly. "I'd have to agree that he does have my eyes and mouth, but he got everything else from you. That's why he is the most adorable little creature ever."

His facial expression suddenly changed. His eyes began to glisten with tears as he reached out his hand to touch her face again. "You and Edward are my world now, Elizabeth. To leave me again would mean to shut me out of my own world."

He noticed that she was a little uncomfortable and was a little hesitant to say anything else, so he quickly shifted gears to change the mood. "When did you two arrive in Atkins?"

"Late last night," she replied, as she slowly glanced back at him.

"And where are you staying?"

"We're at the Palm Hotel." She suddenly looked away again to avoid his eyes and then discreetly added, "I reserved a room for a week."

His eyes shifted away for a moment, too, and then returned to look at her. "So, you're leaving at the end of the week?"

"Yes," she replied quietly, as she looked away again.

A helpless feeling came over him as he tried to comprehend what he had just heard. Was she planning to leave him again? He couldn't bear the thought of her leaving again—and this time with their son. If they left, he knew his heart would shatter. Inside he was screaming and he felt feverish, but he was powerless to do anything about it.

He decided to just breathe slowly to calm himself down. After all, she was still here and he still had the chance to persuade her to stay. He had told her earlier that they were his world and to allow them to leave him this time would mean to shut himself out of his own world. Perhaps God was granting him a second chance. Perhaps this was his opportunity to give her the life she had dreamed of.

He suddenly felt peaceful and calm, as if he had just had a conversation with God. He would just have to be strong and show her how much she and Edward meant to him. He would have to slowly rebuild that bridge that was broken and regain her trust. He felt he didn't have much time, but he was willing to do anything to make her see his true heart and sincere soul.

"Elizabeth," he began, slowly and carefully. "I don't even know how to begin this. I know that I have wronged you and hurt you deeply. I had promised to keep you from harm, but I failed miserably to protect you. I have blamed myself for my carelessness, and I have lived for five long years with the guilt planted heavily in my heart. I'm not asking that you forgive me. I can understand if you never could—"

"Richard, you're not completely at fault," she quickly interrupted.

"But," he cut right back in, "I can't imagine the pain that you had to endure all these years with being alone, pregnant, giving birth, and raising Edward all by yourself. I'm truly sorry, sweetie, for the pain that I've caused. I want you to know that I've missed you every single day for five years. My life without you has been like living in a world without the sun. Since the day you left, my heart never stopped searching and crying for you."

"Richard, please, say no more," she said softly as she gently placed her fingers on his lips. With an earnest expression, she began to explain. "I thought about coming back every day when I first left you. I loved you and missed you with all my heart, but when I found out that I was pregnant, I couldn't come back. I was despairingly lonely, scared, and confused. But I couldn't bear to come back and raise my child in an environment in which everyone was against him. I couldn't bear to see my child suffer just for being who he is. That would slowly kill my heart all over again."

He gaped at her. He now knew that his mother had to have done something far worse than he thought, and he was dying to know what it was. "I'm truly sorry if my mother said or did something to you. What did she do? What did she say?"

Elizabeth felt a knot tightening in her throat. She was afraid of his hostile reactions toward his mother, so she just breathed heavily and continued to stare at the ground in silence.

He gently lifted her face up to meet his. He could tell from her beautiful, sad eyes that she was hesitant to say anything else. He reassured her with a passionate smile and then calmly said, "I understand that there are certain things you'd like to keep to yourself, but there are also things that must be heard in order to prevent misunderstandings. If my mother said something to you that I have no knowledge of, it is probably best if those words are shared between us so that we both are on the same page. I'm wondering if that was why you stayed away for so long."

"I've already forgiven her, Richard. Let's just leave the past behind."

"I know my mother too well. If you could tell me what she said or did to you, at least I could make amends. Please, this would help me find closure."

She gazed at him with tear-filled eyes and sighed faintly. "She told me that she would never accept my child," she said softly. "A child who wasn't purely white, but some sort of a 'half-bred mutt,' to use her words, would only be hated by all sides."

Richard was horrified. How could his mother stoop so low? How could she say that about her own flesh and blood? He reached his arm around Elizabeth to comfort her as best as he could. "Where are the words that could possibly make amends for this?" he cried out. "I'm speechless! If it takes the rest of my life to make up for my mother's despicable, repugnant behavior, I will slowly make it up to you somehow."

Elizabeth looked at him. "Richard, let me beg for forgiveness on her behalf. Let us not dwell on it any longer. Like I said, I have already forgiven her, and you, too, must forgive her. I don't want you to chastise her for it."

Just then Edward ran up to them and interrupted. "Mommy, I'm really hungry. Can we go now?"

Richard reached over to Edward, lifted him, and placed him onto his lap. "Hey, buddy. What would you like to eat?"

"I want to eat *American* food."

Richard laughed amusingly. "Okay, well I know just the place where you can eat all the American food you want." Richard stood and lifted Edward up over his head to set him on his shoulders. Then, he reached out to hold Elizabeth's hand.

As they walked down to the main trail, Elizabeth could guess where they were heading, but she still asked. "Where are we going?"

"We're going to Nancy's," he replied, smiling. "I promised her earlier that I was going to meet her for lunch. She will be *thrilled* to see you."

"Awww, I'm glad you're taking us there. I've missed her dearly. It will be a joy to see her again."

In the company of his beautiful woman and his beloved son, he didn't want the walk to Nancy's restaurant to end. If Edward hadn't been so hungry, Richard could have gone around the park several more times.

Richard decided to walk in by himself. He saw Nancy working diligently on something at the counter and quickly approached her with a jubilant expression on his face. Nancy looked up and was confused to see that he was no longer upset, for she thought all morning about how she would console him upon his return.

"So, how did it go?" she asked, puzzled.

"It was not as I expected," he replied with the same jubilant expression.

"Then why are you so happy?" She squinted her eyes in curiosity. "I was expecting your eyes to be reddened and your face to be all puffy from crying."

"I was in tears earlier, but it wasn't from sadness. I found something far better," he replied.

"Yeah? What did you find?"

Richard quickly grabbed hold of her arm and pulled her around the counter. "Come with me. I'll show you," he said as he led her toward the front door.

"Richard, I have an order to—" Nancy suddenly stopped after they were just a few feet outside the front door. Her heart dropped and her eyes bulged out in disbelief.

"Hello, Nancy," Elizabeth greeted her with her familiar smile.

"*Elizabeth?*" Nancy said hoarsely as if she had been holding her breath for quite some time.

"Yes, Nancy. It's me."

"Are you sure I'm not seeing a ghost?" she said to Richard as she began to weep. She couldn't move. Her feet felt too heavy for her to take even one small step forward.

Elizabeth slowly walked up to her and reached out both arms to gently hug her. "No, Nancy, I'm not a ghost. I'm back."

"You have no idea how much I've missed you, sweetie," Nancy sobbed.

"Trust me, I do know. I missed you just as much."

"I can't believe my eyes, my dear friend. You're still as stunningly beautiful as that first day I met you five years ago."

Elizabeth blushed. "Thank you, Nancy. And you are even more gorgeous than the day I first saw you. It's so nice to see you again."

Nancy glanced down at Edward. "Oh my!" she gasped. "And who is this adorable little guy?" She crouched down to his level to take a closer look at him.

"This is my son, Edward," Elizabeth replied sweetly.

"Goodness, Richard," Nancy said, glancing up at Richard. "He's just a small replica of you! Is my assumption correct?"

"It is, Nance. Isn't he just the most adorable little thing?" Richard proudly exclaimed.

"Hello, Auntie Nancy," Edward said adorably. "My daddy said that you have the best American food in your restaurant."

"Your daddy is *so right* about that!" Nancy replied as she gently pinched his tiny cheeks. "And you can eat anything you want. Are you hungry?"

Edward nodded. "For American food!" he said excitedly.

Nancy laughed. "Well, come on in and let's go eat some *American* food." She took Edward's little hand and led them inside.

They settled at a large table at the back of the room, away from the crowd of customers. Even though Nancy knew that Richard needed this time to become reacquainted with his family, she knew that she also needed to catch up on Elizabeth's life.

"So, what would you like to eat, young man?" Nancy asked, smiling delightfully at Edward.

Edward immediately turned to Richard and asked, "Daddy, can I really eat anything I want to?"

"Yes," Richard said, his heart melting at being called *Daddy*. "You can really eat anything you want to eat, buddy." Richard chuckled as he gently rubbed Edward's head.

"Richard, don't spoil him," Elizabeth said sweetly.

"He's my son, and I'm going to spoil him as much as I can," Richard replied, grinning at Elizabeth.

Edward turned to Nancy and with an ecstatic expression on his face, he said to her, "Auntie, I would like a huge, juicy hamburger, large, greasy fries, and ... hmmm ..." He thoughtfully grabbed his chin with his index finger and thumb like an old man trying to feel his beard. "... a strawberry milkshake. That will be all for now."

Nancy laughed loudly. "That's an *excellent* choice! You have great taste in food, young man." She called out for Jeanie to get started on the order. Then, she turned to Elizabeth and asked, "So, Elizabeth, when did you arrive?"

"We arrived late last night," Elizabeth replied. "I was planning to take Edward to the amusement park today and then come visit you later."

"Hmmm ... I hope I wasn't left out of your plans," Richard chimed in jokingly.

Elizabeth smiled warmly as she glanced at his loving eyes. She gently held on to his hand and softly said, "Not at all."

"It's truly a joy to see you again, Elizabeth," Nancy said. "I've missed you so much. You're always full of surprises."

"I agree with that statement," Richard quickly cut in.

A sudden rush of color filled Elizabeth's cheeks, turning her porcelain-like skin a light pink. She giggled and then nodded, politely agreeing with them on the matter.

"How old is Edward?" Nancy asked curiously.

"He's four. He just had his birthday about a month ago," Elizabeth replied.

"I envy you, Elizabeth," Nancy said sentimentally. "You have an extraordinary man who loves you with all his heart, and a most precious child to brighten your life. These are things every woman would want. Some are just not lucky enough to come close to even dreaming about it."

Elizabeth smiled and nodded. She sat silently and was unable to respond for a moment. "I guess in a way I envy you, too, Nancy. I could never be as strong and as free-spirited as you," she said sincerely.

Elizabeth was delighted. She couldn't express enough how grateful and fortunate she felt to still be receiving Richard's and Nancy's love after all these years. Although Elizabeth was the one who left, her life had not been dandy and splendid. She had struggled immensely on her journey, but she blamed no one for her misfortunes. She was grateful for Richard's understanding and forgiving heart—even after five long years, he was still that very same loving and kindhearted man.

After the meal was over, Elizabeth thanked Nancy for the delicious meal and for her pleasant company, and they rode a cab to the Palm Hotel.

"Why would we go back to the hotel, Richard?" Elizabeth asked as they got out of the cab.

He looked at her with a puzzled and hopeful expression. Then he carefully replied, "I understand that you reserved a room for the rest of your stay here. However, I'd love for you and Edward to stay with me at my apartment. I've missed you so much, and I'd love to spend as much time as I can with Edward."

"Richard, do you really want us to stay with you? Are you sure you wouldn't mind?"

"I'm more than grateful that you came back with Edward. I believe it was my prayers being answered. I thank you for coming back, and I thank you for allowing me to take care of you and my son while you're here. I prayed all morning that you'd allow me to do so."

They then went inside the hotel, where Richard went straight to the front desk and asked for the manager. Moments later, a slender middle-aged man dressed in a fine black three-piece suit came up to them.

"How are you today, Mr. Bennett?" he said as he reached out to enthusiastically shake Richard's hand.

"Hello, Dennis. I'm doing great. Life couldn't get any better than this. And yourself?"

"Business is going great, the weather is awesome, guess I can't complain. How may I help you this afternoon, sir?"

"I need a huge favor."

"Of course, sir. What can I do for you?"

"There has been a change in plans, so I would like for one of your employees to go up to room 411 and pack up everything inside. Then, bring everything to my apartment on Park Avenue. Just inform the front desk when they get there. They will know what to do from there."

"Of course, sir," Dennis said, nodding.

"Oh, and one more thing," Richard said. "I'd appreciate it if you could give Ms. Elizabeth a refund in full for the remainder of her stay."

"Not a problem, sir. Anything else?"

"That would be all. Thank you, Dennis."

"Thank you, sir." Dennis shook Richard's hand and excused himself.

"Do you come here often?" Elizabeth asked, curious. "How does he know you so well?"

"I'm the biggest patron of the hotel," he said proudly and stole a glance at her. Then he chuckled softly and said, "I'm just kidding. My family owns the hotel."

She laughed and gently punched his shoulder as they walked toward the front doors and left the hotel.

"Hey, buddy ..." Richard turned to Edward to grab his hand. "Where would you like to go this afternoon?"

"I want to go to the amusement park, Daddy," Edward excitedly replied.

"The amusement park sounds like a brilliant idea! Off to the amusement park, then!"

Richard reached over to take Elizabeth's hand, and pulled her close as they walked away.

# Chapter Nineteen

Noah's Amusements, located at the southeast corner of Iris Park, was one of the most popular attractions in the city. It was sectioned off by its many types of rides—family rides, thrill rides, kiddie rides, and water rides. With the support and funding of the Bennett Foundation, the park had doubled in size since it was first opened.

Edward excitedly ran into the park ahead of his parents. He dashed around in awe, captivated by all the activities around him. Elizabeth had to call out a few times for him to slow down and to not run too far ahead, but the enthusiastic Edward didn't seem to hear a thing his mother said.

Richard had to increase his pace in order to catch up with Edward. Taking his son by the hand, he led him to the merry-go-round. He put Edward on a horse and sat on the one next to him.

As the ride began, Edward seemed to be a little scared, both of his hands tightly gripping the pole. Richard reached over to touch his shoulder and reassured him that everything was all right. As the ride continued, Edward loosened up a bit and began to enjoy the experience. After about three rounds, his eyes were able to search around for his mother, and he yelled out to her, "Mommy, this is so much fun!"

Elizabeth could not stop smiling as she watched the two of them. Her heart had never been so satisfied as she stood there, seeing Edward right next to his father. She closed her eyes briefly, trying to paint the priceless and special moment on her heart.

After the ride ended, Edward quickly got off and ran to her. "Mommy!" he yelled. "The ride was fantastic! I wanna go again!"

As Richard caught up with them, Edward quickly grabbed onto his hand and nagged him excitedly, "Daddy, let's go on another ride!"

"Sure, buddy. Let's go on one as a family this time." Richard led them to the Ferris wheel. He looked at Elizabeth as she took a couple of steps back. "Aren't you coming with us?" he asked.

"I'm really scared of heights," she replied nervously as she stared at the huge wheel.

He took her hand and led her to the gate. "It will be all right," he assured her. "All you have to do is close your eyes when we reach the top. And then open them when we reach the bottom."

She was still hesitant. "I don't know, Richard. I'm not feeling too good about this."

"Don't worry. You've got us." He smiled sweetly at her.

"Yeah, Mommy, you got us," Edward said. "I'll hold your hand if you're scared."

"I'll go," she agreed, "but only if you'll tell me when we reach the bottom." She looked to Richard for reassurance. "I want to open my eyes to see the two of you."

"Of course," Richard said, still holding her hand as he led them to a cart.

Richard sat in the middle with Elizabeth and Edward on either side of him. Elizabeth had her eyes closed even before the ride started. As the cart ascended, Richard softly whispered to her, "No," and she kept her eyes closed. When the cart had reached the bottom of its descent, he whispered to her, "Yes," and she opened her eyes to look at them.

They had repeated this process a few times when the ride suddenly stopped. She thought that the ride had ended, so she quickly opened her eyes, only to discover that they were at the very top. Out of fear, she let out a quick scream and immediately reached out to hold on tightly to Richard.

He laughed softly as he reached around to hold her. "It's okay. I'm right here and I won't let go," he said softly.

She continued to hold on to him with both eyes closed until they slowly descended to the very bottom.

"You can open your eyes now," he said, chuckling.

She slowly opened her eyes to see him smiling reassuringly at her, and returned his smile with a delightful smile of her own.

"Maybe we should do this more often," he said. "It's the only way to get you to hold on to me and never let go."

She punched him teasingly in the shoulder. He laughed at her and said, "I'm glad you can still find humor in this, after what you just went through." He took her hand again as they ran to catch up with Edward.

Two hours flew by. Richard and Elizabeth were exhausted from all the running around, but Edward was still his energetic self. He remained fascinated with everything that came into view, and he wanted to go on as many rides as possible that afternoon.

As Elizabeth continued to observe Richard and Edward getting on and off rides, running up and down the park after each other, wiping and drying each other's wet hair, and sharing ice cream cones, she realized that Edward had really needed his father, and that Richard needed his son. How could she possibly take her son away from his father now? It would be almost impossible for them to part ways after all this. She suddenly became very quiet.

Richard noticed her change in emotion, so he gently wrapped his arm around her slender waist. "You're awfully quiet. What's on your mind?"

"Oh, I'm just a bit tired, that's all," she replied.

"Are you ready to go home?"

"How could I drag the two of you home when you're just warming up?" she managed to joke.

He laughed and then he pointed at a bench. "Okay, why don't you go and sit down there. Edward still wants to go on a couple more rides. We'll be back in a little while." He leaned over and gave her a gentle kiss on the cheek.

The very same thought she'd had earlier was still on her mind as she slowly made her way to the bench. Why hadn't she considered the pain she would experience after meeting him again? How could she be so careless? Her mind was going crazy thinking about how it was all going to end. Overwhelmed with sadness and guilt, she began to weep silently.

The ride to the apartment was long and quiet. Though she wasn't sleepy, Elizabeth closed her eyes the whole way, pretending to be sleeping just to hide her emotions. Edward was sound asleep on Richard's lap. And Richard, as tired as he was, showed no sign of exhaustion from a whole afternoon of running around with Edward. He still had the energy and strength to make sure the two of them were comfortable.

Thinking about this great man made Elizabeth even sadder. She had longed to be with him for so long, and now she was going to hurt him all over again. She was wrong for coming back, for she never expected all of this to happen. Maybe she felt as though she owed it to Richard to give him a chance to meet his son.

Martin was at the doors to greet them. "Hello, Miss Elizabeth! When the hotel people brought in that ugly bag, I immediately knew it was yours," he laughed. "I've been waiting all afternoon just to see you again. Oh my, you haven't changed one bit. In fact, I must say that you only look more gorgeous than the last time I saw you."

"You're such a sweet man, Martin. I appreciate your kind words and warm welcome. Thank you," she said as she reached out both arms to give him a hug.

Martin shifted his attention to Edward and couldn't believe his eyes. "Oh my! Who is this handsome young man?" Martin asked kindly as he crouched down to gently rest his hand on Edward's shoulder.

"This is our son, Edward," Richard proudly replied.

"Hello, Uncle Martin," Edward said as he quickly shook his hand.

"Oh, goodness! What a delightful surprise to see such a lovely little family," Martin said as he opened the door for them.

As they entered the enormous lobby, Elizabeth had to pause for a moment to slowly glance around. She exhaled deeply, beginning to appreciate all that she had missed for so long. She felt as if she had been gone on a long trip and had just come back home. "It hasn't changed a bit, Richard. It's still as beautiful as I remembered."

Edward interrupted her by running quickly to a small pond in the lobby. "Mommy!" he shouted. "There's fish in it!"

Richard led her to a small bench by the pond. They sat there amused as Edward frantically ran around the lobby, excitedly shouting out to them about every new and interesting thing that he discovered.

Richard looked at Elizabeth for a moment, silently staring into her eyes. "You have no idea how many times I've prayed for this," he said sincerely.

"Oh really?" she said softly. "Just how many times did you pray?"

He smiled. "Too many times to count."

She gently rested her head on his shoulder, trying to avoid eye contact with him.

Edward finally got tired and came to sit by his mother. He quietly leaned his little body into hers and closed his eyes. "My, my," she said, chuckling. "I never thought I'd see this moment coming. It's a surprise to see that you finally got tired."

Richard laughed as he picked Edward up and carried him to the elevators.

When they reached his apartment, he took Edward inside and gently laid him on the couch. Then, he went to his bedroom and brought out a light blanket to cover him.

Elizabeth sighed deeply. She felt a bit strange in this place she had once called home. It was such a comfortable feeling to be inside this apartment again, but a rush of sadness overwhelmed her and she suddenly felt the need to cry. Was it because she missed being here so much that the knot in her heart had all of the sudden come untied? Or was it because she thought she would never live to see herself setting foot in this place again? She closed her eyes for a brief moment to inhale the magnificent scent of this memorable place.

When she opened her eyes to scan the room, she realized that everything seemed to have remained the same as the day she left. Even the pair of slippers that she left at the corner behind the door were still in that very same spot. The only thing that had changed was the fact that her bags from the hotel were now sitting on the living room floor.

She picked up the bags and hauled them to the same room she once called her own. Extending her hand to turn the knob, she noticed that it was locked. "Richard? Why is this door locked?"

He quickly came over to her, reached into his pocket, and took out some keys. As he fiddled with the keys, she could tell he was trying to hide something from her. "You haven't answered my question, Richard. Why was this door locked?"

He sighed deeply and turned away as he quietly replied, "I've kept this room locked for all these years because I hoped that someday you'd come back to it."

She gently turned him around and noticed that his eyes were filled with tears. Immediately, she pulled him into her arms. "Oh, Richard," she cried softly. "I'm so sorry for doing this to you."

After a long, tearful embrace, he unlocked the door and opened it. He entered the room first and then he moved to the side to make way for her. She peeked in as if she was afraid to enter. Her eyes scanned the room for a brief moment, and then she exhaled deeply. He reached over to grab her hand and gently pulled her inside.

"Nothing has changed, Richard," she whispered.

"I know," he replied. "I wanted to keep everything just the way it was."

She stepped forward to check out the bed, the dressers, and the closet. Every piece of her clothing was there the same way she had left it. The beautiful black dress was vacuum packed inside a plastic bag. The whole room seemed like it had been frozen in time, just waiting for her return.

Her eyes were glistening now and her lips began to quiver. "How could you, Richard? How could you keep this room frozen in time for five long years? What kind of a cruel, cold-hearted woman was I to have caused you so much pain? I was so selfish and heartless to have left you hanging like this, but if only you could understand . . ." She began to cry again.

He didn't want to hear it anymore. Her crying made his heart bleed like a rapidly flowing river. He felt a knot in his throat and if he didn't do something about it, he'd also burst into tears. Instead, he reached for her waist and pulled her toward him. His lips covered hers for a long and passionate kiss.

He whispered in between breaths, "What matters is that you're back now." He reached out his hand to cup her cheek and ran his thumb below her left eye to wipe away the tears. He was just about to give her another kiss when they heard a voice behind them.

"Mommy."

Elizabeth turned around to see Edward rubbing his eyes with his little hands. "Oh, hi, sweetie," she said. "Are you hungry?"

"No. But I need a bath," he murmured.

They both laughed, and then Richard went into his room to start a bath for Edward. Richard had always loved children, but he never knew that he could have this strong of a bond with a child. The feeling was so magical and profound that he knew he'd die twice this time if Elizabeth were to leave with Edward.

He enjoyed giving Edward a bubble bath. He washed Edward's hair, scrubbed his back and feet, and then put bubbles on his face, pretending it was his beard.

"Daddy, could I sleep with you tonight?" Edward suddenly asked.

"Sure. Do you think Mommy will be okay with it?"

"I've been sleeping with Mommy every night. I think she needs a break," Edward replied adorably.

Richard chuckled as he poured water over Edward's head to wash away the bubbles.

"I tell Mommy I love her all the time," Edward added. "Do you think that it'll be okay to tell you I love you, too?"

"Yes, I'm okay with it." Richard smiled sweetly to assure him that he really meant it.

"I love you, Daddy."

Richard's heart warmed when he heard those words coming from his son's mouth. He suddenly thought back to his conversation with Elizabeth about what his mother had said to her. How could anyone not love this beautiful little creature? How could his mother tell Elizabeth that this beautiful little boy would be hated?

He looked at Edward with loving eyes. "I love you, too, sweetie, and I mean it. I'm your father, and if someone ever tells you that I don't love you, then don't believe them, okay? You just need to remember that I love you with all my heart, all right?"

"I know," Edward replied confidently.

Richard lifted him out of the tub, dried him, and laid him on his bed. "You go to sleep now, and I'll be back in a little while, okay?"

"Yes, Daddy," Edward replied. Then he slowly drifted off to sleep.

"Good night, my little guy." Richard softly kissed Edward's forehead. Then, he dimmed the lights and quietly closed the door behind him.

Richard went back to the living room and saw that Elizabeth was sitting in that exact spot she used to sit in five years ago. She was sipping a cup of chai. He went to sit next to her and smiled warmly as she handed him his cup.

"That was a lot of work, wasn't it?" she said, smiling teasingly.

"Yes, but I enjoyed every minute of it. I'd give anything to do this every day," he replied ecstatically.

Then she became quiet again. She was so conflicted now that she couldn't say another word, so she stared down at the coffee table for a moment to avoid looking at him.

He sat in silence, staring and smiling warmly at her. "Do you mind if Edward sleeps with me in my room tonight?" he suddenly asked.

She looked up. "Are you sure? Edward hasn't slept by himself since he was born. If you're okay with it and if Edward wants that, I could use a break."

He laughed and took another sip from his cup. He could tell her mind was preoccupied. "Do you still have those nightmares?" he inquired.

She looked at him with a curious expression. "No, not since I stayed with you five years ago. They seem to have gone away somehow."

He continued to stare at her without saying anything. She looked away for a moment and then glanced back at him to see that he was still staring at her. "Is there something on your mind? Or did you just miss me that much?" she joked smilingly.

He laughed softly and then replied, "I missed you, and still missing you dearly even though you're just sitting right here with me."

His whole facial expression had changed now as he leaned a little closer to her to confess what was on his mind. He exhaled heavily and then he sincerely said, "What's on my mind is that I'm scared to experience this moment of contentment, because it might be taken away from me. One day I have my beloved son and the woman that I love more than my own life with me, and then the next day, I'm left with nothing. Elizabeth, that thought scares me so much. I would die twice this time around if you two should disappear."

She was scared, too, except that this time she wasn't just scared for his and her own pain, but also for Edward's. It would break not just two hearts this time, but three. It would scar Edward's heart forever if she were to take him from his father. So she just sat there without a sound, staring silently at her cup.

"I notice your silence," he told her. "Is there something you would like to share? Did I do something wrong today?"

She looked back at him. "Not at all," she said. "You were perfect today. You are perfect every day that I'm with you. I can't ask for anything more from you."

"Then why are you so reserved? Is there someone else? Did you find another person to take my place when you were away?" He was desperate to know, but also terrified of what he might find out.

She looked at him and quietly replied, "Yes, there were others, but none of them ever captured my heart the way that you have." She noticed that he was still not satisfied with her answer. His heart was still unsettled and he was still dying to ask her about the ring. But he was afraid of the answer.

She smiled warmly at him as she reached out a hand to cup his cheek. Then she said to him, "If it gives your heart some comfort, I want you to know that you are the only man that I've ever made love to."

He let out a sigh of relief. Still, the question about the ring needed to be answered. He was definitely scared, but he needed to know. "I have been dying all day to ask you about the ring on your finger," he blurted out. "Are you engaged?" He held his breath, hoping that she'd give him a satisfying answer.

She looked down at the diamond sitting nicely on her finger and smiled sweetly. "So, it was this thing? It was this tiny little thing that had been troubling you all day?"

He raised his eyebrows in surprise. "Of course. That tiny thing caused me a lot of grief today."

She moved her other hand over to touch the ring, and then she slowly slipped it off. She looked up, shifting her eyes to meet his and handed it to him. She could tell that he was confused and didn't know why she had given him the ring. "If you look closely at it," she said "you'll see that the white gold is real, but the diamond isn't. I wore this ring to deter the wandering eyes of men. I just didn't want to be bothered by them."

He slowly brought the ring closer to his eyes to inspect it. He had no idea if the diamond was real or not, but he did know one thing—that she had never lied to him. He had never experienced such profound relief in his life. He felt like his body was floating in midair, that his soul had leaped out of his body and was joyously dancing about inside the room.

He sat there, just basking in his jubilant emotions for a while, and then he looked back at her. "If it's okay with you, may I keep it and give it back to you at a later date?"

"Only if you trade it for a real one," she joked, and they both laughed.

"All jokes aside," she continued, "yes, you may keep it if it gives you some comfort."

They chatted for a while, and then he looked at her with a serious expression. She was a little taken aback by this sudden change. "Is there something else that has been troubling you?" she asked.

He took a deep breath and slowly exhaled. Then he leaned toward her and took her hands in his. "I'm so sorry, sweetie, for what I've done to you. Five years ago, my mother pleaded with me to agree to do a background check on you. I thought that if I agreed to it, then maybe she would leave us alone. I just wanted to put her mind at ease about you so that she'd never bother you again. Even though I knew my mother and what she was capable of, I had no idea what she was planning to do. I'm truly sorry that I've hurt you so much. I know that it may be too late, but I wanted to take this opportunity to apologize to you for what I've done to you. The guilt and the pain have tormented me for five long years. I'll understand if you never forgive me or trust me again."

She listened quietly as he explained to her what had really happened before she left five years before. When he was done, she looked into his deep blue eyes. "I've forgiven you, Richard. I should be asking for your forgiveness instead. I was the one who was being irrational. It was a very sensitive time for me. I was all alone, and my only defense was to run away. It was a flaw that I was not proud of. I'm so sorry for what I've put you through for all these years. Please forgive me."

He quickly pulled her into his arms and held her tightly. "You don't need to ask for my forgiveness. There's nothing to forgive. I'm just blessed to have you back. I want to share the rest of my life with you. If you give me another chance, I promise you that I will spend every day of my life making you happy. I never want to see you shed another tear again."

She stayed in his arms for a brief moment and then she said, "Richard, you must forgive your mother. I know that what she did was very hurtful and cruel, but it was done out of her love for you."

"I haven't spoken to my mother since the day you left," he said despairingly.

She suddenly pulled back to look at him. "You mean to tell me that you haven't spoken to your mother in five years?"

"Yes," he replied. "I told her that if you don't return and that if you can't find it in your heart to forgive her, then she would never hear my voice nor see my face again."

 Elizabeth was stunned by what she just heard. She let out a deep sigh and earnestly said, "I *have* forgiven her, Richard. I can't imagine how devastated she must have felt, knowing that her son wouldn't speak to her ever again. I'm so sorry to do this to the both of you."

"Please don't say that. If only she made an effort to get to know you. She would see that you are my match in every way."

"Well then. Will you please go visit your mother as a favor for me? It would bring some sort of closure for me."

He knew that the bitterness he had for his mother had dragged on for too long. He now wanted to visit his parents and really wanted to show them their grandson. He also desperately wanted Elizabeth to accompany them, but he thought it might be too much too soon for her, and he wasn't going to push it. "Yes, I'll do anything for you," he said. "May I take Edward along? I would like to introduce him to his grandparents."

"Yes, of course. They're the only grandparents he has, and I insist."

"I cannot express in words how excited I am, Elizabeth. I will go visit them first thing in the morning," he said ecstatically.

# Chapter Twenty

It was early morning. The first light of dawn had just peeked in through the windows when Doris and Victor came to the solarium to drink their first morning cup of tea. Though they've been sitting down together like this each morning for the past thirty years, ever since the day Elizabeth left, Victor had not been communicating with Doris in the same way. He was just brief and simple in his conversations with her, and he would talk only if he had to. When he had nothing to say, he would just sit there and stare around the room like she didn't exist.

It had been a very long while since Doris had heard anything from her son, and she had been dying to know how he was doing. There had been many times when she felt the need to ask Victor, but she held her tongue because she was afraid of what he would say to her. She knew she had made a mistake, and she had been living with deep guilt for the past five years. She also knew that she'd carry that guilt with her for the rest of her life. Eventually, though, she couldn't take it any longer. As a mother and out of concern for her son, she decided to ask Victor about Richard's well-being. "How's Richard doing?" she asked quietly.

"I'm sure he's doing well," he replied nonchalantly as he took a sip from his cup.

She looked at him and sighed deeply. "You have given me a short answer every time I ask a question," she said in a heightened tone. "I know I have done wrong, but as a mother I still deserve to know how my son is doing. I was the one who gave birth to him, after all, and I haven't spoken to him in years. I don't even remember what my son looks like anymore."

"I'm glad you finally realized that you are the woman who gave birth to him," he said sarcastically without even looking at her.

She bit her tongue and quietly composed herself before she continued. "I also realize how much I've hurt him. If I can only know that he's doing all right, at least I can die comfortably."

Victor took another sip from his cup and let his eyes wander about the huge room. After a while, he spoke to her without looking at her. "Well, I've spoken with him many times and asked him to come visit you, but I haven't seen him show up yet. It is up to him to decide whether or not he wants to see you."

With a desolate expression, she quietly said, "I miss him, Victor. If I could go back in time to undo everything, I would gladly do it without any hesitation. I only hope that he won't hate me forever. I've wanted to beg for his forgiveness every day for the past five years."

He stole a quick glance at her. He could tell that she was sincere about her words. "Give him time. I'm sure he'll speak to you when he's ready. He's not going to hate you forever."

"You make it sound so easy, but you're not on the receiving end. Do you know how much it hurts? I just want one more chance to get my son back."

He glanced at her again, and this time with a pleasant expression on his face. "You may get your chance soon. I received a phone call earlier from him, and he told me that he wanted to visit us. I hope you've changed your ways."

She quickly gave him an annoyed look. "This is not funny, Victor. What kind of game are you playing?"

He looked at her with an enthusiastic expression. "I'm not playing a game with you. Richard is really coming here. I've just sent out a limo for him."

"Richard is *really* coming to see us? Oh my, what am I going to say to him?" she said in a panicky voice.

"Whatever you do or say, just don't mess it up this time. This might be your last chance," he warned her sharply.

"Of course I won't," she retorted. "Did he say why he's coming?"

"No. He just said he wanted to visit and that he needed for the both of us to be home."

Elizabeth was up early to get Edward ready to go visit his grandparents. She was a little uneasy about him going without her, but she wanted to be on the positive side. After all these years, she wanted to believe that Doris had changed and that perhaps she would adore Edward for who he was. Besides, Richard was going with him, and she trusted that Edward would be in good hands.

Despite all her worries, she still loved Victor like he was her own father. She honestly believed that Victor would accept and love Edward and that he'd be a wonderful grandfather to him. So, she set all her worries aside as she busied herself with dressing Edward up for his special day.

"Mommy, where am I going?"

"You are going with your father to see your grandparents."

"Really? Wow!" he said excitedly.

"Yes, and I want you to be on your very best behavior, okay?"

"Yes, Mommy, but aren't you coming, too?"

"No, sweetie. I'm going to stay home and rest. You go and have fun with your grandparents, okay?"

"Yes, Mommy."

"The limo is here," Richard said as he walked into the room. He reached down to take Edward's hand and then turned to Elizabeth. He desperately didn't want to be apart from her. He was unsure and afraid that she might not be there when he came back. He looked at her lovingly. "Please be here," he said, almost pleading.

She smiled sweetly at him, understanding his concern. "I'll be waiting for you," she replied warmly.

He gently touched her face, caressing it as if for the last time. "We'll be back as soon as possible."

"Take your time and enjoy the day with your parents. I promise that I'll be here when you come back," she reassured him.

"I'll call you later." He reached over to place a tender kiss on her lips, then took Edward's hand and they went out the door.

Richard was delighted with Edward's excited expression upon seeing the limo and at how anxious he was to climb in. If only he could have Edward and Elizabeth by his side every day, he thought, he'd have such a blessed and happy life.

The limo sped southbound on Ocean Boulevard, and within twenty minutes it made a left turn onto Oceanside Road, a private road leading up to the Atkins Mansion. The limo followed the road for a while before making a stop in front of two enormous iron gates.

The driver waved to a security guard inside a small shack a couple of yards away from the gates, and shortly after, the gates slowly opened. The limo continued down the road, and soon a huge mansion, almost like a castle, slowly appeared on the horizon.

"Wow, it's so big, Daddy. Do Grandma and Grandpa live in that castle?" Edward asked excitedly.

"Yes," Richard replied, amused.

"Do you live there too?"

"I used to live there. But now I have a place of my own."

"I could live there forever, Daddy. I would have so much fun there."

Richard gently picked Edward up and sat him on his lap. "Someday, this will all be yours."

"*Really?*" Edward said as a huge grin spread across his face. "Can I put a merry-go-round and a petting zoo in the yard?"

"You can do anything you want." Richard chuckled as he gently pinched Edward's cheek.

The limo slowly came to a stop in the front of the house, and then a man wearing a black suit quickly ran up to open the door for them. "Good morning, Mr. Bennett."

Richard stepped out of the limo and cheerfully greeted him. "Good morning, Carlos." Then he turned back to the limo and held out his hand to help Edward out, and they both walked up toward the entrance.

Marie had been standing at the front entrance for a while awaiting his arrival. It had been years since she had seen Richard set foot in the mansion. "Hello, Richard. It has been too long, honey."

"Hello, Marie. I hope all is well with you," he said kindly. "Are my parents in?"

"Yes, they're in the living room waiting for you."

"Thank you, Marie," Richard said as he led Edward inside.

As they came into the living room, Richard could see his parents standing in the middle with cheerful and enthusiastic expressions on their faces. He was a little nervous, because he wasn't sure how his mother would react to the sight of Edward. But regardless of how she felt, he was not ashamed to show them his son and he would do anything to protect him.

Doris couldn't have been happier to reunite with her son after half a decade. Her heart was pounding joyously and her eyes were glistening in tears. "Richard! I'm so happy to see you!" she cried out as she quickly ran over to give him a long embrace. "Thank you for coming," she added in a trembling voice.

Even though Richard had been furious with Doris for what she had done, he had to admit that he had missed her. After all, she was his mother, and he loved her regardless of what had happened.

Victor also came over to embrace Richard. "Welcome home, son. Thank you so much for coming."

Victor and Doris then inquisitively looked down at the little boy who had accompanied Richard. Silence filled the room for a moment until Richard realized that he hadn't introduced Edward.

Richard looked at his parents with a joyous expression and proudly said, "Mother, Father, this is four-year-old Edward Bennett. He's your grandson."

"How could this be?" Doris whispered as if she was gasping for air.

"Hello, Grandma," Edward waved at Doris. Then, he turned to Victor and shook his hand. "Hello, Grandpa."

"Oh my goodness," Doris said as she knelt down to Edward's level to look at him. "You are adorable."

Edward looked at her with an intrigued expression. "My mommy told me that you are very beautiful. And now that I saw you, my mommy was right. You are really beautiful, Grandma."

Doris was pleasantly amused. Her eyes lit up and she said sweetly, "Oh, really? So, what is your mommy's name, sweetie?"

"My mommy's name is Elizabeth," Edward replied.

Doris's eyes resembled those of a deer caught in headlights. She looked up at Richard and saw that he was smiling and nodding, confirming what she was about to ask.

Her heart began to beat rapidly, not only because she was surprised but because she was so happy. Today, she hadn't just gotten her son back—she had also gained a grandson, and it was overwhelming for her. Tears of joy spilled down her cheeks. She was speechless; all she could do was smile and allow her tears to silently flow.

Edward looked at her, and then suddenly reached up both hands to wipe away her tears. "Grandma, you can stop crying now and just be happy, okay?"

Doris reached out and gave Edward a huge hug. "Grandma is just very happy to see you," she whispered.

Victor stood there proudly, but he was at a loss for words. He considered himself a strong man in every respect, one who could always withstand difficulties. But now he found himself softly crying upon seeing his grandson. How could this happen to his family? he thought. How could he, as a father, allow this to happen to his very own family? It saddened him that his grandson was already four years old, and yet he had just met him for the first time. Victor had missed the first crucial years of his one and only grandson's life. He wept quietly as he knelt down to pull Edward into his large, trembling arms.

Richard was overwhelmed with emotion. Just observing his father made his heart ache. He'd never seen this side of his strong father before. He slowly put a hand under Victor's arm to pull him up.

Victor stood, wiped away his tears, then reached out a hand to give a gentle slap on Richard's shoulder. "Congratulations, my son," he said cheerfully.

"Thank you, Father."

While the two men congratulated each other, Doris stood up, took Edward's hand, and led him to the sofas. She gently lifted him up onto her lap and said with the sweetest smile, "Let me look at you for a moment. Let me see my only grandson." She beamed.

Although Edward looked much like his father, he also resembled Elizabeth. Even though she hadn't said it aloud, Doris had prayed in her heart for Elizabeth's return. She wished to make amends with her, wanting to be a loving mother to her this time.

After Victor came in and sat down, Edward quickly hopped off of Doris's lap and jumped onto Victor's lap. "My mommy told me that you're very nice."

"She did?" Victor replied in an amused tone. "Well, you tell your mommy that Grandpa misses her very much, and that she must come visit me, okay?"

"Yes, Grandpa."

"Marie!" Richard called out to Marie.

"Yes, Richard," Marie said as she entered the room.

"Could you take Edward and show him around the house while I speak to my parents alone?"

"It would be my honor to show young Edward around the house," Marie replied, smiling as she took Edward by the hand and led him out of the room.

"If you don't mind, I would like to congratulate you, Richard. He looks very much like you when you were little," Doris said in astonishment.

Richard smiled proudly. "I know, Mother. When I first saw him, and before I even knew he was my very own, I was as amazed as you are right now. I hoped that he was mine. Then when I saw Elizabeth, I thought I had died and gone to Heaven."

"So she is back?" Victor asked.

Richard let out a deep sigh, and then replied with a sigh, "Yes, she came back. But I don't think she came back for me. She came here because of a promise she made to Edward. I don't think she was planning to come see me. I was in the right place at the right time and just happened to come upon them."

All three of them sat in silence for a moment. Then Doris turned to Richard and said, "Would you be okay with me having a word with her? There's nothing I want to do more than to make amends for what I've done."

"No, Mother," he quickly cautioned her. "She might take offense to it and leave me for good. And this time, I'm not sure what I would do if she and my son leave me."

"But I need to—"

"Please don't," he abruptly interrupted. He looked at his parents with sadness and despair in his eyes. He noticed the curiosity on their faces, and he knew that he would have to let them know more about Elizabeth.

He sighed deeply, and then he slowly explained, "You need to know that Elizabeth is all alone in this world. Her parents, brother, and grandparents are all deceased. I can't imagine the amount of pain and sorrow that she has had to endure all by herself. Because of this, her fragile heart couldn't cope with any more pain, so she protected herself by running away from it. Her only defense was her only flaw. It's just so unfair that someone as sweet, loving, and generous as she had to endure the suffering she has."

Richard paused to wipe a tear from his eye before continuing. "When we first met, she told me that she was on a journey and had been on it for a long time. It wasn't until the day after she'd left that I finally understood what she was saying. She was searching for a family. All she wanted after her long, lonely, and painful journey was to have a loving family like she used to have. I was her only hope, solace, and salvation, and I betrayed her. It pains me so much to know that she has had to endure five more years of pain, caused by the one person who claimed to love her the most. While I sat inside my apartment moping and feeling sorry for myself, she was alone, hurt, confused, and pregnant. While I continued on with my comfortable life, she had given birth to my son alone and struggled to raise him by herself. This is why, mother. This is why I don't ever want her to leave me. She has given me everything, and I desperately want a chance to give it all back to her."

Doris dabbed her eyes as Richard's words cut deep into her formerly cold heart. And for the first time in her life, she had shed tears for someone else besides her own son. She now realized that the pain she had caused her son was insignificant compared to the pain she had inflicted on Elizabeth. She let out a deep, trembling sigh and softly said, "I was wrong, Richard. I've hurt her so much. I know now that the pain that I've caused can never be undone. I would never expect her to forgive me for that. I just wanted another chance, Richard. I wanted a chance to see her the way that you've seen her. I wanted a chance to be a good mother to her, to love her the way I've loved you."

Richard looked at his mother with a despairing but sincere expression. "Thank you, mother, for realizing it now, but I honestly don't think that we're going to get a second chance. Although I think that she still loves me, I also think that there is a deep sense of mistrust in her heart for me. And that worries me."

Silence filled the room. Finally, Doris turned to Richard and asked, "What are you going to do now?"

Richard gave her a helpless look. He had no idea what he was going to do. "I don't know, Mother. I'm so scared right now. I thought that I had gone through it all and that my heart had gotten stronger from my experience, but to be honest, this is the first time in my life that I've ever been this scared. If I lose them both this time, I don't know if I could go on."

Victor gently placed a hand onto Richard's shoulder and assured him, "Don't worry too much. I'm sure she still loves you. You will have to be strong and make her fall in love with you all over again. I know that she will stay with you if she is loved. All she wanted was a loving family, and with the miracle of Edward, we are the only family she has."

"She's leaving at the end of the week. There's not enough time," Richard said desperately.

"How long did it take you to make her fall in love with you the first time?" Victor asked.

"I don't know. Three, maybe four days. I really don't know, Father. "

"Well, you have a week this time. You have plenty of time, and with Edward's help, you're already in good hands."

As they sat and chatted for a while, Edward entered the room and quickly ran up to Richard. "Daddy, they have a piano!" he said excitedly. He took Richard's hand. "Come with me, Daddy. I want to play a song for you."

Everyone stood up and followed Edward to the music room. "I didn't know he played," Doris curiously said to Richard.

"I didn't know either," Richard replied. "But he's a lot like Elizabeth. He just never ceases to amaze me."

Richard picked up Edward and placed him on the bench in front of a magnificent grand piano. "What are you going to play for us?" Richard asked.

"It's a surprise," Edward replied. "It's my mommy's favorite song that she plays all the time."

They stood in anticipation of what a four-year-old might be able to do with a piano. It seemed like the keys were just too big for his tiny fingers. But they watched in amazement as those tiny fingers glided effortlessly along the keyboard as if they weren't even touching the keys. He stroked every key with just the right amount of pressure, creating the most angelic sound they had ever heard.

Richard immediately recognized this piece of music. It was the same piece that Elizabeth had played for him when they were inside the music store. He stood there proudly while his talented son put on an amazing show. However, he also felt a touch of sadness because it brought back some of the memories he had of Elizabeth. He had to turn away for a brief moment to collect himself before he could turn back to enjoy the performance.

After Edward finished the song, everyone applauded and cheered loudly for him.

"You are one amazing young man!" Doris said as she picked him up and set him by her side.

Edward noticed that Richard's eyes were glassy. "What's wrong, Daddy?" he asked in a concerned manner.

"I'm just so happy to hear you play, that's all," Richard softly replied.

"Don't cry, Daddy. I can play for you every day. Mommy taught me lots of songs, but she told me that this one was your favorite."

Richard quickly went over to Edward, picked him up, and hugged him tightly. "Please, God! Please don't take him away from me!" Richard cried out as he embraced is son.


After breakfast, the family went to the solarium and the three adults agreed to pose for Edward to draw a picture of them.

"Since this is the first time I met you, I would like to give you something as a gift from me," Edward said to his grandparents.

"What great idea!" Doris said, delighted. "We'll sit here as still as we can possibly be. You just do what you need to do."

Edward excitedly looked up at them and then he looked down at his paper. He tilted his head to one side, then to the other side. He held up his pencil to trace their faces before he made the sketches on his paper. He made crisscross patterns on the upper half of his paper to help center their faces, then he sketched three ovals right over the patterns. He looked up at them again to see where he should place their eyes, noses, and mouths. He tilted his face to the left and lifted up his pencil to align the center of their faces, then looked down to work again.

After what seemed like a good half hour, Edward lifted up his face with an angelic smile and said, "Okay, I'm all done!"

"Well, show us your masterpiece!" Doris exclaimed.

Edward ran to them with his drawing in his hand. They were all impressed with his artistic talents. Their faces and expressions were drawn out with great and fine details. Even though Edward was just a child and could barely grip a pencil yet, his talents definitely shone through.

"My goodness," Doris gasped. "This is amazing!" She picked him up and kissed him. "We are going to frame this and keep it in the solarium, so that we can look at it every day," she proudly added.

"I'm in awe," Victor said, shaking his head in disbelief. "I've heard of prodigies, but I never imagined I'd have a grandson who was one. I'm truly proud of you," he said to Edward as his fingers teased the hair on top of his head.

"Oh, my gosh! I forgot to call Elizabeth! Will you excuse me for a moment?" Richard said to his parents and then quickly left the room.

Elizabeth was sitting on the couch reading when the home phone rang. She picked it up and was delighted to hear Richard's voice. "So, how did it go?" she asked curiously.

"Great! Edward amazed everyone with his abilities. I'm so proud of him."

"That's wonderful. It's nice to know that he is being so well received by his grandparents."

"I'm sorry that I didn't call sooner. Edward's sketch of us took a while and I couldn't sneak away to give you a call, but we'll be on our way back shortly."

"No, Richard. Stay as long as you'd like. I insist."

"But I miss you already and want to see you."

"You'll see me tonight," she said. "I'll be here, honey."

"It's absolutely honey to the ears when one is being called such," he said, chuckling.

She giggled. "Seriously, Richard, please take all the time you want. I'll see you when you get back."

He hung up and smiled contentedly. He had finally got to see Elizabeth again after half a decade, and not only that, she had brought back his son—one he could only dream of having. What more could he ask for? He was indeed a happy man, and he prayed that he would be this happy for the remainder of his days.

Doris smiled as she noticed the jubilant expression on Richard's face. "So, how did it go? The phone call, I mean," she asked.

"It was great! She insisted that we could stay as long as we'd like."

"She's such a wonderful and understanding woman," Victor said.

Richard and Edward stayed at the mansion until the late afternoon. Lunch with his parents was splendid. Even though Doris had done many cruel things in her life, Richard knew after observing her attitude and how she had treated Edward that his mother wasn't such a bad person after all. She had either learned from her mistakes and had realized that she needed to change, or she just hadn't discovered that sweet, gentle, and kindhearted side of her until now. Whichever it was, Richard decided to let her know how he felt. "I'm proud of you, Mother.

I have always loved you, even during those long years I was away, but seeing how you love and treated Edward today, I can say that I love you even more. Thank you for a wonderful afternoon," he said as he tenderly embraced her.

Doris's tears flowed again, and she wept like a baby in her son's arms. After she finished crying, she managed to say to him, "You do whatever it is in your power to convince her to stay. I would love to help; however, due to my past mistakes, I'm afraid I will just make things worse for you. But I will pray that she will forgive you and will decide not to leave."

On the limo ride home, Richard felt like he was a changed man. He had gone from being weak and helpless to being strong and optimistic. After talking to his mother and observing how she treated Edward, he had the strength to save his life—his life with Elizabeth and Edward.

When they arrived at his apartment and the elevator door opened, Richard could immediately smell the strong aroma of food in the hallway. That smell—that sweet smell that reassured him she was home, waiting for him. How he missed the smell of her cooking filling the hallways of the twentieth floor. His heart couldn't help but jump for joy. It had been too long since he'd had this feeling—the feeling of warmth and love in his heart, the feeling of coming home to not just someone, but to his Elizabeth. He stood in the hallway for a moment to deeply inhale the aroma.

They went inside the apartment and Elizabeth was standing next to the dining table. "You're late," she said, smiling teasingly.

He walked straight over to her and gave her a long, passionate embrace. "You have no idea how much I missed you today."

She smiled sweetly in return, and then shifted her eyes to the table. "I hope you guys are hungry, because I made a lot of food."

He gently touched her face and redirected her eyes toward their son. "Edward ate at the house, but I've been saving my stomach all day for your cooking."

Richard sat there in silence, admiring her as she filled his plate with food. He paid careful attention to every bite of the food and every expression on her face, sealing them in his heart so that he could remember them and cherish them forever.

# Chapter Twenty-One

The sun had just peeked over the horizon and was shining brightly through Elizabeth's bedroom window. She opened her eyes and knew that it was going to be another beautiful day. She couldn't wait to share it with her two favorite people in the world, so she quickly got out of bed and walked to the window.

The sky was clear and blue. The sun was breathtakingly beautiful. She had to prepare now. She needed to spend another memorable day with Richard. She had to try to make as many wonderful memories with him as she possibly could with the few remaining days she and Edward had left in Atkins.

After a quick shower, she went into the kitchen and was about to get breakfast started when the home phone rang. "It's so early in the morning," she whispered. "Who could be calling?" She quickly ran to answer it so that the ringing wouldn't wake Richard and Edward.

"Hello," she whispered softly.

"Hello there. Is this Elizabeth?"

"Yes, this is she."

"Why, hello, Elizabeth, it is so nice to hear your voice again. This is Doris, Richard's mother."

Elizabeth was startled. Her heart began to race faster now, and even though she tried to stay positive, she still feared the worst. After composing herself for a few seconds, she said, "Good morning, ma'am. It's a pleasure to hear your voice as well."

"I hope you have been well."

"I have been doing wonderfully well, ma'am. Thank you for asking. You sound like you're doing great yourself," Elizabeth replied in a cheerful voice, even though she was perplexed and wondering why Doris was calling.

"Say, Elizabeth, I know this is kind of sudden, but if you don't mind, I would love for you to join me for a cup of coffee this morning," Doris said politely.

Elizabeth paused for a moment, trying to comprehend the situation.

"Elizabeth? Are you still there?"

"Yes. Yes, ma'am, I'm still here," she quickly replied.

"Would you do me the honor of joining me for coffee this morning?"

Elizabeth paused again. She panicked for a second, unsure how she should respond to this. Without giving it any more thought, she replied, "Yes. Sure, I would love to." Her words came out so suddenly that she barely knew what she had just said. Perhaps it was her positive thinking that led to her answer.

"Great! We can meet at Gourmet-Gourmet Coffee within the hour. You know where it is, right?"

"Yes, ma'am, I do know where it is, and I'll see you there in about an hour."

"Thank you, dear. I'll see you then."

Elizabeth hung up the phone and realized that her heart was beating fast and unsteadily. Although her brief conversation with Doris was pleasant, she was a little skeptical. After all, the last time they had spoken had been very unpleasant and she ended up being very hurt. Was Doris unhappy about her return? Was Doris suspecting that Elizabeth had come back to claim child support from Richard? Or maybe Doris wanted to prove that her perception about Elizabeth sleeping her way to the family's fortune was correct?

She went back into her bedroom, and as she was getting dressed she felt a couple of warm tears roll down her cheeks. Even though she tried to remain strong, the overwhelming feeling of sorrow began to consume her as she thought about leaving Richard before the end of the week.

She sat on the bed for a while, pondering the best course of action. Whatever was going to happen when she met up with Doris, she knew that she was strong enough to make the decision if she needed to.

Richard woke up and could not believe his eyes. He smiled lovingly at the tiny body sleeping soundly beside him. Never in his life had he dreamed of waking up to something this beautiful. This little creature brought him so much happiness that he felt one lifetime was not going to be enough to spend with him. He gently reached out a hand to comb Edward's hair with his fingers. "My little guy. I love you so much," he whispered as he leaned over to place a gentle kiss on Edward's forehead. Then, he quietly got out of bed and headed out to the kitchen, eager to see Elizabeth.

"Elizabeth?" he called out softly.

"I'm over here," she replied softly from the dining room.

He turned his head and noticed that she was already dressed, as if she was ready to leave the apartment. He stood there with a questioning look on his face, while at the same time admiring her beauty. "Good morning, sweetie," he greeted her cheerfully.

"Morning, Richard," she said, smiling.

"Looks like you're all ready to enjoy the beautiful day?"

She quietly chuckled. "Sorry, this kind of came up suddenly and I didn't have the chance to tell you yet, but I'm going out to meet an old friend for coffee this morning."

"You're going to see Nancy?"

"No. It's just an old friend I met a while back," she replied as she discreetly looked away.

He continued his curious gaze and noticed that she wasn't very anxious to leave. "Would you like for me to accompany you?"

"No, it's just girl talk," she replied, still smiling.

"It just seemed like you'd rather spend time with us this week."

"Of course, I'd rather be with the two of you any day, but this is an old friend and she wanted to see me after all these years."

"All right, enjoy your visit with your friend, and take your time," he said hesitantly, but still maintaining a pleasant expression.

She smiled sweetly. She knew that he couldn't wait for her to return. "I should be back in an hour or so," she said. "I'm sorry about breakfast."

"Don't worry about us. Edward and I needed the time this morning to cook our first meal together."

She reached up and gently caressed his face. "I'll see you when I get back."


As Elizabeth approached the coffee shop, she stopped and hesitated outside the door. After her previous unfortunate experience with Doris, she was nervous and really didn't know what to expect. Taking a deep breath, she gathered up her courage and slowly walked inside. She looked around the room and saw Doris waving at her from a table next to the windows.

Doris quickly stood up and walked over to her. "Hello, Elizabeth dear. It's so nice to finally see you again," she said politely.

"Hello, ma'am. Thank you. It's a pleasure seeing you again as well," Elizabeth said pleasantly, but deep inside, she was dreading what might happen.

Doris turned to the manager and called out, "Marge, please bring us two cups of your finest gourmet coffee!"

They walked back to the table together and sat in silence for a moment, just looking at each other. They were both a little hesitant to speak, for they were both unsure of each other's feelings. Elizabeth felt so uncomfortable that she considered leaving.

Just then the manager brought over two cups of coffee.

*Perhaps if I say something first, it will make this situation a little more bearable,* she thought. She smiled as she took a sip from her cup. "Mmmm... This coffee is delicious. I'm amazed!"

Doris smiled and sat quietly, taking sips from her cup. She was also uncomfortable and at a loss for words.

After Elizabeth took another sip of her coffee, she set the coffee cup down and clasped her nervous hands together. She didn't know what else to do, so she just sat there.

Doris looked at Elizabeth, and with a most sincere smile, she kindly said, "It has indeed been too long. Let me look at you." She slowly reached across the table and grasped Elizabeth's hands, squeezing them with just the right amount of pressure and then gently holding them as she stared straight into Elizabeth's eyes and smiled. "You look absolutely stunning, my dear. I don't know why I didn't see this before, but I hope you'll forgive my old heart," she managed to say in a warm voice.

Elizabeth was surprised at the affection Doris displayed. She had been preparing for an unpleasant and resentful encounter, but this completely caught her off guard. "Thank . . . thank you for the kind words, ma'am," she managed to reply.

Doris went silent for a moment. She took a deep breath and slowly let it out. Still looking into Elizabeth's eyes, she said, "I have a lot to say, my dear, but before anything else, I'd like to thank you for agreeing to meet me on such short notice."

"It's a pleasure to be here, ma'am. Thank you for inviting me," Elizabeth said politely.

Another silence followed as the two continued to smile at each other, as if each was waiting for the other to say something. Finally, Doris let out a soft sigh. "Elizabeth," she said, "thank you for returning with Edward. You have no idea how happy Victor and I were when we met him. You have no idea how thankful we were to learn of your return. It was like our prayers had been answered."

"Thank you, ma'am, for allowing Edward to visit. It meant the world to him."

Doris glanced away for a moment before turning to look straight at Elizabeth again. With an anguished expression, she began to pour her heart out. "I know I hurt you deeply and I don't deserve your forgiveness, but I would like for you to know that I have lived with this guilt for five long years."

She paused to wipe away a tear and then continued. "My cruelty didn't serve me well. After you left, I was miserable. I lost my relationship with my son and my husband—my life never felt so empty. Like you when you had absolutely no one in this world to lean on, I experienced pain and loneliness, only much worse. At least you could accept the fact that you didn't have anyone. I felt worse because I had loved ones who were still living, but they felt betrayed by my selfishness and had walked away from me. They lost all trust and faith in me, which is why I felt so deeply wounded. I'm not proud of my mistakes. Honestly, I've hated myself for years."

Doris paused again to wipe away another tear and then added, "You see, sweetie, it's not only Richard who needs you. I realized that Victor and I need you, too. You are the best thing that has ever happened to our family. Not only did you bring happiness to our lives, but meeting Edward for the first time yesterday, I realized that he is the apple of our eye. He is our pride and joy and will be very much cherished by our family. We love him more than anything in this world, and we will love you, too, just as much."

Upon hearing these heartfelt words from the woman who had claimed she would never accept her and her children, Elizabeth slowly wiped away a tear of her own. "Thank you, ma'am, for accepting him as your own."

Her eyes still glistening with tears, Doris again reached out and gently clasped Elizabeth's hands. "I know that five long years have passed, and I would have begged for your forgiveness sooner, but I didn't know where to find you. I know that I don't deserve your forgiveness, but I'd like a second chance to be a mother to you. I would like for you to be a part of our family, and to share with us your loving and generous heart of gold. This family needs you, and I would like for you to accept us."

Elizabeth remained dumbfounded. As a mother herself, she could now begin to understand the pain in Doris's heart. She could not imagine how miserable Doris must have been after losing her relationship with her only son. Elizabeth knew that she herself would have lived like a dead woman if someone were to cut off her relationship with Edward. As she listened to Doris's painful story, she could not help but cry.

Brushing away her tears, she looked at Doris earnestly. "I forgive you, ma'am. I don't blame you for anything. I'm a mother, too, and I understand why you did what you did. I, too, want only the best for my son."

Doris's face brightened a little, but her sobbing worsened—not because she was sad after hearing Elizabeth's words, but because she was overwhelmed with happiness. She tightened the grip on Elizabeth's hands. "Thank you, sweetie, for your understanding and kind words. You have no idea how much comfort and joy you bring to my old heart. Thank you for coming back to my son."

Elizabeth became silent again. She lowered her eyes to look at the table for a moment before looking back at Doris. With an uneasy but sincere expression, she timidly said, "Ma'am, I need to tell you something. I'm sorry if I gave you the wrong impression. I came back because of a promise I made to Edward. When Edward and I arrived here this week, I had no intension of seeing Richard, because I didn't want to see him in so much pain again. I was planning to stay here discreetly with Edward for only a short week and then go back home."

Doris looked like she had suddenly lost a loved one. She inhaled deeply and then let out a deep sigh. "Surely, you must have known it was fate that brought you and Richard back together again, just like that same fate brought the two of you together the first time? If God didn't intend for the two of you to be together, he would've never allowed the both of you to meet again," Doris said in a hopeful and inspiring manner.

"I haven't thought about it that way . . . maybe you're right, ma'am. To tell you the truth, I'm very confused at this point and haven't thought about what to do next yet."

Doris looked directly into Elizabeth's eyes. "I'm here to beg you on my son's behalf," she pleaded. "Even though he warned me to stay away from you out of fear that you might take offense to what I had to say, I felt that I was to blame for your separation. As a mother, I felt I had to do everything that I could possibly do to make amends for what I did, and try to bring the two of you back together again. Richard has endured an unbearable amount of pain all these years without you. He loves you more than anything in this world, even more than he loves his own parents. He will be gravely affected by your leaving this time and will be forever lost without you and Edward. I'm deathly afraid that if you disappear again, and this time with Edward, Richard would not be able to go on. As one mother to another, I'm sure you understand the pain and anxiety I'm feeling right now."

Elizabeth could see the sincerity in Doris's eyes. She empathized deeply with Doris, because she would've done the same for Edward. Smiling warmly, she said, "I feel your every pain and understand every tear you shed. A mother's biggest fear is to see her own children in pain and to lose their love and trust. A mother's love requires her to do everything in her power to keep her children safe. I do understand your concern. So, let me ask you—what can I do to give you some comfort?"

Doris breathed a small sigh of relief, realizing that this was her opportunity to redirect Elizabeth back to the waiting arms of her son. Still, she was careful with her words. "I know that your trust in Richard has been grossly harmed due to my actions, but I can see in your eyes that your heart hasn't changed. You still love him, and if you look deep into his heart, you'll see that his love for you is as deep as the bluest ocean. It is truly eternal, and I'm envious of that. It wasn't until after you left that I finally understood that all the wealth, power, and status in this world would not bring Richard the happiness that he had when he was with you. I'm truly and deeply sorry to have taken it away from the both of you. It is not an easy thing to live with, and I've regretted it every single day."

Elizabeth looked deep into Doris's beautiful yet grieving eyes and was amazed to see this elegant, powerful woman so helpless and paralyzed. Doris may have shown herself as a strong and competent woman, but she was weak and vulnerable when it concerned her family, especially her son. For this aspect alone, Elizabeth applauded her. She let out a soft sigh and said, "I'll try my best to accommodate your request, ma'am. I'm sorry that I've created this perplexing situation."

Doris's mood was now cheerful and optimistic. She smiled broadly at Elizabeth and said, "Thank you, sweetie, for bringing such joy to my despairing family." She paused for a moment and then added, "By the way, may I ask that you, Edward, and Richard come join Victor and me for dinner this week? I apologize if I am asking too much. But it will be our first get-together as a family, and Victor and I would both be delighted."

Elizabeth smiled warmly at her and then said, "I would love to. I know that Richard and Edward will also love the idea."

Doris looked down at the table for a moment and then she looked back up at Elizabeth. She opened her mouth to speak, but seemed hesitant.

"Yes?" Elizabeth asked. "Is there anything else, ma'am?"

Doris let out a soft sigh. "Elizabeth, Richard doesn't know that I requested this meeting with you this morning," she confessed. "He will be upset with me if he finds out. If you don't mind, please keep this meeting discreet. I will contact him about the dinner arrangements."

"Don't worry about it, ma'am. Our meeting this morning will be kept confidential."

"Thank you, Elizabeth. Is Wednesday night okay for you?"

"Wednesday should be great. I don't believe we have any other engagements."

"Wonderful! Then we'll see you on Wednesday." She stood up to give Elizabeth a hug.

# Chapter Twenty-Two

On the walk back to Richard's apartment building, Elizabeth's mind was still reeling. Her heart was in more pain now than it had been before, because she didn't know whether she should feel relieved, happy, or sad. How could she leave now, after hearing Doris's heartfelt words and desperate pleas? How could she break the heart of Richard's mother—the woman who finally learned to accept her and was so hopeful for her future?

Even though her emotions were jumbled, she did find some consolation, and that was the fact that Doris had accepted Edward. And from now on, he would have a place where he could feel a sense of belonging.

When she returned to the apartment, she was still puzzled. She noticed that Richard and Edward were all dressed up and were sitting in the living room.

"Hey! Welcome back!" Richard said as he abruptly stood up to greet her.

Elizabeth quickly adjusted her expression and squinted her eyes in curiosity. "So, what are you two up to today?"

"Well, Edward wants to visit the City Museum, and then we're going to Chinatown after that. Are you up for it?" He reached a hand over to tenderly touch her face.

"Is that right? Why wasn't I included on your planning team?" she said, smiling now.

"Ahhh . . . that. Well, you see, I'm not the coordinator of this team, so you'd have to ask that young man over there," Richard replied with a charming smile in return.

She chuckled softly. "Aren't you going to work?"

"I called Sam earlier to reschedule all my meetings for next week. I told her that I'm going to be with my family this entire week. There is no way I'm going to leave the two of you alone." Having seen her bewildered expression when she came into the living room earlier, he gently added, "So, how was your meeting with your friend?"

"Oh, that. Well, it was very fruitful and delightful. We had a lot of fun catching up on old times," she discreetly replied as she quickly glanced away to avoid his eyes.

"How did the two of you meet?"

"Oh, we met five years ago inside this building." She glanced away again.

"When I saw the expression on your face this morning, I thought that you were dreading it."

She could sense his curiosity about this friend of hers, so she quickly diverted his attention with a sweet, tender kiss on his lips. "Is it okay to not want to leave my family?" she said, smiling.

"Ummm . . . I'll take that for an answer."

They headed down to the lobby and were cheerfully greeted by Martin as they approached him at the front entrance. "It's the lovely Bennett family! Good morning!"

"Good morning, Martin—I agree with you on this one. Thank you," Richard replied delightfully.

"Say, Mr. Bennett. You got a minute?" Martin said as he gently pulled Richard aside.

"I just wanted to give you a heads up," Martin whispered. "Ms. Denning was here about fifteen minutes ago. I told her that I saw you leave the building this morning, and she was very angry about it."

Richard let out a deep sigh as his facial expression slightly shifted. He had been so happy the past two days that he had completely forgotten about Angela. He knew now that he would have to be more vigilant; there was no way he was going to allow her to ruin his time with his family. "Thank you for the heads up, Martin. I'll just set my phone to vibrate. Please do whatever you can to keep her from coming into the apartment." He gently slapped Martin on the shoulder, then bid him good day.

"What was that all about?" Elizabeth asked, curious.

"Oh, it was nothing," he discreetly replied.

"Richard, for as long as I've known you, you've never lied to me before. I hope you're not going to start now," she teased.

He looked at her and smiled. "You're right, sweetie. I'm sorry. I just didn't know how you would react if I told you."

"Told me what?"

"Martin just told me that Angela was here earlier and wanted to come up, but he had to make up a story for our sake."

"Oh? I wonder if it was something urgent."

"No, I don't think it was anything urgent involving work. Anyway, I would rather she not intrude on my time with my family."

***

The City Museum was an enormous white marble building located at the southwest corner of the park. It had ten large exhibition halls and housed hundreds of exhibits. Admission to the museum was free, and it received millions of visitors every year.

Edward stood awestruck in front of the museum. His eyes bulged out, and his little voice was oohing and aahing as they got closer to the magnificent building. Just observing how happy he was would have made any parents overjoyed.

As soon as they went inside, Edward immediately ran to the Arts Exhibition Hall. Richard and Elizabeth walked around the enormous hall and delighted in the elated expression on Edward's face as he paced from one painting to another.

After a short time Edward ran back to Elizabeth and shouted enthusiastically, "Mommy, you're not going to believe what I've found! It's a Monet! Come with me!" He took her hand and quickly pulled her toward his discovery.

As the three of them stood there studying Monet's *Water Lilies* painting, Edward looked up at Richard and said, "Look how bright the sun shone down onto the lilies. Look how calm the water is, Daddy. Doesn't it look like the water is trying to be super calm and quiet, so that it doesn't disturb the lilies as they bask in the sun? Wow!"

Richard couldn't believe his ears. The concepts his son spoke of were ones that even he, as an adult, couldn't comprehend. Edward knew things beyond his years, and to hear him speak so eloquently gave Richard goose bumps.

"How does he know so much about art?" Richard turned to ask Elizabeth.

She chuckled and then replied, "The museums in Paris were like a second home to him when we were in France." She smiled. "He is actually a very good artist himself. His mind works in mysterious ways. He still has the mentality and curiosity of a four-year-old, but his articulations and perceptions far exceed his age."

"He is truly unique and remarkable, just like his mother," Richard proudly acclaimed.

The Science and Technology Exhibition Hall was next. Richard went to a display table and looked down at a drawing. "What on earth could this be?" he asked Edward.

"Wow, it's a schematic for a basic AM radio, Daddy," Edward replied excitedly.

"Really? How do you know that it's a radio?"

"If you look closely at it, you'll see that this triangle shape here represents the speaker," Edward explained as he pointed out the symbols on the schematic. "Over here is the antenna. These two lines with the arrow through them represent the tuner. This triangular shape over here inside the circle is the detector. These squiggly lines are the resisters in parallel and series circuits."

Richard looked over at Elizabeth in amazement. "What is he *talking* about? Does he know what he's saying?"

She softly laughed. "My uncle Phillip was an engineer. When we lived in France, Edward spent a lot of time with him and learned a little bit about circuitries."

Richard raised his eyebrows. "You have relatives in France?"

"Yes, they're from my grandmother's side of the family. My grandmother had two younger sisters and a brother. I rediscovered them when we were living in France. "

After a few hours at the museum, they decided that it was time to go to Chinatown. On the cab ride there, Elizabeth was a bit tired, but couldn't wait to see this place again. Her heart was pounding in excitement, though she was a bit sad. She missed home immensely, and this was as close to home as it could get.

Richard looked at her and noticed the slight sorrow in her eyes. He reached over to squeeze her hand gently and said, "It has been five years since you've been here. Are you ready to rediscover this place again?" She simply nodded without a word.

They got out of the cab and started toward the entrance. She paused for a few seconds to gaze at the hordes of people and the endless shops and markets. "It hasn't change a bit," she said. She gently closed her eyes and deeply inhaled the sweet, pungent aroma in the air. "I miss home," she said sadly.

Richard put his arm around her shoulders and gently said, "Maybe someday we could go visit your hometown together."

"I would like that," she replied quietly. "I've missed my family so much. I'd really like to go back and visit their graves."

After an hour of sightseeing, Richard decided to take them to Pho Anh.

"Hello, Richard! How you been?" The same Asian woman as before joyfully greeted them.

"Hello, Anh," Richard said. "I'm doing wonderfully well, thank you for asking. How are you?"

"I good," Anh replied smiling. "Good to see you again."

"Anh, do you remember Elizabeth?"

Anh's face lit up. "Oh!" she replied excitedly. "I remember! You still beautiful like long time ago."

"Hello, Anh, it is so good to see you again," Elizabeth said warmly.

Richard smiled as Elizabeth and Anh started in on a lively conversation in Vietnamese. He turned to Edward and asked, "Do you know what they're saying?"

Edward shrugged his shoulders. "I don't know, Daddy. I only know how to speak French, English, and Hmong. Mommy never taught me this language."

After a few minutes of chatting with Elizabeth, Anh turned to Edward and slowly bent down to gently rub his head. "You here to eat pho?"

"Yes," Edward replied.

"Good." Anh pointed to a large table in the corner of the room. "You go sit there and I bring pho to you."

Just moments later, she came out with a cart containing three large bowls. Elizabeth was surprised to see that Anh knew her favorite pho dish, because she didn't remember ordering it.

"How did you know which bowl of pho is my favorite?" Elizabeth quizzically asked.

"I think you must order this one first time you eat here. Richard order same one for many years," Anh explained as she glanced teasingly at Richard.

"Ahh . . . I see," Elizabeth said, grinning at both Anh and Richard.

Elizabeth was just about to begin working on her bowl when Richard suddenly stopped her. "Wait a minute, Elizabeth. Would you allow me the honor of mixing your bowl for you this time?" He quickly moved her bowl in front of him.

"Richard, are you sure?" she asked with a slight frown on her face.

"You don't trust me?" He looked at her with a silly pout that almost made her laugh.

"I have eaten here almost twice a month for half a decade. I've become such a professional at it that I'm even thinking about opening up my own restaurant," he boasted.

She chuckled lightly. "All right . . . I'm sure you're even better at it than I am now."

She watched enthusiastically as he started in. "A little bit of this and this and this and this . . . ," he said as he mixed the sauces and condiments together. When he was all done with the mixing, he brought a spoonful of it up to his mouth for a taste. He made a funny face before adding more chili sauce and a tad more hoisin sauce. He tasted it again and then gave her a satisfied look. He slowly slid the bowl in front of her and smiled charmingly.

Feeling a bit skeptical, she sat there quietly and looked at it for a moment. "Hmmm . . . just wondering if it's safe to eat," she joked with another frown. She took a spoonful of the broth to her mouth and slowly sipped it as he watched and waited excitedly for her approval. She kept her head down for what seemed to him like a whole minute, and then slowly lifted it to give him the news. "Richard, this is excellent! This pho is just *perfect*!"

"I've become quite fond of pho," he said proudly. "I've developed a rich taste for it since Anh showed me how to mix it together."

"Richard, you never cease to amaze me. I'm very impressed."

"Thank you. Is this the first time I've ever impressed you?"

She chuckled amusingly, and then earnestly replied, "Richard, all jokes aside, every day that I'm with you, I just cannot put into words how impressive and inspiring you are to me. And for that, I thank you."

Then she reached out and slid his bowl toward her. "Now, it's my turn to mix yours."

She quickly mixed the sauces and condiments together and gave it right back to him without even tasting it. He looked at it and then looked back at her. The puzzled wrinkles on his forehead seemed like they could become permanent. "Is this safe to eat? You didn't even taste it," he teased.

He took a spoonful of it to his lips: it tasted perfect. *Wow*, he thought. He raised an eyebrow and pretended to be a bit disgusted. After a few seconds, he looked at her and smiled delightfully. "I love it! That's magical! How did you do it without even tasting it?"

"Are you not impressed?" she asked, joking.

"I'm beyond impressed."

While he ate from his bowl, an overwhelming feeling of sweet pleasure filled his heart. He recalled the saying about how the way to a man's heart was through his stomach. However, to him, the way to his heart was through this woman—how she could make his taste buds dance around in his mouth simply by mixing a bowl of soup. If only she could be by his side through every meal, he would eat well and grow to be a very stocky and happy old man.

As he sat there deeply engrossed in his pleasant thoughts, he felt his phone suddenly vibrate inside his shirt pocket. He quickly took it out and looked at the number. "It's my mother," he said, surprised.

Elizabeth and Edward ate quietly while Richard spoke to his mother. Elizabeth already knew what the conversation was about, but she pretended to be oblivious to it. He hung up the phone and looked at her with a hesitant expression.

"Is there something wrong?" she asked.

"No," he quickly replied. He breathed a deep sigh before he continued. "My mother just invited us to join her and my father for dinner on Wednesday evening."

"Oh really? What did you tell her?"

"I told her that we'll talk about it and give her an answer before Wednesday. But that she shouldn't be surprised if you decline the offer."

Elizabeth looked at him. "Richard, that is not a very kind thing to say to your mother. Please call her back and tell her that it would be my honor to accept her invitation."

"Would you really, sweetie? We don't have to go—my mother would totally understand."

"I'm a woman of my word. I've already forgiven her. And yes, I would love to have dinner with your parents."

With a sincere, loving expression, he leaned toward her and said, "Have I told you that you are an incredibly amazing woman? Thank you. I will call her right now and tell her that we're coming on Wednesday. I know that she'll be so thrilled to see you."

With hope in his heart, he just sat there and smiled. He felt as if this was a dream come true for him—to live a happy life with her, Edward, and his parents. Perhaps his fate had been rewritten. Perhaps this was the journey she had been waiting for all her life—to have a family with him. If only he could hold this moment tightly in the palm of his hand and make it come true, he would treasure it forever. However, whether his dream came true or not, she was here now—and that was all that mattered.

# Chapter Twenty-Three

It was late on Tuesday morning and the family was in the living room. Elizabeth went into the kitchen and had just begun cooking lunch when the doorbell rang. "I'll get it, sweetie!" Richard yelled out to her.

He quickly went to the door and opened it. There, outside the door, in full fury, was Angela. Shocked to see her, Richard froze and looked at her, bewildered. He could understand how she had made her way past Martin at the front entrance, but he was stupefied at how she had gotten up to his apartment, especially since she didn't have a keycard to the elevators.

"Richard, what the hell have you been doing for the past couple of days?" she spat furiously. "You haven't answered my phone calls! You haven't been to work for two days now! Your secretary told me that you called and said that you're spending time with your family, so I called your mother, but she was very reluctant to tell me anything! You took me off the guest list again! Are you sick? What the hell is going on?" She was breathing so rapidly that she almost began to hyperventilate in front of him.

His mind was screaming for him to shut the door on her, but his body was paralyzed. He couldn't manage a reply—he just continued to gaze at her as he pondered what to do. He felt helpless, because he knew that whatever course of action he took would ruin the tranquility inside the apartment.

Elizabeth had heard the commotion and was on her way to the door when she heard a familiar voice yelling furiously at Richard. She decided to insert herself into the conversation. Slowly appearing from behind the door, she stopped and stood next to Richard. "Hello, Angela. It's so nice to see you again," she said in a calm and pleasant voice.

Upon seeing her, Angela immediately froze. Her face turned pale, her mouth dropped, and her eyes widened almost to the size of two small donuts. She stood there in dead silence, gazing at Elizabeth in horror as if she had just returned from her grave. Angela opened her mouth several times to say something, but was unable to form any words.

"It's okay. I understand, Angela. I'm very surprised to see you, too," Elizabeth politely said.

Angela quickly snapped out of her trance and replied, "You're not as surprised as I am, that's for sure."

Just as Angela was adjusting to the shock, Edward popped out from behind Richard and stood next to him. "Hello, Auntie," he said, waving his hand at her.

Angela looked down at Edward and immediately raised a hand to cover her gaping mouth. "Wait a minute! What . . .?" She gasped and couldn't finish her sentence.

"This is my son, Edward," Richard said. He had finally found his courage now, so he quickly added, "Like I told Sam yesterday, I'm spending time with my family. Now, would you please leave?"

Even though his voice was calm, Elizabeth quickly scolded him. "Richard, that is not kind!" Then, she quickly turned to Angela. "I apologize for Richard's behavior," she said earnestly. "Please forgive him." With a warm, pleasant smile, she added, "Would you like to stay and have lunch with us?"

"Elizabeth—" Richard tried to reason.

"No, Richard," Elizabeth interrupted. "I insist that she stay."

Angela glanced at Richard and gave him a rebellious and provocative smirk. "Yes. As a matter of fact, I would love to stay for lunch."

With that being said, Angela quickly barged into the apartment, went straight to the living room, and sat on the couch by the windows so that she could have a clear view of the kitchen.

Disgusted by the affection that Richard and Elizabeth showed toward each other in the kitchen, Angela started to have second thoughts about staying. She tried to stay calm, but her anger grew more intense the more she observed them. She slowed down her breathing and tried to keep her mind occupied by gazing about the room, but she found herself glancing back at them every few seconds. Although she felt powerless to do anything right now, she knew that she would get her chance.

"Lunch should be ready in about twenty minutes, Angela. Thank you for being patient," Elizabeth called from the kitchen.

Angela scoffed under her breath as she rolled her eyes.

Edward noticed that Angela was upset about something, so he tried his best to busy himself without disturbing her. He would look up at her every once in a while just to see if she had a change in expression, but to his dismay, she looked even more aggravated by the minute.

He thought that maybe he could help put a smile on her face by drawing a beautiful picture of her. He moved closer to her and knelt down at the coffee table in front of her. He looked at her for about ten seconds and then, he began to sketch a portrait of her.

As he was working hard at his drawing, she just sat there motionless. Feeling a little awkward that this little boy was drawing a picture of her without her permission, she wanted to tell him off. But she didn't want to make him cry, so she just sat still and allowed him to continue sketching.

After a while, Edward stood up and walked around the coffee table to her. He presented the drawing to her and said, "Auntie, you have such a beautiful smile."

She looked at the portrait and was surprised to see that she was smiling pleasantly in the drawing, even though she had sat there with a constant frown on her face the whole time. She thought about the image of her on that drawing for a moment, and then she turned to look at him briefly. She didn't know what to think; her heart was conflicted. She didn't want to like this little boy—after all, he was created by Richard and Elizabeth—but why did her heart tell her differently?

In the eyes and heart of this little boy was something far beyond her comprehension. If he could express her inner beauty in this way despite her outward expression, then he could see far beyond the eyes. Perhaps he had the power to see that even though her beauty wasn't visible, she possessed a kind of beauty only the heart could see. This made her own heart flutter joyously.

"That's how you should smile, Auntie," he said sweetly. She couldn't help but give him one of the most beautiful smiles she had ever shown to anyone.

Elizabeth looked toward the living room and noticed that Edward was talking to Angela. Suspecting he might be bothering her, she called out to him in Hmong, "Edward, koj txhob thab phauj os."

"Yes, Mommy," he replied and slowly got up to walk to the opposite side of the table.

"What did you just say to him?" Angela asked.

"I told him not to bother you too much, that's all," Elizabeth replied with a smile.

"Oh, it's all right. At least he's being nice to me. Unlike his father," Angela said, eyeing Richard.

Elizabeth smiled discreetly at Richard as he tried to ignore Angela's remark.

"This is not a good idea," he whispered to Elizabeth. "You should know that."

"Richard, I bear no ill will toward her. I haven't seen her in five years, and it's very disrespectful to disregard her that easily," she replied quietly.

"I know that you don't have any animosity toward her, but she still has a profound animosity toward you," he muttered. "Her sole purpose is to provoke hostilities between us."

"Then that is her flaw, and we would have to forgive her for that," she whispered.

"What are you two talking about?" Angela asked as she walked into the kitchen.

Elizabeth was startled by Angela's sudden appearance. "I was just telling Richard to be more open and to be kinder to you."

Angela looked straight at Richard. "Thank you. He's been treating me like crap for all these years. He should know that."

Richard bit his tongue, knowing that if he said something derogatory, Elizabeth would scold him again.

"So, Elizabeth," Angela casually asked, taking the dishes and bringing them to the dining table, "are you going to stay here indefinitely?"

"No," Elizabeth replied. "I was planning on staying for about a week."

Angela's eyes suddenly widened at the unexpected surprise. "So you're saying that you're leaving?"

"Yes," Elizabeth replied. She glanced over at Richard and noticed his sad eyes, so she looked straight at him with a warm, loving smile and added, "But I'm not sure at this point. It will all depend on how quickly Richard gets tired of us."

"If it was up to me, I would never, ever want you and Edward to leave," he said earnestly.

Angela quickly gave him an irritated expression as she continued to set the table.

"I hope it's to your liking, Angela," Elizabeth said as they sat down to eat. "It's an old family recipe. It might be a little spicier than you're used to."

"I'm not too fond of Asian food, but I guess this'll do," Angela replied.

"Mmmm," Richard quickly chimed in after tasting a bite. "I really like how these lively spices complement the meat and vegetables."

Angela gave him a quick glance of disapproval and then ate in silence.

"So, Elizabeth," Angela said, without looking at her. "Where have you been all this time?"

Elizabeth sighed softly and dabbed her mouth with her napkin. "Edward and I spent most of our time living in and traveling around Europe, but we also lived in Hong Kong, Seoul, and Bangkok for short periods of time."

Angela noticed a confused expression on Richard's face as he listened in, so she continued to push the issue by saying, "Being so unsettled, it must have been hard to live a normal life, huh?"

Elizabeth politely smiled at Angela. "It was not easy. And at times, it was unbearable, but everything I did had a purpose. I wanted to expose my son to many cultures and the different conditions people lived in. I wanted him to be tolerant of others and not to be ignorant of their unfortunate circumstances. Life should not be taken for granted," she calmly explained, shifting her eyes to Richard, "and for my one and only son—the son of a Bennett and a descendent of Atkins, like his father—I wanted him to be a great man. Perhaps he is destined to do many wonderful things someday."

Richard looked at her with admiration. "You're an incredible mother. I thank you from the bottom of my heart for raising our son to be such a wonderful child," he said.

Angela's attempt to divert and obscure Richard's perceptions of Elizabeth had backfired, so she remained quiet for a moment. She continued to eat in silence as she tried to come up with another provocation.

"So, why did you decide to come back?" Angela asked with a smirk. "Was it because you ran out of money?"

Elizabeth could tell from Richard's irritated expression that he was dying to say something back to Angela. She calmly took hold of his hand to reassure him that she could take care of herself in a civilized manner.

She turned to Angela and politely smiled again. "I look at Edward every day and see the sadness in his eyes because, like any child, he had a strong desire to know his father. It was selfish of me to deprive him of that. Edward is my son, but he is also Richard's son. He needed his father, and now that they have met, I finally realize that his father also needed me." She turned to Richard and looked at him with deep sincerity.

Hearing these words, Richard could sense his whole body quivering with joy. He felt tears stinging his eyes as he passionately said to her, "Yes, I need you. I need you more than anything in this world. I need you by my side to be my companion as we walk this journey together. Without you and Edward, I would be an empty shell—an empty body without a heart and a soul. Thank you for returning to me, Elizabeth. Thank you for making me whole again."

Angela was at a loss for words. She could feel her heart breaking and her dreams shattering. She now knew that it would be easier to capture the wind in the palm of her hand than to win Richard's love.

Although her world had just been darkened by a thousand shadows, she recognized that she needed to be happy for him or her greed and envy would consume her. Of course she was jealous, but she was also human. There really was a soft, gentle side to her heart.

Even though she had never experienced the kind of deep love that existed between Richard and Elizabeth, she now understood that his love wasn't for her. She realized that there would always be a gate separating her from him. Like the stars and the moon, even though they all lived in the same universe, there would always be an unreachable distance between them.

Still, she hoped that God hadn't forgotten her; for she knew that not long after the sun set it would rise again. She hoped that someday fate would grant her heart a chance to experience a happily ever-after fairytale.

Angela politely excused herself and left the apartment, still feeling somewhat defeated. Elizabeth sat in silence with a deep feeling of remorse and empathy for her. Elizabeth looked at Richard for a moment and then slowly said, "I'm sorry, Richard. I was being unkind."

"Why do you say that?"

"My intentions were not meant to be malicious. I knew how she had been hurt all these years. I only wanted her to move on with her life, see her potential, and become the great person she was destined to be. I hope she'll understand and forgive me someday."

Richard reached over to hold her hand. "It was never your fault. If anyone were to blame, it would be me. I was cruel to her. I will make amends for the both of us. I hope someday she'll forgive me for not being able to return her love."

# Chapter Twenty-Four

The Wednesday morning sky was serene: bright and peaceful. The sun's rays cast an attractive picture full of vibrant colors and radiated through the windows, gently waking Richard from his deep and soothing sleep.

He slowly opened his eyes. Then he turned over to search for Edward, being extra careful not to wake him. To his surprise, Edward was not on his spot on the bed. He looked at the clock and noticed that it was already nine thirty.

He quickly hopped out of bed and immediately went to the bathroom to wash up. When he came out of the bedroom, he was a little concerned that he hadn't heard a sound out of either Elizabeth or Edward. Hoping she was still cooking breakfast, he went to the kitchen to see what he could do to help.

As he approached, he noticed Edward crouching down beside the living room coffee table, working hard on his latest drawing. He sketched silently, fully engaged in his most recent masterpiece.

In the kitchen, Elizabeth was busy frying something on the stove. She moved gracefully between the stove and the counter. The food sizzled and a delicious smell filled the room, lingering in the air.

Richard's heart danced blissfully. He had never dreamed of living a life so full of love and contentment. Now that he had experienced such an abundance of joy, he knew he could never, ever feel the same again without it.

He thought how wonderful it would be if everyone could experience a moment as breathtakingly beautiful and pleasant as this. For some, that moment might be the first time laying eyes on someone and falling in love, the first time holding a newborn baby, or the day of one's wedding. For him, if he were to die and be reborn with one memory still living in his heart, he would beg to wake up to see this moment. He would be happy to die a thousand deaths if only God would allow him to wake up to this very moment every lifetime.

"Good morning," Elizabeth greeted him pleasantly. "You seem to have slept well?"

"Yes, a little bit too well. I didn't realize how late it was. I'm sorry I wasn't able to help."

"It's all right." She smiled sweetly. "I was going to have Edward come wake you up so that we could eat, but I thought I would give you a few more minutes. Hope you're hungry?"

"I'm starving. I'll help set the table," he said as he walked over to her.

She passed some plates and silverware to him and then followed him with two large plates of scrambled eggs, sausages, ham, and bacon. They returned to grab another large plate full of pancakes and toast.

"This all looks so good!" he said as he hungrily eyed the food.

Richard sat in his chair as she slowly filled his plate with food. It amazed him that such a simple gesture could fill his heart with so much happiness. Again, he silently prayed that if God were to grant him a moment to wake up to every morning, it would be this moment.

It was late into the afternoon on this beautiful Wednesday, the day the three of them were scheduled to have dinner with Richard's parents. Elizabeth went into her room to get ready for the evening. She had promised him that she would wear the beautiful black dress that he bought for her five years ago, so she went straight to the closet to take a peek at it before she headed to the bathroom for a quick shower.

As she took out the dress from the closet, vivid memories came back to her. Even though she was happy that he had kept the dress for all these years, a sudden pang struck her heart like a nail poking deep into it. She wondered what it would have been like if she had been stronger and stayed with him. She couldn't begin to imagine the pain he endured having to keep all her belongings locked up for this long. If only she had been stronger and more mature then, she wouldn't have allowed him to be so hurt. But now that she had returned and discovered that his love for her had remained strong and was only getting stronger each day, she needed to decide what she should do to make up for all that pain she had caused. Yes, perhaps after tonight, she would know the answer.

She looked admiringly at the dress. It was still so stunning—she found it hard to believe that after all these years, she still loved and treasured it so much. She held the dress in front of her as she peered into the mirror and realized that it was a little smaller than she had remembered. She began to worry that it might no longer fit her like it once did. She let out a soft sigh, thinking that if it didn't fit, she would have to go shopping for another dress, and she wasn't sure she had time for that. She held her breath as she slowly slipped it on. To her surprise, it was just a little snug. It still fit nicely.

After her shower, she lightly brushed on a few strokes of makeup, just enough to brighten up her cheeks and eyes. Then she glossed up her lips. To complete her look, she blow-dried her hair, brushed it down nicely, and allowed it to flow freely against her body. She slowly slipped on the dress, then slipped on her red pumps and grabbed her red purse before going back into the bedroom and sitting down on the chair to take a deep and slow breath.

Richard dressed Edward up in a white polo shirt and a pair of black pants. Then he himself put on a black suit with a nice black bow tie. It didn't take them long at all, so they went into the living room to wait for her. Edward busied himself with his sketching at the coffee table while Richard waited anxiously for Elizabeth to come out.

After several minutes, he could no longer stand the suspense, so he went to her door and softly knocked on it. "Honey, are you ready? I'm dying to see you," he said excitedly.

The door flung open and she stood there in her satin black dress, glistening under the dim lights. Her beauty and elegance sparkled like the stars in a clear August night sky. The gown came down to her knees, flowing gently against her legs. The upper part hugged her feminine body, revealing her smooth, alluring skin. Her shimmery, black hair flowed like a river over her hourglass body.

Richard felt weak as he stared at her, incredulous. How he adored this woman!

She smiled shyly at him as her eyes danced seductively. "How do I look?" she asked.

He took a deep breath and replied passionately, "There are no words that I could use to describe what I see before me. But, there is one word to describe the way I feel."

"And that is?"

"Lucky," he simply replied. "I'm such a lucky man. I'm so lucky to have met such a gorgeous woman. And I'm so lucky to have her love," he said sincerely.

She extended her hand and gently touched his face. "And you think you're the only lucky person in this world?" she said sweetly. "If we were to ask God, his answer would probably be that I'm equally as lucky as you are. I'm just as blessed as you are to have such a wonderful man telling me that he loves me."

As the limousine made its way down Park Avenue toward Ocean Boulevard, Richard could see that Elizabeth was eagerly anticipating the visit with his parents. Even though she hadn't spoken a word about it, it definitely showed on her face, because she had been smiling the whole time. Still, she seemed a little unsettled.

He reached over to hold her hand and smiled warmly at her. "First time in a limo?" he carefully asked.

"You could say that," she replied, smiling nervously.

"Nervous?"

"Just a little," she replied and then tightened her grip on his hand. "More excited than nervous," she added, still smiling.

"Everything is going to be all right. Tonight is going to be your night," he assured her. He was just as nervous as she was, if not more, but he tried his best to keep his composure. In truth, since he wasn't absolutely certain what his mother's intentions were, he was a little anxious that things wouldn't go well. He prayed that Doris wouldn't do anything to jeopardize his relationship with Elizabeth this time. He hoped that he and Elizabeth would be in good hands this evening and that this would be the turning point for their relationship—the moment she would change her mind about leaving and decide to stay with him for the rest of her life.

The limo slowly made a left turn on Oceanside Road, and minutes later it came to a stop at the two enormous gates. The chauffeur waved to the guard, and within seconds the gates slowly opened.

As the limo continued down the small paved road, Elizabeth's mood became lighter. She gazed out the window, amazed at the lush, green fields that seemed to stretch out for hundreds of miles. On each side of the road were an endless variety of shrubs and small trees, all trimmed and maintained to perfection.

The limo continued steadily down the road, and then the chauffeur slowly maneuvered it around a sharp curve as the enormous mansion gradually appeared on the horizon.

Golden rays of light appeared from the setting sun, reflecting brilliantly in the white marble bricks and windows and creating a beautiful, shimmering flame-like light. The dark blue ocean backdrop, the many exotic flowers and vegetation, and a small pond in the front yard combined to make the scene look like a perfect painting.

"It's even more beautiful than how Edward described it to me," Elizabeth said in amazement as her eyes widened at the sight of the majestic building.

Richard slowly leaned over to her. "The Atkins Mansion was built back in the early 1800s, and it took almost fifteen years to complete it. It had thirty large bedrooms occupying the second floor of the north and south wings. It also had an enormous solarium to the east, a large dining room, a music room, a library, an art room, a huge living room, and an enormous ballroom for social events. Outside the mansion were several living quarters occupied by fifteen servants. The mansion sat on a thousand acres of lush green land filled with many exotic flowers, plants, trees, running streams, and a lake. There were also several small paved trails leading to a private forest, a boat landing, a private flower garden, and a private beach. Atkins built the house to impress and humble many of the city's wealthiest people. Over the years, it was passed on from one descendent to another. It continues to be one of the oldest and most prestigious buildings in the entire city."

"It's the most majestic thing I've ever seen, Richard."

"Someday, this will all be ours," he quickly added.

She slowly turned to look at him and said in a faint tone, "Richard, I like your apartment just fine." Then, she turned away and discreetly added, "Of course, if we were to have any more children, we would need something larger."

He couldn't believe what he had just heard. Did he hear her correctly? Or were his ears playing tricks on him? "You have no idea what you're doing to me," he said, reaching an arm around her and pulling her close. "Just hearing those words from you has made me happier than any man alive."

The limo circled around the pond and made a stop in front of the enormous marble steps at the entrance. Carlos quickly came to the limo to open the door for them. "Good evening, sir. Good evening, ma'am. Hello, young Edward."

"Evening," Richard and Elizabeth both greeted Carlos at the same time.

"Are my parents in?" Richard asked.

"Yes, sir," Carlos replied. "They're in the living room waiting for you."

Richard turned around and took Elizabeth's hand, squeezing it tightly for a moment as he stared into her eyes. She stared back nervously and allowed herself to breathe one last deep breath before they continue to the entrance.

"You all right?" he asked gently.

"Yes." She smiled anxiously.

He tightened his grip on her hand and they walked up the steps toward the entrance. Edward followed right along and saw Marie standing at the huge oversized double doors, so he quickly ran over to give her a big hug.

"Why, hello there, Edward," Marie greeted him joyfully. Then, she looked up at Elizabeth.

"Hello, Marie," Richard said. "This is Elizabeth."

"Hello there, Miss Elizabeth. Goodness, Richard wasn't lying. You are truly a beauty," Marie exclaimed.

"Thank you for the kind words, Marie," Elizabeth replied, blushing.

As they walked in, Elizabeth abruptly stopped inside the enormous lobby for a moment to admire the surroundings. The white marble flooring was so shiny that she was almost afraid to walk on it, fearing she might slip and fall.

As she looked up at the ceiling, her eyes were mesmerized by a large and elegant crystal chandelier. Hundreds of crystal pendants sparkled separately. Each of the chandelier's arms firmly held a candle that brightened the entire lobby.

She shifted her eyes to the east and saw a vast white marble staircase that was halfway inside the lobby. The staircase seemed to split into two smaller separate staircases at the landing halfway up, leading to two separate wings on the second floor.

She also noticed that about twenty or so yards beyond the staircase was an enormous open view of lush green vegetation and trees. At a glance, she thought that it was the backyard and she wondered silently about how they would be able to find a door large enough to close that open view if need be.

As her mind was still whirling around dizzily, Richard gently tugged on her arm and said, "Shall we continue?"

"Yes," she replied faintly.

She hung loosely onto his arm as they continued through the lobby. As they walked past the staircase, she stopped again in astonishment. The lush green vegetation and trees weren't out in the backyard of the house, as she had previously thought—they were all inside a gigantic solarium.

The solarium seemed to be three times as big as the lobby. The walls and ceiling were made entirely of glass. Leading away from the white marble flooring were several narrow trails, curving around endless columns of exotic plants and flowers. Stone statues of women, children, and angels appeared here and there—all carrying buckets and seeming as if they were joyously watering the plants. There were also numerous small stone walls, some of which had water flowing out of them, simulating peaceful waterfalls.

In the middle of the room was a giant palm tree that almost reached the glass ceiling. Underneath the tree was a huge circular area filled with several small circular handwoven tables and chairs.

"This is so beautiful, Richard. I could stay in this room forever," she said, gasping as her eyes continuously scanned the room.

He gently pulled her along, with Edward close behind, and they continued toward a narrow hallway. They made a turn to the right and were soon approaching the living room.

The extensive wall to the east hosted several large and beautiful paintings. The opposite wall housed several light-filled windows from floor to ceiling, allowing sunshine to easily stream through. The entire south wall was a huge stone fireplace. The décor helped create a warm and harmonious environment— one that she knew she would enjoy spending some time in.

"Elizabeth! It's so good to see you again!" Doris cried out. She and Victor were standing in the middle of the room, and Elizabeth hoped she hadn't been rude by not noticing them. Doris rushed to Elizabeth with open arms and gave her a warm and loving embrace. "I'm so happy to see you, dear. Thank you so much for coming."

"Thank you for having me, ma'am," Elizabeth politely replied. "You have such a beautiful home."

Victor was behind Doris and stepped forward to give Elizabeth a light kiss on the cheek. "Welcome home, sweetie. I've missed you so much."

"Thank you, sir. I'm delighted to see that you're doing well."

"Hello, Grandma," Edward said, as if he didn't want to be left out.

"Hello, my little angel," Doris said joyfully as she bent down to pick him up. "You have no idea how much Grandma missed you, darling."

"I missed you, too, Grandma," Edward replied, and then he glanced at Victor. "And I missed Grandpa a lot too. I'm glad I got to come back to this humongous house," Edward added, which made everyone laugh. Victor gave Edward a gentle pinch on his cheek, and then he led everyone to the sofas to sit down.

Elizabeth was still a little nervous, so Richard comforted her by gently squeezing her hand. She gave him a quick glance and smiled sweetly as she began to loosen up.

"How are you enjoying your stay so far?" Victor asked Elizabeth.

"I love it here, sir. Richard is so sweet to us, so my being back feels like I'm home."

"This is home, sweetie," Victor said. "We're all happy to have you back home again."

"Thank you for the warm welcome, sir."

"I hope you enjoyed the ride here, dear. I know it is quite a drive," Doris pleasantly chimed in.

"Yes, ma'am," Elizabeth replied. "The drive here was splendid. It was such a wonderful experience. I was completely lost in my thoughts as I observed the beautiful grounds of your residence."

"Thank you, dear," Doris said. "It's an old house, but it's been in the family for generations. Someday, it'll be Richard's turn to tend to it." She looked down and smiled at Edward. "And then it'll be *your* turn."

"I'm going to put a merry-go-round and a petting zoo in the front yard, Grandma," Edward replied enthusiastically.

Everyone laughed again, and Doris picked Edward up and sat him on her lap. "You are quite a creative young man. I would have never thought of that!" She glanced over at Elizabeth and explained, "Every generation has added something to the residence. Victor and I added a flower garden about twenty years ago. Maybe we could take a tour later."

"Thank you, ma'am. I'd be truly delighted to see it," Elizabeth said enthusiastically.

Doris beamed at her son, Elizabeth, and Edward. How she wished that she could turn back the hands of time so that this moment could have arrived sooner in her life.

While everyone was still in the midst of sharing their stories and enjoying each other's company, Marie came into the room to announce that dinner was ready. They all got up and followed Marie out to the hallway.

Doris couldn't wait to share with Elizabeth that she was the main chef for tonight's special dinner. She quickly came up to Elizabeth and touched Elizabeth's arm to slow her down a couple of steps. "I hope dinner is to your liking, dear," she whispered to her. "I personally made the dishes and oversaw tonight's special meal."

Elizabeth turned to her with a grateful smile. "That was very generous of you, ma'am. Thank you for your wonderful hospitality. I'm sure everything will be delicious."

They walked past the staircase and into the large formal dining room. Elizabeth's eyes widened again as she scanned the room. The room featured a twenty-foot-high white Victorian cornicing ceiling and offered an attractive open floor and an unobstructed view of the staircase. The walls were lined with paintings of exotic landscapes and portraits of people whom she could only believe to be the descendants of Atkins.

In the middle of the room stood a massive, long dark glazed mahogany dining table that seemed to stretch from one end of the room to the other. Set on either side of the table were dozens of uniquely hand-carved chairs, plus one large one at each end.

"This table must seat a hundred people!" Elizabeth exclaimed.

Doris chuckled. "Actually, it seats only fifty-two to be exact."

"Are we actually having dinner in this room? It would be a little awkward for the five of us to be sitting at this huge table."

Doris laughed sweetly. "No, I can't even remember the last time we actually ate in this room. We're having dinner in the breakfast room to the right of the fireplace over there." Doris pointed to a small entrance next to the enormous fireplace at the other side of the room.

They walked to the eight-foot-tall stone fireplace and stood in front of it for a moment. On the wall above the fireplace hung a giant portrait of a grayish-haired middle-aged man dressed in a black suit. Elizabeth stared intently at the menacing expression on his face, feeling both intimidation and admiration.

"Who is this?" Elizabeth asked Doris.

"That, my dear, is Mr. Joshua Edward Atkins."

"Wow. Was he an intimidating man?" Elizabeth asked.

"He surely was, but he was also one of the most generous, charismatic, and loving men the city had ever had."

As they entered the breakfast room, Elizabeth began to relax. The room was small but cozy. It had beautiful, white-paneled walls and gold trim with several windows that offered a spectacular view of the pond in the front of the mansion. The table in the room was just about the same size as the one in Richard's apartment. A perfect size, Elizabeth thought.

Richard quickly came around to pull out a chair for Elizabeth. Doris seated herself across from Elizabeth so that she could visit with her while they ate. Then, Doris turned to Edward and insisted that he sit next to her. "Come sit by Grandma, darling," she said as she gently pulled out a chair next to her for him. Richard pulled out a chair for himself next to Elizabeth, and Victor sat at the end between Doris and Elizabeth.

They started out with a plate of healthy green salad and French onion soup. The appetizers were superb—a special dish of escargot and a beef kebab with couscous. The dinner entrée was a tender filet mignon cooked to perfection, served with garlic buttered mashed potatoes and bacon-wrapped asparagus. The dessert was a slice of American apple pie with vanilla ice cream topping.

After they had finished eating, Elizabeth dabbed her mouth with her napkin. "Dinner was amazing, ma'am," she said to Doris. "The food was truly remarkable. You are a very talented cook indeed. I'm privileged to be invited here to have such an amazing dinner with your family."

"Thank you, dear," Doris politely replied. "I'm so delighted to have you join us."

"Mother, did *you* cook this meal?" Richard asked in disbelief.

Doris smiled teasingly at Richard and said, "Richard, just because I don't usually cook doesn't mean that I can't cook. Would it be a surprise to you that I actually went to culinary school to be a chef when I was young?"

"Is that so? It's just that I've rarely seen you in the kitchen."

Doris laughed. "You may not have remembered, but you grew up eating my cooking. I gave Martha my recipes and taught her how to cook using them."

"And all this time, I thought that Martha was such a creative cook," Richard said, chuckling as he stole a quick glance at Elizabeth.

Elizabeth let out a slight giggle and then turned to Doris. "Richard is right, ma'am. You have great talents, and I'm truly impressed."

Doris smiled for a second and then she looked at Elizabeth with a sincere expression. She took a deep breath and then she quietly said, "Elizabeth dear, you don't have to call me ma'am. Just call me Doris. Actually, if you don't mind, I would love for you to call me Mother, because you are a part of this family, too."

Elizabeth quickly looked at Richard. She turned back to look at Doris and smiled politely. "I don't mind at all. Thank you for allowing me to call you that." She paused for a few seconds and then, with small specks of tears forming in her eyes, she quietly said, "Mother."

Doris couldn't believe how happy her heart felt when she heard that word coming from Elizabeth. Her eyes glistened with tears and she could feel the corners of her mouth quiver joyously. She leaned toward Elizabeth and managed to say, "Thank you, sweetie. Finally, this old soul is able to feel complete. From this day on, I will sincerely try my very best to be a good mother to you, and a good grandmother to Edward."

With those words said, Elizabeth's eyes now welled with tears. She let out a deep, trembling sigh. "Thank you, Mother. Ever since the death of my parents, I have missed saying the words Mother and Father so very much. There is nothing in this world that can compare to the comforting feelings of a parent's love, and I want you to know that you are, indeed, making me feel at home. I can comfortably say that I'm feeling like I have a sense of belonging in this sweet place Richard calls home." She paused to slowly wipe her tears before continuing. "A mother's greatest gift is to love and protect her children, and you are already a great mother. Richard doesn't know how lucky he is to have you as his."

She turned her eyes to Victor and tried to say something to him, but she had to pause for a few seconds, because she felt as if something had clogged up her throat. Her heart felt heavy and she clasped her hands together tightly in her lap. Just then, a single tear slowly crept down her cheek as she began to speak. "Father, I'm so sorry for leaving without a word. But believe me, my heart never left for all these years. I'm so grateful that our paths crossed."

Victor reached out and clasped her hands in his. "You don't have to say anything, my dear. Coming home to where you belong is enough."

Richard's heart was exploding with joy. He thought he knew what love was, but with each passing moment his love for this woman only grew stronger. He had always known that her words could move his heart; however, what she just said to his parents had brightened every darkened corner of his heart. He felt as if he were now standing just outside Heaven's gate, about to enter paradise. Elizabeth was indeed his world. She was his living angel. She was his everything, and he silently promised himself that he would never stop loving her. Even if his heart stopped beating, his love for her would live on forever.

# Chapter Twenty-Five

After dinner the evening was still young, so Richard decided to take Elizabeth for a walk in the flower garden. The brilliant sun still hovered along the horizon, creating a gorgeous hue across the sky. Such spectacular color made the flower garden even more beautiful and vibrant. Each flower glowed in the evening sunset, like an outstanding piece of art painted just for the human eyes.

As her eyes roamed every corner of the garden, Elizabeth thought she couldn't possibly be more in love. She halted for a moment to sigh deeply great satisfaction before she said to Richard, "This walk alone could have fulfilled the great desire in my heart, Richard, but thank you for an even more beautiful evening with your parents. I cannot put into words how happy my heart feels at this moment."

"I'm so glad, Elizabeth, but really, I'm the one who should thank you for making my evening so fulfilling."

They stood there wrapped in each other's arms for a couple of minutes, just staring lovingly at each other. He tightened his grip on her waist as his lips gently touched hers. She willingly received his passionate kiss, and then kissed him hungrily in return.

The sun had finally set, and now the clear night sky shone brightly down on them as they held each other tightly beneath the thousands of twinkling stars. Their silhouettes stood stretched over the palette of garden colors, revealing a loving couple in what seemed like the Garden of Eden.

They resumed their slow walk together on the dimly lit trail. The wind from the ocean blew away the hot, humid summer air and replaced it with a cool, perfect breeze.

"Have I told you that tonight was your night, and that I was going to make everything perfect for you?" he said sweetly.

"Thank you again, and just having you beside me is already enough to make this a perfect night for me." She reached over to link her arm in his as they continued the walk in silence.

They soon reached another section of the garden. Elizabeth closed her eyes and deeply inhaled the sweet fragrance lingering in the air. Richard went over to the light switch and illuminated the garden. She opened her eyes and noticed that the whole area was filled with endless rows and columns of flowers in every shape, size, and color. She marveled at the sight of exotic roses, daisies, daffodils, irises, carnations, Oriental lilies, and more. To her eyes, every flower was exotic.

"This is so beautiful," she said in utter amazement. "How many types of flowers are in here?"

"I think around forty—maybe even more. Only the gardener would know for sure."

As they walked along the rows and rows of flowers, she noticed that he picked a couple of the most beautiful blooms.

"Richard, what are you doing?" she quickly asked.

"I'm making a bouquet for you."

"And spoil this perfectly maintained majestic garden?"

"You can't blame me. I haven't given you flowers for five years," he replied with a charming little smirk.

He gathered the flowers together in a bouquet and gave it to her. She happily accepted it. "Richard," she said, "you are the sweetest and most wonderful man I've ever known. Please don't ever stop being who you are."

He gently brushed her soft, silky hair with his fingers. "Even these perfectly bloomed flowers can't compare to your inner and outer beauty," he replied. "Please don't ever stop being who you are."

They finally turned around and started back toward the mansion. As they entered the lobby, they were again greeted by Marie, who took the bouquet from Elizabeth and brought it into the solarium to put it into a vase.

As they walked into the living room, they saw that the family was still inside. Doris and Victor seemed to be wholeheartedly entertained by Edward. Their jubilant laughter was so loud that they could even be heard from the lobby.

As they entered, Doris abruptly lifted her head. It seemed to her that their walk had been very beneficial, and she gave them an expression of approval.

Doris came over to stand next to Richard and said to Elizabeth, "I hope you enjoyed the flower garden as much as I do, dear. It is one of my favorite places to go for an evening walk."

"I absolutely loved it! It was such a beautiful sight, especially when the sun was just about to set. The vibrant color, the crimson sky reflecting off the flowers—there is just something exquisitely lively about it that only the heart can feel," Elizabeth replied.

Doris smiled. "I'm so glad you enjoyed it," she said. Then she hesitated.

Elizabeth noticed this and decided to ease Doris's mind a little bit by kindly saying, "Is there something on your mind, Mother?"

A few seconds passed before Doris spoke. "Elizabeth," she said, "I have a special request. If you don't mind, I would love for you and your family to spend the night. I understand that driving back home isn't an issue for you, but I just feel so complete tonight with my whole family here with me. If it's not too much to ask, I would love to have the three of you stay here tonight."

Elizabeth glanced quickly at Richard. She knew that he would love to accept the offer but was waiting for her to speak.

Richard turned to Doris and said, "Mother, we'd love to, but we didn't bring any personal items with us tonight, and we wouldn't have anything to change into."

"I'm sure we can accommodate you with anything you need," Doris replied optimistically.

"Well, in that case," Elizabeth said cheerfully, "we would love to stay the night."

"I'm so happy to hear that, dear!" Doris said ecstatically. "There are thirty rooms in this house, and you could choose any room of your preference for the night."

"Thank you. I'm very pleased and excited!" Elizabeth exclaimed.

"I'm so glad, sweetie. Oh, and one more request: If you don't mind, Victor and I would love to have Edward stay with us in our room. He told us he'd love to spend the night with his grandparents."

"Are you sure you don't mind?" Elizabeth asked curiously.

"Of course, not at all, dear," Doris replied. Then, she looked straight at Richard with a teasing smile and added, "I know why Edward doesn't like to sleep by himself. Richard was the same way when he was young. I guess Edward got that from his father."

Elizabeth chuckled. "I don't mind it at all. I thank you for your kindness."

Doris smiled delightedly and almost turned around to go back to Victor and Edward, but Elizabeth noticed her unsatisfied facial expression—she still had something else on her mind that she hadn't asked.

As Elizabeth was thinking about what to say, Doris quickly swung around. "Oh, and one more thing, sweetie. I know that I'm already asking too much, but Victor and I would like to throw Edward a late birthday party here at the house. We weren't there for you and him for the first four years of his life, and we would very much like your permission to give him our very first celebration as grandparents."

Upon hearing Doris's words, Elizabeth felt a sharp pain in her heart, as if it were suddenly struck by an arrow, piercing through it. For the past four years, she and her son had been celebrating his birthday by themselves—just the two of them. When she had sung "Happy Birthday" to him, she could see the sadness in his eyes. Doris's offer brought tears to her eyes, and she just allowed them to fall quietly down her cheeks.

Doris was concerned. "Elizabeth? Are you all right, dear?" she asked. "I apologize if it was something I said."

"No, Mother," Elizabeth quickly replied as she raised her palm and wiped away her tears. "You don't need my permission. He is just as much yours as he is mine. You and Father are the only grandparents he has, and I sincerely thank you from the bottom of my heart for the kindness you've shown us."

"Don't cry, dear," Doris said as she took a step closer to pull Elizabeth in for a gentle embrace. "Like I said, I will try my very best to be a good mother to you and a good grandma to Edward."

They went back to the sofas to chat for a while longer. Richard glanced at his watch and noticed that it was getting late. "Wow, I didn't realize that it's already past eleven o'clock."

Doris quickly glanced at her watch and exclaimed, "Goodness, you're so right, Richard. It is almost midnight."

"You and Father should go get ready for bed, Mother," Elizabeth said. "I will make sure Edward washes up, and then I will send him to you as soon as he's done."

"Edward was already taken care of while you and Richard went out to the garden," Doris said. "You and Richard go ahead. Victor and I will just take Edward with us."

They all bid each other good night and left the room.


Richard remembered how intrigued Elizabeth was with the house earlier, so he decided to take her on a tour to the north and south wings.

"This is so wonderful, Richard," she said sweetly, enthralled by everything she looked at. "Thank you for doing this."

She loosely held on to his arm as they slowly walked down the long and dimly lit hallway. As they approached the end of the south wing, she realized it didn't end there—the hallway opened into an enormous room. Once they were inside, he went to the wall and turned on the lights.

There, hanging on the walls, were dozens of portraits of people. There was also a life-size sculpture standing next to each portrait.

"This is the art gallery," he said. "These paintings and sculptures are my ancestors."

"Oh my gosh, Richard!" Elizabeth gasped, looking slowly around the room.

She slowly made her way closer to one of the walls and gazed admiringly at a painting. Then she turned to the sculpture next to it, marveling at the likeness.

As she made her way around the room, she came upon a portrait of a beautiful young woman. There was something exquisitely stunning about this one, she thought. She stared intently at it and noticed that this woman's eyes were dark and exotic, and her smile looked as if it could light up the darkest of nights. She looked at the perfectly carved sculpture and was surprised to see that its height matched her own.

She looked down at the small sign next to it. "Iris Elizabeth Atkins, born 1770, died 1805. So, this was Iris? She was still so young," she whispered. "Wow, she was truly a beauty. No wonder Mr. Atkins named the park after her. Just looking at her gives me a sense of peace and serenity."

He stood silently as he watched her from afar. He knew how much she loved and valued everything new to her, so he patiently stood back and gave her as much time as she needed.

When she had finally walked through the whole room, it was already past midnight. They came back out into the hallway, and then he went and stood in front of a door next to the art room. "This is going to be your room for the night," he said as he reached for the knob and opened the door.

Elizabeth excitedly scanned the entire room. On one end was an enormous canopy bed with white curtains closed all around it. About twenty feet to the left of the bed was a huge stone fireplace. In front of the fireplace were several hand-carved chairs surrounding a small oak table. On the opposite end of the room was a giant oak dresser, and above it was a huge mirror.

"I'm in awe! This is one of the biggest bedrooms I've ever seen. It's probably as big as your whole apartment!" She giggled.

He laughed softly. "Well, there is a room located on the end of the north wing that is almost twice as big as this room. But, it's being occupied by my parents at this moment," he said with a wink.

She smiled at him. "What's behind that door?" She pointed to the door next to the dresser.

"That's the bathroom," he replied. "Would you like to change out of that dress and into something more comfortable? We will continue our midnight tour to the solarium afterward."

She looked at him with a funny expression. "I don't have anything else to change into, Richard, remember?"

He went to the bed and opened the curtains. There, lying on the bed, was her cloth bag.

She gasped. "How did you—"

"I packed some of your clothes and personal items yesterday," he quickly interrupted. "Carlos went over to our apartment and brought your bag here while we were eating dinner. This special evening wouldn't be perfect if we didn't spend the night here. I was just about to ask you, but my mother beat me to it."

"Oh, Richard, you never cease to amaze me." She moved closer to him and gave him a gentle teasing nudge.

Elizabeth needed to refresh herself after the long walk through the garden and gallery, so instead of just changing into her comfortable clothes, she decided to take a quick shower. Afterward, as she was searching through her belongings inside her bag, Richard suddenly opened the door and said, "Honey, are you ready?"

She let out a quick scream, because she was completely naked in front of him. She tightly shut her eyes for a second before quickly grabbing the towel to cover herself.

"Oh my god!" he said as he immediately looked away. "I'm so sorry. I didn't know you weren't ready."

She turned to look at him and then let out a slight smile as she tried to ease the awkward situation. "It's all right, Richard," she said nonchalantly. "It's not like you've never seen me naked before."

He turned his head and glanced at her. He let out a deep sigh of relief and then said in an anguished tone, "I did see you naked, but that was so long ago. I've tried to remember it each day, but it gets more difficult over the years. Now, I only have faded memories of it."

Suddenly she felt a deep pain in her heart. How could she have done this to him? She had left him in so much misery, yet he still thought of her every day and loved her as much as ever. Whatever words she chose to say to him right now might ease his pain, but they would never give him the happiness that he so richly deserved.

She now knew that he was the man she wanted to spend the rest of her life with. She smiled sweetly at him and said to him in a soft voice, "Come here."

He stood there dumbfounded, unsure if he'd heard her correctly. "Are you sure?" he asked, trying to confirm.

"Yes," she replied teasingly.

He slowly approached her, as if he feared she might run away if he walked too quickly. She chuckled at his awkward movements and continued motioning for him to come closer.

He stood nervously in front of her. She was now just a couple of inches from him, with only a towel covering her body. She continued to smile as she gently sat him down on the edge of the bed. Staring deeply into his eyes, she smiled seductively and said, "Describe to me how you remembered my body."

He could no longer help himself. He needed to do something, but the only thing he could do was to gulp down a huge lump that had been sitting in his throat for what seemed like an eternity.

His voice was quivering. "At first," he said shakily, "my recollections of you were so vivid that I could remember every inch of your body, from the firmness of your breasts to the perfection of your lovely womanhood. Over the years, the memories slowly faded and my vision became obscured. I hesitate to tell you this, because I don't want to hurt your feelings."

She slowly leaned toward him and whispered in his ear, "Then, let's do this all over again."

She edged away from him, just far enough so that he could have a full view of her body. Then she slowly took off the towel and let it slip to the floor, completely revealing herself. "Is this what you remembered?" she asked in an alluring voice.

Incredulous, he stared at her body, unable to move, unable to turn away, unable to even breathe. Even though his mind could only remember her as a dream, his heart seemed to recognize this breathtaking beauty. It began to beat more quickly with each passing second.

He took several deep breaths as his eyes slowly looked her over, rediscovering the contours of her slender body. A few water droplets still hung loosely on her soft, silky skin. Her perfect breasts seemed to call out to him. How he desperately hungered to take her firm nipples into his mouth.

Although she had given birth, there were no stretch marks on her toned belly. In fact, he couldn't see a single blemish on her body. She was like a perfect painting—a masterpiece.

"Your body is even more stunningly beautiful than I remembered," he said shakily.

He wanted to do a thousand things to her, but he was afraid. Instead, he stared into her eyes and, like a puppy waiting for a treat, he softly asked, "May I?"

She looked at him as if she had been waiting for a thousand things to happen to her. "Tonight is your night. You may do whatever you'd like, in whatever way you desire," she replied breathlessly.

He slowly reached his hand out to touch her hips and immediately pulled back, as if he was testing a flame to see how hot it was. Then he reached out again and gently placed his warm hands on the sides of her waist, caressing it up and down, reaching around to the small of her back, then around her hips to the back of her thighs. He leaned down and lightly planted butterfly kisses across her belly, slowly making his way up to her breasts. From one to the other, he gently drew her nipples into his mouth, teasing them with his tongue until he could feel her trembling in his arms.

Laying her slowly back on the bed, he softly kissed her right breast, fully enjoying her sweet tenderness as his other hand worked its magic on the other breast.

Moving up to her face, he softly kissed her soft, full lips. Up until now, he had tried to take things slowly, but he couldn't hold himself back any longer. He began to devour her lips, parting them and intertwining his tongue with hers as electric shocks shot through his body.

The anticipation was overwhelming. He parted her slender legs and slowly entered her, immediately engrossed in a sweet euphoria as he pulled back and entered her again and again. After pausing several times to hold himself back, he eventually gave in to what seemed to be the most intense wave of pleasure he had ever experienced. It rippled through his whole being.

***

As they lay in bed together, Elizabeth placed her head on Richard's chest and curled her body against his. He gently kissed her forehead and wrapped his arms around her. "You have no idea how much I love you. I pray to God that you will decide to stay with me and never leave me again," he said earnestly.

She didn't say anything as she slowly ran her fingers up and down his chest. Feeling a sense of uneasiness, he turned to look at her. "What's the matter, sweetie?" he asked.

She sighed. "Oh, Richard," she replied quietly. "I'm so confused right now. My mind says I must return home, but my heart keeps telling me that I'm already home."

He tightened his arm around her body before earnestly saying, "Then you must follow your heart. I promise you that this is just the beginning. From this day on, I promise that we'll live for each moment and each day as if it's our last, so that when we're both old and gray, we won't have any regrets. All I'm asking is for you to grant me this lifetime to love you and to care for you. Please grow old with me, Elizabeth."

With those heartfelt words, he prayed that she would grant him his request, and not slip away from him again. He was thankful that he had been given this second chance to rebuild his dream. Now he just had to make it come true. And he was determined to try—over and over again, until his last breath.

# Chapter Twenty-Six

Richard opened his eyes to the sound of Elizabeth's soft breathing next to his body. He looked at her admiringly as she lay there sleeping peacefully beside him. It had been so long since he had felt the warmth of her body next to his in this way. He felt like he had already waited a whole lifetime for this moment—a moment of awakening, a moment so profound that he felt he had been lifted off his feet.

An orange ray of morning sun beamed down on her silky hair, creating a halo atop her head. She was definitely his angel—a beautiful angel sent down from the heavens to rescue him. For the hundredth time since she had returned, he wanted the hands of time to stand still, so that he could hold this moment and never allow it to pass.

He wanted to stay in bed beside her all day, but he had a lot to do this morning, so he slowly crawled out of bed. Perhaps if he got an early start, he'd be done in no time and could be back to her before noon.

He quickly jotted down a note for her—"I'll be back soon. I love you"— and slowly walked to the window to close the curtains so that the sun wouldn't wake her. Then he slipped quietly out of the room.

He sped in his parent's Maserati down Ocean Boulevard on his way to Cass Jewelers, a prestigious shop located on Summit Drive. He quickly walked inside the shop and asked a clerk for the manager.

A moment later, a balding middle-aged man came up to him and excitedly greeted him, "Good morning, Mr. Bennett. It's such an honor seeing you this morning. How may I be of service to you, sir?"

Richard had brought Elizabeth's ring with him from the apartment the day before. He reached into his pocket and held it out to show it the manager, who took it for a quick inspection. He placed a loupe onto his right eye to examine the diamond closely. "Hmmm . . . I'm sorry to disappoint you, but this diamond is not real," he said.

"I thought so," Richard replied with a huge sense of relief that everything she'd told him was the complete truth. "How many carats is that stone?" he asked.

"Approximately 2 carats," the manager replied.

Richard smiled cheerfully and said, "I would like for you to replace it with your finest diamond."

"Of course, sir," the manager said. "The finest diamond we have right now is a Princess 2-carat signature cut, internally flawless with D color, for about $70,000.00. The setting is free of charge, of course."

Richard was not familiar with the details about the diamond, but he knew he would just have to trust the manager. "We have a deal. I would like it done within the hour."

The manager was bewildered. "Sir, it's very early in the morning. We don't have an actual jeweler on site at this time. The best we could do is about three hours."

"I'm pressed for time right now. If you could do it within the hour, I'll pay a thousand dollars more for it."

"Yes, sir!" the manager said ecstatically. "We'll get on it right away. I thank you."

"Good. I'll be back for it in exactly one hour."

After leaving the jewelry shop, Richard headed straight to his office and told Sam to inform his staff that there would be no work the following day. "It's a paid day off, Sam. Everyone is also invited to attend my son's birthday party tomorrow evening. It will be celebrated at the Atkins Mansion."

"You have a son?" Sam asked, surprised.

"You will get to meet him," he said, smiling. "By the way, please make sure to send out invitations as soon as possible so that everyone is aware of the celebration by this afternoon."

"I'm on it as we speak," she said, starting to type on her computer.

He went into his office and called Angela, James, and Thomas for a quick meeting to go over the weekly reports. He then personally invited them to the Atkins Mansion for Edward's party. Angela wasn't surprised at Richard's news about having a son because she had already met Edward, but James and Thomas were quite dumbfounded.

"Wait a minute, you have a kid?" James asked. "Is this a joke, or when did you do that?" They then turned to Angela and stared at her intently.

"He's not *my* kid!" she yelled out, which immediately put a stop to their stares.

Richard laughed loudly. "Just come to the house tomorrow. You'll see my son and his mother."

After James and Thomas left, Richard asked Angela to stay behind for a brief chat. She was a little hesitant, but she also knew they both needed closure, so she agreed to talk for the sake of their relationship.

"How are you doing?" he gently asked.

Despite a despairing expression on her face, she quietly replied, "I'm doing well."

He reached over and gently took her hands in his. "I'm sorry about the other day," he said sincerely. "I was cruel to you. I truly hope that you'll understand and forgive me. You have been my best friend for as long as I can remember, and I don't want to lose our friendship."

"It's okay," she said politely, though sounding somewhat defeated. "There's nothing to apologize for. I should be asking you for forgiveness. I was the one who was intruding and was rude to you and Elizabeth. I would be grateful if you could please apologize to her on my behalf."

"I'm sure she has already forgiven you, but I will let her know. About me forgiving you, you should already know me by now. You and I are best friends. Our relationship could go sour one day and be pure sunshine the next. That's why we are still friends after all these years."

"I know, Richard. You're the only person who has been able to put up with my crap for all these years. Maybe that's why I bonded so strongly with you. Maybe that's why I was so afraid of losing you."

"You will never lose me. I still love you and will always love you."

Angela looked back at him, small specks of tears forming in the corners of her eyes. With a soft and weak voice, she said, "I finally realized within the past few days that our friendship will be as strong as that first day we met years ago, regardless of what happens between us."

He quietly looked at her for a moment. He wanted to tell her that he was planning to propose to Elizabeth, but he knew that if he broke the news to her now, he would bring more pain to her already broken heart. He paused for a moment to think but finally decided he owed it to her.

Slowly he moved a hand up to her face and gently caressed her soft cheek. He let out a deep sigh, and in an apologetic tone, he said, "The reason why I asked to speak to you alone today was to tell you that I'm planning to propose to Elizabeth, and I wanted you to be the first person to know. I care a lot about you and don't want to surprise you or hurt you anymore. I hope that you'll be happy for us and will give us your blessing."

Angela had her head down while he spoke. When he was done talking, she slowly lifted it to look straight at him. With teary eyes and a tight, crackling voice, she faintly said, "Oh, Richard. Chasing you was like chasing a pot of gold at the end of a rainbow; the more I run after it, the further away it gets. I know now that I could never reach it. I've learned to accept the fact that you and I will never be, and I hope you'll forgive me for everything that I've done to you in the past."

He moved closer to gently wipe away her tears with the back of his hand.

"You are not the only one who was at fault," he said, wrapping his arms around her and gently embracing her. "I have hurt you as well, and I hope that you've forgiven me, as I have already forgiven you."

"Richard, I don't believe I've ever told you this before," she said, as she backed out of the embrace to wipe her eyes. "I'm so fortunate and so blessed to have you as a wonderful friend. Even though we've had our own ups and downs, there has never been one time in my life when I didn't think of you as a good friend. Thank you for always being there for me."

"Always," he said warmly.


Elizabeth woke up to a large, empty bed. Yawning and stretching, she then noticed a small note on Richard's pillow and smiled warmly as she read it. She glanced at the clock and was surprised to see that it was almost nine o'clock. She quickly hopped out of bed and headed straight to the bathroom for a shower.

Hoping that she wasn't late for anything yet this morning, she decided to go see what everyone was up to. She stood at the top of the staircase and looked down into the lobby. It was so quiet, and in this huge house she wasn't sure where to go to find anyone. Luckily, she saw Marie walk into the lobby toward the dining room. "Marie!" Elizabeth called as she quickly descended the enormous staircase.

"Good morning, Miss Elizabeth. I trust that you slept well?"

"I did, thank you," Elizabeth replied. "Do you know where I can find Mr. and Mrs. Bennett?"

"Oh, they're out in the solarium with Edward. Please feel free to join them. I'll be out there with breakfast shortly."

"May I help with anything?"

Marie smiled politely at her and said, "You're too kind, Miss Elizabeth. Thank you for being so considerate, but don't worry about it. I'd rather have you enjoy your morning with the family."

"All right, then. I'll see you in a bit." She smiled at Marie and made her way toward the solarium.

She stood for a moment at the enormous entrance to bask in the warmth of the morning sun shining through the glass ceiling. The air inside the magnificent room was cool and refreshing. Through the golden rays she could make out a clear, blue sky. The endless rows of flowers and plants intermingled with the peaceful sound of the waterfalls as she closed her eyes to fully indulge in the peaceful scene before her.

She made her way toward the giant palm tree and then spotted a tannish cabana about twenty yards to the north of the tree, next to a small pond. She hadn't noticed it there yesterday—perhaps she had been distracted by all the trees, flowers, statues, and waterfalls. Inside the cabana, she saw her family sitting around a large handwoven table.

"Mommy!" Edward yelled out excitedly as he ran over to hug her.

"Good morning, dear," Doris called out cheerfully as she got out of her seat to come and greet Elizabeth. "I trust that you had a wonderful night of sleep?"

"I most certainly did. The bed was so comfortable. When I woke up this morning, I was surprised to see that it was already nine o'clock," Elizabeth replied, embarrassed.

Doris laughed softly and said, "Come sit with us. Breakfast should be out shortly."

"Good morning, sweetie," Victor said as he stood up to give Elizabeth a soft kiss on her cheek.

"Good morning, Father. What a splendid morning in such beautiful surroundings."

While they waited patiently for Marie, Elizabeth was curious about Richard's whereabouts. "I woke up this morning and Richard was not in the bed," she said. "Do you have an idea where he might have gone so early in the morning?"

As soon as the words left her mouth, she thought perhaps she had said something she shouldn't have. She cleared her throat and looked away, but that didn't help the hot sensation that had suddenly rushed to her face.

Doris and Victor smiled at each other, but they didn't want to say anything to embarrass her even more.

"He told us that he had a few important errands to take care of. He took our car into the city and should be back around noon," Doris replied.

Elizabeth nodded, and then turned to Edward and softly rubbed his head. "Did you enjoy sleeping in your grandparents' room?"

"Yes!" Edward replied ecstatically. "They have the biggest bed I've ever seen. Grandma has her own bathroom and Grandpa has his own bathroom."

Doris laughed loudly. "He is such a joy. He brings so much life and laughter into our hearts."


Richard was excited as he reentered the jewelry shop, where the manager politely greeted him and smiled generously as he handed Richard the ring. "This is by far our best, most brilliantly cut stone," the manager proudly stated.

Richard gently held it in his hand and lifted it up to the light to carefully examine it while the manager explained the clarity and the cut of the magnificent stone to him. Richard just nodded as he continued to examine and admire its beauty.

"Considering the time constraint as far as the setting," the manager continued, "I have to admit that it was very well done. It is one of our very best accomplishments."

Richard nodded again. The ring was just as flawless as the woman he was going to give it to. "Thank you, sir," he said. "This is perfect. I'm a very lucky man, and I'm truly excited to present this remarkable stone to my beautiful woman."

The manager then took the ring and placed it inside a small custom-made velvet box. He carefully wrapped it with a pink ribbon and gave it back to Richard, who then paid for the ring and left the shop.

As he walked out to his car, he noticed a mannequin wearing an elegant red dress in the large glass display window of Maya's Designs, the same store where he had bought her the black dress years before. This particular dress draped gracefully down to the mannequin's ankle and was wrapped perfectly around its figure. He knew that the dress could only be worn by Elizabeth, so he quickly went inside.

"I would like to purchase that dress on the mannequin for my wife," he said to the clerk.

"What is her dress size?" she asked.

He hesitated because he didn't know Elizabeth's size. Then he thought back to the time when he bought the beautiful black dress for her from the same shop. Maybe this was the same mannequin that was wearing that dress he had purchased.

"I'm embarrassed to say that I don't even know her size. How long has that mannequin been in the window?"

"At least six or seven years," the clerk replied with a puzzled expression.

He noticed her confused look, so he quickly explained. "I bought a dress here for the same woman, a dress that this very same mannequin was wearing a few years back, and it fit her just perfectly. She is still the same size today. I'll take that dress on the mannequin, if you don't mind getting it for me."

"Of course, sir. I'll be right back with it." The clerk went to the display window and carefully undressed the mannequin. She placed the dress on a hanger and wrapped it inside a large black plastic bag.

"That will be five thousand dollars," she said, handing it to him. "I can ring you up over here, sir."

He followed her to the register and handed her his credit card. She smiled. "Your wife is a very lucky woman," she said.

"Actually," he said, grinning, "I'm the luckiest man in the world to be granted the opportunity to have her by my side."

Soon he was back in the Maserati, zooming down Summit Drive and weaving through traffic on his way to Ocean Boulevard.

After he arrived at the house, he discreetly handed the dress to Marie to bring it up to Elizabeth's room. "I'd appreciate it if you could hide it somewhere in the closet for the time being. I'd like it to be a surprise," he said shyly.

As Marie took the dress from Richard, she couldn't help but chuckle. "That is very sweet of you, Richard, and very cute," she said. "By the way, they are all in the solarium."

"Thank you, Marie," he said and eagerly headed toward the solarium.

As he made his way toward the cabana, he noticed Edward and Elizabeth standing next to the small pond, staring intently at the fish.

Edward turned around and saw him. "Daddy!" he shouted, running toward him and wrapping his arms around his legs.

Elizabeth smiled and walked toward them. "Hello, you. You left so early in the morning with only a note. Must be your way of getting back at me, eh?" she said, giving him a playful nudge.

He gently grabbed her waist and gave her a passionate embrace. "I didn't want to wake you."

They walked back to the table and sat together across from his parents. "You had a long morning—you must be hungry," Elizabeth said as she filled a plate of food for him. He smiled and started in on his meal.

"So, where did you go this morning?" Elizabeth asked as she watched him eat.

"I went to the office and went through the weekly reports with my managers. I also invited everyone to Edward's birthday party tomorrow. And on my way back, I stopped to pick up a few necessary items," he replied, trying to focus on his food.

"A few necessary items?" Elizabeth asked curiously.

"Yes, honey—that is, if you don't mind spending another night here."

"I'm your shadow. Wherever you go, I will gladly follow," she replied half-teasingly and half-seriously.

Richard reached out and gently touched her face. The love and regard for him that she displayed in front of his parents was more than anything he could ever ask for. He wished he knew what he had done to deserve such happiness, and what he could do to stay this happy forever. His respect and admiration for her had only continued to grow and get stronger by the day.

# Chapter Twenty-Seven

Friday—the day of Edward's big birthday celebration—finally arrived. Doris was so excited that she hadn't slept for most of the night; however, she was the first to wake up. She had carefully planned the entire event and wanted everything, from the food on down to the decorative ribbons, to be perfect. This was the most joyous time in her life, because this day was the day that she finally had the opportunity to proudly show off her grandson to her friends and family. She had many precious memories of seeing Richard grow from a little boy into a man. Now, she could re-experience those same wonderful and priceless memories again with Edward.

Elizabeth woke up to the sound of people hustling and bustling up and down the hallway. Remembering that today was the big day for Edward, she immediately got out of the bed, washed up, and headed down the hallway, making her way to the staircase.

Edward was already awake, helping with inflating the balloons in the lobby. As Elizabeth came downstairs, she gave him a smile of approval and headed toward the ballroom. She was excited to see what had been done to it, since this was her first time seeing the magnificent room being set up for an important event. Standing outside the giant double doors to the ballroom, she could already hear Doris's voice calling out orders to everyone inside the room.

As she entered the enormous room, the decorations immediately caught her eye. The lighting was dimmed to allow the brightness from four illuminated chandeliers in the corners to shine through. The giant chandelier in the center, glistening like a golden moon, gave the room a dazzling appeal. Dozens of blue and gold satin ribbons ran elegantly across the ceiling to converge at the main chandelier. From the ribbons hung hundreds of tiny sparkling ornaments and blue balloons, making the entire ceiling look like a sparkling starry night sky.

Rows and rows of round tables and chairs were set up in the ballroom, all covered with delicate white and blue satin cloths.

At the north end of the room was a long table covered in a white satin cloth with blue trimmings and ribbons that were tied into bows and draping down from all four corners. A huge stage was also at the north end of the room, and several musicians were already on it, busying themselves with setting up their instruments.

"They spared no expense on this special occasion for their grandson," she said softly to herself.

"Good morning, dear," Doris said pleasantly as she walked up to her.

"Good morning, Mother," Elizabeth replied, still trying to catch her breath "Wow, this is like nothing I've ever seen before."

Doris was delighted with the compliment. "Thank you, dear. It has been a long time since we've had an event in this room, and I wanted everything to be perfect for my grandson's first birthday party."

"Thank you for going to so much trouble," Elizabeth said, her eyes still fixed on the decorations.

"It's no trouble at all, sweetie. My grandson deserves the very best." Doris looked around the room, then turned back to Elizabeth and said, "I'm curious— did you figure out what you're going to wear tonight?"

The thought hadn't even occurred to Elizabeth until now. Even though this event was a birthday party for a four-year-old, the decorations made it look so elegant and formal. That meant that she would also have to dress appropriately.

She suddenly became a little worried. "I hadn't even thought about it until just now. We were so busy exploring the grounds of this spectacular residence yesterday, and I completely forgot to tell Richard that we needed to go shopping for something suitable for me to wear." She suddenly thought about Edward. "Oh my gosh, that means Edward would need appropriate attire as well."

"Don't worry, dear. You have plenty of time to go shopping today," Doris assured her. "One thing I know about Richard is that he always plans ahead. I'm pretty sure he has something picked out for you already. And don't worry about Edward. We have just what he needs to wear for the evening."

Elizabeth hastened back into her room and noticed that Richard was still in bed. She quietly sat on the edge of the bed with a worried look on her face. He opened his eyes, slowly sat up, and wrapped both of his arms around her for a gentle embrace.

"Good morning, sweetie," he murmured.

"I don't have anything to wear," she said quietly.

Richard rubbed his eyes. "Of course you do. I packed several clothes inside your bag," he joked.

She gave him a serious look. "Richard, I'm not kidding. I don't have anything suitable for tonight, and it looks like it's going to be a very formal event."

He gently brushed a lock of her hair behind her ear and smiled. Then, he slowly got out of the bed and walked straight to the closet. Seconds later, he came back with a huge black plastic bag and presented it to her.

Elizabeth was puzzled but also excited. "Richard, what is this?"

"This was the necessary item I was talking about yesterday," he replied with a charming smile.

She quickly opened the bag, and her eyes grew wide when saw the beautiful red dress. "Awww, Richard," she gasped. "This is gorgeous. So this is what you did yesterday, huh?"

"Something like that." He gave her a teasing wink.

She giggled as she carefully laid the dress down on the bed. "You are so considerate." She gave him a gentle hug and went into the bathroom with the dress.

Fifteen minutes later, she came back out, but in the same clothes she was wearing earlier. She sat down beside him on the bed.

"Didn't it fit?" he asked with a curious frown.

"It fit *perfectly*," she replied, smiling ecstatically. "How did you know my size?"

"Well, the dress was displayed on that same mannequin that your black dress was on years ago. That's how I knew," he said proudly.

"So you went back to the same shop?"

"I just happened to walk by and saw the dress. The moment I saw it, I knew that it belonged to you."

"You are so sweet," she said, leaning over and giving him a passionate kiss. "Thank you, honey. I love it."

"Why didn't you let me look at you with the dress on? I want to see how beautiful you are in it."

She patted his knee and smiled. "You'll get to see me in it this evening. I don't want to ruin the surprise just yet."

He pulled himself back a few inches and let his fingers comb through her long, silky hair. "You're going to look amazing in it, and everyone will be admiring you."

She gently laid her head on his shoulder. "Richard, you always seem to know the perfect words to say to me. My heart dances gracefully every moment that I'm with you."

Elizabeth spent much of the day watching the workers set up for the event. She felt a sense of relief as everyone's jobs were successfully accomplished. When Richard came to join her, she glanced at her watch and noticed that it was already four o'clock, so she quickly told him that she needed to go get herself ready and would join him in the ballroom later.

"Elizabeth, wait." He gently grabbed her hand and turned her around.

"What is it?"

"There's something else I wanted you to wear along with that dress." He led her to a small table inside the lobby, opened the drawer, and took out a small, old jewelry box.

"Here," he said, handing it to her. "I borrowed it from my mother. It belonged to Iris. It has been passed on down to the women in the family for generations."

Elizabeth carefully opened the box and found a magnificent antique necklace. Twelve brilliantly cut oval rubies were separately set in silver, with ten tiny diamonds surrounding each of them. The rubies were perfectly strung together with a gold chain, leading up to a dazzling heart-shaped ruby pendant in the middle.

Inside the box was also a matching set of heart-shaped ruby earrings, each with dazzling diamonds encircling it. Dangling below each heart hung a stunning ruby teardrop.

Elizabeth was breathless. "What a magnificent set of jewelry. It is so beautiful, Richard. I've never seen anything like it before."

"Go try it on and I'll see you later in the ballroom." He slowly leaned over to softly kiss her lips before he walked away.

Richard and his family waited at the entrance to the ballroom, ready to greet the guests as they arrived. James came in first, accompanied by his latest love interest. Richard greeted them warmly and mingled with them for a moment before an usher directed them to a table.

A few minutes later, Thomas arrived with his family. His children quickly learned where the fun was and immediately left them to join the other children.

As Richard stood inside the room, talking with Thomas and his wife, he noticed Angela standing by the door with her parents.

*Angela is quite a beauty tonight,* he thought. She had on an elegant black dress that slightly hugged her slender body, showing off her nice, round bust and slim waist. Her hair was neatly braided and pinned into a seductive updo, with a sophisticated lock of bangs flowing down across her forehead. She was definitely gorgeous and had gotten most of the men's attention as soon as she walked in the door.

Beside her was a very handsome young man who went by the name of Giorgio. He had met Angela a few days earlier on a photo shoot for a project he was hired to model for.

Doris immediately walked over to greet them, and Richard followed right behind her. "Wesley! Charlotte! It's so nice that both of you could be here this evening! And hello there, Angela, sweetheart. Thank you so much for coming on such short notice," Doris said cheerfully as they gave each other hugs and kisses.

As soon as Richard returned to his spot next to Victor, he noticed Nancy and Becca at the entrance with two gentlemen. The women's faces lit up with a pleasant glow as their eyes roamed in awe around the room. Distracted by all the magnificent décor, they stood motionless for a moment.

Nancy had on a flattering tropical green dress that showed off her voluptuous body. Her hair was pinned up into a messy updo with a few curly strands falling out of the pin. Her date was a balding, short, and stocky man who had a charming smile on his cleanly shaved, round face. He wore a blue blazer that clashed with his multicolor pants.

Becca had on a pale pink dress that seemed to be a little too loose for her tall, slim body. Her long golden hair down was left down, swaying freely against her shoulders and back. Her date was a tall, thin young man who seemed to lack a personality. He wore a burgundy blazer with a white dress shirt, khaki pants, and a pink tie.

Richard walked up and cheerfully greeted them. "Ah, my two most favorite people in the whole world! I'm so glad to see you. Thanks for coming."

"Thank you, Richard," Nancy replied. "You're quite a handsome gentleman this evening! Thanks for inviting us." She then noticed that Richard was staring intently at her dress. "Hey, you!" she teased. "This may be the first time that I've actually worn a dress, so consider yourself lucky! And you better not say a thing about how silly I look in it."

He laughed loudly. "Actually, I was just about to compliment you on how beautiful you look in that dress."

She laughed and gave him a hug before introducing their dates. "This is Charlie, and that is Toby."

"It's a pleasure to meet you, Charlie, Toby. Thanks for coming," Richard said reaching out his hand to shake theirs.

Nancy looked around the room for a moment. "I don't see Elizabeth. Is she here this evening?"

"She is still getting ready," Richard replied, looking over at the door. "She should be here shortly."

"I can't wait to see her," Nancy said, smiling.

"Would you like a table?" he asked as he waved at an usher to direct Nancy's group to be seated.

Glancing at his watch every few seconds, Richard waited anxiously for Elizabeth. He was so caught up in anticipation that he could barely stand still. He walked slowly toward the entrance to see if he could see her anywhere in the hallway.

He then froze in place as Elizabeth gradually made her way through the door. He held his breath at the sight of this sweet, sophisticated living angel. She was wrapped elegantly in her glamorous red satin gown, its strapless bodice and sweetheart neckline showing off just enough cleavage to awe any man.

Her long skirt fit perfectly, flaring out from the waistline and draping down into a full skirt at her ankles. Her hair was twisted and pulled up perfectly and elegantly. Her graceful shoulders were pulled back, her hands tightly grasping a black clutch purse.

The lights above beamed directly on her, making her ruby earrings and necklace dazzle and dance. To Richard her beauty was beyond words, like a princess in a fairytale. Only she was not from a fairytale. She was his, and she was standing only a few feet away from him. The thought overwhelmed him, and he had to gasp deeply for another breath of air.

As he walked up to her, she smiled nervously at him. Then she leaned over and whispered sweetly in his ear, "How do I look?"

"There's nothing and no one in this room that could even compare to what I'm seeing before me. There are no words that could describe how I'm feeling right now," he softly whispered back.

She beamed at him and took his arm as they walked to their table. A silence had fallen over the room. For a moment, they were the center of everyone's attention. There were a few whispers here and there, jaws dropping and eyes gazing to admire this beautiful woman who accompanied Richard. As the two of them walked past several tables, Elizabeth kindly greeted the guests and smiled warmly, thanking them for coming.

Doris got up from her seat to greet Elizabeth. "Goodness, you look stunning in that dress! And the magnificent set of ruby necklace and earrings seem to have found their rightful owner. They look simply perfect on you, dear."

"Thank you, Mother," Elizabeth graciously replied. "Thank you for loaning the jewelry to me."

"You're very welcome. The set is one of our family heirlooms. From now on, it will be your turn to take care of it," Doris explained. Then she took Elizabeth over to the table next to them and happily introduced her to Angela's parents.

"Wesley and Charlotte, please meet Elizabeth. Elizabeth, this is Wesley and Charlotte Denning. They are my closest and dearest friends."

"It is a delightful pleasure to meet you. Thank you for being here tonight," Elizabeth said joyfully.

"It is our honor to be here," Charlotte replied.

Elizabeth noticed that Angela was sitting across from the Denning couple, next to a handsome young man.

"Hello, Angela. I'm so glad to see you. Your presence tonight means a lot to us. Thank you for being here."

"Thank you for inviting us," Angela replied, her expression revealing a hint of intimidation. Clearly, Elizabeth was much more dazzling than she was. She looked away to hide her envy.

As Elizabeth walked back to rejoin Richard, she noticed Nancy sitting at a table with her back toward her. She quickly went up to her and hugged her from behind. Nancy immediately turned around to see Elizabeth's smiling face. "Oh my gosh!" Nancy quickly stood up to give her a hug. "You look so beautiful tonight, Elizabeth!"

"And so do you! Thank you for coming, my dear friend. I'm feeling more at ease now that you're here."

"I wouldn't miss this for the world," Nancy replied, hugging Elizabeth again.

Elizabeth turned to greet Becca and complimented her on how lovely she looked as well.

"I hope you're all enjoying your evening so far," Elizabeth said kindly.

"The decorations tonight are absolutely gorgeous. We are enjoying every bit of it," Nancy said. "By the way, this is Charlie and that is Toby."

Elizabeth stood beside Richard as the enormous room continued to fill up with guests. Doris waved at the band to begin performing, which was also a signal for the caterers to serve refreshments and appetizers to the guests.

"This is absolutely beautiful, Richard. Our son's first birthday party couldn't have been any more perfect than this."

He took her hand and gently kissed it. "And I can't be any happier than this—to have you and my son right here with me," he said passionately.

"Oh! Speaking of Edward, where is he?" she asked, looking around the room.

"He is no doubt having the time of his life somewhere inside this room in the company of the other children. This is good for him. I've never seen him so happy," he reassured her.


As dinner was served to the last table, two caterers pushed a cart with an enormous white cake on it into the room and parked it in front of the long table with white satin cloth and blue trimmings, next to the stage. Elizabeth was pleasantly surprised to see that the table was filled with presents.

Looking at Elizabeth, Richard slowly stood up and held his hand out toward her. "Take my hand, sweetie," he said. At first she frowned slightly, realizing they were the center of attention, but then she smiled and nervously reached out her hand to take his. Taking Edward's hand as well, he slowly led the two of them toward the front of the room, stopping next to the cake. She couldn't help but smile as they stood in front of everyone. Richard reached over to accept the microphone from the master of ceremonies. Then he began his speech.

*Good evening, families, friends, and fellow co-workers. We are absolutely delighted to have each and every one of you here to join us at this most special event tonight.*

*First and foremost, we would like to stress our deepest gratitude toward all of you for being here. At any occasion or event, it is the guests who set the tone, and you fine people have definitely created a most festive and vibrant atmosphere this evening.*

*Before I continue, I would like to say that I'm the luckiest man in this entire world. Most of you may not have met my little family before, and I would like to introduce them to you. This beautiful woman beside me is Elizabeth, the mother of my son. And this is my son, Edward.*

Richard paused as the guests burst into applause. He waited a few moments until the room was again quiet.

*We appreciate your being here this evening to support us and to be a part of this joyous time as we celebrate our son's birthday. Even though this is his fourth birthday, it is the first one that I'm blessed with the opportunity to celebrate with him and his mother.*

*I am more than delighted to have each and every one of you here. I want Edward to know that from this day forth, his birthdays will always be celebrated with loved ones, family, and friends.*

*Happy Birthday, my son.*

One of the caterers then brought out a huge candle in the shape of a number four and placed it in front of the cake. Richard lit the candle and on the count of three, everyone inside the room sang "Happy Birthday." Edward blew out the candle in one breath as the crowd cheered and whistled.

Richard took the microphone again and continued.

*I must say that everything that is happening tonight brings me great happiness and is extremely important to me. There is one more thing, however, that I must do before the night is over. It is the one thing I have been waiting to do for five years.*

As silence filled the room once again, Richard turned and looked directly at Elizabeth. She watched as he pulled an old, folded-up piece of pink paper from his pocket. A glimmer of recognition flashed across her face as he unfolded it and began reading:

*From the first time I saw you, I was in love with you. I didn't care about your background, where you were from, or how you lived your life. All I saw was that a beautiful woman was looking at me and thinking about me.*

*I wanted to be everything to you, so that you didn't have to go through life wondering what could have been. I wanted to live a life in which I would look forward to coming home each and every night to you. I wanted to build a home with you and grow old with you.*

*Tonight, I stand here before you as a man who is deeply and*

*madly in love with you. I vow in front of everyone here in this
room that I will devote my whole life to loving you and making
you happy.*

    *Darling, your long journey has ended and you are now home
at last.*

Richard reached into his coat pocket to pull out the ring. Then he slowly
bent down on one knee as he presented it to her.

    *Please, Elizabeth, grant me the chance to live out my promise
to you. Please be my wife.*

The room was quiet before, but now it was so still that if a fly were to slip
into the room, everyone would hear it.

Elizabeth looked around, aware that hundreds of people were gazing at
her, eagerly anticipating her response. She tried hard to hold back her tears as
she looked down at Richard. His pleading eyes were staring intently back at her,
waiting and hoping. She suddenly felt lost and speechless, her hands moist and
quivering. She was still struggling when she heard a small voice behind her.

"Say, yes, Mommy."

She turned around to see Edward smiling at her with a hopeful expression.
She turned back to Richard and took a deep breath, looking directly into his
teary eyes. Leaning toward him, she softly whispered in his ear, "Yes, and I
promise you that from this day forth, I will also spend the rest of my life making
you happy."

Richard stood, his beaming expression evident to everyone in the room. He
then pulled her toward him in a gentle, loving embrace as the crowd burst into
a deafening applause.

The band began to play as Richard, Elizabeth, and Edward embraced each
other. Doris and Victor walked over to them, elated with their son's contented
expression.

"Well done, my son. I couldn't be more proud of you," Victor said
ecstatically. He then turned to Elizabeth and gave her an appreciative, warm hug.

With teary eyes, Doris embraced Elizabeth. "Thank you, dear. I just want
to say that I couldn't be any happier to have you as my daughter."

Still shaking nervously, Elizabeth smiled and lightly nodded at Doris.

As the family bid farewell to the last of the guests, Victor and Doris quietly
sneaked out of the room with Edward, leaving the newly engaged couple alone.
Richard and Elizabeth stood in the middle of the room, deep admiration etched
on both of their faces.

"'Mrs. Elizabeth Bennett.' Ahhh… that sounds so sweet to my ears," he
said.

She smiled warmly at him. "I now have the chance to live out the fairytale."

"Every day with you is a fairytale to me," he said.

She smiled again and then glanced down at her ring. A surprised look flashed across her face. "Richard, you gave my ring back to me."

He gently took her hand and slipped the ring off her finger to look at it for a moment, and then handed it back to her. "Yes. The white gold is real." He paused for a moment before continuing. "But if you look closely at the diamond, you'll see that it, too, is real."

She immediately brought the ring closer to her eyes for a more intense look. "Richard, you did it again—your everlasting power of love. You always manage to surprise me every single time. I love you so much!"

Richard sighed, taking her hand. "Elizabeth, you're my love, my happiness, and my life. If our souls should part, I will keep you in my heart through eternity, and I promise to find you again," he replied passionately. He wrapped his arms around her waist and drew her in for a long, passionate kiss.

# Chapter Twenty-Eight

It was an amazing feeling for Richard to have Elizabeth fast asleep in his arms. Her breathing was soft and steady. Her black, silky hair spread gently across his chest, with a few strands covering her cheek. Carefully pulling away slightly, he propped his head up on one elbow and silently watched her. He wished that this moment would never end and that his tired eyes would never close, so that he could just stare at her like this forever.

He wanted to protect her in every way—he wanted to be her shelter, her safe haven. He gently brushed the locks of hair off of her face and then whispered to her, "I love you so much. It's difficult for me to believe that God has made you mine."

She shifted slightly next to him before snuggling closer and gently pressing her soft body against his. He let out a long sigh and smiled, trying to cherish every minute of it.

All of the sudden, his reverie was shattered by her screaming, "Richard! Richard! They're coming!"

He sat up immediately and noticed that she was gazing at the windows with a horrific expression on her face. "Who?" he asked in a panic. "Who's coming?"

"They're coming, Richard! My god, they're at the window!" she cried out in terror as she grabbed him tightly.

Frantically, Richard looked toward the windows to try to make out what she was seeing. Staring intently, he soon began to see a slight glow outside the curtains in the northwest corner of the room.

A single ray of light burned a small hole through the curtains, consuming them as it slowly expanded. All of the sudden, the entire room lit up as the light burst through the window and became as bright as the sun.

Terrified, Richard tightened his grip on Elizabeth and had to turn his head to the side to avoid looking straight at the light. But it was too bright even with his head turned away from it, so he released one of his hands to cover his eyes.

After doing that, he was finally able to direct his eyes back to the window: was this what had kept coming for her in her dreams? He squinted his eyes and blinked a couple of times as he looked as directly as he could at the light.

As his eyes slowly adjusted to the brightness, he could make out two glowing, formless beings. They were floating effortlessly in midair as they slowly made their way toward Richard and Elizabeth.

He tried to lift her out of the bed and run, but suddenly to his horror the two of them were somehow forced back onto the bed. Lying down now with his arms still wrapped around her, he found he couldn't move. He tried with all his strength to get up, but he still couldn't move—not even an inch. Her terrified screams echoed through the room as she continued to hold tightly on to him, but he felt powerless to do anything. She pressed her face tightly against his chest to avoid looking at the beings.

"Just continue to hold on tightly to me, Elizabeth! Whatever happens, promise me you will never let go! Do you hear me?" When he didn't hear her response, he yelled to her, "Elizabeth, do not let go of me! Do you hear me? Answer me!"

"Yes! I will never let go!" she cried out.

The beings had finally approached them and were now hovering over them. Richard stared in disbelief and horror. He had no idea what was happening and couldn't understand how all of the sudden he could become part of her dreams. Or, the thought occurred to him, was it never a dream? Had this always been... real?

He was desperately trying to comprehend the situation, but everything happened too fast and his mind simply went blank. All he knew was that these beings were here for her and he was not going to let them take her away. He had to save her, no matter what it took.

His heart was beating so fast it felt as if it would leap out of his chest. It seemed every muscle in his body tightened as he tried to find the strength to battle whatever this was that had come for his Elizabeth.

Finally, he managed to find the strength to get to a sitting position. But when he tried to stand, he realized that although the strength had returned to his upper body, his legs were still immobilized. *Even if I can't move my legs*, he thought, *I am going to do everything within my power to protect her.*

"You're not going to take her! You're not going to take her!" he repeatedly shouted as he gripped Elizabeth tightly in one arm and swung wildly at the beings with the other. But his punches went straight through them, as if he was swinging at a puff of smoke. He grew increasingly desperate.

The beings then reached down to them. Richard pulled her as close as he could, reaching one arm across her to protect her. But to his surprise, they didn't grab her—it was his arm they grabbed.

"*NOOOOO!*" he yelled out as he desperately tried to fight them off. But it was no use. He felt himself being lifted and dragged toward the light, his body floating in midair. Each time he struggled to break free, he felt weaker and weaker, as if with every effort another ounce of his energy was drained from his body.

As he moved farther away from Elizabeth, he turned his head back to look at her and could see the tears streaming out of her terrified eyes. Her hands were desperately reaching out to him as she cried out and begged for him not to leave her.

"*NOOOOO!*" was the only word he could scream as his body floated away from her toward the light. He looked back at her again and saw that she was still reaching out to him. As he drifted farther away, her image became smaller and smaller, until she was finally gone.

"Where are you taking me?" he managed to ask in a low, weak voice, but he heard no reply.

He was getting closer and closer to the light now, which was bright and searing hot. He squeezed his eyelids shut to avoid being blinded as the intense heat seemed to set his body on fire, burning through him like the midday sun on a hot, cloudless July afternoon.

"*NO! NOOOOOOO!*" he screamed repeatedly as he slowly entered the light.

His voice became clearer and clearer to his own ears now, and the sound of his screams seemed closer and closer to him, as if he had just come out of a bottomless pit. He kept his eyes squeezed shut and waited for what was going to happen next. He expected to feel an agonizing burning sensation as the light swallowed him, but to his surprise, he didn't feel anything at all.

# Chapter Twenty-Nine

*N*OOOO!" Richard screamed again, but this time his voice sounded different. It seemed to have a different tone, as if he were a completely different person. He abruptly opened his eyes, but everything was a blur. He needed to find out—he needed to see where the beings had taken him. He quickly sat up to look around, but his vision was still blurry. Frustrated, he rubbed his eyes and blinked rapidly several times.

With clearer vision, he began to slowly look around. As he scanned the area around him, he noticed that he was sitting on a small bed with computer monitors on both sides. Soft beeping sounds were coming from the machines that were connected to the monitors. A bright fluorescent light glared down on him from the ceiling behind the bed.

He felt a slight pain in his left arm and noticed that an IV was connected to it, bound to his skin with several clear strips of tape. He looked down at his body and saw that he was wearing a white hospital gown.

There was a slight discomfort in his chest, and he lifted his gown to find several electrical wires connected to round carbon electrodes on his chest. He tried to lean forward but felt a tug on his head, as if something was pulling him back.

As he felt around his head, he noticed that it had been shaven, and there were more wires connected to the top of his head. He tried to pull himself off of the bed, but he couldn't move his legs.

Bewildered, he began to breathe rapidly as his heart rate increased. "*What the hell is going on here?*" he yelled out hysterically. "*What the hell happened to me?*"

A nurse quickly ran into the room. "Mr. Voss, you have awakened!" she said excitedly, but he totally ignored her as he looked around the room, frantically searching for Elizabeth.

"Elizabeth! Elizabeth! What have you done to her?"

"Mr. Voss, please calm down."

"Who the hell is Mr. Voss? My name is Richard! Richard Bennett!" he screamed as he reached to pull the wires off his head and chest.

"Mr. Voss, you need to calm down!" the nurse pleaded before she ran to the door to call for assistance.

Within moments, two huge orderlies ran into the room, grabbed hold of his arms, and tried to pin him down onto the bed.

"Let me go! *Let me go!*" Richard yelled repeatedly, flailing his arms wildly.

A doctor quickly ran into the room. "What's going on?" he said breathlessly.

"Dr. Lewis! Mr. Voss has awakened, but he is hysterical!" the nurse frantically explained. "He tried to get out of bed and has ripped off most of the wires!"

"Mr. Voss," Dr. Lewis said softly to Richard. "You need to calm down."

"Let me go! Let me go!" Richard continued yelling as he tried to fight off the orderlies.

"We need to sedate him before he hurts himself!" Dr. Lewis yelled out to the nurse. "Quick, give me 5 milliliters of B-52!"

The nurse took out a small syringe and inserted the needle into a small brown bottle, filled it with medication, and handed the syringe to Dr. Lewis.

"No! What are you doing to me?" Richard pleaded as he continued to fight to break free. "Please let me go! I have to find Elizabeth!"

Dr. Lewis quickly went over to Richard and injected the needle into his left arm.

Richard was still struggling to break free, but after the drug took effect, he became weak and tired. "My name is . . . Richard Bennett. My name is Richard … Bennett," he said softly as he slowly drifted asleep.

"We need to call his father and tell him the good news," Dr. Lewis said.


"My name is … Richard Bennett," Richard said faintly after he had been sleeping calmly for a few hours. He tried to open his eyes again, hoping that it was just a nightmare and that Elizabeth would be there with him this time.

"Elizabeth?" he called out, but got no reply. He tried to sit up, but he couldn't move his arms. Turning his head, he saw that both of his arms were strapped to the sides of the bed.

"*What the hell is this? What the hell is going on!*" he spat out furiously as he tried frantically to break free.

Just then he noticed an elderly man standing at the door to his room. The man wasn't in a hospital gown, nor was he wearing scrubs. Instead, he was in a neat, three-piece suit with a bow tie.

Richard stopped struggling for a brief moment to look at the man as he slowly made his way toward him.

As the man approached, he leaned over Richard as if he wanted to be closer to him. His eyes were kind and warm, and he seemed to be filled with happiness. He stared down at Richard for a moment, and then his eyes began to glisten with tears.

Bewildered and helpless, Richard quietly rested his head back onto the pillow and tried to collect himself for a moment. Then, he turned his eyes to the man's face and looked straight into his pale, blue eyes.

A rush of curiosity overwhelmed Richard. He slowly turned away and asked, "Who are you?"

The elderly man gently placed his hand on Richard's shoulder and replied in a raspy voice, "I'm your father, Marshall Voss. And you are my son, David."

Richard turned to him with a puzzled expression. "You are mistaken, sir. I'm not your son. My name is Richard Bennett, and my father's name is Victor Bennett."

Marshall gently moved his hand from Richard's shoulder to his face but immediately pulled back as soon as Richard violently jerked his head to avoid being touched. Marshall let out a soft sigh and then went and slid a chair next to Richard's bed. He sat there, staring at Richard without saying anything.

"Where am I?" Richard asked with a deep sigh. "What is happening to me?"

"David, you are in the intensive care unit at Metro State Hospital. You have been in a coma," Marshall carefully explained.

"No! You're wrong again, sir. I was never in a coma," Richard said, shaking his head in disbelief. "I have a beautiful wife and a lovely child. I was taken away from my family and brought here. I want to go back to my wife and son."

"David, it was all a dream. You were in a coma and you just woke up from it."

Richard's eyes grew wide. "That's not true! I was never in a coma!" he said, his voice rising. "My name is Richard Bennett, and I was born in the city of Atkins. My parents' names are Doris and Victor. My wife is Elizabeth and my son is Edward. I don't understand why I was taken away from my family. I don't know what wrong I did or for what reason I'm being brought here, but I beg you to please return me to my family," he tearfully pleaded.

Just as Marshall was about to say something, Dr. Lewis came into the room and asked to speak to Marshall alone. Richard's eyes followed them as they walked out of the room.

"Mr. Voss," the doctor said softly, "I think your son has had enough excitement for today. Let him get some rest. He's got some thinking to do."

Marshall's eyes were fixed on the floor as he let out a deep sigh. "Is it common for a patient to come up with such a story, doctor?"

Dr. Lewis paused and took a deep breath. "I've heard of cases about comatose patients who wake up with completely different identities, but that's not very common. There are others who wake up to their same selves and resumed their normal life. No one really knows what happens to them while they are in the sleeping state. It's a medical mystery that baffles many professionals. I really don't have an answer for you."

"Will he ever get his memories back?"

"I can't really say. Let's just give him some time for now and see what happens."

Frustrated, Marshall slowly nodded, trying hard to comprehend his son's situation. He wanted to stay with him at the hospital, but he knew he needed to leave for his son's sake.


He left the hospital feeling dejected, confused, and worried. At the same time, however, he was overjoyed that his son had come out of his coma. Even though he was frustrated, Marshall had high hopes and was optimistic that his son would regain his memory.

Marshall Maxwell Voss was a very wealthy man and the owner of the Voss Corporation. He grew up in a poor but proud family in the Bronx, the youngest of five children. His father worked as a foreman at a nearby shipping company, and his mother was a stay-at-home mom. Being the youngest, Marshall never had the opportunity to enjoy the luxuries of having new clothes, shoes, or toys. Everything he had was a hand-me-down from his two older brothers.

Marshall learned from his upbringing to be a hard worker. Everything he did, he did it with full effort and with the mindset of succeeding. He started his own business at the age of twenty-five. His shrewd and hard-line tactics made him a fearful figure within the business community. Because of his generous donations to the city's leaders and politicians, he had also become a very powerful member of the elite society. His company had expanded considerably over the years. It now consisted of over four hundred properties, including ten upscale Manhattan apartment buildings and eight companies.

He and his wife Joy were married for fifty years. Together, they had two children, Heather and David. Heather married a wealthy Chinese businessman and moved to Hong Kong. David, on the other hand, was a troubled young man who needed direction and motivation.

Marshall and Joy's enormous residence was in the Eastern Starr Village along the north shore of Long Island. Unfortunately, Joy had passed away two years earlier while David was still in a coma, which left Marshall as the only person to look after him.


Richard lay quietly in bed, still lost and confused. No matter how he tried to comprehend his situation, nothing seemed to make sense to him. How could he just suddenly disappear and then reappear in a whole different world? How could he be both Richard Bennett and David Voss under the same sky?

He tried to recall the bright light and the beings who had abducted him. Why were they also in Elizabeth's dreams? Why were they coming for her? Were they some kind of aliens who were sent to get her but mistakenly took him instead?

His mind drifted back to his beautiful Elizabeth, and he could still feel the warmth of her body rubbing up against his bare skin. He couldn't possibly be dreaming, he thought. But was it possible that he had died? How horrible and cruel if death was this miserable.

He tried to relax, but he couldn't. There were a thousand things on his mind, a thousand questions left unanswered. Perhaps there was a rational explanation of some sort somewhere. Maybe he was in fact still sleeping beside Elizabeth and was just having a nightmare.

"Yes, it's just a bad dream," he said, trying to comfort himself. "Nothing here is real. I'll go back to sleep, and when I wake up, I'll be with her again."

He closed his eyes and slowly fell asleep.

# Chapter Thirty

Richard tried to fill his mind with positive thoughts as he lay in his bed with his eyes still tightly shut. He prayed over and over again that everything was just a dream and that when he opened his eyes, he would be with his lovely Elizabeth again.

He thought he heard something, perhaps a voice—her voice calling him. He felt someone tugging at his arm as if she wanted to snuggle close and be held. He smiled pleasantly at the sound of whispers in his ear, and was sure the sweet whispers belonged to her. He tried to focus on nothing else but those warm and wonderful whispers.

He slowly opened his eyes and sat up to look around, but to his dismay, all he heard were the same beeping noises inside the hospital room. His heart began to beat rapidly again, and he could feel his blood boil as he frantically called out for her.

Why was he still trapped in this hellish nightmare? Frustrated, he let out a scream and slapped his face several times to try to wake himself up, but the pain felt all too real.

A tall, slender brunette suddenly entered the room. She had an attractive face and seemed to be about his age. Casually walking up to his bed, she stood next to him, smiling warmly.

With a bewildered expression, he calmly asked, "Who are you?"

She kept smiling and seemed as if she was really happy to see him. "Hello, David. I'm Mary—Mary Levens—and I'm your physical therapist."

"Why do I have a physical therapist?" he asked, puzzled. "For what reason do I need one?"

"Your father hired me to help keep your muscles from atrophying," she said. "I came here twice a week for over a year now, but unfortunately, each time I was here, you were asleep."

Richard didn't move or say anything at all. He just lay there looking up at the ceiling, trying desperately to make sense of everything.

She could sense that he was not in the mood for therapy, but she needed to do her job. "David, I can totally understand that you're tired and you need some time alone to sort out your thoughts, but if you would allow me to do what I need to do, I promise you that it will only take me a few minutes."

He shifted his eyes to her. "Could we skip therapy for today and just talk?"

She smiled pleasantly at him as she politely insisted, "Why don't you talk and I'll do my best to answer you while we do your therapy."

While she started in on his toes, slowly massaging and bending each of them one at a time, he began to ask his questions. "How did I end up in here?"

"I was told that you were in a car accident and you were in a coma as a result of it," she replied as she worked diligently on his legs.

"Why don't I remember anything?" He squinted and frowned a little as she bent one of his legs a little too far inward.

"I don't know, but you were in a coma for quite a long time. I'm definitely optimistic that you will regain some of your memories," she replied as she continued working on his legs.

"I have all my memories," he said. "I remember everything in my life up to this point. I just can't understand why people keep referring to me as David Voss."

She stopped and looked at him, intrigued. "People call you that name because you *are* David Voss."

He took a deep breath and slowly let it out. "My name is Richard Bennett. Could you please call me Richard instead of David?"

"Of course, if you prefer it, I'll call you Richard."

"Mary, right?"

"Yes."

"Will you please tell me where I'm at?"

"You are in the Metro State Hospital in New York City."

"New York City? How did I end up in New York City?" The question was directed more at himself than at her.

"You live here," she replied with a smile.

He was shocked. He became silent for a brief moment to gather his thoughts before he said anything else. He knew that everything he said would sound weird to her. He also knew that she wasn't going to believe him, but he needed to talk to someone.

He pondered for a while, and then looked at her. "Would you believe me if I tell you that I was born in the city of Atkins and I've lived in Atkins all my life?"

She looked at him with another curious expression, and then gave him a reassuring smile. "I'm sorry. It's not that I don't believe you. It's just that I've never heard of such a city."

Feeling frustrated and defeated, Richard collapsed back onto the bed. Mary continued to work on his legs and arms.

"Okay, good work, Richard, and thank you for allowing me to do my job," she said. "I have about an hour before my next patient. Would you still like to talk?"

He looked at her with a deep sense of despair and then glanced away. "All I have are questions. I don't think you're going to satisfy me with any of the answers."

She slowly seated herself next to the bed, and in a nonjudgmental tone, she softly said, "I'm sorry, Richard. I know that none of the answers I have at this time will satisfy your questions, but I'm a very good listener. If you don't mind sharing, I will sit here and just listen."

Without looking at her, he let out a deep sigh. "I'm very confused right now, and I'm desperately wanting to go back home." Even though his voice was strong, she could see that tears had begun to form at the corners of his eyes.

She didn't know what to say in return, so she kept her promise to simply listen. As she sat there silently listening, she was intrigued by his amazing and captivating story. The love he and this woman, Elizabeth, had shared was phenomenal. She was astonished at how he kept her so close to his heart. His description of every beautiful moment was detailed so clearly that she felt as if she, too, was living in the moment with them. It was a wonderful love story. *This is how a man should love a woman*, she thought.

As she sat quietly, pondering this man's extraordinary dream, there was a loud knock at the door. Two men entered the room.

The tall, blond guy, who was dressed in a white suit with a blue T-shirt, waved his hand in the air as he greeted Richard. "Hey, buddy! How are ya?"

Both Richard and Mary looked at each other with curious expressions. The two men approached Richard's bed and walked around to stand opposite Mary.

"We'll take it from here, sweetheart," said the blond guy, with a flirtatious smile.

Richard didn't know what to say or do. He had no idea who these men were and thought they were somewhat rude and annoying.

"I have to go to my next appointment, Richard," Mary said, getting up. "I'll see you at our next session." She quickly got up to leave, trying not to make eye contact with the men, especially the blond one.

"I'm sorry you have to leave so soon. I'll be looking forward to the next session," Richard said as he watched her walk toward the door.

"Hey, when you're done with your next appointment, how about making an appointment with me?" the blond guy said. Mary turned back to smile pleasantly at them and then quickly left the room.

"How are you feeling, Davey Boy?" the blond guy asked.

Richard squinted intensely before he asked, "I'm sorry, but do I know you guys?"

The two men stared at each other for a couple of seconds and then laughed out loud. The blond guy turned to Richard again and replied, "Sure you do. I'm, Hal, and that's Mark. We're your best buds, dude."

"I'm sorry that I don't remember you guys. I've heard that I've just woken up from a long coma. It'll take a while for my memories to come back," Richard calmly explained.

"Great! When you're all better, we'll go party, get wasted, and get laid by an ungodly amount of chicks—just like the old days," Mark said.

Richard was appalled. There was no way on earth he was going to hang out with these two idiots. How and where did David meet such rude and obscene people? Or was he a lewd idiot, too, just like them? The thought of it gave him the chills.

He wanted nothing to do with them; however, he did desperately need information. Perhaps they could help him learn more about this David Voss that he had been hearing about ever since he woke up.

"Maybe you guys can help me with my memory. If you don't mind, I'd like to ask you a few questions about me."

"Sure thing, dude," Hal replied. "Ask us anything."

"What was I like?" Richard quickly asked.

"Dude, you were the bomb! You screwed almost every chick in the city!" Hal proudly acclaimed.

"Dude, you're the man!" Mark quickly cut in.

"Where did I live, and what did I do for a living? Did I even have a job?" Richard asked.

"Dude, your old man is so loaded," Hal replied. "He owns tons of properties throughout the entire city. You never needed a job."

"What did I do every day?"

"Man, you were so wasted every day. Who knows what all you did," Mark replied laughingly.

"Yeah, sometimes we partied all night at your crib and woke up the next day with naked chicks sleeping everywhere," Hal proudly added.

"Did I even have a family?"

"Yeah," Hal said. "But your mom died two years ago when you were still in the coma, leaving your old man alone to take care of you. A year before your accident, your sister took off with a Chinese guy to Hong Kong and you were pissed as heck. You said that she was no longer your sister because she ran off with that slanty-eyed chink. You also said that you ain't gonna be an uncle to her chinky babies." He burst into laughter.

Richard's eyes widened in shock as he listened to Hal speak about David. Good god, what kind of a man was this David Voss? Was he just an ill-mannered and ignorant bigot who did nothing but drink, party, and screw around? How insulting and unfair to Richard to even be called 'David Voss'!

"Thanks, guys, for your help. If you don't mind, I'd like to get some rest."

"No problem, dude," Hal replied. "Call us when you get back to your crib. We'll come over to help you host the most awesome welcome-back party ever."

"What a waste of human flesh," Richard whispered softly under his breath as he watched them leave the room. He sat up in his bed for a moment, trying to comprehend his ordeal.

"What did I do wrong, God? For what reason did you bring me here?" he asked aloud as he looked up at the ceiling. He placed both of his hands on his face and cried quietly for a moment. Soon his crying became louder and louder.

As he continued to cry with his face deeply buried inside his hands, he felt a gentle pat on his shoulder. He looked up and saw Marshall was standing next to him.

Marshall looked at Richard with compassionate eyes as he pulled him into his arms for a tight embrace. "David, I know it's hard for you to understand everything right now, but in time, your memories will return and you'll see that everything isn't so strange after all."

"I'm so frustrated," Richard said with streams of tears gushing down his cheeks. "I can't remember anything about you or about me being David at all. The only memories I have are sweet and loving memories of Richard Bennett and his beautiful wife and son that he left behind. I don't belong here."

"You are my son," Marshall said softly, his eyes brimming with tears. "You were taken from me for five years, and during those five years I missed you every single day."

Richard looked at Marshall with a deep sense of empathy for him. He himself had lost his son for five years, and he knew how devastating that felt. "I'm sorry, sir. I wish that I could help you bring your son back, but I don't know how to do that. All I know at this point is that I'm not who you believe me to be, and I'm so desperately wanting to go home to my wife and son. My heart and soul are hurting deeply; I wish I could just close my eyes and go back to where I was."

"I know that everything is very difficult for both of us to accept right now," Marshall said, placing his hand on Richard's shoulder. "I'm a stranger to you and you are now a stranger to me, but I cannot begin to express the joy and happiness that fills my heart just to be able to see and talk to you again." He let out a deep sigh. "I will be patient. I will wait for you to return to your old self. That much, I have hope for."

"I understand what you are saying, sir, but my heart is crying so fervently for my family—the loving family I left behind. Even if I have to remain here, I can't promise you that I will ever be the same again. I can't make any promises that I will ever fulfill your dreams of becoming your beloved son—the son you want me to be."

Marshall sat down on the bed beside Richard and looked into his eyes for a moment. Then he slowly reached out one hand to wipe away Richard's tears. "Please give it some time, David. You'll have your memories back, and everything will be back to normal again. You are my only son, and I don't want to lose you again." Marshall slowly stood up, and then bent down to give Richard a gentle kiss on his head. He sighed deeply before he turned around and walked out the door.

Richard sat on the bed, still trying to understand this whole ordeal. What he wouldn't do to see Elizabeth and touch her again. How could God allow him a glimpse of Heaven and then take him away and put him in Hell? Was God punishing him for something he did? Was he doomed to live in this world alone?

# Chapter Thirty-One

Each day after his awakening, Richard couldn't eat, couldn't sleep—he couldn't even smile properly. His life came to a complete halt once again, and this time around was a hundred times worse than when Elizabeth left him. At least then, he still had her room and her personal belongings as memories. He could still revisit the places where they used to go together. He could still walk around places he knew and was familiar with.

Now that he was in a totally new location, a completely changed world where everything was strange and everyone was a stranger to him, the only thing he could do was to focus on the pain his heart was bearing. He couldn't even cry anymore. His tears had either dried up or he was too tired to cry. He was exhausted—tired of trying to remember who he was, not knowing what to do, trying to understand this whole ordeal. He felt so trapped and so out of place—as if he had done something wrong that he was being punished for.

For almost a month, with Mary's help, he had begun to walk on his own and was due to be released from the hospital that afternoon. He was now sitting inside his room, anxiously waiting for Mary's arrival. She had promised him that she would visit him one more time before his release. He had developed a strong attachment to her and couldn't understand why he was feeling so happy each time he was with her. Perhaps, besides Marshall, she was the only person who was there for him. She seemed to be genuinely understanding of his unfortunate predicament.

Mary surprised him when she entered his room with a wheelchair.

"What's this?"

Mary laughed softly. "It's a wheelchair, silly. I'm taking you down to the front entrance in this."

"Come on, Mary, I can walk out of here on my own," he insisted.

"I believe you, but I'm sorry, Richard—it's hospital policy. You have to be wheeled out of the hospital."

He reluctantly got into the chair and she pushed him to the elevator. They went down to the lobby and were soon heading out toward the front entrance. "This is embarrassing, Mary. People are staring."

"Just smile, Richard. This might be the only time you'll ever get to be wheeled by me," she said, laughing. "Hang in there, we're almost done. Just a few more steps and you can get out."

As they exited the front doors, he noticed a black limousine parked inside the driveway. "Where are we going?" he asked.

"Your father wanted you to be at the house for a few days. He wanted you to be fully recovered before you go back to your apartment."

He looked at her with a despairing expression. "Mary, this is the first time that I've been outside this hospital. I don't recognize anything or know anyone except for you and Marshall. I feel so lost in this wide and strange world."

"That's not true. You have friends. I've seen them. They visited you a while back," she joked.

He laughed loudly. "*Really?* Do you really believe that I would hang out with *those guys?* Seriously, I have no clue who they are."

He wanted to ask her to come with him, but he paused, thinking that it might be a little too brash. He didn't want to be a burden to her, but he needed her. He needed her to go along with him to make the transition a little more bearable. He looked up at her with a hesitant but hopeful expression and asked, "Will you come with me to make things a little easier for me?"

She looked at him and smiled. "Of course, Richard. Actually, I was supposed to go there with you, but I'm delighted for the invite anyway."

As they approached the limo, the driver came out to open the door. "How are you doing, Mr. Voss? My name is Ted."

"Hello, Ted. I apologize if I am supposed to recognize you," Richard said as he got out of the wheelchair.

The limo made its way onto the 59th Street Bridge and cruised over the East River. Richard turned his head and was amazed at the picture-perfect view of Manhattan behind him. "Wow, this city is beautiful," he said.

Mary looked at him with a funny expression and smiled. She had seen this view thousands of times, but then she remembered Richard's memory loss.

"I agree," she said. "This is indeed a very beautiful city. The view of Manhattan from here has always been one of my favorites, especially at night when the city is lit up."

Richard became silent and kept looking out the window. He was desperately hoping to see a familiar place, a building, or a sign that could help him with his memories, but there wasn't one. Engrossed in his thoughts, he didn't speak to Mary for much of the ride.

The limo came to Starr Lane and made a left turn. About thirty minutes later, they arrived at the entrance of an enormous white mansion. As the limo slowly made its way along the brick road to the house, Richard noticed dozens of cars.

"What's going on here?"

"Richard, your father had planned a surprise welcome home party for you. I wasn't supposed to tell you, but I do feel that you've had enough surprises already."

He chuckled. "Well, it's not much of a surprise when the rows of cars sort of gave it away now, is it?"

She laughed loudly. "If you could, at least try to act surprised. Your father went to a lot of trouble."

He chuckled again. "I'll do my best to act surprised."

The limo stopped directly in front of the house and Ted quickly came out to open the door for them. As soon as Richard stepped out of the limo, he slowly looked around, hoping that something would spark his memory. But as he'd expected, he found nothing. He turned around and reached out to help Mary out of the limo.

The two of them entered the house and stood in the lobby for a moment. Richard scanned the room, searching for something—anything—that might be familiar. Finding nothing, he continued down the lobby with Mary, soon arriving at the entrance to an enormous living room.

"SURPRISE!" a chorus of voices yelled out as the two of them walked in. Richard was taken aback. He was expecting perhaps a few dozen people, but instead there seemed to be hundreds. *If only I could remember them*, he thought— even just one of them. But he couldn't. They all seemed to be complete strangers to him.

However, despite the fact that no one and nothing seemed familiar to him, the outpouring of love and support filled Richard with happiness. As the guests came up one by one to introduce themselves, he was grateful to find that everyone was so considerate and understanding about his memory loss.

After he had met most of the guests, he was approached by a very pretty brunette with shoulder-length hair. He could see that her blue eyes were rimmed with tears as she attempted to smile cheerfully at him. She was silent, and it seemed as if she was desperately trying to remain composed.

Eventually, she reached out and gave him a long, warm embrace. "I'm so happy to see you again, David," she said as she started to cry. She held him tightly for a moment and then pulled back to look at him again.

Richard was sad, not only because he couldn't remember her, but also because he didn't know how to return her affection.

She noticed his puzzled expression. "I'm sorry, David, I almost forgot. You probably think I'm just another weird stranger. I'm your sister, Heather," she said, half-laughing and half-crying as she wiped away her tears.

"I'm so sorry, Heather. I just don't recognize anyone. I'm happy to see you, too, even though it feels like this is my first time seeing you. But I trust that you do understand my situation," he said sweetly, trying to comfort her.

"It's all right, David. Don't worry about it—I do understand. You just get well quickly, okay?" she said with a sob.

Richard noticed a tall Asian man standing a few feet behind Heather and smiled warmly at him, motioning for him to come closer. He noticed the man's hesitance and was a little puzzled at his behavior. Nevertheless, Richard kept smiling and took a step toward the man, trying to make him feel welcome. He saw a slight change in the man's facial expression as he, too, took a couple of steps toward Richard and smiled at him in return.

"David, I know that we are not the best of friends," the man said, "but I'm truly happy to see you and to know that you are doing well." He noticed that Richard was puzzled. "You may have forgotten who I am. I'm Benny Wong. I'm your brother-in-law."

Richard smiled. "I'm very pleased to meet you, Benny. If we were not the best of friends in the past, please accept my apology. If I could only remember what I did, I would make it up to you somehow. Even though I feel like we've just met, I'm honored to have you as a brother." He reached out and warmly shook Benny's hand.

The overwhelming support from the crowd of strangers both delighted Richard and saddened him. Marshall, Heather, and Benny were all very loving and supportive, and he felt blessed that David had such a wonderful father, sister, and brother-in-law. But Richard felt as if he was adopted into their family. The more he thought about it, the sadder he became. He felt lonely—despairingly alone in a room full of strangers. It seemed to him like a cruel joke that God had played on him and everyone in the room.

Mary had remained behind, near the entrance. She saw Richard in the far corner of the room surrounded by his family, yet to her he seemed to be all by himself. As she walked closer to him, she noticed that his eyes were glistening with tears. She could feel his pain, and even though she was a few steps away, she felt as if she could hear his heart crying.

She quietly walked up to him and took his hand in hers. She squeezed it a bit and whispered softly, "Are you all right?"

He glanced away, trying to hide his tears from her. "I'm okay, really," he replied quietly. "Everything just seems a bit much for me at this time. That's all."

"Everything will eventually start to make sense, Richard," she said softly, squeezing his hand again.

"Thank you, Mary. You are the only friend I have in this whole world. I mean it, and you should know how much it means to me to have you stand tall and confidently beside me."

Richard was becoming tired. As much as he tried to enjoy himself, the evening seemed to drag on and on. He kept looking at the clock, wondering how long the guests would stay.

It wasn't until late in the evening that the guests began to leave. One by one, they approached him to bid him farewell and wish him luck on his recovery. He was very appreciative of their warm and loving words, but at the same time he was feeling a deep sense of despair. He felt he had a story hidden in his heart that needed to come out, but no one would understand or believe him. Therefore, he maintained a cheerful face and politely thanked them as they left the room.

The only remaining guest was Mary, who had promised to stay a while longer. She and Richard walked over and sat on a couch, and Heather and Benny soon joined them.

Richard wanted to know more about who David Voss was, and there was no one more qualified to tell him than David's sister. He looked over at Heather, and with a sincere and curious expression, he asked, "So, Heather, what was I like growing up?"

She turned to him. "Well, you were kind and thoughtful," she said, before quickly glancing away.

"Come on. Tell me the truth," he insisted.

She looked back at him. "Are you sure?" she asked.

"Yes, and be brutally honest," he replied with a smile.

Heather looked straight at him. Then she let out a deep sigh before she began. "Honestly, you were a brat. You were a spoiled little brat who wanted everything and never thought or cared about anyone else's feelings," she said. "You were ignorant, snobbish, inconsiderate, and self-centered. You had no goals, no aspirations in life, and you took advantage of everyone who loved you. All that you've cared about in life is hanging out with your simple-minded friends and partying with them. Honestly, David, you were a very bad person."

"I *was?*" Richard exclaimed, shocked. How could he possibly have been such a person? he wondered. In his other life as Richard, he had always been thoughtful, generous, and compassionate. David led a life that went against his every principle, and he hated that.

"That's the honest truth, David," Heather replied sincerely. "It was very hard growing up with you. I'm sorry to be so blunt, but you did ask for the truth."

Richard was still shocked. He had seen such behavior before in his mother and in Angela. He never thought that he could be anything like them. He sighed deeply. "I'm truly sorry, Heather. I'm sorry for what I've put you through. I wish that I could go back in time to undo everything that I've done. It must have been hard for you to even look at me. It's incredible to me that I have a sister who still loves me after all I put her through."

Heather smiled.

"I'm a new man now, and I promise to be a much better brother to you," Richard said.

"I'm going to mark your words, David," Heather said in a stern voice. Then she smiled again and added, "I loved you very dearly then, and I still love you very dearly now."

Richard turned to Benny. He knew from talking to Hal that David was an insensitive bigot, which had probably caused a great deal of animosity between David and his brother-in-law. Whatever David had done in the past, he was going to apologize to this good man and start anew with him. "Benny, I can't remember what I did in the past, but I'm sure it wasn't pleasant. I'm sorry if I've hurt you in any way. If it's not too late, I would like to start over with you."

Benny smiled warmly and gently placed a hand on Richard's shoulder. "Don't worry about me, David. It has all been forgiven. Let's not dwell on the past. I'm just so happy to see that you're doing well."

Unbeknownst to Richard, Marshall had been standing behind him and was listening in on the conversation. He quietly came over and sat next to Richard. With tears in his eyes, Marshall said, "I don't know what happened to you while you were sleeping, son, but I'm really enjoying this change in you. I only wish that your mother were still alive to see it with me."

Richard felt another rush of sadness. His chest began to tighten and the air felt too thick for him to inhale. He didn't even know this family—why was he so emotional all of the sudden? Could it be that he somehow felt a bond with them but just wasn't aware of it? Or was he sad because he felt sorry for them?

He immediately reached out his arms to embrace Marshall. "Father, please forgive me for being such a bad son to you. I promise you that I will be a better person for as long as you'll be alive to see me. I have a feeling that I wouldn't like who I used to be."

The five of them chatted very late into the evening. When Richard saw Mary glance at her watch, he asked, "Mary, if you don't mind, could I speak with you alone for a moment before you leave?"

Mary looked at the others, who smiled at her with approving eyes. "Sure, David," she said as she got up and followed him to the hallway.

"What is it?" she asked curiously.

He looked at her with an expression of desperation. "I have a silly, childish request. I really don't know these people. Besides Marshall, this is the first time that I've ever met Heather and Benny. Would it be too much if I ask you to spend the night here? It might make it easier for me."

"I'm sorry, Richard, I've got an appointment early in the morning. I have to get back home," Mary hesitantly replied. "Besides, I didn't bring anything to change into and I don't know anyone here either, besides you and Marshall."

She noticed the disappointment on Richard's face. "I'll tell you what," she said. "After the appointment tomorrow, I'm free for the rest of the afternoon. Why don't you get some rest tonight, and when I'm done with my appointment, I'll come back here."

"You promise?" he asked.

"Of course, I promise."

"Then you should go. It's getting very late."

"Good night, Richard," she said and walked out to the waiting limousine.

Richard went back into the living room to say good night to everyone, and then Marshall led him to David's childhood bedroom. Richard was quite impressed with the decorations. The blue walls were plastered with paintings of Superman, Batman, and Spider-Man.

He looked over at an enormous oak dresser and saw several model cars displayed on top of it. To the left of his bed was a black nightstand with a dimly lit small lamp. Even though the room hadn't been used for years, it was kept up quite well. It seemed to be frozen in time, just waiting for his return.

"Thank you, Father," he said quietly as his thoughts drifted back to his other life. He felt a tear trickle down his cheek as he wondered if Elizabeth or his parents would try to keep his apartment clean and dust-free, waiting for his return.

Marshall noticed his son's sadness, so he gently placed his hand on Richard's shoulder and squeezed it a little. "Welcome home, son. Don't think too much—just have a restful night. Tomorrow will be a new, fresh day."


Richard lay in his childhood bed tossing and turning, unable to sleep. The mattress was soft and comfortable, but it was his first time in this strange bed.

He got up and went over to the window. The moon was bright and full in the night sky. As he stared out into the vast universe, he pondered his life.

"So, this is it?" he whispered. "*This* is who I am? I'm a stranger in this world. I'm a stranger to myself. What will become of me? What *must* become of me?" Tears rolled silently down his cheeks.

# Chapter Thirty-Two

R ichard? Wake up. Wake up, Richard," said a sweet, angelic voice—a voice he knew. A voice he loved listening to.

He slowly opened his eyes to see Elizabeth's smiling face looking down at him as his head was resting comfortably on her lap. "Elizabeth? Is it really you?"

"Yes, it's me," she replied softly, gently combing her fingers through his hair.

"I've missed you so much," he said with a soft sob. "Please don't leave me again."

She smiled warmly and reached out her hand to gently place it on his chest. "I never left you, Richard. I'm right here, inside your heart. The love you have for me will always be here with you, my darling." She paused for a moment before letting out a deep, trembling sigh. "Now," she continued, "you must wake up."

*Why must I wake up when I am here with her now?* he asked himself. "I'm awake now. I woke up to you," he said softly.

She reached out a hand to cup his cheek. "You must wake up. You must wake up and fulfill your destiny. Wake up, Richard. Wake up." Her voice seemed to grow louder and louder.

A bird was chirping loudly as Richard opened his eyes suddenly and sat upright in his bed. He glanced at the open window and noticed the sun was high in the sky. He looked around, only to discover that he was still in David's room. Elizabeth was just a dream. It had all seemed so real for a moment—her touch, her sweet whispering voice, the warmth of her body—it all seemed like she was really there with him. How could he wake up to this emptiness? How could he move on from here?

With tears in his eyes, he began to wonder how he could possibly live the rest of his life feeling this lonely and empty. If the only way to see Elizabeth was in his dreams, then he wanted to sleep forever. His head slowly sank back to the softness of his pillow. His eyes closed again, and his heart ached as he tried desperately to fall back to sleep. But he couldn't.

He thought back to the dream and couldn't understand why she was telling him to wake up and to fulfill his destiny. Was she trying to give him some kind of a clue about how to get back? What was his destiny? Was he ever going to find it? All he knew was that he was desperately lost in this strange world and unable to understand who he was.

After despairing for a while, he got dressed and went downstairs to the living room, and noticed it was empty. He went back to the hallway and followed it to a set of double doors at the far end of the house. The doors opened into an enormous backyard. With the afternoon sun shining just over him, he squinted his eyes and looked out at the horizon where the ocean met the sky. The view was breathtaking.

As he continued scanning the area, he saw a large white gazebo about fifty yards away, near the shore. From afar, he could see that a couple of people were inside it. *That's probably where everyone is*, he thought as he quickly walked toward it.

As he approached the gazebo, he could see Marshall, Heather, and Benny inside, but Mary was nowhere in sight. He felt slightly disappointed. Not that he wasn't happy to see them; he was just hoping to see Mary there because he was most comfortable with her.

"Hey, good afternoon, little brother," Heather said cheerfully as he entered the gazebo.

"Did you sleep well?" Marshall asked.

"Yes," Richard simply replied.

"You must be hungry. We'll be having lunch in here soon," Heather said as she reached a hand over and rubbed the top of his head.

He smiled warmly at her and then went over to look out the windows of the gazebo. "Did Mary come?" he asked as he stared at the horizon.

"She called and said that she was going to be a little late," Marshall replied.

"I like her, David," Heather said with a smile. "She is kind, smart, and very pretty." Richard turned to her and smiled. Then he quickly turned back to look out the window again.

He looked out another window and spotted a small figure outside the rear doors of the house. *That must be Mary*, he thought. He watched in excitement as her long and slender legs slowly strode toward the gazebo. She smiled as she noticed him eyeing her through the windows.

"Hello, Mary. Thank you for coming," Marshall said joyfully.

"Hello, Mr. Voss," she said. Then she turned to Richard and greeted him kindly. "Hello, David. How are you doing today?"

"I'm doing much better. Thanks for being here," he replied.

"You're just in time for lunch, Mary. I hope you're hungry," Heather said.

"I'm starving," she replied as she glanced at Richard.

After lunch, Richard decided to take Mary out to explore the grounds. He had no idea why he wanted to go for the walk. All he knew was that there was an overwhelming urge in his heart—an urge to find something to help ease the lingering pain within it.

As they walked away from the gazebo, he turned to her and said, "I would love to show you around here, but like you, I'm not familiar with this place. I'm just as lost as you are." She laughed sweetly as they continued down the narrow trail that led to the beach.

They were just a few hundred yards away from the house when they reached the base of a rocky hill.

"Let's climb that hill!" she said excitedly.

Richard looked up the hill. "It looks kind of steep," he said, hesitating. "There could be loose rocks."

"Where's your sense of adventure, Richard?" she asked, smiling teasingly. "You just follow me." With that, she began to slowly ascend the hill.

He stood still for a moment and was surprised at how easily she maneuvered her way up the rocky terrain. He took one last look at the hill and then slowly followed after her.

After reaching the top, they stood there for a while. Richard was silent as he stared down at the Voss Mansion. The windows of the enormous house sparkled brightly in the sun. He shifted his eyes to the ocean and the blurred line between it and the sky. The vast horizon stretched for miles, as if to suggest that the possibilities were infinite in this world. The beautiful ocean backdrop and the acres of green vegetation made the Voss Mansion look eerily similar to the Atkins Mansion.

"Are you okay?" Mary asked gently.

"Yeah," he replied faintly.

"Richard, whatever is troubling you, you know you can trust me."

He looked away from her and quietly said, "I grew up in a house very similar to this."

Mary's eyes grew wide with excitement. "Richard!" she said. "Could this mean that your memories are returning?"

"No, Mary. I have no recollection of this particular area or this house. What I meant was that this view reminded me of my home in Atkins," he explained.

She remained silent for a moment as she tried to comprehend what she had just heard. "So you grew up by the ocean, in a house like this one?"

"Yes, but the view from afar was way more breathtaking than this view. It would take me all day to describe it to you."

She paused for a few seconds. "Richard, I'm very curious," she said. "Were you in the city of Atkins your entire life?"

"Yes. I really don't belong here," he replied despairingly.

"Do you remember anything about being David Voss?"

He let out a deep sigh, and then replied, "All I can tell you is that David Voss is a stranger to me. I recognize myself—Richard—in the mirror. I feel myself inside my heart, and I know my family and remember each and every one of them like I know the fingers on my hands. I'm Richard Bennett. What I don't know is the reason why I was brought here."

"Who brought you here?" She was now very curious.

He glanced at her for a second and then glanced away. "Even if I tell you, you wouldn't believe me."

"I promise to keep an open mind."

He studied her for a moment before drawing in a deep breath and releasing it slowly. "There was a very bright light at my window," he explained. "As the bright light expanded, I saw two formless beings come out of it. I tried to fight them off, but they were too strong and they took me into the light. The next thing I knew was that I woke up at the hospital."

Mary listened, fascinated. Every moment he had lived in his other world was described in perfect detail, making his story seem so real.

As a person who was educated in the medical field, she was skeptical and was trying very hard to find a logical explanation to this. But she also had a strong spiritual upbringing and was intrigued by the possibility of an afterlife.

They continued on a small worn-down path and came upon a cave underneath a rocky cliff. She wanted to press forward, but he stopped her. "Wait!" he exclaimed. "I remember something about this place."

"What?" she quickly asked. "What do you remember?" She waited patiently, not wanting to interrupt his thinking.

"There's something familiar about this place," he said with his eyes fixed on the small entrance. "I have a strong feeling that I have been here before."

They walked to the cave and entered it. Inside they could see a small, old chair on the ground next to a huge rock that resembled a table. Next to the chair was a kerosene lamp. Both of the items looked as if they hadn't been used in years.

As they approached the rock, they noticed something written on it. The words, written in what appeared to be white chalk, read, "David's Place. Keep Out!"

"This is so strange, Mary. This place looks so familiar to me, but I don't remember ever being here."

"Richard, if you can remember this place, that might prove that you are David."

"It couldn't be," Richard mumbled, bewildered. "I remember everything about my childhood back in Atkins, and I know that I'm Richard, not David."

"But doesn't it give you some sort of comfort that your memories are beginning to return?"

"I don't know," he said despairingly. "I don't know who I am anymore."

She gently placed a hand on his shoulder. "I'm sorry, Richard. I wish I could give you some kind of explanation."

"Let's get out of here, Mary. This place somehow gives me a weird vibe."

They left the cave and continued on down the trail. As they approached a large brown house, they noticed a huge black dog growling and running straight toward them. They had no choice but to brace themselves for an attack.

As Richard frantically looked around for something to defend them, he heard a woman's voice calling for the dog. "Gus! Stop! Come here!" The dog stopped and ran back in the direction of the voice.

A few seconds later, a woman appeared from behind the house. She was tall and slender, and seemed to be the same age as Heather.

Her eyes widened when she saw Richard. "David? Oh my god! David, is it really you?" she exclaimed as she quickly ran to him and gave him a big hug.

Richard was so caught off guard that he immediately took a couple of steps backward to catch himself from falling. "I'm sorry, but do I know you?" he asked puzzling.

The woman took a step back and gave him a confused look. "I'm Emily. Emily Maxtor. You used to come here all the time. You and my younger brother Paul were best friends." She stopped and looked him over. Could she have been mistaken about this guy? she wondered. Was he not David? But he looked just like David.

With an even greater confused expression on her face now, she asked, "Do you not remember me? Do you remember Paul?"

He looked at her, equally confused. "Emily and Paul . . ." he pondered. "You'll have to forgive me. The names and even your face don't ring a bell at all."

Emily looked at him with a sympathetic expression. "It's all right, David. I heard about your accident. Anyways, Paul will be thrilled to hear that you're out and about."

Emily quickly turned to Mary and introduced herself. "Hello. I'm sorry for being so rude. I'm Emily."

"It's nice to meet you. I'm Mary."

"So, where is . . . Paul?" Richard quickly cut in.

"Paul lives in Florida with his family now. He got married shortly after your accident."

"Oh," Richard said. "Is he doing well?"

"Yes, he's doing very well. He owns and runs a tourist business in Miami, and I heard that it is also doing very well."

"What about you, Emily?" Richard asked.

"Well, I'm still home with my parents," she replied with a deep sigh. "I'm still single and searching. It's hard to find Mr. Right when I'm always home, taking care of things."

"Well, you've always been the responsible one," he said quietly. "And you've always taken care of your parents for as long as I can remember." He instantly froze as soon as he heard his voice saying those words. He had no idea why he'd just said that. How did he suddenly remember that she was the responsible one in her family, when he had only met her a few minutes ago? There was something eerie about the whole interaction. *What's going on here?* he wondered.

Mary, too, had a puzzled expression on her face.

As he continued staring at Emily, a sudden rush of anxiety overwhelmed him. His mind was filled with agonizing questions. Was it true that he had been dreaming the whole time he was in the coma? Were Elizabeth, Edward, his parents, and even Angela—were they all a mere dream? No. He couldn't bring himself to believe that his life in Atkins was just a dream.

Richard felt the need to leave, so he politely excused himself and motioned for Mary to continue their walk. The afternoon was getting warmer, but the breeze from the ocean was cool and refreshing. The sound of the gentle waves was calming and soothing. Still, Richard remained disconnected. He stopped and stood silently, his eyes again staring out at the horizon.

Mary knew he was lost in his thoughts. "Are you all right?" she asked, but he paid no attention as he looked up at the sky. She asked him again as she reached out a hand and placed it gently on his shoulder.

Startled by her touch, he suddenly snapped out of his trance and quickly turned to her.

"You seemed like you were very far from here. I'm just wondering if you're okay."

"Oh, I'm just a little confused, that's all," he replied faintly.

"A little confused is an understatement. Your mind seemed to be millions of miles away."

He smiled warmly at her before turning his attention back to the horizon. After a while, he looked at her and said, "It has been a long day. Are you ready to go back?"

"I was just about to ask you the same question," she replied, smiling.

They followed the shore back to the gazebo. Marshall, Heather, and Benny were still inside, enjoying the cool ocean breeze.

"So, how did the walk turn out?" Marshall asked.

"It was a very pleasant walk," Mary replied. "The weather was beautiful, and the ocean view was fantastic."

"We came upon a cave at the base of a cliff. Do you know anything about that cave?" Richard asked Marshall.

"Oh, yes," Marshall replied. "That cave was your favorite hideout place when you were little. Whenever I couldn't find you here, I would go to the cave and you would always be there."

"Did you guys make it to the Maxtor house?" Heather asked.

"Yes. We met Emily there," Mary replied.

"Oh, really," Heather said. "How's Emily? I haven't seen her for quite some time now."

"Looks like she is doing well," Richard replied.

"That's good to know. I was planning on visiting her and her parents before Benny and I leave for home."

"'Leave for home'?" Richard asked, frowning. "When are you going back home?"

Heather noticed the despairing look on his face, so she took a step closer to him and gently caressed his cheek with her hand. "We're going back this Saturday, David. Benny and I have some business to tend to."

"We'll be back in about three months," Benny said as he gently placed a hand on Richard's shoulder to reassure him.

It had been a long afternoon. This first walk in Richard's new world had been perhaps the loneliest walk he had ever taken, even though Mary had been with him.

Mary soon excused herself, leaving Richard alone with his new family. He still felt strange around them, but he needed them now because, besides Mary, they were his only source of comfort.

# Chapter Thirty-Three

Two long weeks had gone by and Richard still couldn't believe that it was all just a dream. His mind had not been able to rest, his heart had not been at peace, and his eyes had not been able to close for more than a few hours every night. He felt like he was abandoned by his own fate and was trapped somewhere deep and dark and that he might never get out of. Even though he strongly believed that he was from Atkins, he knew in his heart that he would have to eventually accept that his whole life in Atkins was merely a dream—a fantasy created in his mind while he was sleeping.

Heather and Benny had gone back home. Marshall asked that Richard stay at the Voss Mansion for a little longer, but he needed to leave. He felt the need to go searching for some answers, or he would never be at peace.

He wished that Mary could be with him to make things more bearable, but he hadn't seen her for a long while. She was always too busy with her job and didn't have time to swing by or even return his messages. So he tried to accept that he would need to endure all his struggles alone.

Today was his first day back at his apartment on the Upper West Side. He looked around it to see if there was anything he could remember, but nothing looked familiar.

Tonight was going to be the longest night for him since he'd come out of the coma. He was now in a strange place, sleeping in a strange bed with totally strange surroundings—and he was all alone. As much as he wanted to try to adapt to this strange new world, he felt like he was invisible in it. He felt like an abandoned child, left alone in a strange place to care for himself.

The next morning, he slowly woke up to the blaring sounds of car horns and car stereos outside his window. Getting out of bed, he pulled the curtains aside for a view of the street. As he stared down at the congested traffic, he was suddenly reminded of the streets of Atkins.

If Atkins was just a dream, a fantasy created by his own mind, then why was his heart so unsettled? Why was his mind so unwilling to forget? What was going on with him?

He suddenly felt the need to leave the apartment. He needed to go somewhere—anywhere—to ease his despair.

He left the building and was soon wandering on a crowded street with no destination in mind. As he ventured off, he began to relax a little. Though everything looked so strange to him and he had no idea where he was going, there was something familiar about these streets. They were overcrowded and filled with life, just like the streets he had walked a thousand times in his make-believe city of Atkins.

He was enchanted by the endless hordes of people scattering everywhere, frantically trying to get where they needed to be. He could imagine how Elizabeth must have felt when she first walked up and down the many tangled streets of Atkins.

As he was just about to cross a busy street, he saw a woman who bore a striking resemblance to Mary standing outside the entrance of a restaurant. He hesitated for a moment, but then he decided to call out to her.

The woman didn't turn around. She hurried away and went into the restaurant. Was that not Mary? Or could it be that she just didn't hear him through the rush of people and the loud noises from the passing cars?

He was a little doubtful, but the woman had to be Mary. Her hair, her body, her height, and even her walk—everything about her was so similar. *Perhaps she just didn't hear me*, he thought. He quickly walked toward the restaurant and went inside.

The woman seated at a table in the middle of the room was indeed Mary. With a smile, he walked up to her and stood before her. She suddenly looked up and was surprised to see him. "Richard?" she gasped.

"Hi! I thought it was you," he said excitedly.

"It's good to see you, Richard. What brings you to this area?"

"I went back to my apartment yesterday and decided to take a tour around the city today. I would like it very much if you could show me around."

"I would love to, but . . .," she said, then frowned slightly. "I'd have to do that another time."

"Not a problem. Whenever you're available," he said. "Have you had lunch? If you don't mind, maybe I could join you?"

She paused for a few seconds and then hesitantly replied, "I wouldn't mind, Richard . . . but I'm here with someone."

Suddenly a voice behind him said, "Excuse me, sir. Can I help you?"

Richard quickly turned around to see a neatly dressed man standing in front of him. Feeling awkward, Richard wasn't sure what to say.

"David, this is my boyfriend, Adam," Mary said. "Adam, this is David Voss."

"Hello, David. It's nice to meet you at last," Adam said pleasantly. "Mary has been telling me a lot about you. Would you like to join us?"

Richard composed himself for a second and then quietly replied, "It's nice meeting you too. I saw Mary walk in, so I came in to say hello to her. Thank you for the invite, and I'm sorry to intrude. You both enjoy your lunch. I'm just out and about for a breath of fresh air."

"Are you sure? We don't mind," Adam said.

"I'm sure. Thanks again and you two have a great day." Richard slowly turned around and walked away.

He left the restaurant with an overwhelming feeling of anxiety. He couldn't comprehend why he was feeling so dejected about what had just happened. Was he falling in love with Mary? he wondered. How could this be? Maybe, in a way, she reminded him of Elizabeth—her gentleness, her understanding, and her warm personality. Or maybe because she was the first person he had connected with since he woke up and she had comforted him. Whatever the reason, he knew that he felt very vulnerable. All he wanted to do at this point was to get as far away from the restaurant as possible.

As he walked quickly down the street, his mind was filled with questions that he had no answers for. He didn't know where he was going. He had no idea what it was he was searching for or what he was hoping to find. *I'll just have to keep on walking*, he said to himself, *and see where the road takes me.*

He stopped at an intersection and stood there, silently staring. People walked up and down the street, crossed the intersection, came and went, but he just stood there as still as a statue. Although his mind wandered, his body didn't move an inch. He wondered what crime he had committed for him to deserve such abandonment.

Finally he decided to continue down the street and was soon overwhelmed by a strong odor of exotic Asian spices. He closed his eyes for a moment and inhaled deeply. This pungent odor was the sweetest scent in the world to him.

He sniffed the air a couple of times to see which direction the aroma was coming from. Following his nose, he walked a few more blocks and noticed the sidewalks were filled with hordes of Asian people. The signs on top of the many businesses, shops, and restaurants were written in Chinese characters, similar to what he saw in the Chinatown in Atkins.

*So, there's a Chinatown here in this city?* he asked himself. *Is there a reason I stumbled in this direction? Maybe there are some answers here to my thousands of questions.*

As he slowly maneuvered through the crowded streets, stopping here and there to gaze at the surroundings, the loneliness in his heart slowly melted away.

He was suddenly reminded of how Elizabeth reacted upon seeing Chinatown. Now, he finally knew how she felt. He, too, felt like he was home.

As he was basking in all the sights and sounds and smells, he came upon a small shop with a sign that read "Mai Lin–Spiritual Reader" above the window. He stopped for a moment. Although he knew he didn't believe in any of that stuff, he was still intrigued.

Still feeling very skeptical, he decided to go inside anyway and give the woman or whoever was doing the reading a run for their money.

"Good afternoon. Are you here for a reading?" asked a young Asian girl inside the shop.

"Yes," he simply replied.

"Okay, have a seat over there and my grandmother will see you in a moment," she said with a pleasant smile.

He sat in the chair next to a small statue of a Buddha. A plate of fresh fruit was placed in front of it. He could smell the odor from the burning sticks of incense that were placed beside it. He suddenly remembered that Elizabeth once told him that Asian businesses often have a statue of a Buddha inside their shops. They would burn incense and put a tray of food or fresh fruit in front of the statue as an offering to bring good luck to their business.

Richard was bewildered. If everything about his life in Atkins was just a dream, then how did he know these things?

"My grandmother is ready to see you now," the young girl said as she came back to the room.

Richard smiled nervously as he got up and followed her to a small, dimly lit room in the back of the shop. He seated himself in a chair at a small table in front of an elderly Asian woman. She smiled warmly at him and then she looked to the girl.

"My grandmother speaks no English, so if you're okay with it, I will have to be the translator for the both of you."

"No. I don't mind at all," Richard said. "I'm glad that you are here to translate."

The elderly woman quietly stared at him for a moment and then said something to the girl in Chinese.

"My grandmother wants you to go over there and pick three flowers, and then bring them back to her," she said, pointing toward a huge pot in the corner of the room.

He nodded and walked over to the flowers. He could see that there were many varieties inside the pot—red, white, yellow, violet, and pink. He carefully examined each flower for a moment, wondering which would be the best choices. Since he didn't know what the colors represented, he decided to just randomly grab three without looking. He closed his eyes and let his hand decide for him.

After he finished grabbing the third flower, he slowly opened his eyes to see that he had chosen three beautiful red flowers.

He brought the flowers back to the elderly woman. As she reached over to take the flowers from him, she took a tight hold of his hand. She held on to it for a moment as if she was trying to transfer some kind of energy into him or out of him, and then slowly released it. She pointed to the chair in front of her and motioned for him to sit.

Richard felt his body turn suddenly cold, and he began to tremble. As he seated his quivering body down on the chair, his eyes were fixed on her, and he wondered what was going to happen next.

The woman clasped her hands together around the flowers. She closed her eyes and whispered softly to herself as if she was saying a prayer. After about a minute or two of whispering, she opened her eyes and said something to the girl. The girl listened carefully and then turned to Richard.

"You are not who you are. You are not from this world. You are from the other side."

Richard's eyes widened and his breathing quickened. He opened his mouth slightly to ask a question, but he was instantly interrupted by the elderly woman. The girl turned to him once again to interpret the woman's message.

"Your soul had been reborn on the other side, but your life here has not ended. You have left your world and cannot go back."

Richard couldn't believe his ears. How could she have known this? His mind began to reel as he blinked through the tears in his eyes. "How I can go back?" he quietly asked.

The girl turned to her grandma and had a short conversation; then she turned back to Richard. "My grandma doesn't know," the girl said. "But she does know death is not the answer. If you take your own life, you will never go back to the place where you came from."

Richard was desperate. "She must know *something*," he pleaded. "There has to be a way back, and I'm begging her to help me. I'm willing to do anything she asks of me."

The woman seemed to understand what Richard had said. Not waiting for a translation, she replied through the girl.

"My grandmother said that your journey will be long. You have very bad karma and you must repay it."

He paused for a few seconds. Then, with a despairing look, he slowly asked, "What is my karma? Could you ask her that? And how can I repay it?"

The elderly woman spoke with a smile on her face now and with her hands waving excitedly in the air. Even though Richard didn't understand what she was saying, her words sounded like music to his ears.

"She said that she can't tell you what your karma is. You will have to find that out on your journey. She also said that you are a great man and you'll do many wonderful things. You are here until your destiny is fulfilled."

His eyes began to fill with tears, and as he wiped them away he suddenly remembered Elizabeth's words for him to wake up and fulfill his destiny. He turned to the elderly woman, and with an earnest expression he asked, "What is my destiny? What do I need to do to fulfill it?"

"My grandmother can't tell you what your destiny is. You must also find it on your journey. It will lead you back to your home."

His heart was crying, not because he didn't know the way back, but because he now knew that it wasn't all a dream. Elizabeth, Edward, and his parents were all real, and he might just get a chance to go back to them.

He let out a deep, heavy sigh at the thought and felt a sense of comfort from what he had just heard. He looked at the elderly woman with gratitude in his eyes. She didn't know him. He was just a complete stranger to her, and for her to be able to know that much about him and his life thus far was truly amazing. At that moment he knew what he needed to do—he had to take on his journey alone and fulfill his destiny, so that he could return to his world someday.

As the girl led him back to the front of the shop, she turned to him and said, "You know, sir. I used to be skeptical about my grandmother's gift. But through the years, after hearing her relay messages to so many people and hearing her predictions about their lives, I've learned to believe her. You, for example, are a total stranger to her, and hearing her reveal your life story that way—to me, that's not bluffing. You even confirmed it yourself. I truly believe that she has a special gift."

Richard nodded in total agreement and said, "Your grandmother is a remarkable woman. Her gift is astonishing. Don't ever doubt her. By the way, what is your name and how old are you?"

"My name is Kate, and I'm 16."

"It's been a pleasure meeting you, Kate. How much do I owe you?"

"$30.00," she replied.

As they approached the front, he noticed that the room was completely empty. He turned to her and asked, "I'm curious, if you don't mind sharing, how much business do you get on a daily basis?"

"Not very much," she replied sadly. "The rent is going up, and I'm not sure if we can stay open much longer."

"Are you just helping your parents out? I'm sorry if I'm being nosy."

"It's okay," she replied. Then she looked at him with a painful expression, as if she was going to cry. She sighed softly. "My parents died when I was very young," she said. "My grandmother raised me all by herself. She is getting very old and can't do anything else except use her gift."

Richard reached out and gently placed a hand on her small shoulders, trying to comfort her as best as he could. "I'm sorry to hear that. I'm sure when you're all done with school, you'll be able to support her," he said kindly, trying to give her some hope.

"I graduated early from high school, but I can't go to college because we have no money and I have to take care of this business by myself. Everything is really tough right now. We're behind on our rent, and I'm not sure what will happen to us if the landlord kicks us out," she said, her eyes brimming with tears.

His heart melted as he stood there listening to her. How could such a young woman have such an enormous burden? She should be out enjoying her life instead of worrying so much about how she and her grandmother were going to survive. He wanted to do something to help ease some of her worries. He looked at her with a warm, comforting expression on his face, and then he softly asked, "How many months are you behind on the rent?"

"Three months." She lowered her eyes. "I'm sorry to tell you all this, but I guess I just needed to talk to someone."

He smiled sweetly at her. "Hey, it's okay to say what's in your heart. I feel lucky to be able to hear your story. By the way, my name is Richard . . . I mean, David."

She looked at him with a curious expression. "Was Richard your name when you were on the other side?"

"Yes," he replied, smiling sweetly.

"What is it like over there?"

"It's beautiful. Everything is beautiful. I have a beautiful wife and an adorable son."

She looked down and quietly said, "I hope someday I'll get to see my parents on the other side. I miss them so much. I'm in desperate need of direction, and they're not here. I don't know what to do." She finally began to cry.

Richard couldn't hold back any longer. He reached out and pulled her into him for a comforting embrace. "Everything is going to be all right. You're on a long journey, just like me. Someday, you'll get to see them," he said.

After crying on his shoulder for a few minutes, she backed away slightly. She looked at him and smiled faintly as she wiped away her tears. "Thank you for being so kind. I'm really sorry for doing this, but I've been keeping everything inside for so long. My grandmother is getting very old, and I don't want to worry her."

"It's quite all right. Sometimes, all you need is a good cry and everything will be a little better. By the way, do you know who owns this building?"

She let out a deep sigh. "The Voss Corporation purchased this building about three years ago. They've been raising the rent ever since they bought the building. I think they're trying to drive everyone out so that they could put some high-end shops in here and some expensive apartment units upstairs. They don't care about people like us. My grandmother and I will have nowhere to go. We will be homeless if they kick us out."

He paused for a second, humiliated by the business practice of his father's company. He knew that he was the one person who could save good people like Kate and her grandmother from complete destitution. This was so wrong, and he was not going to stand by and let it happen.

"I see. Well, I'm thinking that maybe I can do something about it. Don't worry about it or the rent right now," he said with a bright smile as he handed her all the money in his pocket.

"Richard, this is $300.00. You only owe us $30.00," she said, surprised.

He smiled politely at her. "Keep all of it, and buy your grandmother something special. I'll be back in a couple of days."

"You're too kind. Thank you, Richard," she said, her face a combination of joy and surprise.

As he took a cab back to his apartment, he felt heavyhearted about Kate's story. He understood how businesses were run, but the thought of so many people being affected had been bothering him ever since he left the shop. Kate, a young girl being raised by her grandmother—this story sounded very familiar.

Everywhere he went, everything he did, he always ended up with Elizabeth on his mind. He was not going to let his father's company throw Kate and her grandmother out on the streets. They were good people who were simply trying to survive.

It was late in the afternoon when he arrived back at his apartment. As he sat on his couch trying to process everything— Kate and her grandmother, what Kate's grandmother said to him, Elizabeth's words telling him to fulfill his destiny—he felt a tear creep silently down his cheek and land on the back of his hand.

He blinked his eyes a couple of times as he replayed his visit with Kate and her grandmother. The grandmother's words rang loudly in his ears, as if she was sitting there right across from him: "You are a great man and you'll do many wonderful things." He smiled sadly and blinked away a couple of tears.

Then he sat down at the computer and began to research the Voss Corporation. Being a brilliant businessman himself, he knew that he could run the business and use his position to make a difference in many people's lives.

# Chapter Thirty-Four

Richard arrived at the Voss Building and stood there for a while, staring at the enormous structure. As he passed through the entrance, he noticed two security guards sitting behind a large desk inside the spacious lobby. They seemed quite alert and were very watchful of people walking in and out of the building. He walked straight to the desk and asked the guards for directions to Marshall's office.

He got out of the elevator on the twentieth floor with a smile on his face. In a way, he couldn't wait to see Marshall. Perhaps David had been here a thousand times before, but this was Richard's first time, so he decided to start off with a smile.

In the southeast section of the building, a young woman was sitting at a fancy desk in front of a large set of double doors.

"Hello," Richard asked in a pleasant tone. "Is Mr. Voss in?"

"Yes, Mr. Voss is in his office. May I ask if you have an appointment?" the woman replied kindly.

"No, I don't, but—"

"Sir, Mr. Voss is very busy," she interrupted. "You have to have an appointment. He will not see anyone without one."

Richard smiled politely and cheerfully explained, "I'm sure he'd love to see me. I'm his son, David."

"Oh? I'm sorry, sir," she said, blushing. "You must forgive me. I've only been working here for a couple months."

"It's all right. I've been gone for five years, so we've never met," he said.

"Should I let him know that you're here to see him?"

"No," Richard replied as he walked to the doors. "I'd like to surprise him. Thank you."

He quietly entered the office and saw Marshall sitting at his desk, looking at a huge stack of papers. He was so engrossed in his work that he didn't notice Richard standing in front of him.

"Good morning, Father," Richard said cheerfully.

Startled, Marshall looked up, and immediately smiled brightly. "David! What a pleasant surprise! What are you doing here?"

"I was bored, so I decided to come back to work. I do work here, don't I?" Richard asked in a puzzled tone.

Marshall let out a soft sigh and replied, "Well, you do have an office in this building, but you rarely came in."

"I see. Well, I guess it takes being in a long coma for a man to change," he joked. "I want to come back to work more than anything right now, Father. If you don't mind, I'd like to see my office."

Marshall looked at him with an apologetic expression. "Since your accident, I've hired someone else to run the everyday operations, and he has since taken over your office. I'm sorry, David."

"It's not a problem, Father. Just give me a cubicle, and I'll be happy with it."

Marshall paused for a long moment. "No, David," he finally said. "You can have my office."

"What do you mean by that?" Richard asked curiously. "Where will your office be if I take over yours?"

Marshall became very quiet and still. He looked at Richard with a sad and anguished expression on his face. Then, he slowly stepped around his desk to put a hand on Richard's shoulder. "David," he explained, "I've been working hard all my life to build this business for you and Heather. I wanted to make sure that you and your sister were well off and never had to struggle through life like I did. When you got into the accident and were in the coma, all my hopes and aspirations ended. When your mother passed away, I saw myself as an old man who continued to go to work every day with nothing to gain. All the wealth, power, and status meant nothing to me anymore, since I didn't have a family to share it with. I prayed every day that you would wake up so that I could see you once again before I join your mother. And now that you are awake, I want you to handle the business and run it the way you see fit. I want to retire and start enjoying life, because I don't have many years left. It breaks my heart that I will be retiring alone without your mother."

Richard's heart felt heavy and his eyes glistened with tears. He didn't know this man well enough to have a strong father-son bond with him yet, but he knew how it felt to be a father. He would have done the same for Edward. He would have worked hard his whole lifetime, too, just so that Edward wouldn't have to struggle to survive.

Richard had been looking down while he was listening to Marshall. He reached his hand up to wipe away a tear. "Don't worry about the business, Father," he said softly. "I'll do my best to make you proud of me."

With teary eyes himself, Marshall looked at him and said earnestly, "I'm proud of you already, David. I'm sure your mother is watching from above and is proud of you, too."

Richard reached out and gave Marshall a soft, loving embrace. As he hugged Marshall, Richard was convinced that this man had to be his father. Who else could possibly display this kind of emotion toward him? And who else could make Richard this emotional? From now on, he would have to go on living as David and do his best to make Marshall proud.

He then thought about David's mother, and how he would have loved to know her. If only he could see her once, to give her some comfort and closure.

Richard looked at Marshall. "Father," he said sincerely, "Forgive me if this is inappropriate, but it has been on my mind for a couple of days now and I feel the urge to ask you. You already know that I can't remember anything from my past; therefore, I have no recollection of my mother. If you don't mind, I'd like to go visit her. I want to let her know that I'll be fine and for her not to worry about me anymore."

Marshall sighed and smiled. "That's a great idea, David," he said softly. "She'll be happy to see that you've awoken and are doing well."


A short while later, they were riding in a long black limousine down Sarasota Road on Long Island. As they slowly approached the end of the road, Richard could see the entrance to a huge cemetery ahead. He stared at the rows of tombstones, his restless mind wondering what he would say to David's mother. Would she understand and accept him as her son?

He let out a deep sigh. Then he felt Marshall's hand on top of his, taking it and lightly squeezing it. He turned and saw a comforting, reassuring smile on Marshall's face.

The limo came to a stop at the bottom of a small hill, and Marshall led Richard up to a huge white marble gravestone. They stopped a few yards from the headstone and stood there quietly.

Marshall stayed back as Richard approached the stone and noticed the inscription on it: "Joy Voss, Loving mother and wife." His throat suddenly felt tight as he acknowledged his mother silently in his heart.

Marshall took a few steps forward and stood in silence for a moment before he began to speak softly to her. "Have you been well, my dear? Although it has only been a week since I last saw you, it has seemed like a month. I've missed you dearly, but then I think you already know that."

Marshall tried his best to keep his composure. But the overwhelming emotions were too much for him, and he broke down in tears. Richard stood there helpless, as he watched the love that his father displayed toward his mother.

So this was how life had to be, he thought—one person leaves and the other person is left lingering alone in the world? He thought about his own life and how Elizabeth was probably lingering alone in a lonely world as well. He brushed away a tear.

After several minutes had passed, Marshall wiped his eyes and quietly said, "I brought someone here to see you, my dear. David has returned, and he would like to say hello."

Richard lowered his head for a moment before he began to speak. "Hello, Mother. I'm here. Your son is here to see you." His heart felt like it weighed ten pounds, and his voice cracked as he continued to speak to her. "I'm so sorry, Mother. I'm sorry that I made you wait for so long. I'm sorry that I came back so late. And I'm so sorry that I didn't get a chance to say goodbye to you before you left."

The tears flowed down his cheeks. Even though he had never met this woman, he felt weak with emotion. Reaching down, he placed both hands on the headstone to steady himself. Then he just stood there, crying and holding on to the stone.

After a few minutes, he was able to regain his strength and composure. "I promise you, Mother," he said, "from this day on, I will live my life to the fullest and become everything you would have wanted me to be. I promise to make you proud of me." With that, he began to cry again.

After a while, Marshall gently placed a hand on Richard's shoulder. "I know that you're determined to begin work, David, but this has been a tiring day," he said. "We are both drained from this visit. Tomorrow you can shadow me at work. I will request a conference with all the company managers in the building, and I will make it known that you will be in charge of the business from now on."

Even though Richard was eager to start work, he had to agree with Marshall. He needed the afternoon to rest his heart and mind. He needed to go back to Chinatown to inspect Kate and her grandmother's building and find some good reasons to support the decision he was going to make.


Richard woke up bright and early the next day. He was so determined and excited to be at work that he felt his mind hadn't rested at all the whole night.

He walked into the conference room with a great sense of confidence. He delightfully greeted everyone, making sure that he didn't miss anyone as each manager walked in.

After his introduction, Richard spoke positively and diplomatically as he shared his vision of the future of the company. His words were so eloquent and articulate that everyone was impressed. As Richard spoke, Marshall's heart swelled and he beamed with pride. He couldn't help but wonder what had happened that had changed his son so drastically.

"The first order of business is to leave the Rass Building in Chinatown just as it is," Richard said, referring to the building he had visited the day before.

"But, sir, we have spent so much time and money on that building," said a man neatly dressed in a blue suit. "We already have the contractors in place, waiting to renovate the building. The amount of money that we'll be making from that place will be astronomical." The man cleared his throat. "My name is Simon, by the way. I'm the vice president of operations."

"It's nice to meet you, Simon," Richard said. "Thank you for voicing your concern, and I'm grateful to have such dedicated people working for the Voss Corporation. I appreciate the time and effort you put into getting the building renovated for better use. However, the Rass Building has been a part of Chinatown for over a century. Some of the shops were there long before we were even born. I will not tarnish this company's reputation by driving those businesses out. We will renovate the building, but we'll keep everything the way it is."

Richard paused. "I understand that in order for a business to succeed," he continued, "it must continue to grow. The most important goal for a highly successful business is to make money. But to me, it is equally important to gain the trust and respect of the customers and the public. With that being said, I'm delighted to announce that the rents on those shops will be reduced. Our loyal customers and tenants have helped us succeed in this business thus far. In return, we will help them succeed as well. Thank you for your understanding."

Richard turned to Marshall and said, "I'm sorry, Father, but I want the people of this city to look upon the Voss name and reputation with a sense of hope, and not of fear and resentment."

Marshall was surprised to hear such words of compassion from his son, as he continued to marvel at the ways his son had changed. He smiled and said, "I'm proud of you, David. You have my full support."


Sally, Marshall's secretary, was still inside the office after everyone had left. "Is there anything else you would like for me to get before I leave?" she asked as Marshall and Richard came out of the conference room.

"Sally, I just want to inform you that you are now David's secretary," Marshall said. "I trust that you will take very good care of him, as you have done with me."

Sally smiled pleasantly and replied, "Thank you, sir. It will be my pleasure to work with him."

"Sally, please just call me David," Richard said politely.

"Certainly, David. I'm looking forward to working with you."

Marshall looked at Richard and said, "Is there anything you'd like Sally to prepare for your first day tomorrow?"

Richard turned to Sally and said, "Yes, there is something I'd like you to do."

"Sure. What do you have in mind?"

"As I walked around Chinatown simply observing, I came upon the Rass

Building. There is a family business there that got my attention—the Mai Lin Spiritual Reader shop. Please write the owner of this shop a letter to inform them that their debt has been forgiven, and that they also don't need to worry about the rent any longer. We will take care of it, and if they have any questions, they can contact me directly." He paused for a few seconds, and then he cheerfully added, "There's one last request. I wanted to set up a trust fund for Kate, so that she may go to any college of her choice."

Richard turned to Marshall. "I'm sorry, Father, that it took me so long to step up as your son. I promise you that you won't regret this."

Marshall smiled and nodded approvingly. "I always knew that you would make me a proud father someday. There was absolutely no doubt in my mind."

# Chapter Thirty-Five

Richard's heart felt empty and alone as he watched the sun gradually appear above the horizon. Its golden rays slowly crept upward, painting over the imaginary line where the earth met the sky and spreading its vibrant colors across thousands of miles. As its warmth melted away the morning mist, a vast, lush green field slowly appeared.

Far off in the distance, he could make out a small female figure standing on top of a large grassy hill, waving at him, motioning him to come to her. His heart suddenly felt a strong urge to be with her. "Wait for me," he pleaded. "Please wait for me."

A split second later, he was standing at the bottom of the hill. He slowly ascended it with the desperate hope that she was still there.

At the top of the hill, the woman appeared vividly before him. His eyes widened and his heart began to beat rapidly as he looked at her. She seemed so familiar to him, and her gorgeous smile could light up every shade of darkness in his heart. There was only one person who could have such a strong effect on him.

"Elizabeth?" he managed to say—the one sweet word that brought him so much happiness.

"Hello, Richard," she said, smiling.

"Elizabeth?" he gasped. "Am I dreaming?"

"Yes," she replied.

She smiled again—that same captivating smile that his heart remembered so well. Her radiant face was as peaceful as an angel, but her eyes were filled with a deep sadness.

"Have you forgotten about me, Richard?" she asked despairingly.

His lips began to quiver and his eyes glistened. With a broken voice he replied shakily, "No. I've never forgotten about you. I've thought of you every single day, every single moment. There are no words that could express how much I've missed you. I love you so much, Elizabeth."

She lowered her head to stare at the ground for a moment; then she lifted it to look at him again. Her mouth opened slowly, as if she was going to say something, but she hesitated and closed it. She then gazed so deeply and intently at him that it felt as if her eyes were piercing deep into his soul. Holding back tears, she managed to say to him, "Richard, I must go away now. I have to leave you."

"*Why?* Please don't leave me, Elizabeth!" Richard begged her. "Please don't go away!"

"You must wake up now," she said softly.

"No, I don't want to wake up! I want to be with you! I want to sleep forever and be with you!"

"I know, my darling, but I must go now. You must find me." She sobbed softly as she slowly disappeared into a thick, heavy mist.

"Elizabeth! Please don't go! Elizabeth! *Nooooo...!*"

Richard awoke to the sound of his own voice screaming desperately.

Sadness filled his aching heart, and he began to cry. "Why, Elizabeth? Why must you leave? How will I ever find you? Please tell me how to find you!"

He dragged himself out of bed and walked to the living room. Sitting on the couch, he tried to comprehend his dream. *Why did she have to leave?* he wondered. *She said she had to go—but why? What is happening to her?*

After a while, a thought occurred to him: could it be that she, too, had been pulled into the light, and had also awoken from a coma?

"I must find her," he said faintly. "Maybe she is waiting for me somewhere."

But how was he going to find her? He had no idea where to begin. His heart and mind were struggling so much that he felt helpless.

Then he remembered Elizabeth's nationality. She had told him that she was—what was it?—*Hmong* and that she was from Minnesota. He wasn't sure if such a group of people even existed.

Richard rushed to his computer to do a quick search. To his surprise, there was a group of people called Hmong, and the biggest population of Hmong people was in Minnesota. "That's my first step. That's where I will begin my search for her," he said excitedly.

He quickly called Sally and asked her to reserve a flight to Minneapolis as soon as possible. "Yes, car and hotel reservations, too, please," he told her.

After hastily getting dressed, he decided to take a cab to Mai Lin to consult with her about his dream. As he entered the small shop, he was again cheerfully greeted by Kate. "Richard, I cannot express enough thanks for what you did. I'm so grateful to know that there are still people like you out there." She smiled, and gave him a big hug.

"It's my pleasure, Kate," he said. "You don't have to worry anymore. I will make sure that you and your grandmother are comfortable from now on. By the way, is she in?"

"Yes, I'll tell her that you're here."

They walked into the back room. Mai looked up and tears came to her eyes. "*The wonderful things you do for others will not be forgotten,*" she said through Kate. "*They will accompany you and guide you throughout your journey.*"

Suddenly Richard felt a little uneasy. He remembered hearing those exact words before, but he couldn't recall who had said that to him. With a thankful expression, he reached out to hold her fragile hands. He smiled politely at her, trying to convey his gratitude. Mai slowly wiped away her tears and listened as Kate carefully translated Richard's dream to her.

Mai turned to him and said through Kate, "Your dream, the woman in your dream is real, but you'll be in great sorrow when you find her."

Richard's eyes opened wide. "What do you mean, I will be in great sorrow?"

"You will know the reason when you find her."

"*Will* I find her?" he asked.

"Yes, you already know where she is," Mai said. "You just need to take your first step in reaching her." Then she looked directly into his eyes and said, "You must not give up hope, even though sadness and despair will accompany you on your search."

Although Richard felt somewhat heavyhearted after hearing this, he also felt lighter. He now knew that Elizabeth was real and that he would be able to find her. It didn't scare him to hear that he would be in sorrow after he'd found her. He was determined to find her, and if for some reason she couldn't remember him, he would be more than happy to spend the rest of his life trying to win her heart and her love all over again.


As Richard walked into his office, Marshall cheerfully greeted him. "Good morning, David."

"Good morning, Father."

"Did I hear that you're going to Minnesota?"

"Yes. I feel the urge to find someone who is very dear to me. I believe we were both in a coma together, and that she, too, might have awakened from it."

"That's very interesting," Marshall said. "How did you know or meet her?"

Richard had to pause for a second. He needed to take a deep breath before he began to try to explain it to Marshall. "It's a long story, Father. I know that you'll find it hard to understand. I'm still trying to understand it myself. Maybe there are some hidden reasons behind all of this, and maybe I will be able to find some answers to all this confusion."

Marshall simply nodded. "I understand, son. Do what you must do, and don't worry about anything else. Just promise me that you'll let me know if you need anything."

"I promise," Richard replied, relieved. "Thank you for being so understanding and supportive."

"So, how long will you be gone?"

"I should only be gone for a few days. Maybe a week or two at most, but I will call you and let you know if that changes."

Sally walked into the office holding an envelope. "The plane ticket along with the car and hotel reservations are all inside. Your flight departs in three hours, so you should hurry home and start packing," she said.

"Don't worry, I'm just going to go like this. I'll buy some clothes once I get there," he said with a smile as Sally nodded and left the room.

"So, do you truly believe that this person is not just a figment of your imagination?" Marshall asked.

"It's very hard to explain right now, Father. The truth is, I don't know for sure, but I need to find out. If she turns out to be real, then my life will be complete."

"Really?" Marshall asked, puzzling. He wanted to press for more information, but he thought better of it and simply said, "Well, I can't wait to meet her. Please give her that message when you find her."

"I'm sure she'd love to meet you, too. You would be the first person I would introduce her to." He gave Marshall a hug before he left the office.


Richard had a thousand things on his mind while he sat quietly on the plane ride to Minnesota. He pondered over and over again how and where he would begin his search for Elizabeth. His heart and mind were overwhelmed with thoughts of her. Right now, she was the only thing that mattered to him.

He thought about what he would say to her, how she would react to seeing him, if they would be able to pick up where they left off, or if he would have to start again from square one. Even if she didn't know or remember who he was, even if when she saw him she didn't like him the way she once did, even if she was still in a coma at a hospital—none of that was important to him. What was most important to him was to find her. Everything else would happen in due time.

He arrived in Minneapolis at about two o'clock in the afternoon. As he drove his rental car out of the airport parking lot, he was despairing. All he knew about her was that her name was Elizabeth Vang, and that she was from Minnesota. What if that wasn't her name? Like him, she might be a completely different person under a different name in this world. Would he still be able to find her?

He crossed the river into St. Paul and drove up 7th Street on his way to the Royal Crown Hotel downtown.

After he checked in, he noticed that one of the employees standing inside the lobby was of Asian descent. He approached the man and respectfully asked him if he was Hmong.

"Yes, sir, I'm Hmong," he replied. "May I help you with something?"

"Forgive me if I am being ignorant, but could you possibly direct me to a location where there would be a large gathering of Hmong people? Perhaps some restaurants or shops? Anywhere where I might find many Hmong people."

The employee smiled pleasantly at Richard and said, "You don't have to go far. If you go north about five blocks from here, you'll come to University Avenue. Walk down University Avenue, and you'll see that there are many Asian businesses on both sides of the street. Many of them are Hmong businesses."

"Well, that doesn't sound too difficult," Richard said, feeling relieved. "Thank you, sir."

The employee nodded and smiled. "Not a problem, sir. Good luck to you."


It was around four o'clock before Richard finally reached University Avenue. After he had walked a block or two, he came upon a variety of Asian shops and restaurants on both sides of the street.

A strong aroma of pungent spices was in the air, and he remembered how Elizabeth had once described this place. He felt like he might even see her walking on the street somewhere. He looked closely at every woman he saw, but unfortunately, no one resembled his Elizabeth.

He went into several shops in hopes of finding her, but she was nowhere to be found. He saw many beautiful Asian women as he continued on his walk, but he didn't see any who compared to Elizabeth.

After a while of searching, he began to worry. He felt like he was looking for a needle in a haystack, but he was not about to give up hope. He knew that it was not going to be easy, but he had a whole lifetime to search for her.

As he was walking in and out of shops, looking at people, he noticed a sign above a small restaurant with a single word on it: "Pho."

"So, pho is a real dish?" he whispered.

He went inside and sat at a table by the window. A young Asian waitress came over and he quickly ordered a bowl of pho, as if he already knew exactly what he wanted. After his food was ordered, he looked around and noticed a cart with a tray of sauces and condiments on it. Everything looked so eerily similar to what he had seen in the Chinatown in Atkins. He was so fascinated by the tray he didn't even notice that his bowl of pho had arrived.

The waitress set down the large bowl in front of him, along with a platter of condiments consisting of bean sprouts, some fresh basil, a few slices of jalapeño peppers, and a slice of lime. As he took a quick glimpse at everything, a feeling of déjà vu came over him and he suddenly felt a little dizzy.

"May I help you with anything else?" she asked. "Is this your first time eating pho?"

"Yes. I mean, no. I've had it before in my"—he paused in mid-sentence— "hometown and have developed a fond taste for it. Pho is one of my absolute favorite dishes."

"Please let me know if you need anything else."

"Thank you."

Instinctively, he mixed the bowl of soup as he had routinely done many times before. The soup was delicious—just as soothing to his soul as it had been many times back in Atkins.

While he was eating, he noticed a young Asian police officer sitting four tables away from him. He could see the officer's name embroidered onto his uniform with bright yellow letters that read, "K. Vang."

"Vang," he said quietly. There was no better person to ask than a police officer, he thought. Since his last name was also Vang, maybe he could help. If not, maybe he could help direct him to someone who might know Elizabeth's family.

He needed to get the officer's attention, so he quickly motioned for the waitress to come over. "I'd like to pay for that officer's meal," he said.

After he had finished eating, the officer approached Richard and thanked him.

"It's my pleasure, officer," Richard said. "Often times we forget to thank our heroes for the hard work they do."

The officer smiled. "I appreciate your kind words. Even though I can say that this is my job and it is what I love to do, a word of appreciation does inspire us to want to do even better for our community."

"I agreed wholeheartedly, sir," Richard said, extending his hand. "My name is David Voss, by the way."

"Oh . . .," the officer said as he shook Richard's hand. He paused, looking at Richard with an intrigued but surprised expression. "Well, it's a pleasure to meet you, David. My name is Kenny."

Richard contemplated whether or not to ask his question. He wasn't sure if it was appropriate just yet. But he knew this might be his chance. "If you don't mind," he said slowly, "I'd like to ask you a couple of questions, sir."

"Of course," Kenny said curiously. "I'm not sure how much I can help you, but I will do my best to answer your questions."

Richard smiled warmly and took a deep breath before he began. "Well, I'm new in town. In fact, I just arrived here about three hours ago. There is someone I'm looking for—someone who is very dear to me."

"What's the name, may I ask?"

Richard paused. "Well, I noticed that your last name was Vang. The person that I'm looking for has the same last name as yours."

Kenny softly laughed. "I'll do my best to help you, David, but my last name is very common. There are thousands of Hmong people with the same last name here in St. Paul. May I know her full name and maybe a physical description?"

Richard took another deep breath. "Her name is Elizabeth," he carefully explained. "She is taller than most Asian women. She has long, black, silky hair, and has the most captivating smile. She has very beautiful eyes—big, pearly round, and dark brown. She lived here with her grandmother, I believe. It's embarrassing that I don't even have a picture of her."

Kenny listened with an intrigued expression on his face as Richard gave his detailed description of Elizabeth, and was silent as he thought about how to answer Richard. He opened his mouth as if he was going to speak, but only let out a soft sigh.

Finally, he slowly shook his head and said, "I'm sorry, David. I don't know anyone by that name. And other than her height, that physical description you gave me fits almost any Asian woman out there. Good luck on your search." Kenny thanked Richard again for the meal and walked out of the restaurant.


It was still early in the evening and the sun was still shining brightly when Richard headed back to the hotel. As he walked into the lobby, he felt he hadn't accomplished anything yet. His heart was empty and he still felt like he was a world away from Elizabeth. How could he have thought that finding her would be easy? Despite feeling hopeless, Richard hadn't given up.

While he was inside the lobby, he was approached by the same Hmong employee he had met earlier. The employee mentioned a place called Phalen Park, which was located in the area of the city known as the "East Side."

"It's quite a popular hangout place for many Hmong people," he said.

Richard decided to check it out. He quickly headed to his car and was soon driving toward the East Side. A short time later, he came upon the beautiful grounds of Phalen Park. He took a left turn onto Phalen Drive and parked in a huge lot next to a large brown beach house.

He walked along a paved trail until he came to a small beach at the southwest corner of the lake. *This area is eerily reminiscent of Lake Iris*, he thought. He glanced around and examined the entire area, focusing mainly on the faces and figures of the many Asian women. To his disappointment, none of them resembled Elizabeth. He continued down the trail and slowly walked around the lake.

About thirty minutes later, he saw a small island on the northwest side of the lake. A little stream that flowed out of the lake was split in two, surrounding a small piece of land. The two streams merged back together at the northwest corner to reform into a single stream that flowed into a smaller lake.

On the island he saw people playing volleyball in a small field. He also saw several picnic tables and the area was filled with people—adults as well as children—running around, barbecuing, playing, fishing, and just enjoying the evening.

He walked across the small wooden bridge to the island and soon found himself in the midst of all of the action. He wandered around the whole area with an intense hope of finding Elizabeth. But to his despair, she was nowhere to be found.

As the sun slowly set on the horizon, he knew that he would have to return to the hotel. His heart felt a slight chill as he walked back to his car, but he was never going to lose his hope of finding her.

# Chapter Thirty-Six

It was May 25th, a beautiful spring day in the city of St. Paul. The breeze was gentle and refreshing, with the perfect amount of warmth from the sunlight pouring through the puffy white clouds. The smell of the air was freshly cultivated with a sweet odor of food from the restaurants.

Richard was beginning to lose hope. It had already been almost a week since he had arrived here, and still he had no clue as to Elizabeth's whereabouts. However, today was a new day—a new, bright, and beautiful day that somehow gave him a spirited sense of hope. He felt a little more optimistic about his search for her today than he had in the last few days, because May 25th was the day he had found her twice.

As he walked down University Avenue and approached the southeast corner of Arundel Street, he saw an Asian police officer wrestling with a man on the ground. Richard could see that the officer was struggling to control the man and was in desperate need of assistance, so he quickly ran up to them and asked the officer if he needed help.

"Yes! Get on top of him and grab his arm!" the officer shouted through his breath.

Richard quickly placed his knee on the suspect's back and pinned him to the ground. Using both his hands, he grabbed the suspect's right arm and bent it to the small of his back. He held the man's arm in that position until the officer was able to handcuff the suspect.

Filled with adrenaline, Richard and the officer were breathing heavily as they slowly got to their feet. After what seemed like a long time, the officer finally turned to Richard and thanked him.

"You're quite welcome, Officer. I'm glad I was able to help," Richard replied, smiling.

A crowd of people had gathered to watch the scuffle, which annoyed the officer. He shouted at the crowd in a language that was somewhat familiar to Richard.

As the crowd slowly dispersed, the officer turned back to Richard and explained. "All these people just stood still and watched while I was fighting with this guy, and none of them even thought about helping me. It's just pathetic how this society has become. I'm truly grateful for your help, sir."

"Again, Officer, I was glad that I was able to help," Richard replied modestly.

The officer looked at Richard with a curious expression. "Have we met before?" he asked with a curious frown.

Richard noticed the name on the officer's uniform and immediately remembered having met him at the restaurant the day he arrived. "Ahhh ... Now that I take a closer look at you and your name, I believe we met about a week ago inside a restaurant."

"Oh, yes, now I remember. You paid for my lunch and now you also came to my assistance. I'm truly indebted to you, sir."

"It's not a problem, Officer. I'm just doing my good deed for today."

The officer laughed. "Just call me Kenny. And you're David Voss, right?"

"Yes—you have a good memory, Kenny."

"Well, in my line of work, you have to have a good memory. Just like this guy here. I remember seeing a picture of him at roll call a couple of days ago and knew that he was wanted for a felony assault."

"Your line of work is quite dangerous," Richard said. "Well, you take care of yourself, Kenny. Please be safe." He turned around and began to walk away.

"David! Please wait a minute!" Kenny called out.

Richard stopped abruptly and quickly turned around. Kenny took a few steps toward him. "I'm just wondering if you have found the person you were looking for?"

Richard let out a deep sigh and then slowly replied, "Luck hasn't been on my side at all. I've tried so hard to find her, but I still have no clue where she might be."

"Just out of curiosity, may I ask you what your relationship with her is?"

Richard chuckled. "You might think that I'm crazy, but what I'm about to say is the honest truth," he replied. Then he paused before continuing. "It may seem like I hardly even know her, but the truth is, she was about to be my wife."

Kenny stood there in silence, his bewildered eyes fixed intently on Richard.

Richard noticed this, so he quickly added, "But hey, don't worry about it. This is a big city, and I kind of expected that it wouldn't be easy to find her. However, I'm not giving up yet. I haven't lost hope, and I'm confident that I will find her somehow, regardless of how long it will take me. I have a whole lifetime to search for her."

Kenny remained quiet as his eyes shifted to the ground. He let out a deep sigh, and then he lifted his head to look at Richard. "I knew her," he said quietly.

Richard couldn't believe what he'd just heard. "Kenny, if you know her, then please help me find her! There's nothing I want more in this world than to be with her!" he pleaded.

Kenny looked at Richard for a moment. "Do you have time for a ride?" he quietly asked.

"Yes, of course. I have all the time in the world."

"I need to book this guy, and then I'll take the rest of the day off. I'll come back for you, and we'll go on that ride."

"Thank you so much, Kenny. I will just wait around here."

As Richard watched Kenny drive away, he was filled with a profound sense of happiness—the kind of happiness that made him feel renewed and recharged. He felt a sense of completeness, as if he had finally achieved something extremely important in his life. For many moons he had dreamed of Elizabeth, but had only awoken with empty arms. He couldn't touch her or feel her next to him, but now it seemed he would finally get to hold her in his arms again. The feeling of anticipation was so overwhelming that he began to pace back and forth, waiting anxiously for Kenny's return.

About an hour later, Kenny's car rounded the corner. Richard quickly jumped in, and they were soon going west on University Avenue. A short while later, Kenny took a right turn onto Logan Drive and drove north for about fifteen minutes.

A little ways ahead, Richard could see an entrance to an enormous park. As they got closer, he noticed the sign on two huge iron gates that read "Logan Cemetery." His heart suddenly stopped. His eyes widened and he felt like the world around him began to spin rapidly.

"What's this?" he asked in a whisper.

"I'm still praying that I'm wrong, but you can confirm whether or not she is the person you're looking for," Kenny gently replied.

"This is a joke, right?" Richard asked again. Now there was a sense of panic in his voice. "How can this be?" he asked, more to himself than to Kenny.

Kenny kept on driving silently, his eyes focusing straight forward as if he didn't hear a single one of Richard's questions.

As they passed through the gates, Kenny carefully maneuvered his car around a curvy road and a beautiful field of lush green grass came into view. The scene looked very familiar to Richard. *Have I been here before?* he wondered. As he quietly pondered where he had seen this field of green, he finally remembered: it was in his dream. Everything was eerily similar to the field that he'd dreamt about a few days earlier.

Kenny stopped the car at the bottom of a large grassy hill, and he slowly turned to look at Richard. He noticed Richard's puzzled face and his miserable and horrified expression, so he gently placed his hand on Richard's shoulder and quietly asked, "Are you all right?"

Richard had sunk deep into his seat in disbelief and hadn't moved since they arrived at the hill. He just sat there, staring straight ahead.

"Should we leave?" Kenny asked gently.

Richard slowly turned his head to Kenny. "No," he faintly replied. "I have to find out."

As they slowly made their way up the hill, Richard felt a chill shoot down his spine. His chest felt compressed and he was breathing rapidly. His heartbeat was fast and unsteady. He felt that if he didn't try to control his breathing, he could just pass out right there, halfway up the hill.

Richard stopped walking for a moment to catch his breath and as he exhaled deeply, he looked up and saw a large oak tree at the top of the hill. His eyes began to focus closely on what lay beneath it. There, underneath the tree, stood an upright headstone. His knees weakened, his whole body began to tremble, and he felt a surge of grief—even though he hadn't yet seen whose headstone this was.

As they walked up to it, Richard had to gather all his strength and courage to focus on the picture that was embedded in the headstone. He froze, and his face went pale as a ghost. He couldn't even cry. Not even one tear—no anguish. Not a word. He just fell straight to his knees in complete disbelief.

That picture on the headstone. That smile, that beautiful face—it was the face he had missed so much . . . the face he had traveled such a long distance in search of. His beautiful Elizabeth had been here, lying beneath this cold, damp dirt—not in a cozy house, but under an oak tree. His agonized heart was furiously pumping blood through every vein. He clutched both hands tightly against his chest and screamed so loud that he could feel his ears vibrate.

After a while, he slowly reached up both hands to gently embrace the headstone. Tears were streaming down his cheeks now as he sobbed louder and louder, until his cries were so loud they filled the whole cemetery.

Kenny stood in silence as he observed this man's profound sadness. He gently placed a hand on Richard's shoulder, and with a low, soft voice, he said, "I'll give you some time, David." Then, he turned and made his way down the hill to wait by his car.

Richard slowly wiped away his tears so he could clearly look at Elizabeth's picture. After a while, he managed to say to her in a low, broken, and shaky voice, "I've found you, Elizabeth. I've finally found you." He paused. "Why are you here? Why are you beneath this cold, damp dirt when you could have been in the warmth of my arms? Why didn't you wait for me?"

He closed his eyes and a few more tears fell. *How am I ever going to live without her?* he wondered. The pain of seeing her like this was unbearable. Yet, in his heart, he somehow knew that he had accomplished something: he had finally found her. And from here on, he would never be apart from her again.

About an hour later, Kenny came back up the hill. "David, it's getting late,"

Kenny said softly as he put a hand on Richard's shoulder again. "We have to go now. This place will be closing in a few minutes."

Richard was reluctant, but he knew that they had to leave. He slowly wrapped his arms around Elizabeth's headstone and gently kissed her. "You sleep now, my darling, and I promise I will see you again."

"Are you all right?" Kenny asked as they walked back to the car.

Richard let out a deep, trembling sigh. "I loved her with all my heart," he replied as he wiped away his tears.

"I loved her, too, David," Kenny said in a soft, desolate voice.

Richard stopped and looked at Kenny, his eyebrows raised slightly.

Sensing Richard's confusion, Kenny quickly explained. "Her name was Leela. She was my sister—my only sister—and I loved her dearly." Kenny's eyes were brimming with tears. "There's not a single day that goes by that I don't think of her."

Richard's relief was quickly replaced with profound sadness for Kenny. He slowly glanced away to focus on the walk as they came to the bottom of the hill and got into Kenny's car.

"I hesitate to ask this," Richard said, "and I'm not sure if I'm ready for it, but my heart is dying to know. I need to ask you about it for my heart's sake." He took a deep breath. "Please tell me how she died."

With an anguished expression, Kenny quietly explained. "My sister landed a job in New York City. She was so happy about it and couldn't wait to go to the big city." Kenny paused for a second and sighed before he continued. "On the day that she got there, while walking down Broadway toward Times Square, she was struck by a car. She was in a coma after the accident. After several months in the coma, she was flown back here so that we could be closer to her. Over a year ago, we finally decided to end her suffering and let her go."

Richard paused for a few seconds to allow the news to all sink in. Then he asked, "Are your parents still with you?"

Kenny glanced away and quietly replied, "No. Our parents died when Leela and I were very young. My grandmother took care of us." He smiled sweetly as he continued. "Growing up with my sister was an absolute treat. I was the younger brother, and she was always very protective of me. She wanted me to do the right thing, and I never once disappointed her. When she got that job in New York, she was so happy. She told us that when she got situated, she would come back for us. I was so proud of her." He discreetly wiped away a tear.

Kenny turned to look at Richard. "How did you come to know my sister?" he asked, intrigued. "She never mentioned you, but the emotion that you expressed back there told me that you loved her just as much as I did."

Richard lowered his head and folded his hands in his lap. "You wouldn't believe me if I told you," he said softly.

"Try me, David. I would believe anything at this point," Kenny said as he drove away from the cemetery.

Richard looked out the window for a few seconds and then took a deep breath. "My name is not David," he said as he turned to Kenny. "In fact, I didn't even know who this David Voss was until I woke up in his body. My real name is Richard Bennett, and I was born in the city of Atkins. I met your sister in Atkins. But her name wasn't Leela. Her name was Elizabeth."

Kenny kept his eyes on the road the whole time and remained silent. After a long pause, he glanced over at Richard and said, "I'm guessing the city of Atkins is one I wouldn't find, even if I searched for it all my life, right?"

"Yes, it is in a world only your sister and I would know," Richard sadly replied.

Upon hearing Richard's reply, Kenny didn't seem to be shocked or surprised. It was as if he somehow knew and understood what Richard was saying.

"She was everything to me, much like she was to you in this world." Richard's voice was unsteady as the wonderful memories came rushing back to him. "We had everything going for us back in our world. We were going to be married. We even had a son together. Can you believe that?" He shook his head and wiped away a tear.

Kenny glanced at Richard. "Was she doing well in . . . Atkins?" he asked. "I've missed her so much."

"She was a strong, independent, and amazing woman, and while I was with her, she was doing very well." Richard paused and looked out the window. "But after I was brought back to this world, I really didn't know what had become of her. And that is what's killing me so much."

"Can't you go back to her?" Kenny asked. "I would hate for her to be alone."

"I desperately want to go back to her, to my son, and to my family, but I don't know how," Richard replied helplessly.

Kenny went silent for a moment. Then he looked at Richard again. "I'm not sure how you feel about this, but I think that my grandmother can help you find your way. She is a shaman, and she is highly respected in the Hmong community."

Richard gave Kenny a faint smile. He was willing to try anything at this point.

# Chapter Thirty-Seven

W*hat is hope?* Richard thought long and hard about that while he and Kenny were on their way to Kenny's house. He had done almost everything in his power to find his beloved Elizabeth, and in the end this was what he ended up with? His pain, his sorrow, and his anger escalated. He felt he had been betrayed by his optimistic heart.

When he had lost all else, he had at least maintained a small thread of hope. Now that even hope had betrayed him, his life seemed meaningless.

He was so tired and was starting to have second thoughts about meeting Kenny's grandmother now. He didn't want to be disappointed again. If this was his destiny, he no longer wanted to fulfill it. Elizabeth was gone—what was left in this world for him now?

Kenny drove quietly, his eyes focused on the road. He wasn't going to say anything at all because he, too, was emotional beyond words. He took a quick glance at Richard and seemed to read his mind. "Don't lose hope just yet," he said in a comforting voice. "Even if there's not a way for you to return to her, I'm sure there's a reason you were left behind. Maybe you're needed here to accomplish something."

Richard didn't want to cry anymore, but his teardrops were too stubborn to stay put. As he wiped them away, he thought about his life and began to despise it. He felt trapped. Was he being punished for something that he had done? Maybe Kenny was right—maybe there was a reason why he was left behind. If he was being punished, he needed to find out what he was being punished for. Now he felt a strong urge to see Kenny's grandmother.

They arrived at Kenny's house in the part of the city called Highland Park. Kenny parked the car on the street. Richard looked around and noticed that the houses on this block were old and small, but they were clean and well maintained.

As he slowly stepped out of the car, his mind was filled with the images of Elizabeth walking in and out of this house at some point in her life. He could almost see her opening the door and running out to greet him. As the images faded, his heart felt like it was being slashed and pierced with a sharp blade.

Before he led Richard up to the front door, Kenny turned to him and said, "I don't know how much you believe in these kinds of things, but I will at least introduce you to my grandmother. It will be up to you and her to figure out your fate. And yes, she does speak English." Richard smiled and simply nodded his head.

As they stepped through the front door, Richard stopped. The living room had an eerie look and feel to it. By the wall, on the opposite side of the front door, stood a huge altar that was decorated with hundreds of gold and silver Chinese papers. The altar itself was made of five hand-carved wooden platforms. The ends of the platforms were supported by two large, flat, ornate wooden boards. The largest platform was filled with numerous small white cups, which were filled with some sort of liquid. Next to the cups were several small exotic ornaments that had red strings attached to them. In the center of the main platform was a large white bowl filled with rice to support several standing sticks of incense.

On one side of the altar hung a large, round gong with a mallet. On the other side hung a short, broad sword made of copper, with several red strings attached to the wooden handle. Near the ceiling, several pieces of white yarn ran from the top of the altar to each side and corner of the room, resembling a huge spider web.

Richard was impressed and amazed by the altar, but he could also see how it might terrify someone.

"*Pog, kuv los tsev lawm os!* (Grandma, I'm home now!)" Kenny called out in Hmong.

A short time later, a frail elderly woman came in through the kitchen door. She looked at Richard with an intrigued expression. Then, she turned to Kenny, and with a raspy voice, she asked, "Who is this young man?"

"His name is David. He is here to see you."

"Ah, good. Come sit by me," she said, gesturing Richard to the altar.

Richard walked over and seated himself on a wooden bench next to her.

She smiled pleasantly at him and asked, "You come for a reading?"

"Yes," he replied quietly.

She took three incense sticks and held them in her hands, then closed her eyes and quietly mumbled some words as if she was saying a prayer. A moment later, she opened her eyes, lit the incenses and set them inside the large white bowl. She clasped her hands together and mumbled some more words.

After a few minutes, she turned to Richard and slowly reached out, grasping his hands in her fragile ones. As she held his hands, she stared intently into his eyes as if she was looking deep into his soul. Then she lowered her head, closed her eyes, and began to speak softly to herself.

Richard waited patiently. After a moment, she lifted her head to look at him again. Her eyes widened. "You are from the other side," she said.

"Yes," he said as he leaned forward with anticipation.

The grandmother lifted up her hand to touch his cheek and with tears in her eyes, she said, "You have been with my granddaughter."

"Yes, and I loved her very much," he replied with tears of his own.

"I see a child. You and my granddaughter have a child together."

"Yes, we did," he said softly.

She gave him an empathetic expression as she placed a hand on his cheek again, gently caressing it. "The question in your heart is how can you go back home? The answer is that you cannot. You have karma in this life and you must repay your karma."

He lowered his head for a moment, for he was expecting to hear this. He closed his eyes, and then he opened them and looked at her. "Do you know anything about my karma and how can I repay it?"

She looked at him despairingly. It seemed as if she wanted to tell him, but something was holding her back, stopping her from doing it. She let out a deep sigh and replied, "Yes, but I cannot tell you. All I can tell you is that you'll find it very soon. Once you've found it, then you'll know what to do."

He slowly leaned over to look into her eyes. Desperately he asked, "If I repay all my karma in this world, this lifetime, will I ever get a chance to go back to her?"

She nodded her head and replied, "You have a good heart. You must wake up and find your destiny. Fulfill your destiny, and you will go back."

His heart was suddenly lifted with a sense of hope. But he still couldn't understand why they—Elizabeth, Mai, and now the grandmother—kept telling him to fulfill his destiny. How could he fulfill his destiny when he didn't even know what it was or where to find it? He was desperately hoping that Kenny's grandmother would tell him. He pleaded with her, "Do you know what my destiny is? Can you tell me?"

The grandmother nodded and softly replied, "Yes. But I cannot tell you that either." She leaned over and, with a serious expression on her face, she added, "If you cannot find your destiny and fulfill it before you leave this place, you will go to a different place. There, you will linger forever and will never be able to find that place you called home."

Upon hearing those words, his heart sank. The walls of despair were beginning to close in on him, suffocating him and draining him of every ounce of hope and faith. He looked devastated by her words. His eyes started to tear up again and he began to cry quietly in front of her.

*For a grown man to be crying like this*, the grandmother thought, *his heart and soul must truly be sincere.* Although she did want to give him more information, she knew his destiny was prewritten and he would have to find it himself. The laws of the heavens could not be broken, and she was helpless to do anything about it.

She thought long and hard about how she could help him. Then she let out a deep sigh, leaned over to him, and whispered in his ear, "I cannot tell you, because the laws of the heavens forbid me. But I can tell you that your destiny is already in your heart. You have not yet opened your eyes to see it."

She sat back and paused for a moment to look into his questioning eyes. Then she slowly leaned toward him again and whispered, "My granddaughter is your soul mate, and she cannot go back without you. She is waiting for you in a different place. You must follow the path set for you by my granddaughter. You keep her close to your heart, and then you will find your destiny. Your destiny will take you to her. And then she will take you back to that place you called home."

She smiled warmly at him and gently placed a hand on his shoulder to reassure him. "It was written for you by the heavens. It is not your time yet. You are a great man, and you must live your life as a great man. You must fulfill your destiny, and when the moment arrives you will go back to the time in which you found your greatest happiness. There, you and my granddaughter will begin your lives once again."

With a warm and comforting smile, she reached out both her hands to caress his grieving face. "When you see my granddaughter, you tell her that I will see her again."

"Yes. Yes, I will," he replied with a spirited sense of hope.

She got up, still holding his hand. "Now you must come eat dinner with us, my son," she said as she led him to the kitchen.


The dinner was amazing. Now Richard understood where Elizabeth's cooking skills came from. He couldn't take a single bite without remembering her. He ate with tears in his eyes the whole time, and the grandmother noticed it. She reached over to touch his hand and said, "When you miss her, you come eat Grandma's cooking."

Richard suddenly felt a slight cool breeze caressing his cheek, and another tear rolled down his cheek. Maybe this is Elizabeth giving me her approval, he thought. "Thank you, Grandmother," he replied softly. "The food is delicious."

They ate quietly for a moment, and then Kenny decided to ask Richard something he'd been wondering about. "If you don't mind sharing, Richard," he said, "I'd like to ask you how you happened to meet my sister on the other side."

Richard looked at Kenny with a pleasant smile. The memory of him meeting Elizabeth for the first time filled him with such happiness that he couldn't wait to share it, especially with Kenny and his grandmother. "When I was inside a restaurant, I saw a beautiful woman sitting at a corner table, and I instantly fell in love with her. I was intimidated by her beauty, though, because I thought that there was no way I could ever have a chance with her. However, I found out later that same day that she was the sweetest woman I had ever met. She was not only gorgeous, but also a very respectful woman with a gentle and kind heart. After that day, I just knew that my life would never be the same again without her." Suddenly his gleeful emotion shifted as he despairingly added, "I just don't know why I was taken away from her. I've missed her every single day."

The grandmother turned to look at him. "Did you see the light, too?" she slowly asked.

"Yes, and that was when I left her behind," he replied with a sudden rush of curiosity. "When we first met, she told me about her dreams. She said that the light came for her every single night, and she couldn't sleep. I thought that maybe she was just having nightmares, so I tried to comfort her as best as I could. But on the night of our engagement, the light came for her again. I thought that she was having another nightmare, but when I saw it with my own eyes, I couldn't believe that it was real. Then, I saw two ghostly beings coming out of the light to take her. I tried to protect her, but I was too weak. They took me into the light, and I woke up in this world." He wiped away a tear.

Kenny's grandmother let out a deep sigh. "Her soul had already passed on and had been reborn on the other side. While her body was sleeping, I tried many times to bring her back. I've done everything I could, but she was very strong and stubborn. When her body died, she could no longer come back."

Richard was confused. "I still don't understand the light. Will you please help me understand what exactly the light is?"

"Yes," she replied. "The light was my shaman spirit and energy that traveled on a journey to find her and to bring her back. I have negotiated with her spirit in the underworld, I have sacrificed animals, I have given spiritual money, and I have battled for many years. But I lost the battle. Her soul could not return and I knew that, so I decided not to make her suffer any longer. Though I missed her dearly, I had to let her go so that her soul could start anew on the other side."

"So you were the one who brought me back?" Richard looked at her with an intense expression.

"No," she replied. Sensing his frustration, she gently placed a hand on his shoulder to reassure him, and then she carefully explained. "I was only looking for my granddaughter, and I had stopped a long time ago. The light that came that night was not for her—it was for you. Your will and your body were very strong in this world. Your body woke up, so you had to come back."

"Then why didn't the light come for me every night like it came for her?"

"The light that came for her was my shaman spirit. The light that came for you could not be forced upon you until your body woke up."

Richard took a deep breath and slowly let it out. "I'm so confused, Grandmother. Why was my soul reborn if my body was still alive? Why didn't my soul stay with my body?"

"When the body sleeps, the soul moves on. The soul will always be searching for a way to be reborn and start anew. But, if the body wakes, then the soul must come back. It is the law of the heavens."

"Were you on life support when you woke up?" Kenny asked.

"No. I wasn't," Richard replied. "Why?"

"My sister was on life support the whole time she was in a coma. Her body was too far gone, and it couldn't sustain itself without the support of the machines. We were going to end her suffering months after her coma, but Grandma insisted that she could bring her back. Four years into it, Grandma finally lost hope and had given up. We decided not to let her suffer any longer and to let her go."

Suddenly, everything started to make sense to Richard. Elizabeth once told him that she no longer had the nightmares and was confused about it. The nightmares didn't stop because he had protected her. They stopped because her body had died and she couldn't be brought back. Richard then thought about himself. Why didn't his body die? Why did he have to come back to this?

He became silent and no longer seemed to be interested in asking any more questions. He wanted to trust his fate and live with the promise of hope in his heart once again. How could he not, when all he wanted was to believe that he would someday return to his world, his home, and his family? Could he really trust this elderly woman? She seemed to know so much about him. Everything she told him was true and made sense. He would have to keep this hope deep inside his heart and just trust that God would decide his fate for him.

Richard let out a deep sigh. "The one thing I wish for more than anything in this world," he said, "is to see her and to feel her one last time. I want to remember her and cherish that moment for the rest of my life as I set off on my journey alone."

Kenny looked at his grandmother and pleaded, "Grandma, please help him."

Richard turned and looked at the grandmother. "Grandmother, I would do anything to be granted the opportunity to see her again. Will you please help me?"

The grandmother was very hesitant, but she could see the immense despair in Richard's eyes and felt the sincerity in his plea. She slowly said, "There is a way, but it is too risky and I don't want my granddaughter to linger on for eternity."

Richard gave her a puzzled look. He wanted nothing more than to see his Elizabeth one more time, but if it meant that she would be in danger, he didn't want to risk that. "What do you mean when you say it's too risky and that she would linger on for eternity?" he asked.

The grandmother quietly explained. "I trust you, but I don't trust the human heart. There are too many temptations in this world, and the heart may stray. Once your heart strays, my granddaughter will be left walking the grounds of eternity alone forever."

Richard got out of his chair and went down on his knees. His tears rolled down his cheeks as he desperately begged for the grandmother to help him see Elizabeth again one last time. "I don't know how else to prove to you my sincere and undying love for her. All I can do at this moment is to kneel down in front of you and give you my word that I truly and sincerely love her with all my heart. If temptation should win my heart over one day and I break my promise to you, may my soul be left wandering the grounds of this earth alone for eternity instead of hers."

"Is your love for her that strong? Words are not just words. Promises are not to be played around with. Spirits have ears, and everything in this world has a spirit—this means the spirit of the house, the spirit of a tree, the spirit of a rock, even the spirit of the wind may have heard your promise. I hope you understand that," she sternly warned him.

"My promise is not just an empty promise," he replied with teary eyes.

"If I help you, then you must stay true to your promise and never stray away from it. If you break your promise and fall in love with another and get married, your soul will linger on in a different direction. You and my granddaughter will never meet again. Is that a risk you are willing to take?"

Without hesitation, he took her hand and held it tightly in his, and then he earnestly said to her, "May the spirit of this house and every spirit in this world be my witnesses. If I break my promise, may my soul linger on alone for eternity."

The grandmother was satisfied after hearing his words. She slowly got out of her seat and took his hands. "Then come with me and we shall begin," she said as she led him back to the altar.

She took three gold and silver Chinese papers and carefully folded them into three small canoe-like figures. Then she took another paper and carefully cut it into two small figures that resembled two people holding hands.

She took out a needle and asked him to hold out his hand. He cringed as she poked the needle into his index finger and a small drop of blood began to ooze out of it. She slowly placed one drop of the blood onto the chests of the two figures and a drop of blood on each hand where the hands joined together. Then she placed the two figures and the canoes on the platform. She bent down to the floor where the incense sticks were kept in a bag, took out six of them, and put them next to the figures.

She sighed softly and turned around to look at him again. "The canoes will take you to her. The figures are your blood oath to her soul. Your soul will forever be joined with hers. If you break your oath, both of your souls will linger on in eternity without finding each other." She paused for a moment, then sighed deeply as she continued. "Are you sure you want to go through with this? There's no turning back once we begin."

"I'm sure. I want to see her more than anything," he replied without hesitation.

She turned around to face the altar and then lit three more incenses and stood them inside the bowl. She placed the items on the platform next to the bowl. "Come and kneel down beside me," she said, still facing the altar. "When I begin to pray, you close your eyes and think about her, and about your love for her."

While she prayed, his heart melted as he thought back to the first time he saw Elizabeth sitting all alone at Nancy's restaurant. He thought about the many nights she patiently waited for him to come home so that they could eat dinner together. He thought about seeing her again with Edward and the overwhelming happiness that the two had brought him. He thought about the morning that he woke to see his son in the living room and Elizabeth in the kitchen, getting breakfast ready for them. Tears flowed out of his eyes as the wonderful memories came rushing back.

"Okay, it's done now," she said.

"I'm sorry," he said with a confused look, "but I didn't see her."

She smiled sweetly at him. "You're not going to see her tonight. Bring these items to her grave very early tomorrow morning," she said as she placed the paper canoes, the incenses, and the two paper figures into a small cloth bag and handed it to him. "When the first light of the sun comes over the horizon, you will burn these items and then lie down next to her grave. You will immediately fall asleep, and then you will be with her."

# Chapter Thirty-Eight

The moon was bright and full as it sat silently up in the darkness of the vast sky. The thousands of twinkling stars stood proudly behind the moon, graciously illuminating the world below.

On the drive back to his hotel that night, Richard thought the evening somehow looked fresher and brighter than any other night since he had awoken from his coma.

Although he knew he needed to stay focused on the road, Richard's mind refused to focus on anything but Elizabeth. He thought about what he was going to say to her and about how tenderly he was going to hold her in his arms again. He had missed her so much that even if he were to just stand before her and look at her, he would be completely content.

After arriving at his hotel, he went straight to his room, his mind still buzzing with all the things he wanted to say to her. Suddenly he remembered the book *Pride and Prejudice* that he had bought at a store the other day while he was searching for her. He quickly rummaged through his bag and took it out. He remembered what she had said about how she enjoyed reading romance novels and that this book was one of her favorites. He had lied to her when he said he had read the book; the truth was he had never read it. Perhaps now he could spend some time reading it to her and enjoying it with her.

He lay quietly in bed and tried to fall asleep, but his heart and mind were too full of thoughts, emotions, and memories. He tried to focus on sleeping, but his restless mind was continually interrupted by images of her beautiful face, her gorgeous smile, and her sweet, angelic voice. How was he ever going to fall asleep? Eventually, his body succumbed to the fatigue, and he drifted off.

***

Slowly, Richard opened his eyes to the start of a brand-new day—the first day of the next chapter of his life. As he lay in bed, an overwhelming sense of peace filled his lonely heart and traveled deep into his soul. He knew that he was no longer alone. His heart was no longer empty. Even though she was not there with him, Elizabeth's spirit was there to comfort him.

Elizabeth or Leela—it didn't matter to him which name she had. They both would sound sweet to his ears. Through her, he was grateful to have met her family, and with their help, he would be able to see her again.

He quickly got dressed, gathered the bag of items that Kenny's grandmother had given him the night before, and went downstairs to the garage. He started the car and headed down University Avenue.

The world was still dark and quiet—not even the birds had awoken yet. There was a slight chill in the air and the morning mist was still low and thick, but he kept his eyes focused on the road ahead. After traveling on Logan Drive for a while, he spotted the entrance to the cemetery, and his heart began to feel restless with excitement.

On the right side of the road he noticed a little flower boutique about a block from the cemetery entrance. He thought that it would be nice if he could get her some flowers—in Atkins, he'd often come home with a new, fresh bouquet of flowers for her.

He wondered if it was too early in the morning for anyone to be in the shop. After stopping the car, he got out, walked over, and peeked through the shop window. To his surprise, he spotted a woman inside. He opened the door.

"Good morning!" he called out.

"Morning!" the woman replied with a smile, approaching him.

"Wow, you sure start your day early."

She chuckled pleasantly. "I'm a morning person, so I just like to come in early. How may I help you?"

"I would like a bouquet of flowers. I know that it's a little early, but I really hope that you'll have one ready."

"You're in luck. I've just finished arranging one."

Delighted, Richard quickly paid for the bouquet and then jumped back in his car.

As he slowly maneuvered along the curvy cemetery road, he was reminded of the sweet times when he couldn't wait to get home to see Elizabeth—the feeling of love and contentment in his heart as he would stop by the flower vendor to get her a bouquet. How he wished that his life hadn't changed so much. He sighed deeply and refocused on the road.

As the large hill slowly came into view, he could see the oak tree standing proudly on top of it. Staring up at it, he silently wished that he could be the tree. He would be her protector, just like he promised, and would shield her from the wind, the rain, and the harsh beams of the sun.

He parked his car at the bottom, grabbed the bag of items and the bouquet, and quickly ascended the hill. Standing in front of Elizabeth, he gently laid the bouquet of flowers next to her. He stood back up to look at her, and then, with a soft painful sigh, he began to speak to her. "Hello, my darling. You look so beautiful, as always."

Struggling to keep his composure and not break down into tears, he slowly sat down next to her and reached out to caress her picture with his fingers. He just sat there, gazing into her eyes as if she could see him and feel his tender touch. He gently rested his head on her and reached his arm around her. He closed his eyes for a while as he embraced her, and then opened them to await the first light of the sun.

It didn't take long before a dark orange glow appeared in the horizon. His heart could no longer rest now, and his hands began to tremble as he flicked the lighter. He tried and tried again, but the lighter only sparked slightly. Suddenly he became fearful: if it didn't light, he'd lose his chance to be with her. He couldn't give up now. It had to work. He flicked it desperately again and again until finally the spark became a flame.

He quickly burned the items and waited until the flames subsided and the smoke from the incense began to fill the air. Then he lay down next to her headstone and closed his eyes.

Suddenly he heard a voice telling him to wake up. He thought that maybe someone else had ascended the hill and had stumbled upon him, so he kept his eyes closed and tried to concentrate solely on sleeping.

"Richard, wake up," the voice said again. This time it called him by his name, and he felt it deep down from his heart.

"Elizabeth, is it you?"

"Yes. It's me, Richard. Open your eyes."

"Am I dreaming?" he asked.

"Yes. You're dreaming."

He slowly opened his eyes, desperately hoping to see her sitting there in front of him, but he noticed instead that he was standing in the middle of a lush green field. The thick grass stood proudly up to his waist. He felt calm, peaceful, and carefree standing there as the cool breeze gently brushed the blades of grass against his bare arms. His heart beat peacefully inside his chest as he drew in a deep breath of fresh air.

The sky was clear and blue. The warm rays of the midday sun teased his hair and blinded his eyes.

He suddenly felt the urge to call out for her. "Elizabeth?" he said softly at first. "Elizabeth! Are you here?" he called out louder.

"Yes, Richard, I'm here," she finally replied.

He looked around, frantically searching for her, but he couldn't see her anywhere. "Elizabeth! Where are you?" he said in a panicky voice.

"Follow the path, Richard."

"What path? I don't see a path anywhere."

Glancing down at his feet, he noticed that he was standing on a small dirt path. The path began where he stood and continued ahead through the tall grass.

He didn't take time to think; he instantly knew that he had to follow it. He didn't know his destination, but he didn't care to know. As long as she was at the other end waiting for him, he would follow it anywhere.

He walked straight ahead for a while, stopping a few times to gaze at the breathtaking scenery. After a while, the path slightly curved and led him up a large hill.

As he ascended, he looked up and noticed a woman at the top, standing next to a small wooden cottage. The sunlight shone brightly on her, making her white summer dress sparkle and glisten. His heart began to beat faster now as he picked up speed. Fearing that if he even blinked or looked elsewhere he would lose sight of her, he kept his eyes firmly fixed on her the whole time.

As he approached her, her face came into view—the face of an angel, the face of his one and only Elizabeth. He stopped in front of her and stared at her silently for a moment. He didn't know what to say or how to begin his greeting. There were no words that could express the happiness he felt just being able to stand there in front of her. He sighed deeply and finally managed to utter one trembling word: "Elizabeth."

She smiled that same captivating smile—that same smile that he had missed and loved so much.

"I've missed you so much. I've missed you beyond words," he said with gentle tears streaming down his cheeks.

"I've missed you, too, my darling," she said, tears forming in her own eyes.

He took a step closer to her and slowly reached for her, hoping that she would accept his embrace with open arms. To his surprise, she reached out for him, and before he knew it, she was in his arms, holding on tightly to him. He could no longer control his emotions, and he began to sob in her loving embrace.

"I love you so much, Elizabeth," he cried out. "I don't want to be apart from you again. My heart can't stand the pain anymore."

She gently placed her hand on his cheek, caressing it like she used to do. "I love you, too, my darling. My heart longs for you every single moment."

After a long embrace, she took his hand and led him to a small wooden bench next to the cottage, where they sat down. *What a beautiful cottage*, he thought to himself as he slowly looked around. It looked cozy and comfortable, but it seemed too small for two people to share.

"Is this your house?" he asked.

"Yes, I've lived here for as long as I can remember," she replied. "It seems like they picked the perfect spot for me. I have a breathtaking view of the entire valley from up here. I've also been very fortunate that the sun, the rain, and the wind have been kind to me. My house is still in great shape. It's like I have a protector."

They sat in silence for a moment. Then, his eyes focused on the edge of the hill, and wandered far beyond it. She sensed his curiosity, so she took his hand. "Come with me, I'll show you around."

They walked over and stood on the edge of the hill. He gently wrapped his arm around her waist as he stared down at the valley below. He marveled at the lush green grass swaying back and forth as if it were dancing to the sweet music of the gentle breeze. The green field seemed to stretch on forever, but there were no trees or flowers anywhere.

He looked along the horizon at the perfect alignment between the heavens and the earth. Glancing up at the sky, he noticed that the midday sun was still shining directly above them; it seemed as if it hadn't moved at all. *Maybe there are no nights and no darkness here*, he thought. *What kind of a place is this that even time seems to stand still? Is this Heaven?*

Gazing at this unruffled serenity brought a deep, peaceful happiness to his heart. How his heart longed to be with her in this beautiful paradise forever.

"Thank you for bringing me flowers, Richard," she said. "Now I can start my own flower garden. I will plant every flower that I receive from you, and I will enjoy its beauty and its fresh, sweet scent for as long as I'm here."

He turned to her and gave her a charming smile. "I know how much you love flowers, and I've always loved giving them to you." He looked down at the grassy field, wondering if he could spot anyone. "Are there others down there in the valley?" he asked.

"No. I'm the only one here," she quietly replied. She tried to maintain a cheerful expression, but he could sense her sadness.

Suddenly a deep rush of sorrow filled his heart as he thought about how sad it must be for her to be in this beautiful place all by herself. Is this the eternity that the grandmother told him about? Is this where she will be lingering forever if he breaks his blood oath promise to her? There was no way he would do that to her now. He couldn't possibly leave her alone in this place forever.

They walked to the other end of the hill and stood by the edge for a while. She took a deep trembling breath as she stared silently to the east. He could sense her desire to leave this place, so he shifted his eyes in the same direction, seeing a beautiful valley below a set of hills. The sun's bright rays shone directly down onto the valley, creating a majestic glow. "What's over there?" he asked, pointing to the valley.

She let out a soft, anguishing sigh, her eyes still fixed on the valley. "Over there is where I want to go," she replied.

"Are there people over in that valley?"

"I don't know. But my heart longs to be over there with you."

"Maybe we could go there right now," he said. "All we have to do is leave this hill."

"No!" she replied in a fearful tone. "We can't go beyond the foot of this hill. If we leave, we'll be lost in the darkness forever. You must trust me."

They stood there for a while before going back to the bench. He could still sense her sorrow and wanted desperately to cheer her up. Then he thought about the book, and pulled it out of his pocket. "I brought a book that I want to read to you."

"Really? Which one?" she asked curiously.

He showed it to her. "*Pride and Prejudice*," she said as she took it from him. "It's my favorite, Richard. Please read it to me."

She gently laid her head on his shoulder as he began to read the book out loud. She listened intently and melted away in the flow of the beautiful words. Richard was reminded of those sweet moments he had with her when they sat together on the bench at Atkins Peak.

He was filled with so much love and happiness, yet the deep anguishing feeling of despair still lingered in his heart because he realized this was merely a dream and it was going to come to an end soon. He wished that things hadn't changed so much and that he could be with her like this for eternity. The only thing he could do now was to cherish this moment so that he could treasure it forever as he continued on his long and painful journey alone.

"I've heard that this story ends happily," he said, setting the book down. "Do you think every story should end happily?"

"I do believe that every life does end happily if one lives it to the fullest," she softly replied.

He looked at her for a moment, and then he couldn't hold back his despairing emotions any longer. "Why are you here, Elizabeth?" he said with a sob.

She slowly reached up to caress his face. "Don't cry, my darling. I'm here to wait for you. I will not leave without you."

"The thought of you being in this place all by yourself is so painful to me. I'm here now, and I want to stay here with you forever."

"I will be all right," she said quietly. Then, with a sad and desolate expression, she gently added, "You must go back. You must go back and live your life to the fullest."

"I don't want to go back. A life without you is not worth living."

"Please don't say that," she said with tears in her eyes. "I will always be in your heart. Wherever you go, I'm there with you. You have a whole lifetime ahead of you. You must trust me, and you must live happily. Your journey may be long, but you will never be alone. You must complete your journey and then come back to me."

"But I found you!" he said. "My journey has been completed, and—"

"You've just begun your journey, my darling," she interrupted. "Our paths could diverge forever if you don't fulfill what was prewritten for you. You mustn't forget that. Now it's time for you to go back."

"What if you're not here when my time has come?"

"I will be waiting for you. You must fulfill your destiny so that you'll be sent back to me," she said as she embraced him tightly one more time.

A beam of light broke through the protection of the tree and cast its warmth across his face.

Richard opened his eyes and instantly stood up and looked around, but Elizabeth was nowhere in sight. He realized then that he had awoken from his dream. He quickly glanced at his watch: it was already late in the evening.

"The cemetery will be closing in twenty minutes, sir!" the groundskeeper shouted out to him.

He closed his eyes again and imagined embracing her one last time. He softly kissed her as he said his last words to her: "You sleep now, my darling. I promise you that I will bring you flowers so that you can finish your garden."

He looked at the large tree with the deepest of gratitude. "Thank you for protecting her," he said.

# Chapter Thirty-Nine

Richard flew back to New York the next day. Another chapter of his life had ended. Even though it wasn't what he expected and he had prayed over and over again for a better ending, he was content that he was able to find some measure of peace in his life. He was disappointed about his fate, and the path that had led him to this point in his life, but he was glad to have found some sort of closure to this chapter.

His wounded heart would never be healed. The memories of losing the one person that he loved the most would be forever painful to him, yet he understood and accepted the fact that everyone loses at least one loved one in their lives. But that didn't mean life should come to a halt.

Even though he had no idea how he was going to continue to exist with this engulfing void in his heart, he knew he needed to go on living, both for Elizabeth and for himself.

He was still a little skeptical about life after death and about what happens to the soul after it leaves the body. He still wondered if what he saw of Elizabeth's life in the underworld was real. Was it just a dream he had? Or perhaps it was what he *wanted* to see? He understood that everyone's perception of the underworld was different, but could one's soul simply leap out of one's body and enter into a different world or dimension? His head began to spin as his mind struggled with the mysteries of life after death.

Then he wondered: what would happen to his soul if he decided to pass on by his own will? Would he end up in a different world and have to live another lifetime without Elizabeth?

He thought about his karma. It boggled his mind to think about the kind of a person David used to be. What had he done in the past that would cause him to have to live a whole lifetime in order to repay all of his karma? He needed to find out the reason for all of this, so he left his apartment for a walk to clear his cluttered mind.

With no destination in mind, he just kept walking down the street to see where it would lead him. After a while, he found himself on Broadway, heading south toward Times Square. Then, as he stood at an intersection, an eerie feeling suddenly came over him.

He remembered what Kenny had told him when he was back in Minnesota. In his mind a recording of Kenny's words began to play clearly about his sister being struck by a car in this area. He couldn't imagine her lying lifelessly somewhere on these streets. He couldn't bear to imagine the pain and suffering she went through. A rush of despairing sadness struck deep into his heart as he broke down in tears. "Why, Elizabeth? Why did you have to come to New York?" he cried.

After a while of drowning in his despair, he sighed deeply and vowed to himself that he would never return to this heartbreaking part of town again.

As he walked away, he was suddenly reminded of his own accident and was determined to find out what had happened that night—what had David Voss done? There must be a police report about the accident on file somewhere.


Richard walked into a nearby police station and was greeted by a female officer at the front desk. "Hello, sir. How may I help you today?"

"Hi, my name is Rich—I mean, David Voss. I was in a car accident five years ago, and I'm wondering if you still have a report on file?"

"And your name is David Voss, right?"

"That's correct, ma'am."

"I would have to check. This might take a little while," she said as she began typing on her computer.

As he stood there silently, his heart began to pound heavily and his body trembled slightly. There were so many unanswered questions, and he was desperately hoping that this report might bring some answers.

After searching for a while, the officer finally looked up at him with a pleasant smile. "I think I've found it. Just give me a minute here. I need to confirm it, and then I will print you a copy."

Richard waited nervously. He didn't want to expect too much out of the report because he didn't want to be disappointed again. But why was he feeling so tense and uneasy? He watched as the officer read the printout. Then he noticed a sudden change in her facial expression.

"Is there something wrong, ma'am?" Richard raised an eyebrow in curiosity.

She let out a sigh as she looked at him. "Well, it looks like this was a very bad accident and someone else, besides you, was seriously hurt."

"Are you sure?"

"You're David Voss, right? I'm pretty sure this is the right report."

"Oh my god!" he gasped. "How could this be?" He felt that his heart was going to stop. His knees began to shake, and he could feel his whole body weakening with each passing second.

The officer quickly came around the desk to grab hold of his arm. "Are you all right, sir? Do you want me to call an ambulance?"

"No, please don't. I'll be okay," he replied, trying to steady himself. "I was just a little shocked at what I heard, that's all."

"I could give you this copy of the report, but I'm not sure you'd be able to understand it. It has a lot of police jargon in it."

"Then could you help explain it to me?" he asked.

She looked at him and smiled warmly. "You're in luck today. The detective who was investigating that accident is still here in this building. Maybe you would like to speak with him?"

"Yes," Richard replied. "Could you please get him for me?"

"Of course, sir. Why don't you go have a seat, and I'll let him know that you're here to see him."

Richard slowly made his way to the lobby and sat down, his mind deeply engrossed in his thoughts. Is this the karma that he was told of? Was the accident his fault, and did someone die as a result of it? And if that person did die, how was he ever going to repay this karma?

About ten minutes later, a sharply dressed middle-aged man approached him. "Mr. Voss?"

"Yes," Richard replied as he slowly lifted his head and looked up.

"I'm Detective Mueller. I understand that you wanted to speak with me about your accident?"

"Yes, sir. I apologize for showing up like this. I didn't expect it to be something this awful, and I didn't know I was going to need to speak to you at all. I appreciate your making time to meet with me."

"It's not a problem, sir. I'll be glad to answer any of your questions. Please, follow me."

Richard followed the detective into his office and sat down next to a small desk. "So, Mr. Voss," the detective said. "What would you like to know?"

"Well, sir, I was in a coma after the accident. I woke up five years later and have no recollection of anything. In fact, I have no memories of my life at all prior to the accident. I guess I'm here for some answers and hope that something will spark my memory."

"I'm sorry to hear about that," the detective said, reaching into his filing cabinet and taking out a manila folder. He paged through it and then placed it on the desk. "This is a copy of the official accident report. Would you like to look at it?"

"If you don't mind," Richard said.

"Take your time."

Richard picked up the folder and took out the papers. The detective noticed the confused expression on Richard's face, so he took the papers from Richard. "Let me paraphrase it for you," he said. "On a Saturday night, at approximately 11 p.m., you were heading down Broadway, toward West 48th Street. At that time a pedestrian was crossing the street against the light, which forced you to swerve out of the way to avoid hitting that person. Your car spun out of control and went into the intersection. Because your car was a convertible and you weren't wearing a seatbelt, you were ejected and your body hit a light pole. Your car crashed into a building on the other side of the street and came to a stop there.

"Unfortunately, it also struck a young woman who was crossing the street on the other side. There were no witnesses at the time. And the pedestrian who supposedly crossed the street against the lights was not there either when the responding officers first arrived."

"Oh my god," Richard gasped in horror. "Was that young woman all right?"

"You were both taken to the same hospital. She was in critical condition and was in a coma as well."

"Do you know if she is still at the hospital?"

The detective shook his head. "Her family eventually took her back home with them, and that was the last I've heard."

"I'm so sorry," Richard said faintly.

"Well, you *should* be!" the detective suddenly said in a harsh tone.

The detective's sudden outburst made Richard uneasy. He could tell that the detective was holding back from saying more.

"Is there something else, sir?" Richard asked puzzling.

"Yes, there is. But because of your family's close connections with the department, I'm not in the position to say anything else. Have a good day."

"Please, sir!" Richard pleaded. "If you know more about this, then please tell me. I promise you that I will not mention it to my father or your superiors. I'm just here to find out what I've done. I need some answers and some closure."

The detective slowly picked up the papers and looked at Richard with a sincere expression. "This report," he said, holding up the papers, "was the official version, but as an officer who has been investigating accident scenes for many years, I have my own version of the accident. Would you like to hear it?"

"Please."

"Before I begin, I want you to understand that I'm not accusing you of anything. I wasn't there to witness it. I'm just sharing my professional opinion."

"I understand."

The detective looked straight into Richard's eyes and said, "Off the record, I think that you were high—you were speeding and you weren't paying any attention to the traffic lights. You saw that the light was red at the last second and you panicked. You tried to stop, but your car was going too fast. It spun out of control into the intersection and struck that poor woman, who just happened to be in the wrong place at the wrong time."

Richard covered his face with his hands and hung his head in shame. "How did you know that I was high?" he asked woefully.

"There were traces of cocaine and cannabis inside your vehicle."

"What's cannabis?" Richard asked.

"Marijuana. The common street term would be 'dope.' Unfortunately, a toxicology test was not performed on you due to your family's close ties with the police commissioner and many of the other higher-ups. I had no other choice but to confirm the official version of the report to satisfy everyone's interests." Richard sensed the resentment and disgust in the detective's voice as he placed the reports back into the folder and then handed it to Richard.

"I'm so sorry," Richard said. "The word 'sorry' can't even scratch the surface of what I'm feeling right now. I have no idea what kind of person I used to be. I'm just so ashamed of myself and for what I've done."

"Well," the detective said, "apologizing to me won't do any good. You need to track down that young woman you injured and make it right."

"I have been planning on making things right ever since I came out of the coma. In fact, coming here was my first step toward redemption. By the way, do you have any information on this young woman that could help me find her?"

The detective pointed to the folder in Richard's hand. "Her personal information is somewhere inside the reports. This case was closed years ago, and I have not been updated with any current information on her."

"Thank you for your time, sir," Richard said sincerely as he got up and walked to the door.

"Hey!" the detective called out to him. Richard abruptly stopped and slowly turned around. In a stern voice, the detective said, "I don't make great choices myself, and I'm in no place to give advice, but I'll give you my two cents. You seem very sincere and truly sorry about your mistakes. This is your second chance at life, so stop being a spoiled little brat. Do something right with your life."

Again, Richard looked at him with a deep sense of shame. Without another word, he simply nodded and quietly left the office.


On the long walk back to his apartment, Richard was consumed with agonizing torment and shame. He knew in his heart that these feelings would be his constant companions as he retraced the life he once lived. He knew that he would have to repay everything he had done during his careless and reckless years.

About an hour later, he finally reached his apartment. Feeling mentally exhausted, he sat down on his couch. He couldn't stop thinking about the accident, and his heart couldn't stop bleeding for the poor young woman and her family. He turned his head to stare at the manila folder that he had placed on the coffee table, and decided to open it.

He was on the third page of the report when his eyes fell upon two words that sent his whole world crashing down on him. His heart weakened and his vision blurred. Two words on the page—two sweet words—would torment him for the rest of his living days. "Leela Vang," he murmured faintly.

*"I killed you,"* he whimpered. *"I was the one who killed you!"* he cried out loud.

# Chapter Forty

Richard tried to open his eyes, but the sunlight streaking through the window painfully blinded them. He turned his head away to avoid the glare, and then got up from the couch and looked outside. The sun had already traveled far above the horizon. *How long was I out?* he asked himself. He looked at his watch and noticed that it was almost nine o'clock. He had been sleeping not just for a few minutes, but for sixteen long hours.

He could feel pain, not only in his heart, but all over his body. His legs and arms were still tingling from lying down in the same position for so long. His head seemed to wobble as he tried to hold it up. He reached up to touch his puffy and sore eyes. He could feel a trace of rough, crusted residue on his cheek and realized that he had cried himself to sleep.

He sat down again and leaned forward, his hands holding his head as if they were trying to keep it from falling off. But all the aches in his body couldn't compare to the burning agony in his heart. He felt sick to his stomach thinking about the suffering he had caused. Because of his bad choices, his flaws, and his wrong decisions, in the blink of an eye he had hurt so many people.

He had broken his mother's heart—she had lost hope while waiting for her son to come out of his coma. When she died, he had made his father a lonely soul. He had profoundly wounded Elizabeth's grandmother's heart by taking away her granddaughter, the orphan she had raised. He had also injured Kenny's heart forever by stealing the life of his only sister, the only family that Kenny knew. Most of all, he had murdered his own heart by killing the one and only person he loved most in the world.

He hated himself and wished that he hadn't survived the accident. He didn't deserve to live after what he had done. Now he was told that he had to live out this lifetime to repay his karma. How could one lifetime be enough to pay for all the suffering he had caused? He had no right to return to Elizabeth after this. How dare he?

As the thoughts and questions cluttered his mind, he could no longer hold back the rage and disgust he had for himself. He cried out, grabbing his head and twisting it back and forth.

He thought about the night of the accident and wondered why he was out driving at such a late hour. Was he high? Where was he going? Why was he speeding?

He needed to find out more details. He knew that with his unacceptable behavior, he could never ask for forgiveness, but he wanted to know the truth so that he could do everything in his power to pay for his sin, to repay his karma.

He began to turn his apartment upside down, searching for something—anything—that could possibly spark his memory about the night of the accident. He searched high and low, even digging into drawers and behind furniture.

After a few hours of digging, he came upon a small black address book tucked in back of the top drawer of the large dresser inside his bedroom. He flipped through it. Could this book hold a clue?

"Was this really mine?" he said aloud in disgust as he went through pages and pages of women's names and phone numbers. He noticed that some names were marked with a small star next to them. He cringed with shame. "My god, I was such a dog!"

As he continued to look through the book, one particular name caught his attention. "Hal," he murmured. He suddenly remembered the two guys who visited him while he was at the hospital. "That's right. Hal claimed to be a good friend of mine," he whispered.

Richard grabbed his phone and called Hal's number, praying that it hadn't changed. A male voice answered the phone. "Yo, this is Hal."

"Hey buddy, this is David. How's it going?"

"Yo, Davey Boy! How the heck are ya?"

"I'm still not doing too well," Richard replied. "I was wondering if you could help me with something."

"Anything, dude. What's up?"

Richard paused for a few seconds, trying to come up with something to say.

"Yo! You still there, buddy?" Hal asked.

"Yeah, I'm still here," Richard quickly replied. "I've got a question about the night of my accident. I know it has been five years, but I'm wondering if you remembered anything about it."

"Yup, I was on the phone with you right up to when you crashed. I even heard you scream, 'Oh, shit!' And then your phone went dead silent."

Richard paused for a couple of seconds to allow it to sink in. "Really?" he asked. "So then, do you know why I was out driving that night and what our conversation was about?"

"Yup," Hal said. "I was at this awesome party and met two hot-looking chicks. I bragged to them about you, and they were dying to meet you. I figured that we could bring them back to your crib and maybe get some booty later on. I called you and you were already high, but you wanted to join me. You were taking your sweet time getting here, and the chicks were getting pissed. I called you again and told you to hurry up. I was still on the phone with you when you got into the accident."

Richard listened intently, feeling disgusted and ashamed. The detective was right about him being high.

"Hey, buddy, are you still there?"

"Yeah, I'm still here." Richard quickly snapped out of his trance. "Thanks for your help. I'll call you some other time."

"Let me know when you're feeling better, dude," Hal said. "I'll throw a huge welcome-back party for you and we'll booze it up. I'll make sure that the hottest chicks are invited, too. You better be well and be ready for some serious drinking."

"Sounds like a plan. Thanks." Richard hung up with the intention of never talking to or seeing Hal again. There was no reason to. Just the thought of him hanging out and drinking with that group of friends made him sick to his stomach.

How could he have been so irresponsible? His rush to get another score under his belt had caused the death of the person most precious to him. Not only was he physically injured, but his heart had been scarred for the rest of his life. How could he ever forgive himself for being so foolish? How was he ever going to overcome this guilt?

He thought about Kenny and Kenny's grandmother and couldn't imagine the pain that they had gone through. How was he going to face them now and tell them that he was the irresponsible monster who had taken the life of their beloved Leela? But what pained him most was facing Elizabeth, knowing that he was the one who put her there in that place—that lonely place underneath the tree. "Don't ever forgive me. Please don't forgive me," he murmured softly in between sobs.

What should he do now? he asked himself over and over. He briefly contemplated suicide, but quickly decided against it. If he killed himself he would be a lost soul forever, and he had already vowed to never break his promise to her. If he committed suicide, she, too, would be a lost soul, doomed to wander a dark and endless path for eternity. Besides, only a coward would take the shortcut and commit suicide to be free of the pain, torment, and suffering. He didn't deserve to be free from it. He must endure it and live to pay for what he had done.

Suddenly Richard felt a strong sense of urgency to let Kenny and Kenny's grandmother know what had happened. Even if they would hate him forever, they still deserved to know the truth. Doing that, Richard decided, would be a small step toward his soul's redemption.

He thought about calling them, but he realized it would be cowardly to break such terrible news over the phone. "No," he said aloud. "I'm going to look them in the eyes and tell them. I'm willing to face whatever consequences will come to me. I owe them this much."

He went straight to his computer and booked another flight to Minnesota.

# Chapter Forty-One

It was early Sunday morning—a lovely, golden morning with the young sun barely peeking above the horizon. Richard had just arrived in St. Paul, and it seemed things had changed since his last trip. The beautiful scenery that he had fallen in love with appeared unfamiliar to him this time. The hotel was still there, and everything was in its correct place, but somehow things seemed different this time around.

He felt as if he had been floating in the nothingness of an odd world for the past few days as he tried desperately to balance his emotions. He wanted to be strong, but the deep throbbing pain in his heart wouldn't subside. Even though his mind couldn't remember the tragic event, his heart would never let him forget. He pulled out his phone to call Kenny.

"Didn't you just leave?" a voice on the other end said jokingly.

"Yes, Kenny, but I've returned," Richard replied. "I have an important matter that I need to discuss with you and Grandmother."

The drive to Kenny's house seemed to take forever as Richard tried to think of a way to deliver the news. He expected the worst and hoped that they would never forgive him. He knew that if that happened, for some reason his heart would rest a little easier.

As he neared Kenny's house, he decided to park his car about a block away to avoid being seen just yet. He waited silently in the car for several minutes, trying to gather courage. Then he stepped out of the car and, with the manila folder in his hand, he slowly made his way up to the front door.

"Richard, it's so nice to see you again," Kenny said cheerfully as he came out of the house to greet him.

"Hello, Kenny," Richard said faintly.

"I didn't expect to see you back here so soon, but anyways, I'm really glad to see you."

Richard let out a deep sigh before timidly saying, "I have a very important matter to discuss with you and Grandmother. That's why I came back. Is she inside?"

"Yes, and she is very happy and excited to see you again."

Richard stepped inside and noticed that Kenny's grandmother was sitting on the couch. Her pleasant smile was warm and soothing, and it immediately gnawed at his agonizing heart. She loved him and even called him her son; she had no idea that he was here to break her heart all over again.

He looked at her and tried to muster a smile, but it quickly faded as he lowered his eyes to stare at the floor. He just wanted to hold his breath until he could no longer feel the pain in his heart anymore.

"Richard, come to me, my son," she said invitingly, holding out both arms.

Without a word, he slowly walked over to her, set the folder on the table, and knelt down in front of her. He placed his hands on her lap, rested his head on them, and began to sob softly.

She gently placed both hands on his head and carefully lifted his face to meet hers. "Don't cry, my son. I love you, too," she said with a comforting voice.

He could barely believe the words that this wonderful woman had just said to him. How could he have killed her granddaughter and still be taken in as a loving son? How could he be so cold and heartless to come back here, only to leave a scar in her heart forever? Still, he knew it would have been even more heartless to remain in New York and keep all of this a secret.

He wiped away his tears and sat next to her on the couch, looking intently into her warm, loving eyes for a moment. Then he picked up the folder and held it out.

"What's this?" Kenny asked with a quizzical look as he reached down to take it from Richard's hand.

"This is the reason I'm here today, Kenny."

Kenny opened it and pulled out the papers. He slowly looked at them and then he shifted his eyes to Richard. "When did you get this report?" he calmly asked.

"Two days ago," Richard replied with teary eyes. "I've been agonizing over it ever since and wished a thousand times that it wasn't true, but it is true. I'm the one who is responsible for Leela's horrific accident. I'm truly sorry," he said with a choked-up voice.

Kenny took a deep breath and slowly asked, "And you're here to apologize?"

Richard felt helpless and didn't know what else to do, so he simply nodded. "I know that words couldn't possibly make up for the pain and sorrow you both go through every day of your lives without her, and I will understand if you can never forgive me." He paused to wipe his eyes, and then continued. "I am also suffering, and words alone could never express the guilt and torment I am going through right now."

Kenny slowly set the folder on the table and turned to Richard. "You are a better man than I thought, Richard."

Richard looked at Kenny with a puzzled expression.

Kenny let out a deep sigh. "I read this same report years ago, right after the accident. I read it over and over again and had never forgotten the name of the person who took my sister away from me and my grandmother." Kenny glanced away for a moment and then turned and looked intently at Richard. "At the restaurant when you introduced yourself to me as David Voss, and then you asked me about the whereabouts of a particular woman, I knew that you were talking about my sister. Right then, I wanted to punch you in the face. But I didn't. I simply told you that I'd never seen her before, and I left that day with the hope that I would never see you again. Through some strange twist of fate, our paths crossed again and you came to my assistance. After that, I could sense the sincerity in you, and I knew that you were really here to make amends for what you did. That was why I decided to take you to see my sister." Kenny gently placed his hand on Richard's shoulder, and with a warm, loving expression, he said, "We have already forgiven you, Richard. That was what my sister would have wanted us to do."

Richard leaned back on the couch and began to weep quietly. Kenny's kind words made him feel even worse; he didn't want Leela's family to forgive him. Even if they did, he could never forgive himself.

Suddenly, he felt a gentle touch on his shoulder. He looked up to see that Kenny's grandmother had moved closer to him. She reached out and wrapped him in a warm, comforting embrace.

"Cry, my son," she said warmly. "Cry out all your pain and sorrow today, and be done with crying come tomorrow. From this day on, you will live a happy life. You will do many great things. You will give and will also receive great things."

In the comfort of the grandmother's arms, Richard was slowly able to let out all of his sorrow, his guilt, and his torment. One by one, each painful emotion made its way out of his heart to be released.

"How could I ever receive great things, Grandma? I don't deserve anything."

"You have found your karma," she said as she wiped away his tears. She gently touched his grieving face and added, "You are not that man anymore. You are a great man from the other side. You must fulfill your destiny. Then you will be with my granddaughter once again."

He gave her a despairing look. "There is no one else I trust more than you, Grandma. But how can I fulfill my destiny when I don't know what it is? I don't even where to look or how to find it." He glanced away to stare at the folder, and then added, "I fear that I won't find my destiny before I leave this world and I will never be with her again."

"It is not as hard as you think," she said calmly.

He looked at her quizzically.

She smiled warmly at him. "It is not as hard as you think," she repeated. She leaned closer to him. "My granddaughter had already opened your eyes. She had taught you every day when you were with her. She started preparing you for your journey a long time ago."

Sensing that he was still confused, she reached out a hand and touched his chest. "My granddaughter's spirit lives within your heart. She will guide you throughout your journey. Follow what's in your heart, and you'll find your destiny."

As he pondered what she'd just told him, she said, "Always try to remember this: *The wonderful things you do for others will not be forgotten. They will accompany you and guide you throughout your journey.*"

Richard's eyes widened. He knew that he had heard those exact words before. The first time was from the elderly Chinese woman who was selling shoes. The second time was from Mai, at the shop. And now, it was Elizabeth's grandmother who told him this. *There's got to be some sort of connection to all of this*, he thought.

Before he could say anything, she reached down and grabbed hold of his hands, squeezing them tightly in hers. "No more bad news," she said. "I want to share with you something that only I know."

He waited with great anticipation. He knew from her joyful expression that she was going to tell him something wonderful.

She smiled lovingly and leaned over to whisper into his ear. "When you see my granddaughter again, tell her that I will be reborn on the other side as her daughter. My time with her is not over. This time, she will be the one to take care of me."

Richard's eyes widened again, and he looked at her with a bewildered expression. Before he could ask the question, she'd already confirmed the answer. "Yes," she said smiling. "You will find your destiny very soon. You will be with my granddaughter again."

With an ecstatic expression on his face, he slowly wiped away his tears. "Thank you, Grandma. I will tell her about you. We will cherish and love you with all our hearts."

Richard's heart was filled with joy and liberation. These two kind and understanding strangers that he had just met a few days before had now become his loving family. For the first time in his life, he knew that he would have a loving brother and a loving grandmother. Maybe, in a way, he was already repaying his karma. Maybe Elizabeth had led him to her family so that he could look after them the way she would have if she were still alive. He silently made a promise to himself that he would love and cherish them for the rest of his life.

Still, even after this news, he felt somewhat uneasy. Much of the torment in his heart had melted away, but there was still a gloomy cloud hovering over him.

He needed to be with Elizabeth, because there was an overwhelming urge deep inside his heart to ask for her forgiveness.

He left Kenny's house with the promise of returning later on in the evening for dinner with the two of them.

Richard parked his car at the base of the large hill. He got out and as he looked up, he could see the large oak tree standing proudly on the hill, waiting as if it was expecting his arrival.

He slowly ascended and came to a stop as he saw her headstone standing there, all alone, underneath that huge tree. Just as before, seeing the lonely headstone caused a deep and agonizing pain in his heart—except this time the pain was a hundred times worse, because he now knew that he was the very reason why she was there.

He stood there silently, looking at her picture as the tears fell silently down his cheeks.

After a long while, he opened his mouth. "Hello, my darling," he said, his lips quivering. His knees weakened and his body began to tremble. He dropped to the ground and knelt in front of her. With both hands cupping his face, he cried, "*I'm so sorry!* Please forgive me. I'm so sorry . . ." No words came out after that—only the sound of his cries. He continued crying for a long time, and then everything went dark.

"Wake up, Richard," a voice said softly.

Richard slowly opened his eyes to see Elizabeth's smiling face looking down at him. He then noticed that his head was resting comfortably on her lap, and she was gently combing her fingers through his hair.

"Elizabeth," he sobbed softly.

"Yes, it's me," she whispered.

"Why am I here? Am I . . . dead?"

"No," she assured him. "I was granted another chance with you."

She continued combing through his hair. How he appreciated just being in her arms—he could stay like this for eternity. "How I've long for this moment," he sobbed. "I want to stay like this forever."

"Shhh . . ." She gently placed her finger on his lips. "I know," she simply said.

Richard slowly sat up and noticed that they were in the middle of a beautiful valley filled with soft, luscious green grass. The sun was high in the sky, hot and vibrant, but in her refuge, he felt pleasantly cool and safe. The sight of this beautiful yet empty place brought tears to his eyes once again as he suddenly remembered his cruel and selfish act—the act that had resulted in her being here.

"I'm so sorry. I've done such a cruel thing to you," he cried. "Please forgive me."

"There's nothing to forgive," she said with a warm and comforting voice.

"But I did this to you. I put you here in this lonely place."

She reached over to tenderly touch his cheek, trailing her fingers down to his lips to stop him from speaking. With a warm and loving smile, she softly said, *"It was our fate to meet this way.* I've forgiven you with all my heart. Please don't dwell in your pain any longer."

"I miss you so much, Elizabeth," he said as he wiped away a tear. "I don't know how you managed to live every day without me. Without you, I died a little every day."

"I know that you'll come back to me. I've lived every day with this hope in my heart. That is how I managed," she softly replied. "You must fulfill your destiny, and we will be with each other once again."

He turned away in despair. "How am I to ever find my destiny? I don't even know what it is."

She reached over to turn his face back to meet hers before explaining. "Everyone was put on earth with a destiny to fulfill. Everyone also has free will to change what was written for them by the heavens. Some will find their destiny and live a full and contented life. Most will never find it and will live an unhappy life, powerless to change their fate." She sighed softly, and then continued. "I can't tell you what your destiny is because it was written for you and only you. But you will find it as you continue on your journey."

Richard turned and stared at the horizon. He thought about how beautiful this place was, yet it was not to be shared with him. The more he thought about it, the more trapped and suffocated he felt. He was so helpless and powerless to change his fate. He let out a deep, agonizing sigh and then, with quivering lips, he said, "I want this to all end. I want the hurt and torment to end. I don't think I can go on another day with this pain lingering in my heart like this. Even though my heart is still beating, I feel like I'm dead."

"You must be strong," she said, caressing his face with the back of her fingers. "You must fight this pain every day. You will never be alone on your journey." A cool breeze mixed with her gentle touch on his face. He closed his eyes and slowly surrendered himself to the beautiful stillness of the moment.

Suddenly, his heart came to life, beating gracefully to the sweet sound of her humming. He immediately recognized the tune as the same one she had played for him once in the city of Atkins. Her sweet, soothing, angelic voice continued as he drifted off to sleep.

Richard woke with a heart full of love and sweet memories, but his arms were empty. He sighed sadly as his eyes opened to a world filled with nothing.

*"I've forgiven you,"* whispered a gust of wind blowing from the leaves in the tree above him. The voice seemed so clear to him that he stood up and looked around, only to discover that he was all alone.

He looked at his watch and noticed that it was already seven o'clock in the evening. He had been out cold for almost four hours. *My time with her was too brief,* he said sadly to himself. However, it was a beautiful memory that he would treasure for as long as he was alive.

He gently caressed her picture on the headstone. "Thank you, my darling," he said. "Thank you for forgiving me. I promise you that I will never dwell on the past again—I will only live for the future. You sleep now, and I promise I will see you again." Then he leaned over and tenderly kissed her.

# Chapter Forty-Two

Richard arrived back in New York City around one o'clock in the afternoon the next day. What began as an unimaginable nightmare had blossomed into a whole new and beautiful beginning for him. He felt blessed and fortunate that he was granted the opportunity to meet Elizabeth's family. How compassionate they were to have forgiven him and to have granted him another chance to better his life after the awful crime that he had committed. How kind of them to not resent him, to not hold grudges against him, and to not seek revenge. Instead, they embraced him and accepted him into their family, and they were willing to help guide him toward the right path, so that he could be with their beloved Leela once again. Through them, he had learned how to embrace forgiveness, and also learned that letting go of one's anger, grudges, and bitterness meant living a healthier, happier, and peaceful life.

He pondered over and over what Kenny's grandmother had told him about his destiny: that Elizabeth had already opened his eyes and had taught him every day. She said that the wonderful things he would do for others would not be forgotten, and that they would accompany him throughout his journey.

As he was deeply engrossed in his thoughts, a sudden realization emerged from deep inside his soul, overwhelming his heart and mind. How could he not have seen this before? All those times when he was with Elizabeth, he had always been in awe of her generosity and her loving and forgiving heart. How could he not have realized this before? He remembered wishing that Angela would be more like Elizabeth, and at one point he even told Angela that Elizabeth had opened his eyes, heart, and soul to seeing the beautiful things that the world had to offer. Now, he finally understood why Kenny's grandmother had said that Elizabeth's spirit lives in his heart, and that he must follow what's in his heart.

He now knew what he must do. He had to live the life that she would have lived. She was waiting for him in that beautiful paradise. And to get to her, he would have to follow the road that she had already paved for him. She was his journey, his karma, and his destiny.

He was excited and felt like a brand-new person. He decided that he needed to go see his father, so he went straight to the Voss Building from the airport.


Richard opened the door to Marshall's office and saw him sitting at the desk, deeply absorbed in his work.

"Hello, Father," he said excitedly as he walked in.

"David!" Marshall replied with a joyous expression on his face. He immediately stood up and came around his desk to give Richard a big hug. "So? How did it go?" he asked. "Did you find her?"

"Yes, I did." Richard was beaming.

"Well? Where is she? I'd love to meet her."

Richard suddenly became quiet for a moment and then he looked at Marshall with a despairing expression. "She's not here, Father. She has passed on."

Marshall just stared blankly at Richard. He didn't know what to do or say to comfort Richard, so he simply said, "I'm sorry, David. I'm very sorry."

"It's all right, Father. I would have been very happy if she was still alive, but I'm still happy that I finally found her. Through it all, I was able to find closure."

They stood in silence for a few seconds, and then Marshall softly asked, "Who was she? Where did you meet her?"

With a grieving look on his face, Richard replied, "You remember my accident five years ago? She was the person that I hurt."

"Are you sure?" Marshall asked, puzzling.

"It was confirmed. I read the police reports. After the accident, she was flown back to Minnesota to be with her family. She died there over a year ago."

Marshall let out a deep sigh and then placed a hand on Richard's shoulder. "I'm so sorry, David. It must've been very hard and painful for you to go about this alone, but I'm very proud of you for doing this."

"Thank you, Father. I was very hurt when I learned that she was no longer in this world, and then it nearly killed me to discover that I was the one who ended her life. But that wasn't all. Because then I had to face her family and confess to them that I was responsible for taking the life of their precious child."

Marshall slowly nodded. "I know that it doesn't help for me to say that I understand your pain, but I'm sure it was not an easy task. As a father, I'm also in pain every time my children go through tough times. My deepest condolences also go to the family of that poor woman. As a father, I also understand their pain. I hope they will learn to forgive you someday."

Richard looked at Marshall with tears in his eyes. "They are the most understanding and forgiving people, Father," he said. "I don't believe I deserve to be forgiven, but they did forgive me. They were kind and gracious enough to even accept me into their family. They are wonderful people with a beautiful culture. The tremendous guilt and pain in my heart were lifted away, and I've finally found some peace within myself."

"No matter how long it takes for you to repay the gratitude that they've shown to you, I'll be with you every step of the way," Marshall assured him.

"Thank you, Father." Richard reached out and embraced Marshall. Wiping away tears, he chokingly apologized. "I'm so sorry, Father, that I put you and Mother through hell all these years. I know that words cannot even come close to explaining how I'm feeling right now, but I want you to know that I'm no longer the man I once was. I will never take life for granted, and I will only make you proud from this day forward."

"There's no need to apologize, my son," Marshall assured him. "Just having you here and hearing you say those words have made me a very proud father already."

Richard left Marshall's office with a new sense of purpose. He felt whole and complete, and believed in his heart that he had finally found his place in this world—that he was at last on his way to fulfilling his destiny. He silently made a promise to himself that he would fulfill his purpose in this world and build a stairway that would lead him back to Elizabeth—to his Heaven. It didn't matter how long it was going to take him; he would never stray away from this purpose.

He decided to go for a long walk around the city—the city he now called his home, the city where his long journey had begun.

He walked for hours without a destination, but he didn't care—he just wanted to start his new journey. Soon he came upon a small restaurant on the Upper West Side. He hadn't eaten anything since he'd left St. Paul early this morning, so he decided to go in for a meal.

While he was looking over the menu, he heard a familiar voice, "Hello, Richard." He glanced back up to see that Mary was standing in front of him.

"Mary!" he exclaimed. "How are you?"

"I'm doing well, and yourself?" she said.

"I'm doing great!"

He noticed she seemed uncomfortable about something, so he tried to think of something to ease the situation. "Are you by yourself today? There's an empty seat here. If you don't mind, I would like some company."

"Thank you," Mary replied with a faint smile.

She sat across from him and just stared at him in silence for a moment. She seemed like she wanted to say something to him, but she held back.

"Is something wrong?" he politely asked.

She looked back at him with a sincere expression "Look, Richard," she said. "I'm really sorry about what happened before, with Adam. I—"

"There's no need to apologize," he said, quickly cutting her off. "I am the one who should be apologizing to you. I should have been more considerate of your personal life. I'm sorry I put you in an awkward situation."

She smiled sweetly. "I didn't mean to make it seem like I was leading you on. I should have known that you were very vulnerable at the time, and I should have been more careful."

He smiled politely. "It's not your fault at all."

"So, does this mean that we are still friends?" she said.

"Of course—you're the only friend I have," he assured her. "By the way, where's your boyfriend today, if you don't mind my nosiness?"

"He's back home in Minnesota."

"Minnesota?" Richard said, surprised.

"Yes, he's a doctor, and he is doing his residency at the Mayo Clinic in Minnesota," she replied. "Is something the matter?"

He chuckled. "I just came back from Minnesota a few hours ago."

"Really? Why were you there, may I ask?"

Richard looked at her. "I went to Minnesota to search for someone."

"Is that right?" Mary said. "Did you find that person?"

"I did, but it wasn't a sweet experience. In fact, it was a painful and traumatic one. But it was a rewarding and liberating experience that changed me in many ways."

"I'm sorry to hear that it was painful, but I'm glad everything is resolved," Mary said.

"Yes, you could say things are resolved. While I was searching for that person, I also found myself and I know I will never lose myself again. I'm proud to say that I am now a changed man, and I believe now that I have a whole new purpose in life."

# Chapter Forty-Three

Richard slowly opened his eyes to the warm sunshine pouring in through the windows. He turned his head a little to allow the bright rays to brush across his cheek. As he lay there with the warmth on his face, he knew that it was going to be a day full of promise. He thought about getting up, but his body ached, and he collapsed back into the soft bed and closed his eyes, listening to the birds singing outside the window.

He still wished he could open his eyes to see Elizabeth every morning, but he had accepted the fact that he was going to walk his journey alone. Even though she wasn't here to share his bed and to hold his hand, she was never far from his heart. He could feel her presence, he could see her in his dreams, and he looked forward to going home to her soon.

It was May 24th. Tomorrow was going to be his day—a day so special to him that in fifty long years he had not forgotten it. Even though his aged body was weak and frail, he was not going to let tomorrow pass by without seeing her again.

After a moment of struggling to get out of bed, he was finally able to move himself to the edge of the bed. He sat there for a moment to allow his body to recover, and then he slowly reached for his cane. When he got to his feet, he felt a wave of dizziness and had to sit back down on his bed for a while longer.

Every morning was a struggle for him to get out of bed, but he never complained, because each day he was a day closer to being with his Elizabeth again. Even though he ached to stay in bed, he knew he had to get up so that he could get ready for the next day. He had been waiting patiently all year long for this significant moment when he could visit her once again.

Using his cane, he brought himself to his feet and slowly walked to the bathroom. The warm water from the faucet felt refreshing as he splashed it on his face. Then he stopped for a moment as he gazed at his reflection in the mirror.

He sighed softly. His once magnificent and strong body was now hunched over. His once clean-cut, handsome face was now fragile, wrinkled, and darkened with age spots. His once brownish hair was now grayish and silvery.

As he thought back through the previous fifty years, he smiled with contentment. If he had to walk alone on this path again, he wouldn't have done it any differently. He had lived his life to the fullest and had done many great things. He wouldn't leave behind any regrets if he were to suddenly leave this world.

He had set up many foundations to assist those who were less fortunate in the city and around the world. He had created several programs to help orphans, both in New York City and in other cities. He had turned most of his properties into affordable housing for those in poverty. He had traveled to Thailand many times and created a hospital there and several schools for Hmong refugees who were still living in camps. He had become a leading advocate for Hmong people, lobbying the Laotian government to improve their living conditions.

He wouldn't have lived his life any other way. He even wanted to do more, but his old body couldn't handle it anymore. Perhaps he would do more and give more in his next lifetime.

He slowly walked out of his room and could smell a sweet aroma coming from the kitchen. Amy, his personal assistant, had just finished cooking his breakfast and had placed several dishes on the dining table for him.

"Good morning, Mr. Voss," she said, greeting him cheerfully as always.

"Good morning, Amy," he replied in a raspy, cheerful voice.

"How are you this morning, sir?"

"Well, it took a while for this old body to get going, but I'm doing better now."

"Maybe you'll feel even stronger after breakfast," she said with a smile as she helped him to his chair.

He nibbled on some eggs and then exhaled deeply, feeling a little nauseous. He set his fork down, clasped his hands tightly together and just stared down at the food. Then he picked up his fork and took another bite, but he wasn't able to eat much, so he laid his fork back on the table.

"Is there something wrong, sir?" Amy asked in a concerned manner.

"No, Amy. The food is delicious, but unfortunately, I just don't have the appetite for it," he replied. Then, he turned to her and said, "Did you make all the arrangements for my trip to Minnesota? It's very important."

"Yes, sir," she replied. "Everything is arranged. Jessie should be here in two hours to accompany you to the airport." She looked at him with a slight frown. "I'm sorry for asking this, sir, but I'm very concerned about you. You have been very tired lately, and I'm not sure it's a good idea for you to travel at this time."

"Don't worry, sweetie," Richard said softly. "I'm really looking forward to this trip. My visit to Minnesota on May 25th is one that I've never missed. I will be all right, dear."

Amy sighed. "Again, I'm sorry if I'm being nosy," she said, "but if you don't mind sharing, why do you go there every year? Even though I've only been with you for three years, you're like a father to me. I'm curious, and I'm concerned for your health."

Richard smiled at her. "I go there to be with the woman that I loved. May 25th is the day I met her, and I go there to be with her every year on our anniversary."

"Were you married to her?"

"Not exactly," he replied. "We were going to be married, but we were parted. All I have left are my fondest memories. I go there to bring flowers to her grave and be with her every year."

Amy smiled. "That is a beautiful and inspiring story, sir, but it brings tears to my eyes. I can't imagine what it would feel like to not be with the person that I love so dearly for so many years. I'm so sorry, sir. I truly admire you. I admire your devotion."

"It's like she never left my side, Amy. It's just a matter of time now before I go home to be with her again."

She paused after hearing that. "Mr. Voss, you have to promise me that you'll come back. I'm going to miss you so much."

He slowly reached out his hand to hold hers. "I'll be all right. I've lived a great life."

It wasn't long before Jessie arrived to accompany Richard on his trip. He took Richard's luggage down to the lobby. Amy walked with Richard and helped him get to the elevators.

As Richard was just about to get into the limo, Amy reached over to give him a hug. Tears flowed down her cheeks as she embraced him, clinging tightly to him like a child hugging a parent. Somehow, she knew that she might not see him again.

He gently wiped away her tears with the back of his hand. "Don't cry, sweetie. Thank you for taking care of me. I will be all right." He tenderly touched her face and added, "I've created a trust fund for you to go to college, and that fund will take care of you for the rest of your life. Please live your life to the fullest and enjoy every moment of it."

The plane ride to Minnesota seemed to take longer than usual, and the energy was slowly draining from Richard's body. He spent the entire ride sleeping and was awoken by Jessie after the plane had landed.

On the long ride to the hotel in downtown St. Paul, Richard fell asleep again in the limo and was awoken by Jessie's voice: "Are you all right, sir? If you're not well, we can go to the hospital."

"No, Jessie," Richard assured him. "I'm quite all right. I'm just tired from the long trip, that's all."

They arrived at the hotel, and Richard went immediately to the bedroom to lie down.

"Sir, are you hungry? Should I order dinner for you?" Jessie asked as he peeked into the room.

"No, Jessie. I'm not hungry. You should order dinner for yourself," Richard replied breathlessly. "I'm going to go to sleep now. Please wake me when the sun first appears in the morning."

"Yes, sir," Jessie replied. "You have a good night."

# Chapter Forty-Four

It was the early morning of May 25th. The sunrise painted the horizon in a brilliant orange, pink, and yellow hue that stretched like a masterpiece for thousands of miles across the sky.

As the limo made its way through the enormous gates of the cemetery, Richard looked out the window, his vision becoming clearer and clearer now as the world came alive. The silhouettes of the hills, rocks, and trees slowly disappeared and gave way to stunning shades of green and brown.

He was mesmerized by the beauty of the lush vegetation as the sun smiled graciously down upon it. He stared out into the distance—*how beautiful this place is!* he thought. He was excited, as if he was just seeing it for the first time, even though he had made numerous trips here every year for the past fifty years.

While the limo slowly maneuvered its way along the curvy road, he could see the large oak tree standing proudly on top of the hill, like a shepherd watching over its flock of sheep. When the limo came to a stop at the bottom of the hill, Jessie immediately got out to open the door for Richard.

With the help of his cane in one hand, Richard slowly pulled his aching body out of the seat while the other hand tightly held a bouquet of flowers. He stood there for a moment and then slowly stretched his back to ease the stiffness and pain. He looked up at the large tree and knew that he was going to struggle to reach his destination, but he was not going to let anything keep him from getting up that hill to be with Elizabeth.

He let out a deep sigh, and with the support of his cane, he steadily walked up the hill. It seemed to take an eternity, and he had to stop several times to catch his breath. But he was not going to give up.

"Do you need help, sir?" Jessie called out to him.

"No. I'm all right," Richard called back. "I've done this every year!"

With sheer determination, he finally made it to the top and slowly approached Elizabeth's headstone. He stood in front of her for a moment before laying the bouquet of flowers next to her. Then he reached over to softly caress her picture. "Hello, my dear. How are you? You still look as beautiful as the very first day I met you," he said in a low, raspy voice.

He sat down beside her and slowly leaned against her. "I've missed you so much. I've missed you every day for fifty years."

Tears formed at the corner of his eyes as he thought about his deteriorating body and that he might no longer be able to visit her and bring her flowers. He closed his eyes and drifted off to sleep next to her.

"Sir? Are you all right?" Jessie asked as he gently shook Richard's shoulder. But when Richard showed no sign of waking up or moving at all, he tried to wake him up again. "Mr. Voss? Mr. Voss! Are you all right?"

Richard just lay there peacefully, as if he had been touched by an angel. Jessie was panicking a little now, so he shook Richard's shoulders again, hoping to wake him up this time. Eventually Richard began to slowly open his eyes.

"It is now four o'clock, sir," Jessie said. "You'll miss your flight if we don't leave now."

Richard slowly reached for his cane. "Thank you, Jessie. Give me just a minute to bid my farewell." Richard felt rested and refreshed. He couldn't believe how much strength he had gained by just being by Elizabeth's side. He leaned down and gently kissed her, and then he whispered faintly to her, "You sleep now, my love, and I promise I will see you again."

As they left the cemetery, Richard felt his strength draining again. He didn't want to do anything except closed his eyes and sleep.

"Would you like to stop somewhere else, or should we just go straight to the airport, sir?" Jessie asked.

"I'm very tired, Jessie," Richard faintly replied. "Let's go back to the hotel tonight, and it would be great if you could please reschedule our flight for tomorrow."

"Yes, sir. I'll call the hotel to let them know that we're coming back."

When they reached the hotel, Richard went straight to his room. He felt so weak and exhausted that he could barely make it to his bed. As he struggled to pull back the covers, he heard a soft knock at the door. But he was too tired to even talk, so he just closed his eyes and collapsed on the bed.

The door slowly cracked open and he heard Jessie calling his name in a low, faint whispering voice from what seemed like a long distance away.

"Mr. Voss? Are you okay, sir?" Jessie asked as he entered the bedroom. "Mr. Voss?" he called, but Richard was too sleepy to respond. "Mr. Voss, sir?" he called again.

"Yes, Jessie?" Richard finally replied breathlessly.

"Sir, would you like me to order dinner for you? You haven't eaten anything all day."

"I'm not hungry, Jessie. Please, order dinner for yourself and I'll see you in the morning," Richard replied in a tired voice.

"You must eat something, sir. It's for your health and your strength. You need to gain your strength for tomorrow's flight."

"Just bring me a glass of water and I will be fine, Jessie."

Jessie returned a few minutes later with a glass of water and helped Richard sit up for a drink. "Sleep well and I'll see you in the morning, sir," Jessie said as he left the bedroom and closed the door behind him.

As Richard lay sleeping, his spirit was joyful and content, but his body was weak and exhausted. It seemed as if he didn't have an ounce of energy left in his body. His breathing had become extremely labored and he had to open his mouth now to gasp for air, like a fish out of water.

Richard was frightened and attempted to call Jessie for help, but he couldn't manage to say anything. He tried desperately to pull himself out of bed, but he couldn't move.

Suddenly an overwhelming feeling of peace and calmness filled his heart, and he willingly closed his eyes. He took two deep breaths and slowly let them out. With his third breath, he smiled happily. His next breath never came.

"Richard, wake up," a voice called to him.

"Hmm . . .?"

"Wake up," the voice called out again.

"Elizabeth? Am I dreaming again?" he asked.

"No, Richard," she replied softly. "Wake up."

He slowly opened his eyes. He was standing in the middle of the same lush green field that he stood in fifty years ago when he had first visited her grave. How he had wanted so desperately to return to this beautiful paradise again, but he had never been able to. He closed his eyes for a moment and tried to relax and just indulge in the tranquility of this place—a place where he knew she existed.

He slowly opened his eyes again to find himself standing on the dirt path he had stood on long ago. Excited, he followed the path to the bottom and then immediately ran up the hill as fast as he could.

As he approached the top, he stopped, noticing the breathtaking view. It was definitely different now from when he first saw it. The whole hilltop was covered with thousands upon thousands of beautiful, lively flowers.

"She did have her garden," he whispered joyously.

He walked a few more steps and saw Elizabeth standing in the middle of the field, smiling that same captivating smile that he had missed for so long. All those years of missing her and longing for her, and here she was—standing there, so gorgeous. She took his breath away once again, just as she had done that first moment he laid eyes on her fifty-something years ago. His eyes moistened with tears as he ran to embrace her.

"I've missed you so much, Elizabeth! How I've longed for your touch, for your smile, and to hear your sweet voice again," he cried out loud.

She reached out and wiped away his tears, and with tears in her own eyes she softly said, "You're here now, my darling. Your destiny has been fulfilled. We're finally together again."

"I've always kept you so close and dear to my heart throughout my long and painful journey," he said in a shaky voice. "I've struggled along the way, but I endured it bravely because I knew that it would lead me back to you. You don't know how happy my heart is to know that you have waited all these long and lonely years for me, my love."

She reached out and gently placed a finger on his quivering lips. "Shhhh... I know," she said warmly. "You are my soul mate, Richard, and I would never leave you behind."

She took his hand, and they went to the edge of the hill. As they stood there, staring far out at the beautiful horizon, she turned to him and said, "I've waited for you for so long. I've never lost hope that you would find your way back to me. Now we can leave this place together."

He looked at her despairingly. He had just arrived in this beautiful place— why would he want to leave? "Leave?" he said. "Why must we leave? I want to spend an eternity with you here."

She turned to him and softly said, "I know, my darling. But we have to leave this place." She leaned out and gave him a tender kiss, and then she added, "We have to go finish our journey together."

"Where are we going?"

She pointed east to the picturesque valley below the set of hills. "We are going to that beautiful valley over there. It is there where we'll spend the rest of our lives together." She turned to him and added, "Do you remember when I told you I wanted to go there with you?"

He suddenly remembered standing in that spot with her fifty years ago, and remembered how her heart longed to be over there with him. He silently nodded.

"Now we can go, Richard. We can go over there together."

He took a deep breath as he gazed at the horizon. "It seems so far away. How are we ever going to get there?" he asked.

She smiled sweetly at him, and then softly replied, "Just close your eyes, Richard. We'll be there when you open your eyes."

He closed his eyes and held on to her as tightly as he could. This time, there was no way he was going to ever lose her again—not now, and not ever.

# Chapter Forty-Five

The morning was quiet and peaceful. A splash of fresh yellowish-orange light was peeking through the window. Richard squinted his eyes just a little and then hid his face under his pillow to avoid being completely consumed by the bright rays.

His body was still very tired, and his eyes were still shut. He didn't want his beautiful dream to be disturbed, but he needed to wake up. After such an unbelievable dream, he suddenly felt the urge to reconnect himself with reality. He felt the need to strengthen himself mentally, physically, and spiritually so that he could continue on with his journey.

He slowly opened his eyes just a little to get them adjusted to the bright sunlight. He moved his arm out from under his comforter and reached his hand across the mattress to feel the edge of the bed. His heart ached as he lay in bed, trying to once again recall his beautiful dream.

It was so disappointing to not wake up in the arms of his lovely Elizabeth, but instead alone in his large, empty bed.

He pulled himself up and realized that for some reason he didn't have to struggle much this morning. He sat on the edge of the bed for a moment to allow the pain in his body to pass before getting up to his feet, but again he was surprised to feel no pain at all this time. *The long night's rest must have helped a great deal*, he thought. Or maybe the magnificent dream had revived his strength somehow.

He quickly reached for his cane but discovered that it was not there at the side of the bed like it had been every morning. *Maybe Amy took it and forgot to put it back*, he thought.

He quickly hopped to his feet with very little effort. Then he carefully walked to the bathroom like he did every morning, looking down and rubbing his eyes.

He turned on the faucet to let the water run for a while before he gently tested it with his hands to see if the water was warm enough. Then, he splashed the warm and refreshing liquid onto his face. He felt stronger now and even more alive as the soothing water touched his skin and washed away the tiredness.

He slowly opened his eyes, expecting to see his old wrinkled face. But to his surprise, he was staring straight at a total stranger—a young and familiar face, one he thought he had seen in his younger years. He closed his eyes and thought that maybe he was beginning to see things in his old age. He lifted his hands to touch his face and rubbed his cheeks up and down.

He kept his eyes closed and took a deep breath before opening them again. He was astonished to see that the young man in the mirror was still there, staring back at him. He frowned at the reflection, and it frowned back.

"Hmmm . . . am I still dreaming?" he whispered to himself. He slapped himself a couple of times, feeling the palm of his hand sting his cheeks. It all felt too real to be a dream, he thought. What was happening to him?

He stared at the man in the mirror for a long time before the realization hit him: he looked exactly like the young Richard Bennett, the man he once knew and had always believed himself to be. He didn't know if he should feel excited or sad. Had he died? Why was he seeing this fifty-year-younger image of himself?

He quickly left the bathroom to look for a shirt to throw on and walked to the bedroom door. He was excited to see if there was anything else he could find that might explain the odd reflection in the mirror.

As soon as he opened the door, he could smell the wonderful aroma of food coming from the kitchen. He noticed the hallway looked familiar, but he couldn't pinpoint where he had seen this place before. Maybe he had become forgetful in his old age. It must be Amy in the kitchen cooking breakfast for him, he thought, because she knew he hadn't eaten anything for a couple of days now. "She's such a sweetheart to worry so much about this sick, old man," he whispered as he made his way down the hallway.

Toward the end of the hallway, he suddenly stopped dead in his tracks and his heart skipped a few beats. Tears came to his eyes as he stood in silence. There was his son, Edward, crouched down by the coffee table inside the living room, working hard on his latest masterpiece.

He then turned his head toward the kitchen to search for someone else. His heart seemed to stop beating now as he saw her—his love, his life, his destiny, his Elizabeth—inside the dining room, working diligently on setting the table for breakfast.

Tears streamed out of his eyes as he remembered what her grandmother had said to him:

*"You must follow the path set for you by my granddaughter."*

*You keep her close to your heart, and then you will find your destiny. Your destiny will take you to her. And then she will take you back to that place you called home… Fulfill your destiny and when the moment arrives, you will go back to the time in which you found your greatest happiness. There, you and my granddaughter will begin your lives once again."*

He tried to approach her, but his feet seemed glued to the floor. His legs were too weak to move. Then she turned around and smiled sweetly at him.

"Good morning, stranger," she said sweetly as she approached him.

"What day is today?" he asked as he turned away to hide his tears from her.

She smiled sweetly again. "It's Wednesday, silly. We're going to go meet your parents for dinner tonight." Then she squinted in curiosity as she noticed the tears in his eyes. "Is there something wrong?" she asked as she gently turned his face back to meet hers.

He was confused by her words, so all he could do was just stand there, silent and motionless. How could she not remember the tragedy that had happened to them, when it was the most difficult memory for him to forget?

He wanted to tell her everything about his long and lonely journey and about the many years that he struggled in order to be with her again. He wanted to tell her about her grandmother and her brother, but now he knew that this wasn't the time to do that. Besides, it would be hard for her to understand. So he just slowly wiped away his tears and replied, "I've missed you so much, that's all."

"Richard, you're acting like you haven't seen me for ages," she said softly as she reached up and tenderly stroked his cheek. Then she pulled him into her arms for a tight embrace.

She was still a little confused to see him acting like this, so she pulled back a bit to look at his face again. She could feel his body trembling. "Was it a bad dream?" she asked softly. When she heard no reply, she continued. "I'm sorry, I didn't know you had a bad dream."

He hugged her even tighter now. "I love you, Elizabeth. I love you so much that I don't think I could survive another day without you."

"I love you, too, honey," she replied sweetly. "I'll be here with you until we're both old and gray and can't recognize each other anymore. And even then I will still be with you."

He cried again as he held her. He feared that this might be just another beautiful dream, and he might wake up to an empty world again.

He pulled back so that he could look at her beautiful face again. She reached up to brush a lock of hair off his forehead and then slowly trailed her finger down to his lips. She tenderly kissed his moist cheek.

Looking into his eyes as if she were piercing deep into his soul, she whispered, "Your eyes look as if you've been on a long journey. I understand."

He slowly combed his fingers through her long black hair and then softly caressed her face with his quivering hands. "You have no idea how long of a journey I went through to come back to you," he whispered.

He then gave her a passionate kiss—a kiss that expressed his love for her after fifty years of longing. He was going to kiss her as passionately as this every day for the rest of his life, because he understood now that even though love could be given, it could also suddenly be taken away.

# The End

www.ingramcontent.com/pod-product-compliance
Lightning Source LLC
Chambersburg PA
CBHW060517180626
46817CB00002B/391